ELEPHANT SHOE

J.S. EDGE

J.S. EDGE

For Daniel and Winnifred Nightingale.
Always in my heart.

MY BROTHER, EVERYONE. REAL STAND-UP GUY

The ice took us off the road; the tumble crushed the car roof; the tree caved in the driver side door. My best friend, Tate, suffered a hefty blow to the head, dislocated right shoulder and fractured wrist. Me, two cracked ribs and a broken shin.

My parents died.

That was six years ago. I was eleven.

My brother, David, was twenty-one. And on that day, he became all I had. Freshly orphaned; injured and traumatised. He was then all I had, and I needed him.

Unfortunately for me, I wasn't all he had. He had his girlfriend, Melissa. He had their unborn child. He didn't need me. Nor did he want me.

Two weeks later, as David settled his new family into our home, I was sent away. 400 miles away. From my small rural town in Devon, from everything I'd ever known, to Newcastle and into the care of grandparents who were barely more than strangers.

I can count on my fingers the number of times I've seen my big brother since, and I can take off two for the number of times I've spoken to him.

David Alston is —no shadow of a doubt —my least favourite person on the planet.

Understandable, right?

And so, imagine my horror when I arrive home from a sweet afternoon's skating jaunt with Jody, utterly beat and hankering after the leftover lasagne I know is waiting for me in the fridge, to be surprise attacked by the sight of the heinous tosspot sat at the kitchen table. All self-assured cockiness, an older, more expertly put-together version of me. Looking way too comfortable. Greeting me with the ugly *"We need to talk"* line no one ever wants to hear.

Yeah, it's that shoved off a cliff kinda horror.

I gape. For way too long.

"Uh...There appears to be an undesirable besmirching my seat, Suzy," I say (and sound not at all as impressive as my brain convinced me I would), transferring my eyeballing to the woman sat across from him. Gran's best friend and our upstairs neighbour. My ally...or so I'd thought. Wringing guilt from her bony hands, I see betrayal etched in every wrinkle of her heavily made-up face. My, how it stings. "Why?"

David sighs. "Really, Michael?"

I grit my teeth.

Holding my gaze, Suzy purses her lips, collects the two empty mugs from the table and pushes up from her seat. "Sit down, pet. Tea or coffee?"

"You been colluding against me, is that it?" I'm stood in the doorway, vice-gripping the frame. My feet still skated up; my jacket still on; my shoulder still backpack burdened. I make no move. "All in on it?"

"Jean and Hannah know David's here, aye."

"And Gran?"

She gives a limp sort of half shrug, turning her back to me with an almost imperceptible bob of her head. My temples throb, heart botching some beats.

"You don't take my calls, Michael. What else am I supposed to do?"

Mikey. It's MIKEY! My middle finger tells him, *And, seriously, take the neon-bright hint, moron: Leave us the hell alone!*

I force a breath. "And you couldn't have warned me? No?"

"Do I look daft, pet, eh?" Suzy lays the two mugs on the bench and plucks my 'No.1 Grandson' one from the mug tree. "What good would thata done?"

Wow!

"We're supposed to be a team, Suzy. A *team*. What the f... what were you thinking of?"

"Mikey," (< *see*) "sit your butt down and shut up, would ye love?" She admonishes in her too-sweet voice, filling the kettle then setting it to boil. "Jean won't be back with yer gran for −ooh − least another hour or so. I'm headin' upstairs to get meself ready for work in a mo. Just... give yer brother fair hearing, aye?"

"No."

"Mikey..." I hear a needling mix of plea and warning. Suzy turns, teaspoon in hand, and I catch the apologetic glance she sends David's way before she meets my glare, her free hand fixing on her hip.

She's totally sold me out.

And working off the fact David's been pushed to make the cross-country trip up for a face to face, her tattling must've been slap-around brutal.

I'm shaking my head. Vehemently. No idea how long I've been doing it. "No."

"You're being ridiculous, little brother."

Am I? Am I really? I can barely stand being in the same room as him, can't look at him. His voice offends my ears, and his smell, Christ! The scent of his cologne is everywhere and, with each breath I take, I swear I'm being poisoned. As if I'm gonna willingly sit and let him chew me out. As if he holds any power to chastise me and have an impact. He doesn't belong here. He has no place here. I owe him nothing. *He's* being ridiculous thinking otherwise.

Pushing off of the frame, I swerve a tight one-eighty over the kitchen's linoleum floor onto the hallway's laminate.

"Mikey!" Suzy repeats in a sterner tone.

"Suzy!" I throw back. "I said NO. Make him disappear."

'Least favourite person on the planet', yeah, I understated it. I'd take to bartering with Lucifer for my soul over listening to anything David has to say. Fact.

"Hell. That went...as expected." I hear David grumble as I clump my way back along the hall (storming out calls for an aggressive step, and the clump satisfies where a glide would not), accompanied by the scrape of a chair against the floor.

"Leave it, pet. Won't do yerself any favours pushin' him. Best just lettin' him stew awhile."

I can feel both pairs of eyes branding my back.

"Ah, I'd be a fool to believe any amount of stewing's going to make the slightest difference here, Suzy," David voices my thoughts precisely as I step out the flat and shut (*slam*) the door behind me.

Beyond making my point, I really didn't think this storm out through at all. It's the middle of February. It's freezing cold. And the afternoon's swiftly growing dark into evening. I have zero desire to be out, no idea what to do now I am. Not a hell's chance I'm going straight back in.

Jody comes to her door in spotty pj's and a hot pink dressing gown. Her slippers, hairy grey beast feet. And her curly brown hair's squished flat on one side. Disturbingly, the look's not new to me. I know straight off her answer'll be a resounding no, but I go ahead and ask anyway.

"Joking, right? I've just got shot of you, Miktard. Passing up Zombieland and my snuggly blanket to come back out trawling the streets with you? Hil.Arious."

"Aww, come on, please?" I try out the puppy dog eyes.

She snorts. "Not if your life depended on it."

"But you owe me one."

"Nope."

"I'd do it for you."

"You would not."

I huff out a cloudy breath. "Okay, be that way. But know this: Next time things turn sour in Paul Paradise, you'll get nout from me."

"Yu-huh. Call me tomoz. After 11." Then the door's swung shut in my face.

The chippy around the corner is where her mister, Paul, works. My next stop. I'm freaking ravenous. Reckon, with a bit of badgering, there's a fair chance he'll slip me a freebie just to get me gone. Only...

"What can I get ye, flower?"

Pants to my luck, Paul's not working this evening. Brenda is, and she scares the bejeezus outta me. She once attempted to suffocate me in her ample bosom.

"Yeah, um, I'm good, ta," I say, backing out the door before it's had chance to close.

I consider –briefly –the park for my following port of call. Creepy in the dark, I imagine, probably –*possibly* – full of ne'er-do-wells. And so, at a loss and reluctant to stray too far, a few zips around the block and I end up back on my street.

The lights are on inside my flat...

Situation analysis: Suzy's car's gone from the drive, her first-floor flat dark; so she's gone to work. I've not yet filled in an hour, and Jean's car hasn't replaced Suzy's out front; so Gran's not back.

...Blatantly, David has very much not disappeared. Why, oh, why has he not disappeared?

Taking a perch on a garden wall across the road, I hunker down and wait. And dread the coming blow a little more with each passing second.

The moment I see Jean's old fiesta turn into the street, I'm up and over the road. Sliding to a neat stop at the top of the drive, I wave and smile at Gran as the car pulls up to park. Gran pretends she doesn't see me. *Crap!*

"She's had a bad day," Jean confirms, wearily stepping out the car and rounding it to open the passenger door. "Come on, Evelyn, love."

I watch Gran look all around herself, startled —as if she hasn't the faintest clue what's required of her, before leaning out the door to stare up at Jean. "Ye've tied me up, woman. I canna get out!"

Jean sighs, pressing her lips tight as she stretches an arm around Gran to unclip the seatbelt.

"Your daft jumpers tickling me snozz. Gerroff, will ye."

Jean jerks back, sucking in a sharp gasp, "Evelyn, don't you ever nip me again. You hear?"

Gran cackles.

"Gran?" Moving slowly around the front of the car, catching her attention, I stop by Jean and crouch down. "Let's get in, eh? I wanna hear about your day."

She smiles. I return it, holding my hand out toward her.

"Ah, my little Davey, you made it! Such a handsome face." She pats my cheek.

My smile drops.

Taking tight grip of my hand, Gran shuffles awkwardly out the car. Jean catches her other arm, helping her straighten and balance. "Eee now, Davey, ye wouldna believe the day I've had, pet. Wouldna believe!"

This isn't the first she's called me by my brother's name. I try not to let it bite, remind myself it's nothing more than a slip up. But this time...well, the added affirmation she's been expecting him makes it all the more hurtful. Actually, thinking on it...these past few days I've been Davey more often than not. "It's Mikey, Gran. I'm Mikey."

And of course, as if summoned, David chooses that moment to appear at the front door. Filling the space and scrutinising the scene before him. I've no idea what of anything David's been told, but I'm assuming Suzy'll have said something about Gran. There's a whole world of difference between the telling and the seeing, though, and this, right here, is exactly what I've been sat dreading. Stupid jerk should have disappeared.

6

Gran tilts her head to one side, frowning as she considers my face through narrowed eyes. Then her white eyebrows lift and she chuckles. "'Course it is, dear love. Silly cow that I am, I'm just so tired, ye know?"

I manage a weak smile, drawing her closer to tuck her arm beneath mine, hands still clasped. "Yeah, Gran, I know."

"Bet ye didna know Liz −Church Liz, I mean −she hit me. Didna know that, no? Today. In Hannah's place. Reet across the back of me bonce."

Jean's shaking her head at me. Releasing her hold, she steps back. "Her bags are in the boot, Mikey. Can you grab em? I've gotta get off."

I catch David in my peripheral, starting his way over.

Leading Gran from the car, I raise my voice, "David'll get the bags. I'm gonna get Gran in."

"Bet ye also didna know, Mikey, that awful, scruffy man −the bus driver. Derek or Dominic?" She's raised her voice too. I grimace. "Duncan? Whatever D he goes by. Keeps on tryin'ta court me. Touchin', touchin', always with the touchin'. Telt him no. I'm a happily married woman, I've said. He willna listen. Can ye fathom it, eh?"

"Gran, hey." David approaches, crooked grin fixed on a face that says he's heard enough to be concerned. "David, remember?"

My eyes roll of their own accord. *Sure she does. You're the one with the handsome face.* Bitterness' captaining this ship, oi oi. I guide Gran into a side step of him. She resists.

"Oh my, now, you really are Davey. Jim been taking good care of you, has he?"

"Uh..."

"Gran," I cut him off, "let's get into the warm. David'll follow in a bit." Pulling her forward, I glance behind me. "Open the boot for him, Jean, please. And thank you. Big thank you."

I see Jean nod. "Hiya, David. Looking well."

"I'll clip him if he hasna, mind," Gran calls back as I help her manoeuvre the step in. "You just tell me."

7

Once the door has clicked shut behind us, I clasp her shoulders and wait for her to look at me. *Gently, gently.* "Gran, we lost grandad Jim last year, remember? You know he's not with us anymore. You know it's just me and you now, yeah?"

She looks away, off to her right, and I feel like scum. It's rare for her to forget Grandad's gone. Not sure I'm right in correcting her but I can't risk her expecting him to be asleep in his chair and snapping to a tantrum when he's not. Like the last time. Most especially with David here. Her lip quivers. "I've missed me show, haven't I?"

A short bark of laughter escapes. "It's recorded, don't worry. Bed now, but you can watch it tomorrow, okay?"

"You're ever so good to me, Mikey. Such a good lad."

I hear Jean's car pull away. David comes in while I'm helping Gran out of her coat. "Here you go, Gran," he says, laying her hand, tote and carrier bags down beside my backpack on the telephone table inside the door.

"Jean tried to steal those."

"Jean's your friend, Gran," I say, shaking my head.

"I'm not lyin'. Took em straight out me hand."

"She'll've been helping you out."

Gran tuts. Dropping her coat on an air hook, she takes herself off toward the kitchen. "Can I make you anything, Davey? I can put ye a pie in if you fancy?"

"David's fine," I jump in before he can. "Bathroom, Gran, please."

"Yes, yes." She backtracks along the hall, opening the door to the airing cupboard, then the sitting room. I push the bathroom door, holding it open for her. She steps in and I pull it closed. "You'll make our Davey a pie, won't ye, dear?" She calls.

Do we have rat poison? "Sure thing."

"And if he doesn't take care of me you'll clip him, yeah?"

Clamping down hard on my urge to reward him with a glare, I bend to retrieve Gran's coat from the floor, hooking the hood over an arm of the coatrack. Then, yanking mine off, I hook it opposite for balance. Of course, David ruins it, adding his between ours.

"Oh now, silly, I wouldna clip my boy!"

I grin. Stupidly.

Stepping into Gran's bedroom, David follows me.

Oh, no. No, no, no! Enough is enough. I'm done.

Taking out her long, white nighty from the bedside cabinet, I lay it on the bed before spinning around to face him. "She's tired and you're practically a stranger to her. I've got this, so back the hell off!"

David's leaning against the wardrobe, lips thinned. Unmoved, his eyes slide past me, away beyond my left shoulder. And then the ghost of a smile steals over his face, "I remember the day that was taken."

I glance behind me without meaning to, as if I have no clue what he's referencing. Though I've seen that picture in the silver frame every day I've been here, stood as it always has done atop the cabinet beside Gran's bed.

"Christmas Eve. My first year with Mel. She snapped it."

Our whole family, all huddled together, all dressed in our festive best. Grandad and Gran standing behind the blue sofa, hugging and smiling. Dad beside them, seemingly caught mid-laugh, his arms slung over the back of the sofa, circling Mum's neck. I'm curled up in Mum's lap, most of my face hidden against her chest. Tiny for my seven years, a mass of blond hair as unruly then as now. And David sits beside us; slouched back, cocky grin in place, his big coffee-dark eyes looking directly out —like he's what this picture is all about, the main attraction. Of the age I am now, the resemblance is uncanny, only...well, he's always worked our genes that bit better than I ever could.

My memory of that captured moment is barely a whisper. Think I'd been crying though.

I have the overwhelming urge to turn the photo facedown, or – better yet–shove it away in the drawer. "Ever the smug tool, David, right?"

He does back off then.

If only to free the doorway for Gran to step through. "Oh, you boys and ye bickering. Haddaway wi' yersels."

Thereupon shooed from the room while she changes, I shoulder past David and stalk to the kitchen, dropping onto a chair.

"How long things been like this?" David shadows me in, propping himself against the bench.

My best line of defence here: Denial. I focus on removing my skates. "Dunno what you're on about. Things are fine. We're all fine."

"Gran's not fine, little brother."

"She gets confused sometimes, that's all. We've got it in hand. We have a system. We're doing *fine*."

And we do have a system. Between Suzy, Jean, Hannah and me, Gran's never on her own. Sure, it's not easy, it's not perfect, but it works. And everything's. *Absolutely*. Fine.

"Two days ago, you were caught shoplifting. That's really 'fine' is it?"

Damn.

My fingers fumble.

Dragging in a lung-filling breath, I force my body to slump back down on its release, because, no, *hell no*, he can go screw himself before I let him score a rise from me. "Misunderstanding."

"You were arrested and cautioned."

"Misunderstanding," I repeat. And it was. Seriously. Hannah had phoned while I was in the shop; she was distressed, and I could hear Gran in the background, on the verge of a full-blown meltdown over being asked to take a bath. So, I hot tailed it outta there to get back, sparing no thought for the chocolate digestives, jar of coffee and six magazines I had clutched to my chest. I was caught at the end of the street by security and dragged back to store. The manager was a prick. "Done with and sorted now, so drop it."

"Suzy missed her daughter's baby scan. Because she was stuck in the station. Minding you."

I wrench my skates off and stare down at them, wrestling the freed shame and guilt back into the deep dark pit I'd buried them in. "I apologised. I bought her flowers. And a coke." Okay, so the coke was actually mine. She just took it. But I let her. "Why the sudden concern anyway, huh? No part of this is your problem."

"Michael, I..."

"It's Mikey." My head snaps up to him. "My freaking name is Mikey!"

"Your name's Michael. Mum and Dad named you Michael. That's what's on your birth certificate. To me, you've always been Michael."

"No." My head's started that vehement shake thing again. "To you, *Dave*, I'm a nuisance. And I've always been a nuisance. You made that all too clear when you scrubbed your perfect life clean of me."

For the first time today, I spy a crack in his cool facade. He averts his gaze to his feet, sighs, and then straightens up off the bench.

Without another word, he walks out. A moment later I hear the front door open then snick quietly shut.

Gran calls for me, loud and anxious.

It's ten thirty before I sit down at the table to eat my lasagne.

I'M WOKEN by the smells and sounds of sizzling sausages. And David's voice: "...didn't go well. Never even got to the crux of it. No idea how I'm best broaching that with him."

Then Jean: "It's gonna be rough no matter the hows. But we're here, you know...for the both of you."

I spend a moment burying my head under the pillow, muffling my vicious stream of curses, before throwing back the duvet and pulling myself up and out.

"What time can I expect Mikey up?" I hear David say as I pull on black sweatpants over my Donald Duck boxers.

"Wouldn't count on it being anytime soon, I'm afraid. Not on a weekend," Jean replies.

Batman t-shirt and green hoody on, I shove my feet into my skates and do a rush job of fastening up.

"Guessing you wouldn't advise me waking him?"

"You guess right. Kid's moody enough on a morning. It'd be like poking a bear."

Scribbling a quick note to prop on the telephone table ('J, gone out. Got phone. Call only in event of emergency, otherwise don't bother 'til David leaves. M'), I head straight out the flat. Sneaky quiet.

2

THE AVOID DAVID EXPERIENCE:
DAY TWO

*O*nce again, I'm out and about with absolutely no desire to be. 7.35 on a Sunday. The sky's barely lightened. And it's raining.

My conscience kicks in, making me feel lower than low, before I make it as far as the end of my street. What. Am I even. *Doing?* Deserting Gran; shirking responsibility; not coping...

That's not how it is. Really so not how it is. Honest. But that's how it'll look. That's how David's sure to see it.

I'm handing him ammunition, alongside an open opportunity to spend time he shouldn't with Gran. It's wrong. I'm handling this all wrong.

I should turn back. *'Never even got to the crux of it'.* I don't.

Way too early to call on Jody...or anyone else for that matter. I mean, seriously, nobody should be forced to see this time of a Sunday. It's the day of rest.

Hiding out around the corner until the day's made more of an appearance, I head for the local park.

A few lo-ong hours are filled in with skating, sitting, swinging, sitting and skating; ignoring my phone; getting thoroughly soaked. Then I move on to the supermarket. Distracting my co-workers fills in a good while until the customer count picks up and my boss, Cheryl, politely reminds me of the no-skate-in-store policy and sends me packing.

Next, I brave Hannah's café. A mistake, I realise instantly: Jean's little sister can pull off one helluva wounding glare. Clearly, she's been brought up to speed.

"You're to ring Jean, young man. She's worried sick."

"Mad?" I slide into a tiny booth by the counter and pick up a sticky laminated menu to cower behind.

"You bet your arse she is! Taking off without a word. You know better than that, Mikey. She had no clue what to tell Evelyn."

"I, um, I left a note."

Definitely a mistake.

I stay for the score of coffee and lemon cake, but the harsh verbal bashing and spate of harrumphs I'm subjected to alongside utterly sour the treat. I've been turned on by my whole team. They're all aware of what David did, know how I feel about him. They've comforted me over him plenty enough in the past. Why is it I'm coming off the bad guy in this? I leave without saying bye.

11.50. I call Jody.

"Going through Leeson's in a bit. Me, Paul and Flynn. Come with?"

They're all likely planning to get stoned. Leeson's a ma-hoosive knob-end with a disgusting flat. Paul and Jody will be going at it like the rest of us don't exist. And Flynn...Paul's best friend; he makes me uncomfortable. *Horrible plan.* "I'll be at yours in twenty."

"Uck, make it an hour. I'm literally still asleep here."

Oh, no-no-no, Jody! I grimace at my phone. "Okie-dokie. I'll *literally* be at yours in an hour then."

"Sure thing, chicken wing," she chirps, oblivious.

THE DAY HAS DRAGGED on forever. I'm sucking it up now,

returning home. It's almost six and Gran'll certainly start to fret if I stay out any longer.

Flynn's walking with me the two streets from Jody's, cos mine's on the way to his. I wish he wasn't.

I can feel him watching me as I watch my feet swerving wide and close, wide and close. Our journey's silence is a discomfort I'm content to suffer, but apparently, he's not. "Come on then, how many broken bones you had?"

"Err..." My eyes flick across to him, "what?"

"You know, being a wheel junkie, all those crazy-ass tricks I've seen you pull. Must've broken plenty, right?"

"Nope."

"Seriously?" He doubts me.

I nod. "Never anything from skating."

"Wow." He still doubts me. "You're that good, huh? Impressive."

"I guess." And curses to it all if I don't stumble right then.

Really can't say why he makes me uncomfortable. Cos I've no clue why. It's not that I dislike the guy, he's never given me any reason to. Just...

"I went ice-skating once, when I was eight." A crescent hollow appears in his left cheek. "Snapped my arm. Never been since."

"I love ice-skating."

He chuckles, dimple deepening. "Yeah, figured you would."

...Something about him puts me on edge; I find him stupendously difficult to be around. My eyes drop back to the pavement in front of me. "Jody...um, Jody fell off her board a couple years back. She broke her coccyx."

"Ha! Oh man, I remember that. Proper hilarious!"

"Not sure she'd agree."

"No. Reckon you're right there." We turn onto my street and I stumble over nothing for the second time this short trip. I'm certain the indent to his cheek's now become a crater, his scepticism firming. I determinedly don't check. "You should hang with us more often, man. Today was fun."

"Oh." *Fun?* "Absolutely."

The insincerity that rings so clear to my own ears seems to flit by him, unnoticed. "We're getting some drinks in tomorrow. Pizza. Fifa."

"Can't tomorrow. Working."

"Shame."

It's with a distinct pang of relief that I veer away from him onto the sloped drive fronting my flat. "Another time."

"Another time," Flynn echoes, again flashing his crooked grin as he lifts his hand in a half-wave, half-salute.

I hover by the front door, breathing a little easier the further he moves on along the street. Dark head bowed, hands shoved in his jacket pockets, his stride long and sure, he doesn't glance back. The moment he's turned out of sight, however, and I slide my key in the lock, my gut wastes no time resuming its clench.

Taking a bracing gulp of icy air, I step inside.

David's nowhere to be seen. Instead, Jean and Suzy accost me. And they're not smiling.

I spot Gran napping in her chair in the sitting room, TV blaring too loud. Hannah's sprawled across the sofa, headphones on and book in hand. She fixes me with a knowing look, the set of her mouth doing nothing to soothe me.

I'm in for a dragging over the coals. It's gonna be brutal, I can tell, and there'll be no letting up until I give.

"I shouldn't have heard all this from Suzy, little brother." David's sat across from me in the dimly lit booth, eyes fixed steadily on my face. I'm looking everywhere but back at him.

The pub's quiet tonight. Dunno if that's normal for a Sunday or not. 7pm's probably considered pretty early for drinking anyway, though, I guess. There's a group of four old blokes huddled around one end of the bar, a lone drinker hunched on a barstool at the other end, and two women at a table across the room from us. The bartender too, of course: A rotund, mousta-chioed gentleman.

"No. You're right," I eventually respond. "Suzy should have kept her mouth shut and left you out of it."

"Mikey," he sighs, "Suzy called me because she's worried about you. They all are. Gran too. Worried about the effect everything's having on you, how much pressure you're putting on yourself."

"I'm fi..."

"Fine. Yes, you've said that. Shame I don't believe you."

Whatever debate the men at the bar are having, it's getting heated. One man is leant in so close to another it's almost a kiss – discounting their overt rage. "Shame I don't care."

"You're barely seventeen, Michael. You should be in school."

"Mikey. And please, say that again only louder, *Dave*, I don't think the barman heard you." Raising my pint high, I then take a huge swig, instantly regretting it as my taste buds protest and my face surely gives me away. I'm really not that much of a drinker. Grandad would tell me –often –he'd kill me if he ever caught me drunk. I believed him enough not to test him. And since he died, well... partying doesn't fit all that well into my life. My eyes flick to David. His lip twitches, brows lifting as he takes a drink of his own pint. I take another sip and set my glass down. "What good am I to anyone sat another two years in a classroom? I'm working..."

"In a supermarket."

"Yeah, in a supermarket. So what?"

"You're a smart kid. You should be looking toward uni, and a career."

"It's a decent job, you judgemental prick." I glare at him, then away. "And it's not like I've signed my life over to it. I am smart, yeah, and I don't need school or uni to make something of myself. I work hard, take care of Gran and, actually, I think I'm doing pretty damn great at stepping up and dealing!"

"You are, I'm not disputing that. But you..."

"Whatever, okay? Just...whatever. So I screwed up last week. And sure, it was bad. One stupid misunderstanding and everyone's on my case, knocking me down. I've been blackmailed into sitting here, hearing you out. The hell if I know what use they think you'll be. What use have you ever been?

"But, hey, you go ahead and have at it. Lay into me some, yeah? So then you can go off home tomorrow, back to your family —who, I'm sure are missing you terribly – all smug in the illusion you've done your bit for the cause. Shoot."

"Quit being precious, Mikey." He doesn't raise his voice, doesn't sound angry. Nor upset. He sounds exasperatedly patient, and I kinda want to kick him in the shin just to get a rise outta him. "That's not what this is. No one's out to get you."

I snort. David sighs, takes a drink. Then another.

The two women across the room are preparing to leave. The brunette blows a kiss to the bartender as she shirks into her coat. Mr Mustachio pretends to catch it, pulling it into his chest. The women giggle. I get a whiff of fruity perfume on the refreshing cold blast of air as they exit.

"You're moving back to Yoverton."

His words hang there, over the table between us, threatening, before slowly sinking in. My eyes shift to him first, head following, "What?"

"You and Gran. You're coming to live with us."

I stare at him. He stares back at me. Something's bubbling up inside me, can't figure out what it is. Until it escapes. And I'm laughing. David's face tells me I'm sounding more than a little touched in the head. To be fair, I can hear that for myself. It's wholly unsettling. He reaches across the table toward my arm, I pull it further from him and he retreats.

"It's for the best, Mikey."

In a heartbeat, the giddy's gone. I've heard that line from him before and I'm calling bullshit. I stand, shoving my chair back, hard. "Oh, the hell it is!" It's to my credit I don't full-on pelt it out the door.

David's on my heels, I'm well aware. *Good.*

One step out the door and he has a hold on my arm.

"For the best?" I yank myself free, whirling on him. "Don't you dare. Just don't you...*fucking* dare! I'm not eleven anymore, David. *I* decide what's for the best here. *ME*. And what you just said? Not. It!"

"Gran has dementia, Mikey."

"You think I don't know that?"

"She's only going to get worse. And..."

"And the worst thing you could possibly do is rip her from her comfortable place in the world, you jackass! What is there for either of us down there, huh? How will we be any better off? Our home is here. Here, we have Suzy and Jean and Han..."

"And they're not enough for you anymore," he cuts over me. "They've told me so themselves. Suzy has a family –her first grand-daughter to think of now. Jean's going to be in and out of hospital from next month onwards. Hannah...she can't do any more than she already is; her business and her son demanding time. Told you so too, right?"

"We've already got that all figured..."

"No. No, you haven't. Your plan to work nights to free up their time is exactly what has them so worried. You'll be shouldering too much on your young shoulders and it'll eat up your life. Why do you think they...?"

"Shut up."

"Gran'll have me," he steams on. "And Mel. She'll get to spend time with Sophie. More space, a big garden. It's so much quieter – relaxing. We have a nurse next door and we'll be arranging carer visits. You'll get your freedom back, get to be a teena..."

"Shut. UP!" I start walking.

"Where are you going?"

I know David'll follow me. I know this isn't over and he won't let it drop. But, hell, I need to be moving. Standing there, staring at his big dumb face, I felt... itchy. Too itchy.

As expected, a moment later, he steps up alongside. "You'll have your life back, Mikey."

"What life? I don't have a life in Devon anymore. You took

that. My life is *here* now. And you're trying to do it again." We're approaching his car, parked up on the roadside, and I deviate to the side just to kick his tyre. Pointless, sure. But it needed doing. I don't expect a reaction from him, and I don't get one. "Where's this concern come from anyway? Turning up all of a sudden, like some misguided hero, trying to save our lives, why?"

"If I'd known, I'd..."

"You haven't even visited in over a year —not once in all the time it's been just me and Gran."

"You made it pretty damn clear at Grandad's funeral I wouldn't be welcome."

I snort, shaking my head. "Seriously? That's what you've got? Like I have any sway over you whatsoever?"

He doesn't respond for a long while. I wait him out —I want to hear this.

"I'm at fault there, I know."

Whoop-dee-freaking-doo! "One day, David. One day you spared us when Grandad died. Showed your face at the church then *poof*. And we see nothing more of you after, until you roll in declaring you're taking charge of my whole *fucking* world again!"

"Michael, I didn't mean to leave so quickly after the funeral, you know that. I had no choice, Sophie needed..."

"Yeah. Figures."

"What's that supposed to mean?"

"They always come first, right?"

"They're my family."

He catches his mistake as quick as I do. A swift glance, I can see it on his face. "I'm your family too. Your brother! Why hasn't that ever counted for anything?"

"It has. It does." He touches my arm. *Again.* I jerk away and, *I swear*, if he tries it one more time, I'll be far less reasonable. "I'm trying here, little brother."

Nope. Not good enough. Not even close, big bro. Moving back to be placed last in the pecking order? That's a whole wide world away from what's best for me. "Gran's MY responsibility. It's MY choice to make. I'm saying no. I'm not going. Nor's Gran."

David stops. I continue. I don't look back.

"It's sorted, Mikey. It's happening."

"Go screw yourself, David," I throw back. "I hope you choke on your own hot air."

"I'm sorry."

Racking up quickly to a sprint, I freaking hate how slow my feet are without wheels.

～

ARRIVING HOME, I chuck Suzy outta my flat before calling in to check on Gran in her bedroom.

"Oh, Mikey, you been wi'our David, have ye?" She's in bed propped up on her pillows, the bedside lamp on and a magazine open on her lap. A grin stretches wide across her face. My heart sinks. "Has he told ye?"

"Err...Yeah. But..."

"Thank goodness for that!" She claps her hands. "Cat's out the bag. Eee, ye've no idea how hard it's been keepin' it to meself. Davey made me promise though. I swore I'd keep schtum. And I did well mind, didna have a clue did ye?"

It burns that she kept this from me. "Gran, I really wish you'd warned me."

"And ruined the surprise, dear love? Heavens, no! Excitin', ain't it? You and me on a new adventure, eh?"

I settle on the edge of her bed and wrap my freezing cold hand around her warm one, resting on top of her lavender duvet. "You can't want to leave, Gran?"

"I'll have a garden. You know how long it's been since I hadda garden? I'm gonna plant a tree, Mikey. For my Jim. Davey says I can. Says he knows the perfect spot."

I sigh. Leaning over her, I rest a quick kiss on her forehead and then stand. "Goodnight, Gran."

3

HOSTILE TAKEOVER

ap. Tap. Tap.

I startle awake with no idea of where I am. I sense too much space; odd smelling space. I'm facing the wrong way and the mattress is much too soft beneath me. There's absolutely squat all familiar about this room. *Enter: Panic.*

Tap. Tap. Tap. I flinch.

Then: "Wakey, wakey sleepy head," comes a high sing-songy voice.

I snap to, and my panic instantly solidifies into heavy despair. *Urgh!*

Yeah, it happened. It happened head-spin fast.

Yesterday −only ten days on from taking David's shattering blow −I returned to my hometown of Yoverton. My old house, my old room. I hate what they've done to the place.

"Uncle Mikeyyy?"

The kid learns sharper than her Dad, that's for sure. Not especially keen on her inclusion of the 'Uncle' title, though: Suggests a relationship we don't have.

She barrelled into me with a leg hug last night. I wasn't about to shove the dinky five-year-old (six?) off me, but −hell −it was completely weird. See, I've only met Sophie once before, when she was, like, three or something and David brought her up to Gran's for a week. I didn't spend any time with her, didn't talk to her; there's no way she remembers me. I'm a stranger to her and I'd really appreciate her treating me as such.

"Yeah?" I croak.

"Good. You're alive." The door swings open, blasting my unprepared eyes with light from the hall. I squeeze them shut, cursing. "Naughty words." I'm scolded. "Breakfast time. Up, up, up."

Cautiously squinting open one eye, I find the small intruder stood not two feet from my face, grinning at me –creepily. I pull my duvet up tight around my chin. "Get out."

"You said to come in."

"I said: 'Yeah?'"

"Yeah," she nods.

I groan and close my eye. It's too early. Much too early. "What time is it?"

The bed dips and I'm quick to scoot away, closer to the wall. "Um, eleven and six?"

"O.Kay..." I throw my hands up over my head. "Kid, I just really wanna go back to sleep." *For as long as it takes for this God-awful nightmare to be over.*

"Can't. It's wakey time. Mummy's making breakfast. Gotta get up." She shakes my leg.

"Sophie."

"Uncle Mikey." She continues shaking my leg.

"Alright!" I snap, smacking my arms down on the duvet by my sides. "Alright. Tell your Mummy I'll be out in five, 'kay?"

"Kay-kay." She stops shaking my leg and her weight lifts from the bed. "You like eggs?"

"Sure."

"That's lucky."

I slit my eyes to watch her out. She kinda prances, her long brown ponytail swooshing across her back. Girl really needs to learn some freaking boundaries. "Shut the..." She's gone. "Never mind."

Propping up on one elbow, I reach for my phone on the bedside cabinet, waking the screen. Then I groan and flop back down. *7am. Seriously?!* The kid's up, dressed, and in high spirits at 7am. *Kill me now.*

So I'm not out in five. Nope. I turn over, snuggle down, and go back to sleep. Nobody else comes to disturb me.

~

It's a little after nine when I eventually rouse myself and, pulling on yesterday's jeans and Pikachu t-shirt, venture out from my room. Much later than I'd intended to sleep in for. The house is quiet. Padding softly on the thick beige carpet along the hall and down the stairs, I head straight for the ground floor master room – once my parents', now Gran's.

We were given the Grand Tour when we arrived late last night, as if completely new to the place. Truth is, though, we might as well have been –not a thing remains as I remember it. My parents' former room most especially.

I knock and, in getting no response, tentatively crack open the door and poke my head a small way in. "Gran?" Quick sweep. Empty.

Balls! Curses to me for being lazy. If that prancing pixie gave Gran a ridik o'clock wakeup call same she did...

I hear a raised voice. Gran's raised voice. "I never said that, did I? Puttin' bloody words in me mouth!"

My investigation is halted as the door to the kitchen swings open. Jean quick-steps out, looking rather harried. "Evelyn, I'm going for some now, okay?"

Yeah, see, for all David's big show of great concern, he checked out of his hotel and vamoosed home a day after our pub talk. It was Jean who drove us the hideous eight-hour trip yesterday. She's opted to stay a few days to 'help' Gran settle in'... scored herself a sweet little holiday. (Bitter? Me? Nooo).

"You're a star." I hear David.

"Not the cheap stuff, mind!" Gran follows up.

"What's going on Jean?"

"Oh, hey Mikey. Not half so bad as it sounds, don't fret. Evelyn's a tad impatient for the rest of her stuff arriving. Removal van's due before three, but that's apparently not soon enough."

Well, duh! I'm good with the little luggage I brought with me – skates; laptop; small suitcase of clothes and a backpack of essentials – it's all I need, really. But I knew Gran wouldn't be. Said as much, too.

"I'm popping to the shops, get some bits to tide her over. You wanting anything?"

"Nope." I move to the side and gesture her past, turning my attention to the kitchen beyond her.

"And another thing: I'm not spendin' another goddamned night on that quicksand bed, Davey!" I spy Gran sat at the kitchen table, her back to me. Wrapped in her purple velour dressing gown, her bob of white hair's frizzed up something chronic.

"Rightio, won't be long," Jean says behind me. I hear the front door open then close.

Dapper in dark jeans and grey shirt, David's leaning, arms crossed, against the beastly silver fridge-freezer Gran's facing. He's looking –and I'm sure it's not my imagination –a touch red in the face. "A few more hours, Gran, and we can get you settled in properly, yeah? We'll have your bed set up in there ready for you for tonight."

"Those sheets; what shade would ye call em? Mustard? Awful colour."

"Easily changed." He glances up at me as I enter, seeming expectant of my aid. Sod that.

I scowl at him, secretly elated. Sucks Gran's upset, sure, but could well be we get back to Newcastle sooner than I'd hoped. See, I may have given in –coming here, but I absolutely haven't given up. I expected to endure a couple of weeks while Gran got her enthusiasm for adventure worked outta her system. Day one and she's already ill at ease, with David exhibiting hints of the realisation he's bitten off more than he was prepared for... could well be we're set to head home with Jean in a mere few days.

"Morning, Gran." Moving up behind her, I give her shoulders a quick squeeze. She looks up and smiles. I feel smug as all hell. "Where's..." *the bitch and the brat,* "err, everyone?"

"Mel's getting Sophie to school. She's due back any minute now." David straightens up, crossing the room to the kettle's spot on the gleaming black bench. "Sophie was upset when you didn't come out for breakfast. She'd sorted you a plateful herself."

I shrug, not caring in the least – even as the lingering smell of bacon starts my mouth watering. "While you're on the subject of décor, I have a question." Taking the seat beside Gran, she shoves a plate of biscuits towards me. I choose a jammy dodger. Like hell am I asking David for food. Too much like admitting defeat...or weakness. Petty, yeah. I'm petty. David's filling the kettle at the sink, he glances back at me over his shoulder. "My room: What the hell's that all about?" I've held onto this since last night, too cotton-headed then to address the grievance. Seriously, it's atrocious. All white, royal blue and gold, with pictures of ships on the walls, and even a model ship monstrosity taking up the entire windowsill. "It looks like a sailor's thrown up in there."

Gran cackles. I grin at her.

David sets the kettle down on its cradle and clicks the button. "Mel's parent's sleep in there when they visit."

"And from what planet are they from to consider that an improvement to how it was before?"

"Well, they're not huge Pokemon fans, Mikey." The power in a name is once again evidenced as, on cue, Melissa enters the kitchen through the door from the sitting room.

I snap around.

Even in nothing fancier than jeans and a black off-shoulder sweater, David's wife has an elegance about her that would have most men looking twice: Tall and curvy, her hair a lustrous silky brown and her eyes a brilliant blue; yeah, the woman sure commands attention.

But her current smile could wither flowers.

I'm very tempted to backtrack now, apologise and excuse myself. Instead, I cram the jammy dodger in my mouth and avert my stare down to the glossy table top.

"It's not like we had any reason to expect you to grace us with a visit at any point. Mum and Dad stayed to watch Sophie while David and I honeymooned, and we gave them the go ahead to redecorate."

Ah, so spite fuelled then, I don't say.

A few months after my move up North I was invited back down to meet my newborn niece. My refusal to was readily accepted; everyone figured –very rightly –that it was too much to expect too soon after, everything still so raw for me. But two years later, when I declined a role in David and Mel's wedding, I met with much more resistance. Apparently, I should have been over it by that point. Mel had called and called and called, pleading ('*It would mean so much to David*' and all that kind of crap), coercing a promise from me to show. Of course, I didn't actually show. And two days after their big day, I received a jiffy bag, addressed in Mel's graceful hand, crammed full of pulverised wedding cake. Obviously, her hissy fit wasn't vented through cake-mail alone.

"Chucked all my stuff, huh?"

"Surely you've grown out of all that by now." Her eyes touch on my t-shirt and her brow quirks up. I fold my arms across my chest. "Hey Evelyn. Sleep well?"

"Absolutely, petal. Very well. Very, very well."

Oh, Gran, you disappoint, I side-eye her.

"And no, Mikey, you'll find everything stored safe and sound in the garage."

Everything? Not quite. My favourite thing about my old room, the wall covered in doodles and scribbles, is lost never to be recovered underneath several layers of white paint.

Mel crosses the room to David, passing over an A4 brown envelope. "Called in and collected these for you. Need filling in. Principal Carston's expecting you at four."

"Thanks, baby." He leans forward; Mel leans forward; they kiss; it's a wholly indecent and sickening display.

"I'm redecorating."

"Go wild. Your room again now, isn't it?" Mel puts a step of space between herself and David and, reaching past him, retrieves a pen from a lumpy, clay-slab of a pot beside the microwave. She presses it into his hand. "Here. I'm going to get sorted for work. Get me a coffee ready, please, love."

With that, she waltzes from the kitchen out the door into the hall. "Busy, busy day ahead."

Mel has her own salon in town. *Hair? Beauty?* I don't know. She was waxing lyrical last night, as we were led from room to room, on the outstanding reputation it has in these here parts. And, apparently, David's design business is proving equally as fan-dabby-dossy-awesome. Oh, such pleasure she took in boasting over their successes of these past couple of years. And, urgh, that led neatly into a gushing spiel about just how fabulously well this new arrangement will work out —with David mainly working from home and her hours flexible, '*someone can always be here for your gran*'. I needn't ever worry, she said. The pressure's all off me. *Super.*

I scowl after her.

David joins us at the table, shuffling his chair way too close to mine. I transfer my scowl to him, a very clear warning. He lays the envelope —pen on top —on the table and slides it over to me. "Forms for you. Need doing before our appointment at four."

"'Scuse me?"

"School, Mikey. Monday, you'll be starting Sixth Form at YCS."

The envelope turns to poison before my eyes.

I'm expected to seize freedom? Well, fine.

Grabbing another couple of biscuits, I stand. "Gran, I'm sorry, I need to get out a while. You good?"

Gran frowns, looking from me to David to the envelope and

back. She pats my hand, "It'll be good seein' ye back in school, dear love. Wi' friends."

This place is so very oppressive. "An hour, Gran, please?"

"It's fine," David sighs, "go work it out your system."

I continue waiting for Gran's response.

"So restless, young un. Get yesel' away, then."

"I'll have my phone. Love you."

"Back by three." David calls as I peg it up the stairs to get washed and dressed and retrieve my skates.

I ONCE HAD A BACKBONE. Swear down I did. The hell if I know what's become of it.

The light is still warring against the dark this gloomy Monday morning as I trudge my gloomy way across town, my backpack slung on one shoulder, empty bar one pen. Due to Sophie's insufferable chirpiness, I set out much earlier than I needed to. It's fine, though, really. Gran's had a good couple of days, was all a fluster of excitement for me this morning (*chrissake!*), and, yeah, I'm feeling in great need for as much time as I can get to myself. Time to wallow in self-pity and disgust before fixing on my *smiley-and-approachable* game face.

I know this route. My steps may be slow but they aren't unsure. For all that the house has changed beyond recognition, Yoverton hasn't. Memories are everywhere. It's disturbing in a kinda... uncomfortably comforting way.

Past the newsagent on the corner where I'd spend my pocket money on sweets, trading cards, and comics; down the steep bank that once scraped my backside raw in a daring skate run fail; along by the leisure centre at which I learnt to swim, and the community centre I attended Cubs every Thursday evening. I'd just moved up to Scouts when I was sent away. I refused to join a new group after. Bone of contention for Grandad, though it didn't ever take much for me to nettle him.

Through the play park friends and I would hang out in, new vandalism adorning the old play set; a long row of candy coloured terraced houses. And, up ahead at the street's end, the squat, red brick front of Somerton Primary school comes into view. Ever my journey's end. Before.

Quiet now. Marker of how absurdly early I am. Soon cars will line the roadside, soon children and parents will buzz around the school's tall, green metal fence, eager for the gates to open. Soon Mel and Sophie will be pulling up.

I turn off, climbing the steep stone steps slashing the candy strip in half, onto the far less picturesque housing row beyond. Skirting the stone wall of a church and cutting down an alley...

There.

I stop.

'Yoverton Community School' the blue lettering reads on the large burnt-orange sign across the road from me, indicating the narrow turnoff onto its grounds. My destination today onward.

YCS is the town's only secondary school, in to which all three local primaries feed. It's the school I was always meant for; the school I'd been ten months shy of moving up to; the school all my classmates *will* have moved up to.

I'm no doubt going to recognise a fair few faces today. Makes me all the more nervous. I'm the new kid who's not new at all. I have baggage some will know of, some will gossip of. And there'll be questions aplenty about my years of absence, and more still about my sudden return. *Or* −a mean little voice counters −*possibly worse, you'll be a forgotten nobody, ignored completely.*

At least Sixth Formers aren't required to wear uniform. (Thankful for small mercies and all that, right?)

I curse aloud. Then, checking the road each side, I cross.

Can't believe I'm doing this. I'm so freaking pathetic.

Six years too late, I take my first steps onto the school's long, wood-enclosed driveway.

The grand old stone building comes into sight sooner than I prepared for. Taking a corner past trees, the road widens, and I'm assaulted by it. My step falters and then slows even further as I take stock. The sprawling stately home appearance is tragically offset by the drab-brown additions off to both sides, tarmacked car park, and the tall, spike-topped high fence enclosing all. But, *jeezus*, it's impressive nonetheless. And imposing. Small in comparison to my previous school, but seriously imposing.

A quick check of my phone tells me that, despite my dragging feet, I've a long wait still ahead of me before the gates'll grant me admittance to my first day in hell. The place is practically deserted. There's only me, a small group of younger kids in uniform kicking a ball around the road up ahead, and...

And...

My legs absolutely lose their ability to function. Like, at all.

Tate McAllister.

4

OUCH! A BRICK TO THE FACE WOULD HURT LESS

The surety is instant, and it's absolute.

Tate.

He's oblivious to me. Thankfully. Cos I'm staring, and I'm not yet ready to stop.

Slouching, his long legs stretched out and crossed at the ankles, he's sat alone on a bench a short way along the fence, beneath the bare, spindly trees. Humongous orange headphones on, his head's bowed over a book in his lap (*a comic book?* Yeah, it's totally gotta be a comic book).

Taller. *Obviously*. Easily taller than me, I reckon. His dark hair's shaggy – and looking kinda unkempt (but it suits him). Face too solemn; no hint of that maddeningly easy grin of his. But...

If I harboured any doubt, noticing the black sharpie doodles adorning his jeans would have eradicated it.

I hadn't dared even hope he'd still be around. Hadn't expected him to be. The McAllister's are supposed to be living in New Zealand now. At least according to Mel. *'Could be the last chance you get to see your friend,'* she'd said, part of her attack strategy to get me to her wedding. It'd been the one thing that almost swayed me. Almost. In the end, though, I figured I couldn't handle saying goodbye to him a second time. The first had been hard enough. And I was far too stubborn to cave to Mel's demands.

What happened there, then?

It's only now I'm here looking at him that I grasp just how fully I'd resigned myself to never seeing him again. Were they ever really set to emigrate? Or had that whole tale been a fabrication of Mel's to manipulate me? Seriously wouldn't put it past her.

It takes major effort to make a start toward him. And, once started, it takes just as much effort to rein in my pace.

"Tate?"

Nothing. But of course, headphones. *Duh.*

"TATE!"

He looks up when I'm a mere few steps from him, his forehead creasing as his green eyes fix on me. Eyes so immediately and acutely familiar, the shock I see flash through them must surely be echoed back to him from my own. Thrown off kilter, my insides launch into a frenzy. It's awful. As is the grin that's taken over my face; the assuredly ridiculous grin of a person not in control of himself. And the time I stand before him, looking at him looking at me, stretches out an eternity.

It is a comic in his lap. X Men, I think. That pleases me.

"Hey," I say, and I raise my hand too, cos ¬ya know ¬headphones. "Hi."

I suppose the reaction I'm wanting from him here is along the lines of... well, his eyes should brighten with the return of his signature grin, elation jolting him to his feet. That's not what happens.

The worst I could imagine is for his first words to be 'And you are?' That's not what happens either.

Instead, without a word, he stands, retrieves the tatty backpack from the ground beside the bench, and walks away. Fence to his right, trees to his left, me falling ever further behind, staring dumbly after him.

Finally, I lose the idiot grin from my face.

~

"Psst, Mikey!"

Oblivious, Mr Garrimay continues scribbling drivel on the white board, as he has done most the lesson, reading it out as he goes.

Heedless, I remain steadfastly focused ahead. My pen poised over a sheet of lined paper, as it has been most the lesson, unmoving.

Today has sucked in all the ways I anticipated it would. I've gotten myself lost to the consequence of embarrassing lateness; been forced to introduce myself in every class; been pointed at, whispered about and openly questioned; and, in fourth Maths (as if GCSE resit wasn't bad enough), I was seated beside Gary Tinwell – a beast who hasn't at all changed his bullying ways since I knew him in Somerton.

And then there's Tate McAllister. Providing the crappiest crap topping to all that suck.

"Oi! Alston." Something pings off the back of my head.

I'm now in last period History, my eyes lasering the dark head sat two rows in front. He must be aware of it. *Turn around, bell-end!* He must be itching to, if only to glare at me.

It was in a History lesson we became friends. Way back in year two, when paired up on a Motte and Bailey Castle project. To be fair, we perhaps could well have been friends long before then, when we met in nursery, if not for my proclivity to bite (allegedly, I bit Tate *a lot*-a lot in nursery. Enough for his dad to insist we be kept apart). By year two, though, I'd long since moved beyond my rabid dog aspirations, and our model turned out awesome; Mrs Lumsbury picked it as one for the display by reception, a great honour. But right as the finishing touches were being added, I accidently dropped a paint pot on it, crushing the tower and splurging red paint all down one side. Gaping at the destruction, tears threatening, I didn't dare turn to Tate, and all I could think to say was, "whoops."

His crazed burst of laughter was the extreme opposite of the reaction I'd been expecting from him. "Blood! Blood everywhere!"

Then, without warning, I was laughing right along with him, a riot of giddy hiccups chipping away the lump in my throat. "But I ruined it," I said, gesturing at the mess in case he'd somehow missed the gravity of the situation.

He stuck his finger in the spill and dabbed it on my nose. "Making it was the fun bit."

And from that day on, we'd been inseparable.

Until I left.

This is the second class I've been in with Tate today, seen him several times around the corridors too. He's given me nothing. Pointedly ignored me, in fact. Even when I took the seat beside him in second period Study, he did a top-notch job of pretending I didn't exist. Impressive, really. Cos I sure as hell didn't make it easy for him. Reminisced on the good old days of our youth; summarised my Newcastle years; lamented on the wreck of my room; and then, finding the one-sided conversation an unrewarding struggle, switched tack to joke telling in the hope of surprising amusement from him. Not a word; not a glare; not a glance.

Squat. All.

I'm livid.

Maybe I should ping something off his head.

So I left and we lost touch. Time passed and we moved on. Now I'm back −unexpectedly; and he's still here −unexpectedly. It's weird, I get that. I do. But it's not like I'm demanding immediate best friend reinstatement. Surely, I'm at least due...

I jump as the bell sounds, marking the end of class.

"Everyone needs the board notes written down before leaving." Mr Garrimay bellows over the sudden explosion of chatter and scraping chairs.

Tate remains bowed over his desk, pen moving furiously. I'd never have pegged him as the conscientious student type. All toil and no trouble, where's that attitude sprouted from?

I release my pen onto my blank paper.

A body drops into the vacant chair beside me and then my arm is jiggled, knocking my chin from its prop on my fisted hand.

"You not hear me, space cadet?"

I turn my head partway to the petite, freckle-faced, curly haired blond to my left, keeping Tate in the edge of my vision.

"Thought anymore about coming with us?" Lyndsay appointed herself as my guide when I mistakenly stumbled into her fourth period English class instead of my Maths. She's taken the role very seriously. "Come on, you know you want to."

"Hey, nope. Can't. Sorry."

"Aww, Mikey! We're just going to the View. It's fun. You can free up half an hour, right?"

The View: Top of the bank overlooking the play park one side and the stream the other, good vantage point to see out across much of the town. David spent many of his evenings there as a teen.

I remember, once, being woken up and dragged from my bed by Mum. Cos David had missed curfew and I had to go with her to collect him (don't know where Dad was that night. Working late probably). Mum'd pulled into the small parking area beside the play park. Left in the car, I'd watched her storm up the long bank, and then, ten minutes later, watched her frogmarch my stumbling-drunk and angry big bro back down it. He fell across the backseat and immediately puked in the footwell.

And I remember, another time, Tate sending me up on a dare to ask David for a couple of quid. I made it only far enough up to spy the gaggle of loud and loitering big kids at the top and, chickening out, I tripped over my own feet in my flight, rolling a majority of the way back down. Tate thought it hysterical.

Really is kinda depressing how very, very rooted such things are here. Primary to Secondary –the park to the View.

Pretty sure all that's there is an old three-sided rusty metal shed, a few picnic benches, and a tyre swing. *So much fun.*

I sigh. "Lynds…"

"Newbie, you can't be turning down social opportunities."

"Absolutely, I know. But today's no good for me." Annoyance leaks into my tone, which is unfair. She's been nothing but friendly. *Overly friendly.* I try again, aiming for a more regretful sound, "sorry, but cheers anyhow." I fail.

Her friend, Stephanie —a loud-dressing redhead I vaguely recall from Somerton (Lyndsay's a Redstow Primary kid; considered our rival, once upon a time) – stops beside the desk. "You ready?"

Lyndsay jiggles my now-desk-rested arm again, quirking a brow. I shake my head. "Fine." I catch her eye roll as she stands, perky smile unfaltering. "I'll try again tomorrow."

Tate's standing too, freeing his orange headphones from his bag then cramming his books in.

"Wait." I halt Lyndsay's move away, grabbing her sleeve. She looks down at me expectantly. "Will Tate be there?"

"Who?"

Stephanie snorts and nods her head —none-too-subtly —in his direction. "You know. McAllister, there." She says; pointing too, for good measure.

I cringe, frowning at her. And then whip around to check Tate for a reaction as Lyndsay laughs, loud, and says, "Mac? Wow, now that would be interesting." But nope, no reaction, he's leaving.

Loading my books into my arms, I grab up my bag.

"You changed your mind?"

"Try me again tomorrow," I call back as I hurry after my swiftly departing, uncooperative best friend.

"Oh, Steph, I'm seriously in love with his Geordie accent."

For the gazillionth time, girl, I do not sound even remotely Geordie!

"He doesn't have an accent, Lynds." I get Steph's backing.

By the time I make it through the crowded hallway and out the school, Tate's lost to me.

~

I WALK into the house to find Jean violently thrusting Henry Hoover over the hall carpet. And crying.

Hurrying to the socket, I flick the power off. She startles when Henry cuts out.

"Oh, Mikey. Hi." Her attempt at a smile is pathetic.

"Have you...have you got a fat lip, Jean?"

Dropping the hoover hose, she slaps a hand over her mouth. And dropping my bag to the floor, I step toward her, frowning. "What happened? Where is everyone?" Without Henry Hoover's hum, the house is deathly quiet.

Shoulders slumping, she scrubs her hand over her tear stained face before lifting her gaze to me. "David had a meeting in Exeter. He's caught in traffic coming home. Shouldn't be long. Mel's on school run. Be home soon, too."

Tremendous. My hands clench at my sides. "So Gran's...?"

Her eyes flick toward the door of the master bedroom. "Mel asked if she wanted to go with her to collect Sophie. Evelyn was enjoying tea and cake, watching last night's Corrie, so I said it'd be best leaving her be." She sighs and runs her tongue over her swollen bottom lip, averting her eyes. "Five minutes after Mel left, your gran decided she really wanted to go. There was no reasoning with her, you know how she is once she starts. She's shut herself in her room, and I think she's pulled something across it cos it ain't opening."

Breathe, Mikey, breathe. I start for the door. Jean beats me to it, blocking the handle. It's then I notice the brown splotch down the front of her cream blouse. "And you?"

"It's nout. Really."

Shaking my head, I step into her.

"Evelyn's cup," she concedes, tightly, taking a step back, freeing up the door.

"Goddamnit, Jean." My fist connects with the wall. "*Fuck!*"

"Mikey!"

I take the handle, turn, and push, but it doesn't budge.

"Gran!" I knock, "Gran, it's Mikey. Open the door."

Nothing.

"Come on, love." Jean tugs on my jacket sleeve. "Leave her to calm down, and you come calm down some too, eh?"

I knock again, harder. "GRAN! You okay in there?"

More nothing. And then, just as I raise my hand for a third knock: "Where on God's green earth've ye been, boy?"

"School." I shoot an accusatory glare at Jean, having no one else to direct it at. "I had to go to school, remember?"

"Oh, school. How lovely for you. Everyone's got to go somewhere lovely 'cept for me. Not allowed out, me."

I lean into the door and shove. "What have you blocked the door with? Come out, Gran, please?"

"Haddaway wi'ye!" Leavus alone, man."

"Need to..." Another failed shove, "talk. Can you..."

I'm cut off by the front door slamming wide open against the wall and Sophie barrelling in.

"Uncle Mikey! Have fun at school? I did. I gotta new liberrerry book."

"First day, and I come in to find her locked up in her room!" I explode as Mel follows her daughter in, her hands full with small pink coat, umbrella, wellies, bag, and a weird, brightly coloured, cardboard...thing. "Great arrangement. Working so freaking well."

Setting her burden down on the shoe rack, Mel passes Sophie her school bag, all the while scolding me with her eyes. "Sweetheart, go on upstairs and start on your homework, could you? I'll be up in a mo."

"I wanna do my homework when Uncle Mikey does his. We can help each other."

"This ain't gonna work. You get that right?" I shirk Jean's hand off my shoulder. "It's stupid!"

"I just need a quick word with your Uncle Mikey first, alright?" Mel nudges Sophie toward the stairs and then straightens. "What happened, Jean?"

"Gran threw a cup at her."

"Oooh, really? Why'd Nanny do that, Uncle Mikey?"

"Kid, do one, would ya?"

"Take no notice, Sophie." Now I feel Jean eye-scolding me, too. "Your Uncle needs to watch his mouth and use his head more. Do as your mammy says, and I'll sort you a nice slab of choccy cake for when you're done, hmm?"

Sophie huffs. Her steps are markedly less bouncy than her entrance, her stink-eye impressively venomous, as she passes me. I hear her stomp up the stairs, muttering, "I'm not doing my homework, so HA! I'm gonna practice my numbers instead."

"You better start watching your tone around your niece, Mikey." Mel snaps as soon as Sophie's topped the stairs. "That was well out of order!"

I shrug, turning back to the door and half-heartedly shoving my shoulder into it. "Open the door, Gran. We can talk about my day if you want?"

"Boy, swear to God, you wanna let me alone!" Gran bellows. Something smacks off the inside of the door and I recoil back. "Sick of folk botherin' me. Sick of ye always, *always* on my bleedin' case. Sod off."

I blink. Rapidly. Clenching my jaw, I draw deep breaths through my nose, trying to force back the lump suddenly obstructing my throat.

Jean rubs my back, "Don't, love."

I whirl back around on Mel. "We were alright. Doing fine as we were. You just had to mess, didn't you? Screw you all to hell, I hope you're happy!"

5

SO THAT'S HOW IT IS, HUH?

*S*torming into the living room, door slamming behind me, I drop down onto the sofa and press my face into the arm cushion, my hands clenched together behind my head.

I can faintly hear Jean and Mel discussing the recent happenings out in the hall. Their voices infuriatingly calm and reasonable. Not what this situation warrants at all.

A few minutes later, I hear the door open and then the edge of the sofa, by my feet, depresses. It's Jean, the waft of rose tells me. I don't move.

"We know better than to take it to heart, Mikey. Drive ourselves mad if we took it all personally."

Of course I know that. I say nothing.

"You reacted appallingly. You know better than that too, don't you?"

Duh.

She pats my leg. "Talk to me. You and me, that's what we do, right? Turn around."

I don't. Silence stretches. Jean waits.

Then: "We shouldn't be here, Jean."

"What?"

Lowering one arm and turning my head to the side, I repeat myself.

"Oh, love, I know it's hard. And I know, adjusting to the change, it's not gonna seem like it. But this is the best..."

"No."

"It is." She squeezes my ankle. I move it away. "David's made mistakes, I'll grant you. But he does care, I honestly believe that. Him and Mel, you need them. Evelyn needs them. They're family."

"No." From my position, I can see the framed photo on the mantelpiece of me and David. I could only be a few months old in it, cradled in David's arms. Baldy baby, I looked ridiculous. It's one captured memory in amongst many: Ones of Sophie; Mel with Sophie; David with Sophie; the happy family; and a montage of wedding pics. The one and only photographic documentation on display of the time I considered David my family. Nothing of Mum and Dad up there. Says a lot. "*We* were family, Jean. You, Suzy, Hannah. Gran and me."

"You think I betrayed you? Let you down?"

"You did!"

She sighs, shifts her weight. "It hurts that you think that."

I burrow myself back into the sofa arm.

"Evelyn's deteriorating, love. She's not..."

"Don't!"

"Look...truth is...is I'm not dealing with it. I've tried, for you, but it's killing me. Sounds selfish, I know, but you were..."

"Don't!" I shove up, swinging my feet around her to the floor. "Don't. Don't dare make out like I wasn't dealing either. Cos I was."

"Try to understand, Mikey. Give this a chance..."

"Jean," I cut her off. I'm feeling way too close to storming out again. It's becoming a ridiculous habit. And, really, I'm much too weary to be doing any more of it. "I don't want to talk. Can we not? Can you leave me be?"

She considers me awhile, concern creasing her brow. Clearing

42

her throat —once, twice —she pushes up to her feet. "Mikey, I'm... going home. Tomorrow, first thing."

My head whips up. Something like panic flaring. "What?"

"I thought I'd help Evelyn settle in. But I'm not. I'm not helping anyone."

I turn away, fixing on a photo of David holding a tiny, pink baby-groed Sophie with a fluff of dark hair —set right beside the one of him holding me. His idiotic grin stretches ear-to-ear in this one. My eyes burn.

"You're a good kid, Mikey, and I love the bones off of you. I'm not turning my back on you. None of us are. You're mad now, but... don't you forget that, alright? We're still here for you. For you both. Only a phone call away." She sighs. Clears her throat again. "This is going to work out, I truly, *truly* believe that. And...and you've got some being young to do, love, don't forget that either."

I don't release baby Sophie from my fury until I hear the door click softly shut. Then I flop back with an almighty vocal unleashing, punishing the sofa cushion.

GIVING myself a few minutes to pull it together, I make a move out the living room. Try on Gran again. No matter everyone else and their crap —whatever, I'm not letting her down.

I'm halted outside her room by voices within it. Trying the handle, the door swings easily open.

"Calmed down now, have you?" Mel's perched on the side of Gran's bed.

Gran's in bed, fully clothed under the duvet, looking for all the world like she's having the jolliest of jolly times. "Could you givus awhile longer, dear love? Melissa needs my advice. Personal, ye know."

Mel smiles at her, patting her hand, receiving Gran's smile in return. "If anyone can help me out, I'm sure it's you." Then she looks back to me as if to say, *'run along now, no need for you here'*.

"Um..." Something lead-heavy drops into my stomach from outta nowhere, "sure. Yeah. I'll...I guess I'll be upstairs."

~

"WHAT'S UP, MIKEY?" Lyndsay's slowed and turned, noticing I've dropped behind our little lunch-hall headed group, drawn up by the large sash window looking out across the Quad.

"All's good," I wave her off, "I'll catch yas up."

She joins me, following my gaze. "Weirdos. As if it's picnic weather."

I nod. It may not be raining now, but it has been. And it's far from warm out. There's a half dozen tables lining the far side of the green, along the drab brown Sixth Form block. Only the one is occupied.

Tate wasn't at the gates this morning, leaving me with a long and lonely wait. Nor was he in second period study. No sign by lunchtime, I'd pretty much marked him off a no show for the day. But there he is.

"Guys," Callum calls back, slowing Steph and twitching his long nose in an effort to straighten his specs. "The queue'll be getting longer by the second. No time for dawdling."

Tate's not alone. There's a girl sat across from him, her back to me, jet black hair sleeked over one shoulder. The white shirt collar visible above her blue coat and the grey trousers tell of her being younger. I see her slide something across the table to him. See him glance down at it. And then he's laughing. It's not his full-on, creased-over-and-spasming laugh I've countless amusing memories of, but it's genuine.

I feel a smile tug at my mouth, even as my gut sours. *I failed to even prompt a smile.*

"Cal's right, ya know." Lyndsay nudges my shoulder with hers. "Come on."

"I'll catch yas up," I repeat, already started down the hall toward the door leading out. "Won't be a mo."

"Tsk, suit yourself."

Stepping out, I'm spotted quickly. And all evidence of his good humour vanishes. *Ouch.* The girl turns as Tate averts his attention to capping the pen in his hand. Her charcoal eyes catch on me and hold.

Honey toned skin, wide cheekbones and a small pointed chin: It takes me only a breath to place her. Adele Saunders. All grown up.

I know she knows me too, I can see it. But I get no smile, no *'hey, Mikey, good to see ya'*. A frown pinches her brow.

Adele was −likely still is, I don't know −Tate's next-door neighbour. A year our junior, she attended the Catholic school −St. Paul's. We'd let her play with us sometimes. Not often; generally, we found her annoying. In truth, I'm irked now just looking at her.

I start my approach.

Tate stands, snatching up his bag from the bench beside him.

"Oh, hells, no. Tate, don't you dare," I call, speeding my pace.

Frown deepening, Adele whips back around to him. He shakes his head. Then, collecting a notebook from the table, he strides away.

"TATE! Adele...?"

"Don't bother, Alston." Adele cuts me off, gathering her own stuff from the table as Tate disappears down the alley between the Sixth Form block and the music wing.

"Explain, please," I say, my voice shamefully unsteady.

Hitching a shoulder, she follows after him. "He's not being subtle, is he?"

Okay, yeah, I dislike her immensely.

IT'S NOT until leaving school at the end of the day I next see Tate.

I'm walking out with Lyndsay and company, having softened my View rejection with an agreement to walk alongside as far as the park (it's sort of on the way anyhow). The group's idling along at snail's pace. Steph's a few paces ahead, sloshing through puddles with her clunky lime green boots. Callum's behind, practically clipping my heels, talking louder than necessary on his phone to –I suspect –his mum. Lyndsay's pressed in close to my right side, talking about me right across me to the big, surly guy with a blond faux-hawk (Andrew?) on my left. Only half listening to her, I'm discretely scanning the mass exodus of students surrounding us, searching for a dark head peeking above the rest. It's not until a rogue football whizzing past my face jolts my attention to the bordering woods, however, do I spy him.

It's the bright orange of his headphones that catches my eye.

Tate's not among the herd trudging the driveway. Only a short way up ahead, his steps as unrushed as ours, he's cutting his own path through the trees.

"Mikey went to primary school with Steph," Lyndsay's saying, a teasing tone to her voice. "He was a right troublemaker, she's told me. Prone to huuuge temper tantrums. And, oh, this one time, apparently, he..." She stops short and I feel my jacket sleeve catch, promptly liberated. I've picked up my pace, pulling ahead. "Mikey?"

Cutting across Possibly-Andrew, I lope into the trees. "I'll be back. TATE. HEY!"

I catch him up, reaching for his arm to get his attention. I've barely even touched him when he grabs my wrist –hard, whirling on me. The expression on his face is one I'd never have thought him capable of, it's more than a little, um...terrifying.

"Whoa, man, ow."

There's a flicker of *something* as he looks me over, and he frees my wrist, but he doesn't wind down. His eyes fix a touch south of meeting mine, guarded, intense. He takes a small step back. "Why...shit...why can't you just take the fucking hint?"

Words! He spoke words to me. Progress. "I'm stubborn. Or maybe dense." I rub my poor wrist, glancing from him to it to his stupid obstructive headphones. "Can you take them off?"

"Don't want to talk to you, Mikey."

And my name! Forget context. "Why, Tate?"

His jaw clenches, eyes flicking past me and returning with renewed hostility. I won't back down. "The past is the fucking past. Leave me there. I'm...It's...no." Shaking his head, he drags in a long breath through his nose. His voice is toneless, and he's speaking as though rusty at it; slow and stammering. But his words aren't lacking in clout, that's for sure. "You seem to be alright... doing alright for friends. And this? Here? It's heading you for social suicide."

Okay, at that I do kinda back down; glancing behind me to see that, yeah, my new buds are all gathered at the kerbside, staring at us. Their expressions vary, but none are encouraging. Possibly-Andrew is looking especially disapproving.

Tate's words sink in. With them, the realisation I've perhaps been viewing this whole situation with blinkers on. It's troubling.

"Tell me why?" I ask again, swerving back around.

Tate's walking away, further into the trees, his stride considerably quickened.

"TELL ME WHY?"

He doesn't turn.

I choke back a savage growl of frustration, gritting my teeth to hold it there. *Goddamnit!* Why is he being such a tool? The one upshot to my forced return, and he's failing me spectacularly.

"Wow. That has to burn some." A breakout of sniggering draws my attention back around to the group of spectators gathered on the driveway. I find Steph and Callum looking unabashedly entertained, and Lyndsay appears to be working hard on holding her face straight. "But, hey, if it makes you feel any better," Steph continues. "You got more from him there than any of us ever do."

I blink. "It doesn't."

Surly Faux-Hawk doesn't appear even remotely amused. Thick brows cinched close, he rakes his gaze over me, chilling my insides. "Mac don't play nice with others, mate. Waste of time."

If I frown anymore, I'm fairly certain my face'll cave in on itself.

47

"Guy creeps me out," chimes in Callum with an exaggerated shudder, not helping.

Lyndsay's expression sobers, shifting to something dangerously close to pity. "That's enough, guys," she cautions, narrowing her eyes at Callum before starting her way toward me. "Mac was his friend, cut him some slack. Ready to move on, Mikey?"

I start to nod but stop, Lyndsay's choice of words lodging a screw in the cogs. She takes hold of my elbow and I flinch. No. No, stuff em. I have no intentions of moving on anywhere, and no one's gonna make me. Whatever their issue, I don't care, it's theirs not mine. And whatever Tate's issue, well —I cast a glance over my shoulder, marking the point I saw him last —I'm not through with him. This guy's not so easily repelled. No siree.

Freeing my arm from Lyndsay's grasp, I pull back, "I'll see you tomorrow."

"What?"

"Sorry," I add, sidestepping past her.

"Hey!"

Speeding to a jog, I feel eyes trained on my back as I hit the driveway far ahead of the others.

Tate McAllister will be my friend again. My best friend. I'm decided. Tension eases from my muscles. I slow to a brisk walk. *It's decided.*

"Until tomorrow. Dickwad." I mutter into the trees.

6

MY BAD

*O*nly, Tate doesn't show for school the next day. Or the one after. Friday neither. I'm concerned, and the only one who seems to be.

Steph's told me he's absent often, and she suspects he's skiving. But when I think of the Tate I've seen in class, head buried in his text books, or fervently scribbling notes, or hawk-eyed on the teacher, that theory really doesn't fit too comfortably with me. When I ambushed Adele in the science corridor yesterday, she'd simply shrugged and told me it was none of her business and even less so mine. Then she'd shoulder barged past me (and for a small girl, she's got the power of a freaking truck).

I did consider calling at his house last night. Went so far as to skate up and grab my jacket. Chickened out halfway down the stairs. Having him slam the door in my face at the house I could once walk into without knocking? Ouch! No thank you. Plus, I don't know if he still even lives there. And also, his dad never was much of a fan of mine.

Not that I can say Tate's presence acts to brighten my day, but without him —without even the slightest chance of seeing him, cornering him, talking to him, making headway —the latter half of this week has felt like a dismal, purposeless waste of time.

My life outside of school has not been any more attributed with point. Hurrying in each afternoon only to be side-lined, told I should be out socialising and *'having fun'*, it's maddening. Worse, because I haven't even *felt* needed. Gran's been busy planting trees and colouring with Sophie, making friends with the nurse next door and having her hair done at Mel's salon. I'm missing Jean. She hasn't called. Suzy has, I refused to talk to her.

So, come Friday afternoon, I find myself trekking up the long bank to the View.

Lyndsay walks beside me, her arm linked through mine. I don't have the heart to un-link it, even though I'm having to walk infuriatingly slow to stay paced with her. She'd sulked at me for an awkward hour or so the morning after I ditched her. I bought her an apology Twix from the school's vending machine.

In electric blue mac and her lime boots, Steph's leading the way with faux-hawk Alex (yeah, turns out his name is Alex, not Andrew. And, also, he's an utter tool); Mousey Callum's winging Lyndsay's other side; and half a dozen more senior YCS'ers shadow behind.

"Relax, would ya?" Lyndsay bounces her shoulder off mine.

"I am relaxed. Just cold." A half-truth: It is freaking freezing. I can see my own breath puff out. Now, see, I get that Yoverton has little to offer in the way of fun, but surely, *surely* there's better can be found than this exposed hilltop hangout, right?

"And you claim to be a Geordie? You're not supposed to get cold."

I make a concerted effort not to roll my eyes. "No. I've never once made any such claim, Lynds. My gran's Geordie. Mum and Grandad were Geordie. I am as Devonian as you are. And I'm very cold."

"And grumpy."

Yes, and grumpy. Alright for her: Baby pink hat over her blond curls, scarf tucked around her neck, her hands snug in matching mitts, she's looking delightfully toasty. "Remind me again how this'll be fun?"

"Jeez, Mikey!" She laughs, rubbing my arm ineffectually. "It'll be warmer in the shed, yeah? And if you're still chilly, we can snuggle together."

A sigh slips out. I cough to cover.

The View turns out to be not as hideous as I anticipated, to be fair. It is actually pretty sheltered and snug within the three-sided shed. There's even some chairs stashed inside, saving my arse from the cold, hard concrete floor. Someone sets their phone up with speakers, filling the close space with music (God-awful boom-boom-boom music), and a couple of resourceful boy-scouts even thought to bring torches along. It being Friday, there's also alcohol passed around —though, for all I know, that could be the way of it every day of the week. The light weight I am, I take two cans of cider from Callum and endeavour to stretch them out. Lyndsay seems to be of like mind, setting two of her own down between our chairs.

"You good?"

"Yeah, I'm good," I admit.

And she beams.

We've been here a couple of hours, and I'm about a third the way through my second can, enjoying the first half-decent tunes I've been exposed to tonight (annoyingly Alex's pick), and listening in to a couple of year eleven's debating whether or not i-phones are better than Samsungs, when Lyndsay returns to me from a stint outside watching the kick about a few of the guys are having.

"I've got to get home for dinner. Don't suppose you'd mind walking me, would you?" She looks at me expectantly before rushing on, "I mean, if you're not ready to go yet, that's completely fine, don't worry."

"You live the next street from me," one of the year eleven guys is quick to interject, standing up behind her. "I could walk you."

Lyndsay ignores him, fixed on me.

"No. Yeah, absolutely." Putting my can down, I attempt to free myself from the rust coated, bent-all-out-of-shape chair I've sunk deep into. I fail miserably. "Just...givus a sec here."

"Here." Lyndsay shoves her mitted hand out toward me, trying not to laugh. She's not much help but, together, I finally extract myself.

The chair is punished with a mean kick. "I should get back too, so," I grab up my bag, "yeah, good to go."

The i-phone supporter casts a scowl my way before sinking back down in his seat.

Coming up to 6pm, the sky's already fairly dark. It's a shock to the system, stepping out of the shed's protection into the harsh evening air. I burrow my head down into my jacket collar and ram my hands deep into the pockets. Lyndsay's quick off the mark linking her arm back through mine.

"Thanks, Mikey."

"No problem. Where's Steph, like?

"Oh," her arm tightens around mine, "Steph won't leave until everyone else already has."

"Ah."

"You'd come again, right?"

"I guess." I can sense her side-eying me. "Yeah. It... wasn't awful."

"Oh, high praise indeed. But good, I'm glad."

It's not far to Lyndsay's house. *Thank God*; cos the illusion of a comfortable silence we've got going on is wearing mighty thin fast, and there's only so many times we can glance at each other and smile before it becomes absurd.

"This is my street," she says, drawing to a stop at the corner of the neat terraced row. "So..."

"So..." I pull my hand from my pocket, breaking our arm link, "see you Monday, yeah?"

"Mikey, are...?" She huffs, clouding the air, looks away and then back with a smile in place. "Are you free anytime this weekend?"

"Err?"

"Would you like to do something? With me, I mean."

Jeezus, where has all my oxygen gone?

The smile I'm sure she must think she has looking ultra-solid and cocksure is exceptionally jittery; becoming more so the longer my speechless silence drags out, until it finally peters away and she averts her gaze. Even under the garish orange glow of the street-light, I can see her pale, freckled face heated a precious shade of pink.

Don't know why I'm so surprised, really. It's not like she's been especially subtle in her interest. I guess I just kinda figured *–hoped* *–*if I ignored it, it would quickly...like, drop off and go away. Walking her home clearly was not my best move ever. That Twix was dumb, too.

"Wow, okay." She steps away from me. "Too forward. Forg..."

"Yeah. Um, yeah," I blurt, startling the both of us. "You want to go out? When?"

With a shaky little laugh, she prods my chest. "That's your call, Mikey."

"Right." I flounder. "To...tomorrow? Cinema?" *Idiot! Too soon, too tragically unoriginal.*

"That sounds awesome." Tugging my jacket sleeve, she starts us walking again. "Only if you're sure you want to, though?"

"Absolutely. Looking forward to it," I lie.

I tense as she appraises me. "You're an awful liar."

"I am *not* lying," I lie some more. "Honestly."

"Then...awesome."

"Yep, awesome."

It's not that I don't like her. Lyndsay's nice. Really *nice*. Just... I've only ever got into 'things' with girls I've known well as friends first. And even then, it's never worked out so great. My last girl-friend was Jody. That was over a year ago. After close-on three years of friendship, we lasted less than a week as a couple. And, really, it was horrendous. I barely know Lyndsay.

Could make the difference.

I muster a pathetic smile for her, circle my awkward arm

around her awkward shoulder and walk her the few steps to her gate.

Yeahhh, doubt it.

～

"AND YOU'RE positive you're going to be okay?" David says, side-stepping me to grab his car keys from the tray on the shoe rack. "She's grouchy today."

"I'm gonna assume you're extracting the urine."

"Mikey, I'm not having a dig. I just feel real lousy dropping this on you. It's Saturday, you should be free to..."

"Socialise and have fun. Yeah. Them's the rules, right?"

"Sophie, hurry up!" He shouts up the stairs. "We'll call for pizza on the way back, shouldn't be later than five. Mel, you ready?"

"Just helping Evelyn find her slipper. Won't be a sec," Mel calls from Gran's room.

"So, any do's and don'ts for me?" I ask. "Heaven knows what ballyhoo I'll get into if you don't set some ground rules down."

"I trust you."

Well, that's laughable. "No. No, you don't."

"Uncle Mikey!" Sophie prances down the stairs in a puffy red dress, ringletted hair bouncing, an oblong box clutched to her chest. Stopping sharp in front of me, she thrusts it out. "For you. It's chess."

"Err..." I step back. "No. Thanks. But no."

"Nanny likes it, Uncle Mikey. Really, really. It puts her in a good mood."

"I've plenty of my own tricks for cheering up Gran." I glance reproachfully down at the chess set she's still brandishing at me. A Sonic the Hedgehog chess set. "What the hell kinda six-year-old plays chess anyway?"

"I'm actually extremely very good at it," she retorts, lifting her chin with too much haught. "But don't worry if you don't know the rules. Sometimes I forget, and it's still fun when you make em up."

I snort.

"Put it down on the stairs, sweetheart," Mel says, emerging from Gran's room and cutting me a glare. "Mikey might change his mind. We've got to go."

They're on their way out to lunch with a client of David's and his family. For a date forgotten until approximately an hour and a half ago, David's of the mind it's a super big deal. Left behind alone with Gran, I'm of the mind it's the giver of a most welcome breather.

"Don't be stubborn, little brother. Call if there's a problem."

"Yu-huh. Y'all take your time now."

No sooner has David stepped out the front door after Mel and Sophie, than: "Davey?" Gran calls out. "Need some help in here. It's stuck!"

Sighing, he looks set to come back in. I swing the door shut on him, flicking the latch lock.

"David's gone out, Gran. Can I help?"

"Oh, Jesus wept! Where's he gone? How long?" I hear a bang, and then, a moment later, she appears in the doorway with dusty streaks down the front of her cardy. "Mikey, dear love, call him back."

"What is it you're doing? I'll give ya a hand." I start toward her.

Her eyes widen and she glances back into her room. "No, no. You're no good." She steps out into the hall, slamming the door behind her. "It'll hav'ta wait. I need Davey."

"Oh." I stop short; I take a long, deep breath. "Okay." *She doesn't mean it. It's nothing personal.* I take another. "Gran, um, how do you feel about chess?"

"I NEED YOUR ADVICE," I greet Jody when she picks up the call on the sixth ring. "Please."

"Oh crap. What's the dealio, Miktard?"

I cross the bedroom to my open door, sticking my head out. I left Gran in the sitting room, catching up with her shows; all's still quiet. "I have a date sort of thing tonight, and I'm..."

"Right, yeah, that's a big problem. Givus her number, and I'll talk some sense into her."

"Har-har! I'm bricking it a little here, Jody. Can you switch tack to pep-talk mode? Tell me it won't be as horrific as I'm thinking it will?"

"It probably will be, though. You want me to fill you with lies?"

"Yes."

"Uck!"

"I want supportiveness and I want useful pointers," I say.

"Useful pointers? Let's start there. What you gonna wear?"

"I don't need your help with what to wear, Jody. You dress like a tramp."

"Whoa, prick! One more comment like that and I'm hanging up. And wiping all memory of you from my mind. You know I don't even especially like you anyways, right?"

For all that Jody's fun company —a rather superb skating companion, she's actually kind of a pretty rubbish friend. Not the greatest person to talk anything through with. But it's not like I have the luxury of choice. "Okay. Sorry. I'm sorry. Forgive me please."

"I grant you a pass. One pass. What I was just going to *usefully* point out was... well, as much as you love your Wile E. Coyote shirt —and as truly, *truly* splen-diferous as it may be, don't wear it."

"Firstly, I don't appreciate the sarcasm. And secondly," I glance down at my Wile E. Coyote shirted chest (red, it features Wile tied to a launched rocket, the tagline reads 'I do all my own stunts'; it's awesome), "you can't diss on this tee."

"HA! Knew you'd be wearing it. So predictable. Seriously, I advise you to change. Or has the hole on the shoulder magically repaired itself?"

I side-eye my shoulder like I genuinely expect that it may have done. *Nope.* "You're terrible at this."

"Uh, what did you expect?"

"Yeah, point. My bad."

"So...aside from certifiably insane, what's this girl like? It is a girl, right?"

"Nice, Jody, real n..." I'm cut off by an almighty crash downstairs. It's closely followed by a gut-wrenching scream.

"Mik...?" My phone drops from my hand, thudding off the thick carpet.

"GRAN!" I launch out the room.

7

CAN'T BE HERE

*S*tumbling on the stairs, one foot tripping on the other, I plummet down the entire flight on my arse. All air thwacked outta me, I catch the banister on the second off last step, reclaiming oxygen in gulps.

The wailing –Gran's pained wailing –sirens out at me. *Her room.* The door's ajar. I scramble for it on hands and knees.

I've not passed the threshold into this room since my return – the only element familiar to me being the placement of the bed; I spare no time dwelling on that needling discomfort now.

Sprawled across the floor on her side, arms enfolding her head, she's shaking and crying and –*oh God* –bleeding. There's blood on the cream carpet. The smell of urine invades my nose as I fall down beside her.

"Gr-Gran? Gran?" I try, ever so gently, with uncooperative fingers, to prise an arm from her face. "What happened, Gran? Where're you bleeding? I need to see. Let me see, Gran, please let me see." She clasps her head tighter. The noise; she's making such an awful noise. A tear falls free of my nose, I don't see where it falls.

I look about for...for...*something.*

The toppled chair... the box peeping out over the edge of the wardrobe... Gran's barely-utilised walking stick hooked into the top of it...

"What were you doing? Gran, what the *fuck* were you doing?" I slam a shaking hand over my mouth. "Oh. Oh no, I'm sorry. I'm so sorry."

∾

"DAMN, MICHAEL. ASSAULTING A SNACK MACHINE?"

I drag in my lungs' fill of the fresh air, the first proper breaths I've managed in a long while. They should be soothing me. They're not. My eyes are trained dead ahead, focused on the little girl, dark hair in plaited pigtails, who's spinning circles across the pavement someway further along. Unintentionally, she's adding to the chaos in my head.

"You want to explain to me what the hell that was in there?" David draws us to a halt beside a grassy bank and, releasing my arm from his vice-grip, steps in front to stare me down. I attempt to rub all lingering sense of his touch off of me, but I'm pretty certain he's given me a set of finger-shaped bruises. "What on earth were you thinking?"

Can't even force a shrug, I'm wound up so tight. I paid for crisps from a vending machine, the crisps weren't delivered, and the enemy part of my brain convinced my body to freak. Now David's pulled me out the hospital. Literally pulled. Need to chat, he'd said. His definition of 'chat' is very different to mine. More a scolding to my ears. Not that I'm especially listening to him. Still not even looking at him.

I can see the kid beyond his shoulder, spinning around and around and around. The screwy notion I somehow know her holds its bite, viciously gnawing away at my brain like a rabid freaking dog, and though I realise I shouldn't be staring at her, I can't not.

"The way you were going at that machine...if it were anyone

else but me caught you, you could have been done for criminal damage," David continues, background noise.

My hands are clenching and unclenching at my sides.

There's no way I could possibly know her. No way. Makes zero sense. I'm acquainted with precisely one kid in Yoverton. One. Sophie. And there's no wiggle space for debate on that. Meaning this girl, well, she absolutely doesn't have any place in which to fit. Yet...

It's exceedingly frustrating. Infuriating, even.

A tiny glimpse into how Gran must feel so much of the time, a merciless little voice needles into the mix, *with all those simple connections refusing to click into place for her.* I grit my teeth, inwardly scowling at my brain, as a sharp punch of anguish explodes in my chest.

"In away from the road, Megan." I hear a man's deep voice call from somewhere. The girl casts a quick glance over her shoulder before whirling herself closer to the building.

Megan? Nope, nothing.

"Not to mention the damage you could have done to yourself. You listening?" I readjust my focus a teeny smidgeon in David's favour. And feel instantly worse for doing so. He's shaking his head, his expression one of serene, implacable judgement. Would be so satisfying to punch him in the face. If only I could muster the energy. Behind him, Megan stops spinning and starts dancing. "Your behaviour's completely irrational. You realise that right?" David steams ahead. "Gran's fall shook you up, I get that. But... seriously, help me out here, little brother. A couple hour's observation and Gran's good to come home. Scare over. She's okay."

Okay? A derisive snort escapes me. Is he really so dense?

Gran's bitten through her tongue; sprained her ankle. Concussed, perhaps —the hospital's monitoring her a while. Yeah, sure, at the doctor's assurance, she's suffered nothing of any major concern today. But *'Okay'*? No, she most certainly is not. And I'm not being irrational.

David didn't hear Gran's gut-wrenching wails; he wasn't there, crouched by her side, terrified by his uselessness; he's not the one who was so consumed by panic he could barely make it through the 999 call. Is David swamped with guilt for failing her —yet again? Nope.

The only hint he's even rattled at all is in the way he's smoothing his hands up and down his jean-clad thighs. And that's likely more due to me. "Nothing? You've nothing to say?" Zero concern in his tone.

I bite the inside of my lip, my gaze yet again straying past him. Kid's no longer on the move but she's far from still, shifting her slight weight from one foot to the other as she's scanning around herself with the expectant concentration of someone trying to find someone. Her eyes pass right over me without a single dot of notice spared. *What in all the seven hells is it about her?*

My obstinate silence prompts a heavy sigh from David. A sigh that makes me all the less willing to *help* him out.

Because I shouldn't have to explain myself to him; how hard it is for me to breathe inside this place, how the echoes of my previous experience here —the pain, the fear, the loss —suffocate me. If he had the first clue about me, he wouldn't need me too.

Another sigh. "You know, everyone —you included —would find life a whole lot pleasanter if you were to lose this bad attitude of yours." He moves his head directly into my line of sight, filling my vision. I recoil. "Hows about you give it a shot, huh?"

My temples are throbbing relentlessly. Christ! What am I even doing? Stood outside, subjecting myself to this patronizing 'disappointed parent' routine of David's while obsessing over some kid...

"Mummy! Mummy!" She's calling —squealing really – jumping up and down by the curb, skinny arms raised high over her head and waving. "I see Mummy's car!"

...Some random girl who, really, I could only have chanced upon once —in the park or the newsagents or out in the street – somewhere, my messed up, overly wrung out brain magnifying the significance.

Her. David. *Seriously?* I throw my head back, glowering at the mackerel grey sky. This, this is not what I'm freaking here for. "I need to go back in."

"No." David hooks my elbow as though I'd made some move to walk away. I hadn't budged. I do now though. Wrenching free, I take a big step back and slam him a look of undisguised loathing. I see the muscle jump in his jaw. "You don't. You need to get a grip."

"Screw you!"

Oh, that startles him. Seems I have a little juice left after all.

"You're no good to Gran like this."

I laugh in that vapid way people do when there's nothing funny, interlocking my fingers behind my head so I can't do anything rash. My hair's damp with sweat. "And us out here yapping's helping her how?"

"Go home." It's not a request. My eyes narrow to iddy biddy slits, daring him to repeat it. Expression turning a little wary perhaps, voice softening, he does. "Just go home, Michae...Mikey. There's really no point to us all hanging around here. Mel can take you. Or I'll give you bus fare. Taxi fare, even."

I'm shaking my head before he's done speaking, adamant. Sure, there's nothing I'd like more than to escape the hospital, get my skates and expend all this away. But I'm not going on David's order, like a shamed child. And I'm not going without Gran. "You go home."

"I'm not the one falling apart."

"I'm not the one dead inside."

"'Scuse me?"

"You heard."

His jaw pressing tight, I see the muscle jump again —one, two three times before he next speaks. "You're impossible."

"Yeah? And you're abhorrent, so..."

"Can you please, for once, try to be reasonable?"

"Can you please, for once, quit pretending you care? Quit pretending you're this really top bloke who's sacrificing oh-so-much for us —his needy, damaged *family*? We mean nothing to you. You think I don't know that? Think I don't know our only purpose here is to make you feel better about... about yourself?" I didn't mean for my voice to rise so high. It breaks at the end there too, which I hate. I clear my throat. "It's sickening. You truly *fucking* sicken me."

He opens his mouth. Shuts it. I see −actually *see* −him swallow down his comeback. Instead, he eyeballs me for a long disturbing moment −as if expecting an apology. My eyes refuse to lock on his. I'm not retracting what I said. He provoked me, he deserved it. And I meant every word. I should be walking away now, leaving David stood here, alone, feeling the fool, returning to where I ought to be −where I'm needed. But no amount of glaring at my feet is spurring them to move.

With a mighty growl, it's my stomach that breaks off the strained silence (and my enmity for the thieving-piece-of-crap snack machine reignites).

David's quick to pounce. "If you won't go home, at least take a break. Check out the cafeteria. Eat. Get a coffee. Yeah?"

I haven't eaten since breakfast, and that consisted of only a handful of M&Ms. I'm ravenous. I watch his hand slide into his jeans pocket, towards his wallet; all slow and purposeful, so as to tempt me. And, *damnit,* I am tempted. But − "I'm about two seconds away from taking off my shoe and chucking it at your head, David. Swear down." −am I even actually capable of stomaching anything right now? I have my doubts. And is chancing it worth allowing David any sort of victory here? Nope.

Bowing his head and shaking it, he retrieves his hand, empty. "None of this is easy for me either, you know?" His tone's soft − deliberately so. It's a tone, I imagine, well suited for talking wannabe jumpers in from ledges.

I curl my lip in what I hope at least resembles a wounding sneer. "And it's lies such as those that've blackened your soul."

Wish I had chucked my shoe at him, he sure wouldn't be chuckling away to himself then. I dare a glance up...and hastily jerk back as his arms launch into an abrupt skyward swing, I catch not the merest hint of amusement on his face. Then, hands slamming down against his sides accompanied by a huffed "Whatever", he's brushing past me. And stalking away.

What. The. Actual...? I turn, my mouth gaping a tad until I realise and slam it shut, eyes tracking him along the path. He walks with his head down, shoulders slumped. And for the teeniest flicker of a millisecond, I find myself perhaps kinda feeling a pinch bad about myself. That gets shut right down.

"Yeah! *What*ever!" I call after him. Not a great feat of scathing genius, granted, but it's passable for purpose: Prick's dragged me out here, pushed all my buttons like only he can, stolen *MY* storm off and −urgh, I feel dirty −almost manipulated an eeking of remorse from me. Like hell is he getting to take the final word too. He doesn't spin and stomp back. In fact, disappearing around a corner, returning to the A&E entrance, I'm not even spared a final glance.

My body sags, bone weary. My legs feel brittle. Far too brittle to cope with keeping me upright, never mind moving. There's a distinct possibility I may just fracture into a gazillion pieces any minute now. *Curse him. Curse him times infinity.* I scowl at the point David passed out of sight, attempting to anger fuel myself. Then, hitting the heel of my hand off my forehead a few times, I force a start after him.

I don't get far: Three tortured steps in and a figure caught in the fringe of my vision rams my feet to a dead halt and snaps my head to the right.

There.

A sudden fierce jolt of giddiness sends me woozy.

Even dressed...*wrong*, with a smart grey pantsuit and shiny black heels replacing the once-typical abundance of contrasting coloured layers, it takes no work whatsoever for me to identify the petite brunette weaving her way through the car park. Approaching, one hand clutching the straps of a huge black bag to her shoulder and the other held up high, she's mirroring the wave of...

My eyes whip to the girl bouncing on her heels at the curb side. *Oh. Holy...*

I *don't* know this kid. I've definitely, most assuredly never seen her before anywhere ever. When I left for Newcastle, she wasn't so much as the whisper of a thought. But... jeezus! The dark hair; the shape of the face, nose, mouth: These I *do* know. Very well. Seems incomprehensible, suddenly, how she could have had me so flummoxed cos it's so freaking obvious.

"Hurry, hurry, Mummy!"

"I am, I am, Angel!" Pausing at the far side of the road as a car slips past, Megan's mum −Tate's mum −Laura casts a brief glance left and then right, and her wide, warm smile glides over me like a rainbow through the gloomy sky. Such a welcome sight, I feel the knot of my insides loosen a fraction, enough for me to pull off a smile of my own. She doesn't see it though. Doesn't see me. Attention swiftly returning to her daughter, she readjusts the bag on her shoulder and starts across, "I'm hurrying as quickly as these silly shoes will let me."

It's not a conscious decision to move closer, but I don't stop myself when I realise I'm doing it.

Megan's on the move too, bounding from the curb onto the road with skinny arms stretched wide.

"No you don't, young lady!"

The kid and I freeze mid-step and turn our heads simultaneously as a man, huge and gruff as a bear, half his face hidden behind coarse dark hair, steps away from the hospital wall into view. Tate's Dad. My hovering foot drops to the ground as if pulled to a magnet. My stomach drops too. The giddiness dies.

"Hey Graham," Laura greets him.

"You're late," Graham responds. "Again."

Megan nods, backward stepping to his side and clutching his hand. Her impish grin is so much like young Tate's, it's eerie.

Smile drawing discernibly and disconcertingly tight, Laura joins them on the pavement. "Well, I'm sorry. I can't control the traffic."

The act of breathing has become something of a challenge again. And it has nothing −okay, only a little −to do with the appearance of Mr McAllister and his unnerving stormy grey eyes.

There's this unpleasant, ominous tension thickening the air.

Outside of a hospital —a place no one visits for the fun of it, ever —only three of the four McAllisters are stood before me...

And Tate's been off school.

Tate's missed school a lot.

Tate's become an ill-tempered, self-styled outcast.

I scan around me —along the length of the red brick building and out across the car park. But nope. Tate's nowhere to be seen.

I'm straight to the worst-case scenario. My brain truly is my worst enemy.

"It's okay, Mummy, we forgive you," Megan says, the only one seemingly oblivious to the heavy atmosphere. Laura strokes her hair affectionately. "Will he get to come home today, do you think? I hate it when he has to be here ages!"

"I know, angel," Laura replies, smoothing her thumb over the girl's cheek. "But the doctors take good care of him, you know that, right? He won't be home today, but soon. Promise."

I remain standing statue still. Continue to not explode into shards, which, under the circumstances, I feel is rather commendable.

"We've left the boy waiting long enough." Graham juts his chin toward the building. "Come on."

Suspicion confirmed: Tate's dying.

8

EAU DE CARLSBERG

I clock Adele as soon as we enter the pub.

It's early Sunday evening and I'm out with Lyndsay. My cancelling of our date had gone only so well as to postpone it for 24 hours. Cinema plan dumped, we're instead spending the night watching her cousin's band, Desperate For Aces, perform in the Red Bull Inn —the most popular of Yoverton's few drinking establishments among the town's youngsters, situated on the corner of its pathetic front street.

Adele's stood at the bar with a blue-haired giant and an excessively pierced giantess. No Tate. Disheartening. The three are engaged in quiet conversation, though Adele's animated expressions and busy hands lend a seeming of rowdiness to the words I can't hear.

"You're going to love these guys, I swear." Lyndsay tugs on my elbow. I survey the rest of the large room as she leads me toward a small table centre-front of the stage, then I eye her dubiously. For all her enthusiastic insistence of Desperate For Aces' talent and local popularity, the deadness of this place tonight casts immense suspicion toward the contrary. With a bright smile, she pulls herself out a chair and slides her coat off over the back of it as she gracefully sits.

The girl's looking really very pretty tonight. Impossible not to notice. Her fair bouncy curls loose across her shoulders and her petite figure flatteringly snug in a lacy black dress, pink heels notching her height up some inches; she's clearly put in the effort.

Almost makes me feel bad. Almost.

I showered. And heeded Jody's advice on the Wile E. tee, plumping for a safe, plain black long sleeve instead. That's as far as my effort stretched.

But no. Cos, see, I have a plan for how this date'll go and impressing her socks off is not it. This mix up I've created is gonna get straightened out, full stop. This girl is getting big-time Friend-zoned. When the evening is through, I do not want for even a teeny tiny ember of uncertainty or hope to exist in her sweet, blond head.

Shirking out of my jacket and hitching my ill-fitting jeans up over my hips, I settle in the seat opposite feeling spotlighted and awkward under her keen study. I flash a smile and then swiftly move my gaze back to the bar. Adele and her friends have moved. Swivelling in my chair, I spot them surrounding the quiz machine in the far corner, their backs to the room. Still only a trio.

"So are you okay going to the bar?" Lyndsay asks, snapping me back to her. I dart a glance toward the dreadlocked barman pumping a pint, visible beyond her shoulder. "I'll go if... if you'd rather not."

I would rather not, in all honesty. Even though I'm not far off, it would take a great leap of imagination to pass me as eighteen without ID. But, giving a sharp shake of my head, I stand. Slim though my chances may be, Lyndsay's are surely zero. "What would you like?"

"A white wine please," she says, reaching a hand down toward her bag under the table.

"No," I halt her, "I've got this."

Beaming, she straightens up.

"Be a mo, then." Clearing my throat and rolling my shoulders back, I cross the room with a firm stride. *Let the humiliation commence...*

...No humiliation occurred. For which I am both relieved and disgusted. This place should most assuredly not still be open and trading.

Lyndsay jams her phone into her coat pocket on my return. "Thanks," she says, taking her large white wine from me with both hands.

I set a pint of cider on the table and slide into my seat. "You're welcome."

Lyndsay takes a drink and smiles. I take a serious gulp, draining a good fifth of my pint in one go, and turn my head so she won't notice my eyes bugging out of my head as I suffer from it. Silence reigns.

Swigging another, much smaller mouthful, I set the cider down and check my watch, then I let my eyes roam the mostly empty pub. Adele's still by the quiz machine, still not with Tate. I check my watch again, and this time register the time: 18.50. *Jeezus! It's gonna be a long night.*

Drawn back to Lyndsay by her prickling attention, I tug my sleeve down over my wrist and school my face. "You look lovely tonight, by the way." It's only fair to acknowledge it, I figure, given the careful consideration she's obviously put into her appearance. After all, my plan is to draw a line between us, not to insult or upset her. And 'lovely' isn't a particularly amorous word, is it? She can't be led on far by that.

"Give it half an hour or so, this place'll be heaving," Lyndsay says simultaneously with a confident nod.

"What?"

And over me once again she says, "oh. Thanks." Her smile turning coy-ish, gaze dropping to the table, a light pink flushes her cheeks. *Damn,* it's a fine but fuzzy line I'm treading. "Just... I know it's looking bad now, but we got here super early cos I wanted to bag us good seats. Give it a little while, though, and the room will be rammed. You'll see."

"Okay." I flick a look over my shoulder at the double doors which have not opened to admit any one since us. "Awesome."

Yet, true to her word, forty agonisingly long and stiff minutes later, the pub is filled to standing room only. It's pretty suffocating. Appears practically the whole of YCS is here —at least from year nine upwards —mixing in alongside a generous smattering of (barely) legal-aged adults. Adele's settled herself at the bar. Two more people have joined her party, but neither of them are Tate. The band have arrived and are up on stage, setting up their equipment.

"Derek's only two years older than me, you know. Wouldn't think it, right?" Lyndsay's fondly fixed on the broad-shouldered guy unpacking the drum kit; hair shorn short, he has colourful tattoos visible up both arms and around his neck. "We were so close growing up. But now...well, you know, with the band and everything, he's always crazy-busy. I only really get to see him when I come watch him play."

There's a distinct slur to her words. I compare her almost empty third glass to my practically untouched second and frown. Her drinks are going down at much greater speed than she allowed for at the View. "That sucks."

"Mmmhmm." She rests her chin in her hand, elbow propped on the table, and lets out a sigh. "Proud of him though, he's totally awesome. Gonna make it big. Like, superstar big. Then I'll be set up for life. S'all good."

"Sounds like a concrete plan there."

"I just wish my mum would...Uck!" Breaking off, she purses her lips tight. "Never mind."

I consider her carefully for a moment, feeling the night's awkwardness spike. "So, um, do they do tours and things? Are they signed?"

Her eyes slide across to me and she giggles. I don't at all understand why she's giggling. A finger points at me from under her chin. "Your hair's adorable."

Oh.

She reaches for her drink with her free hand. I move swiftly to slide it away from her. Thwarted, her hand slams down on the table top and she harrumphs at me.

"Does this place do food? Think I'll go get us some chips or something, yeah?" Leaving her gaping, her glass of wine behind the defence of my cider, beyond her easy reach, I beeline for the bar.

Unfortunately, the once empty bar space is now padded by at least three layers of bodies. Don't even think they *do* do food here, but all pubs stock crisps and nuts and the like, right? I resign myself to quite some wait.

I've been stood for approximately five minutes or so when, off to my left, I see Adele push through the bodies to free herself from the bar crowd. Each of the previous three times I've done the drinks run, Adele's been surrounded, and I've decided against an approach. Now she's broke free, alone, seemingly headed for the ladies' room, I'm quick to grasp my chance.

I intercept her halfway between bar and toilet door.

"What's Tate in hospital for?"

She spins on her heel, her long hair flaring out. I step back. "Christ, Mikey! What makes you think Tate's in hospital?"

"I was there. Yesterday."

"So you saw him?"

"So he is there?"

She rolls her eyes and then her brow scrunches up tight. "Why were you in hospital?"

"There with Gran. She had a fall."

"Oh." Her lips remain in and O for a drawn-out moment. "She okay?"

"Yeah. I mean," I shrug, "I guess so. Shaken up, mostly. Anyway, Tate?"

Adele huffs out a breath, throwing a glance over her shoulder in the direction of the toilets. "Get with it, Mikey, it's too late to reconnect. You've missed out on too much."

"Hey, he could've made an effort to keep in touch too. That's not all on me!"

"Yeah, and that's not on me at all. I'm saying nothing. Not my place, is it?" She moves to walk away.

I grab her arm. Tight. "Please."

Glancing down at my squeezing hand, she scowls and yanks herself free. "Soz."

I watch her continue toward the ladies' room. Door pushed halfway open, she looks back at me, her mouth twisting into a weird half-smile that looks uncomfortable on her face. "He'll be back in school tomorrow. Don't go making it a big deal, 'kay? He won't appreciate it."

The hair stands up on the nape of my neck: I take no reassurance from her words or how she's said them. Specifically asking me not to make it a big deal tells me that, whatever *it* is, it is definitely something big-deal-worthy.

Just as the toilet door swings closed behind Adele, the front doors blast open. My head whips around, in unison with many others', to see Gary Tinwell stagger-fall through the entrance into the group of four guys stood just inside it.

"Ladies and Gentlemen, I have arrived. The night can now truly begin!"

"Brilliant. Just. Freaking brilliant." I mutter to myself, quick-stepping well out of harm's way as he begins shoving a brutal path through to the bar, Ben Baxter and Wayne Dursdale riding in his wake.

Returning to the table a good ten minutes later, I set down packets of ready salted and beefy crisps. Lyndsay's glass is in her hand and empty. Callum is sat in my seat.

"Oh, sorry dude." He nudges his glasses up the bridge of his long nose and makes to push the chair back. "I'll just..."

"Nah man," I drop into the chair between them. "It's alright."

The look I catch on Lyndsay's face as she sets her empty glass down a little sharper than necessary tells me I'm wrong. But then the lights dim, the band take their positions on the narrow stage, the small frontman freeing the mic from the mic stand, and she's on her feet.

Callum leans in close to my left ear. "Aaand we've lost her," he says too loud for being so close, amusement lacing his tone.

I study her until I'm sure the slight sway to her stance isn't likely to bring her crashing down, and then, with a chin jut to Callum, I slump low on the seat, snagging up the beefy crisps.

"Hey folks," the frontman's (surprisingly) deep voice booms through the room, spurring much applause and whooping. "We're Desperate For Aces. It's great to see so many here. Hope you've all got your drinks in and are keyed up to show us some love. Let's kick this off with 'What's Mine Is Mine', should we?"

Lyndsay's clapping like the continuation of the world depends upon it as the first song strikes up. An unanticipated grin tugs stubbornly at my lips.

My gaze drifts over the standing crowd behind me, but I don't catch on Adele's dark head amongst them.

Callum starts singing as the frontman does, loud, and as completely in time as he is out of tune. I see Lyndsay's mouth moving too. And, when the chorus kicks in, she's jumping, her arms going mental above her head.

The Desperate For Aces' set goes on for about forty minutes, and they're actually, legitimately *really* good. Not exactly my usual taste, granted –kinda heavy and a little too screamy in places, but these guys sure do know how to work a crowd. The vibe they've created is pretty damn infectious. Lyndsay's sang along with every song, word for word, aiming the lyrics at me and Callum in turn. She's proven quite amusing to watch –so unreservedly animated, it's been a pleasant distraction.

With the final guitar thrum fading, lights lifting, the crowd eases to relative quiet and Lyndsay finally stills in her seat. Her familiar uncertain smile returns as she scopes the room, as if she'd forgotten and just now remembered she's out in public.

Skipping over Callum, who waggles his eyebrows at her, her eyes settle on me. I push the bag of Ready Salted crisps against her wine glass and she snorts out a laugh. "Great night?"

"Immense!" Callum says, slamming his hands down on the table. "As always."

I fill my mouth with cider, give a thumbs up and nod emphatically.

She nods along with me, smile stretching to a wide grin. "Right then, good. I'm excusing myself to the little girls' room now. And then, um, if you want to go get some more drinks in, Mikey, I'll introduce you to my cousin and the rest of the band. Yeah?"

"Uh," I glance at my near empty glass (crap, where'd that go?), "sure."

Tracking her steady path across the room, I'm given some reassurance that she does appear much sobered. My gaze then strays to the bar as I debate the wisdom of following her instructions. And there's Adele, stood alone, gigantic patchwork bag propped on a barstool as she rifles through it. Getting more drinks will validate me approaching her again, I suppose. If I can figure out a new tack to take, she may be tricked into letting something slip. If...

"Tinwell, stop being a prick and move!" The loud rebuke snaps me back to Lyndsay.

Gary's blocking her path. She steps to the side and he mirrors her. She sidesteps the other way and he does too, all the while smirking. He's clearly wasted, rocking on his feet.

"Come on, Gary."

Gary's a big guy –really big. Granted, he's made up more of fat than muscle, and his cheeks are cherub round with a constant rosy glow, but he's still hella scary. And when he laughs, I instinctively cower down. 'Michaela' is what he had kids calling me in Somerton, came after me almost every day. "No. You 'come on', Lynds." He leans into her, "I jus' wanna talk. Chat a lil, be friendly, you know? Quit bein' rude."

My gaze slides across to Callum and he catches my eye. His

face is completely drained of colour and, seemingly, he's lost all ability of movement.

Great!

I see Lyndsay attempt to turn away, but Gary catches hold of her shoulder and spins her back around to him, stepping in to completely invade her personal space.

"You scrub up real nice, Lynds. You should make an effort more offen."

That's when I find my feet.

Of course, the moment I reach Lyndsay's side, my burst of chivalrous courage disappears. I hitch my jeans up around my waist and widen my stance.

Gary's eyes rake over me, his lip curled. "Piss off, Alston."

"You, err... you ready to go?" I ask Lyndsay, making the mistake of turning away from our threat. This I abruptly realise when a shove to my shoulder sends me careening sideways. I make a frantic grab for a nearby chair and only just manage to avoid my face meeting the floor. My backend crashes into a table, toppling a glass and I feel its dregs soak into my shirt.

"Too far, Tinwell!" I hear Lyndsay shriek.

From hands and knees, I glare up at him. He's greatly amused by himself, his arms lifted high as if welcoming applause. "HA! Epic!"

No one's applauding (discounting his sidekicks). Though many are watching; eyes all around trained on the spectacle that is me. Callum's appeared behind Lyndsay. And, beyond Gary's bulk, I spy Adele. *Superb.*

Lyndsay and Callum take an arm each and I let them help me up. Keeping my head ducked in an effort to hide the scarlet colour of my face, I futilely wipe my sticky hands down my jeans and shake out my top.

Lyndsay presses in close against me, her hand reattaching to my elbow, "you want to wait outside while I grab our stuff from the table?"

My jaw clenched hard, I nod.

"Hey, no hard feelings, eh? Bants, innit? I don't know my own strength is all." His *apology* is followed up with more stomach-churning sniggers.

Head down, teeth grating, a thousand things I want to say to him clogging up my throat, I make my hasty escape.

Lyndsay joins me outside a couple of minutes later, passing me my jacket as she shirks into her own. "You okay?"

"No damage but to my pride." I force a smile.

"Tinwell pulls crap like that all the time, don't worry about it. And I appreciate you coming to help me."

"Yeah, well..." I shrug. *Some help I was. And Adele saw. Word'll get back to Tate. Not that he'll care. But I do.* "Home?"

"Oh." She takes a step and stumbles. I catch her. Her head dropping against my chest, I hear her hiccup. *Oh, sweet jeezus,* not quite as sobered as I'd thought then. And, as I fumble my footing under her weight, I realise perhaps neither am I. *Goddamnit, fresh air!* "Okay, sure."

Gently, I manipulate her off of me. "Callum not coming?"

A funny sound erupts from her throat. "Nope."

9

PIGGY THE PUP

"So," Lyndsay eventually breaks into the silence as we amble our slow way along the street. "Before. What were you, um, talking with Adele about?"

I glance across at her. Didn't think she'd noticed that. Head bowed, she's watching her feet, arms wrapped tightly around herself. "Tate." I catch her side-eying me, dubiously. "Just asking her, you know, what his deal is. She's the only one I've seen him talk to, thought she might be able to help me out."

"And —*hic*—did she?"

"Nope."

She nods. We lapse back into silence for several long beats. Then, with a heavy sigh, she lifts her head and asks, "seriously, Mikey, what's *your* deal with Tate?"

I flinch, my brow furrowing.

"I'm sorry, I mean, I know you guys were friends when you were little and all," she rushes on, screwing up her face in a way that's probably supposed to be sympathetic before returning her gaze downward, "but... listen, okay?" Hiccup. Deep breath. Grimace. Head shake. *This is gonna be nasty.* "Mac is not good people." *Yep.* I glare at the side of her head. "Not that I'm claiming

77

I know him all that well or anything; don't think I've ever even actually spoken to him. But, seriously, I've seen and heard plenty enough to know that guy is not someone to mess with."

I stop. "Like what?"

Her own step falters and her eyes dart up, meeting mine. "Huh?"

"You said you've seen and heard plenty. Like what?"

"Oh. Right." She starts playing with a lock of her hair, wrapping it around her finger and letting it spring free. "Like...Drink. Drugs. He's..."

"Nope." I laugh, shaking my head. Then I'm striding away. "That's bull."

"Hey, like I said, I don't really know Mac. The drink and drugs thing, that's just what I've heard. But, Mikey." Hurried steps bring her back to my side, she hiccups and mutters a grumble before continuing, "I do know a few who have suffered on his bad side. He's super volatile, you know? Unstable. The guy just flips. Over nothing. Goes totally cray-cray."

I flick up a hand. A warning. But it would seem drink makes her bold, she keeps right on talking.

"And, besides, hasn't he told you himself to leave him be? Not too nicely either, was it?"

I see Tate. Stood before me. His hand gripping my wrist, expression hard, challenging me with a full on scary intensity. I press my eyes closed against it. My steps slow.

I feel Lyndsay's hand on my arm, a soft touch. "I'm..." Hiccupping again, she draws in a long breath and holds it. I can practically hear her mental count to ten before she releases it in a loud gush. "I'm not trying to upset you, sorry. Just...let's change the subject, should we? Forget I said..."

"I didn't have friends when I was a kid," I cut her off abruptly. Because, no. I can't forget what she's said when it's so completely wrong and out of line, when it's planted this image of Tate in my head that I don't want and now can't shift. No. I'm not leaving it at that. I need to set her straight. "For a long time. None. Shocking right?" She blinks at me –a few times, her lips slightly parted. I drop my eyes to the ground. "The weird kid, that was me. The one who'd cry in class or kick off when things didn't go my way. The one who still carried a stuffed toy around everywhere and played with an imaginary friend at break. No one would sit with me in class, work with me, play... I didn't get invited to parties or asked round for tea."

"Aww –*hic*–Mikey!"

I give her comment no acknowledgement, continuing on over her. "Then Tate gets moved out of his class and into mine. He wasn't exactly finding school an easy fit either. Him, mostly because he'd do whatever the hell he wanted and didn't give a toss for the consequences. His teacher couldn't handle him. And, see, I guess it was that attitude he had what led him to me. Like, he'd stand for no one telling him what not to do and who not to be friends with."

That first day of his in Mrs Lumsbury's class, it was the Motte and Bailey Castle day. I remember all too well how the announcement of group work had made my heart sink. I remember how startled I was when Tate pulled up the seat beside me. And how fingers-and-thumbsy the pressure of having a partner made me.

I ruined our impressively grand model that afternoon. Worse, my Piggy the Pup suffered too, his dirty white head and front paws soaked in scarlet. The poor dog went unnoticed at first, because I was too caught up with Tate's bizarre laughing fit and baffled by my own. My amusement quickly died when I did see him, though. I heard other kids sniggering, saying things like *"Urgh, Michaela's crying again!"* and *"He's such a dumb baby"*.

But, then, Tate stood up, snatching Piggy the Pup by his tail and dragging me up to my feet with him. He sped me from the classroom, ignoring Mrs Lumsbury bellowing after us. And in the boys' toilets, we scrubbed that stuffed mutt in the sink until the soap ran out and only the merest hint of pink remained on his fuzzy head, then we shoved him down behind a radiator, out of sight, to dry...

With a sharp tug on my arm, Lyndsay snatches me from the memory, and the vague smile playing lightly on my lips flickers into something much more self-conscious. She motions toward the low garden wall to her left and steps away from me, perching herself down on top of it. She pats the space beside her. I've made her sad, it would seem. Awesome. Real fortunate that I'm not fussed on impressing her, I guess. Portraying myself as pitiful and pathetic was never my intent either though.

"Things got better then. So much better. Tate," I settle myself beside her, crossing my legs at the ankles and staring up at the cloudy, dark sky, "well, he made me feel less of a loser, you know? Less...faulty."

"Hmm." And that's all the response I get for a long while. I can feel her eyes appraising me. Then, shuffling closer into my side, she softly says, "you –*hic* –don't owe him."

Wow. I tense, somewhat stunned. She's not took what she was supposed to from that at all! What with the stuff she's told me in the Red Bull tonight about her and Derek, I thought she'd at least've *kinda* got it. The cousins were important to each other once and, even though they've drifted, Lyndsay's determined not to let him completely drop from her life, and that's not so vastly different to this, is it? Dropping my head and shaking it, I stand. "Come on. Let's get you home."

"Mikey?" She reaches an arm out toward me but pulls short of making contact when I turn to her, retracting it to her side and pushing herself up from the wall. "I think I really need to –*hic* –tell you some stuff, and you need to hear it –so you'll understand, but, um, you're not gonna like it much." She pulls on a strand of her hair, straightening the curl to her collarbone. It pings instantly back up to her neck on release. "Just...don't shoot the messenger here, okay?"

Shuddering against a sudden chill, I shove my hands in my pocket and start walking. Lyndsay apparently interprets that as an invitation to wrap her arm around mine and forge ahead:

"Okay, so back in year ten, Gary was giving Mac a bit of a

rough time. Claimed he'd caught Mac doing something...uh, dodgy, spread it all around the school. It got −*hic* −oh for the love of... it got pretty ugly."

"What something?"

She presses her lips tight, studying me as she seemingly deliberates, and then gives her head a brisk shake.

"No?" I frown at her.

She shrugs sheepishly, "Alex has a half-brother, Craig −same age, different mums. He's not at YCS anymore; didn't stay for sixth form... Well, thing is, he was also a part of the nasty little rumour. Alex − *hic* −would kill me if I stirred all that up again. It doesn't even matter anyway, no one really believed it −Tinwell's so full of crap."

My stubby nails bite painfully into the palms of my hands. But, whatever, Tinwell *is* so full of crap. I can imagine well enough what tosh his nasty mind concocted. "So Mac hit the beast, is that where this is going? Cos the prick got no less than he deserved so far as I figure."

"Well, no." I raise a disbelieving brow at her and she rushes on, "I mean, yeah, sure, he deserved a smack, but no, that's not what happened. That's the thing. Craig kicked off about the whole thing big style. But Mac, he did nothing. It's just like you said −he didn't seem to give a single toss."

My brow knits, head tilting. Yeah, her point is entirely lost on me here.

"He −*hic* −disappeared from school a short while after so, actually, maybe it did get to him more than he let on. Only, he was gone ages. Like at least a couple of months, I think. We all sort of figured he must have left.

"But then, one morning, totally random, he was back. And that's when..." She draws up her shoulders, huffing out a foggy, hic-rupted breath as they drop down. "Within a few hours, he'd given Tinwell a black eye. So bad, it swelled completely shut.

"Over the next few days, he also lashed out at Alex and shoved Craig up against a wall. I heard about him tipping tables over, chucking chairs across classrooms, ripping up text books and the like. He had Mrs Callows in tears one day." My knowledge of how to walk deserts me mid-step, I gape at her. She flashes me a small, sorry smile before continuing, "I'm surprised Adele still talks to him, actually. Cos half the school witnessed him –*hic* –screaming in her face to *back the hell off away* from him or she'd regret it. He punched a hole in the wall behind her head, real scary." That image of him, all fierce hostility, takes over my head again and I shudder. "She was mortified. I was mortified for her. It was awful.

"And then Mac vanished again. Expelled for sure, I thought. But, nope. Returned a week later." She starts us walking again, slowly. "Everyone – pretty much – sharp learned it best to just keep a safe distance. And, seriously Mikey, he seems more than okay with that."

Stroking her mitted hand down my arm, she slides it into my jacket pocket alongside mine, takes hold and squeezes. We continue on in silence –this silence a one that feels thick as all hell. Even her hiccups give up in it. I'm well aware of the non-too-subtle glances she sends my way every few seconds, but I make no effort to meet them. I'm supposed to respond, I get that, but I have nothing. It's disturbing, what she's said. I cannot even begin to process...

It's not until we reach her terraced street that Lyndsay next speaks, "you're not that weird kid anymore, Mikey." It takes me a second or two to reboot my brain and grasp her meaning. "You have friends. And, well, we all think you're pretty ace."

Just wait until the novelty wears off, I don't say, choking back a snort. I am very much still that weird kid.

And I'm wishing I hadn't shared that now. Don't know what possessed me. Feeling especially vulnerable, I suppose; what with Gran, and Tate in hospital, and Gary-Dickwad-Tinwell. And, although I appreciate her sentiment, she didn't at all get where I was coming from with it. I'm also wishing she hadn't felt the need to unload all that she did onto me. Did I really need to hear it? Cos all it's doing right now is seriously messing me up. And she's given me no why's to work with.

"You're not mad at me, are you?" She asks after another weighty pause that I'm sure I was meant to fill.

Kinda, yeah. I shake my head.

We're only a couple of doors away from her house now —so close, and she draws us to a halt. "Sure?"

"Just...tired, I guess," I respond pathetically. Unconvinced and probing, she holds my gaze for a small torturous eternity, pouting a little. "Didn't sleep too well last night." (Actually true) "You sure you aren't mad at me?"

Genius move, there, with the flip-around. Her expression turns confused, "what do you mean?"

"I know you were looking forward to speaking with your cousin."

"Aww, don't be silly! That's not your fault. I really enjoyed tonight. I mean, aside from Tinwell's contribution of course. You've shown me a great time."

"Yeah?" I don't get any reading of insincerity from her. *Well done, Mikey.* I clear my throat. *Big congrats.* "Yeah, good." I deflate. *Tonight has gone so swimmingly to plan.*

Although, she could mean...

Hand remaining pocketed with mine, she moves in to me. "Thank you."

"Uh," I attempt an unaffected shrug. Not easy when your shoulders have cemented into place. "Welcome."

And then, lifting up on to tippy toes, her lips are pressed against mine, her free hand squeezing the back of my neck, and I feel the barest darting touch of her tongue breaching my mouth.

...Nope. She clearly does not mean in a 'friends' way.

It's over before I have chance to react, which is probably a good thing.

I realise my eyes have closed. Snapping them open, I find her a mere breath from my face. She lowers herself and puts a sliver of distance between us, a nervous half-smile quirking her mouth.

No clue what my face is doing, but whatever it is, Lyndsay appears reassured by it, the twitchy smile morphing into a wide grin –almost smug. "You're a difficult guy to read, Mikey Alston."

Apparently so. My lips feel weird. I want to rub them, but I'm smart enough to realise that would be a bad move. "I don't try to be."

She releases me, giggling a little, and I stand dumbly still, watching her walk away. At her gate, she looks back at me and waves, "I carried around a yellow rabbit called Tee-Tee til I was ten. It's not so strange. I still have her, she's on my bed. Night, Mikey."

"Night."

I don't have Piggy the Pup anymore. He was lost to me in the car accident. Along with everything else I treasured.

10

OH, WHAT A PICKLE

*L*yndsay pats the vacant seat beside her as I weave my way through the grand, vaulted-ceilinged lunch hall, around tables and loitering bodies, toward her. "Took your time."

I flash her something I hope at least resembles an apologetic smile as I slide my tray of food onto the cramped table, and the moment I yank out the chair to sit, she shuffles hers up closer beside me. If my discomfort is as obvious as I think it must be, Lyndsay refuses to acknowledge it. I have no idea what to do with this. It's not territory I'm accustomed to. Peeling back the lid of my pasta pot, I stab in a fork and make a concerted effort to decipher the conversation elsewhere around the table.

Unfortunately, I find no way to fit myself in: Callum and Alex are deeply involved in a discussion of their upcoming football plans with a bunch of people I don't know, and I'm not much of a football fan; Steph is turned in her seat debating with Ashleigh −an extraordinarily ditzy girl I sit two seats over from in English Lit. − over whether she should risk bleaching her hair and pink tipping it. I feign interest in Alex and Callum regardless.

Tate's back in school today −just as Adele said he would be. He skipped second period Study, but I've spotted him twice around the corridors. Once with Adele outside of Mrs Callows' Psychology classroom, sat side by side on the floor passing notes. And then on his own exiting the science block.

I barely slept last night, thinking on all Lyndsay told me. *Drink. Drugs. Violence.* Could he really have changed so completely? Perhaps his hospital stay was due to something like an overdose. Or a bar fight that hadn't gone his way. Harm he's inflicted on himself.

I hate these thoughts. Despise them. Feel like they're poisoning me. The hard, green eyes of a stranger searing away the warm, expressive ones of my best friend.

'You don't owe him.' Lyndsay'd said. But don't I?

Tate was the kid who stuck up for me against everyone telling him he was dumb for doing so. With the roles reversed now, how can I even be entertaining the idea of giving him less?

Acid-yellow nailed fingers are clicked in my face, "Oi!"

I blink.

Steph retracts her hand, sitting back in her seat across from me.

"Hey you," Lyndsay laughs, bumping her shoulder off mine. "Go anywhere nice? Steph's asking if you've got your name down for Thursday's History trip yet. You have, right?"

"Uh... yeah." It's hard to concentrate. I'm feeling kinda sick.

"Rats!" Steph clicks her fingers again before crossing her arms. "I'm gonna get stuck here alone, aren't I?"

"Just sign up, Steph. Come with."

"And have my mum embarrass me? No ta!"

"Your mum's not so bad." Lyndsay throws a look my way, rolling her eyes.

"Oh, she so is! You've no idea. She'll be leading the tour all like 'and my Stephanie once got her head stuck between these bars, here, and we had to call the fire service to cut her out', or 'Stephanie, sweetheart, remember when you were five and you wet yourself right beside this WWi exhibit?'"

Dissolving into giggles, Lyndsay drops her head on my shoulder. She leaves it there as the giggles die down.

I stand up, jolting her off of me, my chair screeching back over the tiled floor.

"Where you off to, Alston?" Steph asks as Lyndsay starts to rise up after me.

"I..." I glance toward the double doors. "Toilet."

Walking away, I hear Steph say, "are you not, like, sick of him doing that already, Lynds? He's like Dynamo only without the astounding wizardry."

Yeah. Once my New Guy novelty wears off, I'm gonna be left with no one.

Free of the lunch hall, out in the Languages corridor, I take out my phone and call Jody.

"Hi, you've gone through to answer phone. Please take this as a sign Jody doesn't want to talk to you. *BEEP.*"

~

"Hey, Gran." I settle down next to her on the sofa. It's the first time I've managed to catch her by herself since...since The Incident on Saturday. It's like they're guarding her against me. "What you doing?"

"Oh, Mikey, bless ye, sweetheart." She pats my leg, only half turning her attention from the TV, "could ye shufty forward and get me that doofer thing, dear love?"

I reach and snatch up the remote from the coffee table, pointing it towards the obnoxiously large flat screen. "What do you want on?"

Gran turns fully to me now, frowning. "For Chrissake, pass it here! I know how to bloody work the thing."

Without argument, I pass it into her impatient hand and watch her jab a couple of buttons, her eyes returning to the screen. She mutters a few choice curses, jabs at several more buttons then huffs out a breath and slams the remote back into my lap.

"Don't get why they have to make em so flammin' complicated. What on earth was wrong wi' 1,2,3,4, eh?"

I swallow back my amusement as I point the remote and tilt my head at her.

"I want that thing wi' whatshisname in, that crime thing. It's him what was in that period drama I liked, ye know the one. Suzy told me to watch it."

"Errr..." The remote droops and I stare at the side of her head until she looks at me. "I've no idea, sorry."

She raspberries at me, throwing her hands skyward, but as they drop her frown returns and she's studying me curiously. "What on earth's the matter wi' ye, boy?"

"Nothing, Gran. I'm good," I say, frowning back at her.

"Ha! Try that again but make it believable, eh? Yer lookin' all sorts of peevy. Somethin's the matter."

Pressing guide on the remote and averting my gaze to the TV, I snort.

"Tell me. Now. Or so help me..."

"Okay," I cut her off, resting my head back on the sofa. My insides are doing a little happy dance: She's herself. Shrewd and snipey, big hearted but hot headed, *this* is my gran. And a proper talk, like she once held me to regularly of an evening, is exactly what I hoped for. I appreciated our talks far less than I should have, I'm acutely aware of that in this moment. I take a breath. "Okay. Gran, do you remember when I first moved in with you and Grandad? I used to talk about my friend, Tate?"

"Oh, my dear love, how could I forget? Ye had me worried sick with your bawlin' over that un."

I narrow my eyes, preparing to argue, but I'm quick to realise I have no argument. Lifting my head, I set the remote down on the sofa arm and swivel around to better face her. "Well, he's still here."

"Not in Australia?"

"New Zealand." I shake my head. "He's at YCS. In a few of my classes. Only...he's changed."

"Wey, I should think so. Puberty does that."

"Yeah, but no. It's something more than that."

"Cut with the prattlin' on and just spill, will ye?" She lightly slaps my knee. "What's the issue?"

"I don't know exactly. I suppose *that's* my issue. It's just..."

The sitting room door slams open and in flounces Sophie. "Here you are!"

"Oh!" Gran's hand jumps to her chest as she whirls around. "Oh, it's you, little pup. Scared the life outta me!"

I shoot poison tipped arrows at our mini intruder.

"Hey Nanny." Sophie skips around the sofa to stand in front of us. "Uncle Mikey guess what."

"Nope."

Gran budges over, smacking a hand down in the space between us. *No, Gran, no. Why?!* Sophie's straight in there, wedging herself as far back into the sofa as she's able, and knocking me with her bony elbows and knees several times in the process. The space Sophie is squeezing into is super tight, but I stay put.

"Guess what," she repeats, big brown eyes −so like David's −*like mine* −fixed on me.

"Nope."

In a blink, her brow turns Neanderthal. "Guess. What."

"Go. Away," I retort, my tone a touch harsher than I intended.

"Michael Spencer Alston!" Gran's swift to admonish.

I wilt.

Sophie's eyes turn real sad real fast, and she turns them on Gran. "I just wanted to tell Uncle Mikey something exciting. He'll really like it."

And then Gran has her hardest stern eyes set on me. "You tell us, puppy. I'm sure he'd love to hear yer news."

"Okay." There's no hesitation, and an immediate reinstatement of her impish grin wipes all trace of dejection from her manipulative little face. "My Daddy says that when I'm biggerer, he's gonna get me some skates just exactly like Uncle Mikey's!"

"Oooh, well now, that is excitin'! Hear that, dear love? This young un's wantin' to give you a run for ye money. Reckon you could be better even at skatin' than yer Uncle Mikey one day then, darlin'?"

"Mmm, yep, I think so. I'm almost brilliant on my Hello Kitty ones."

I stand, shaking my head. *Five minutes with Gran: So much for that.* I make a move toward the door through to the kitchen. *Left-over pizza's a pretty poor substitute, but it'll do.*

~

TATE SHOWS up to Study on Tuesday morning. But, because I made the mistake of arriving first, he's seated himself as far from me as the Sixth Form library study area allows him to, seeming to press himself into the wall at his back to add a significant extra few millimetres to the distance between us. Headphones on and text book open on the table in front of him, he may as well be wearing a tabard saying, 'DO NOT APPROACH!'

I'm deliberating an approach.

"Alright, Alston?" I start, my chair jerking back, as, out of nowhere, Gary appears before me, blocking my view. "So, you and Lyndsay Webb, huh? Punching above your weight, but well done."

"Tinwell." I clap my notebook shut and reach for my bag. "You're not even in this class."

"I'm just wondering how your girlfriend would feel about your shameless eye-raping of McAllister, there."

"Lyndsay's not..." I slam to a stop. Because —I'm a beat late in catching —his goading use of the 'girlfriend' term is whole worlds from the most disturbing part of his sentence. "What the hell, Gary?!"

He puts his hands up, palms out, and a wince-inducing sneer curves his lips. "Hey, calm down. No need to worry yourself, Michaela. It can be our little secret. Though, between you and me, I think you should go for it. Seriously. Think you've got a real solid chance with your buddy boy over there. Made for each other: Both freaks, both fairies."

"What. The actual. Hell?" I stand before thinking the move through.

Resting his thick knuckles onto my table, Gary leans in toward me. I jump back a step or three.

He guffaws, flashing me a wink before straightening up and turning away. "Filthy cocksuckers are taking over." I hear him say as he struts out the library door.

Heat's scalding my face, my pulse drumming in my ears far louder than can be healthy. I do not, *do not* look across at Tate.

And then somehow, unwittingly, eyes drawn by the will of demons, I do.

Our gazes lock for the briefest of brief moments, his expression unreadable yet discouraging, before a blink refocuses him down to the open book on his desk.

He saw.

I slump into my seat and reopen my notepad.

Could he have heard too?

~

"SINCE WHEN HAS YOVERTON HAD A MUSEUM?"

"Since...I don't know when." Lyndsay turns to me, "but don't go getting too excited, it's horrendously dull."

"Figures." I sigh.

This Museum of Local History is located somewhere on the outskirts of Yoverton. We've been walking toward it for approximately twenty minutes and have passed by all the parts of town I'm familiar with. Now I'm finding myself in territory little known. The upper-class side of town. Big fancy houses, many with gated drives, generously spaced, large expanses of trees between providing privacy; there's not much to see. The path we're walking allows for no more than two abreast, running alongside an incredibly narrow, winding road. Traffic is sparse.

"Steph's mum does the tours though, and she's legit hilarious, so it shouldn't actually be too unbearable."

"How much further is it?"

"Not far. But it's a really nice walk, Mikey. Just enjoy it."

"Right."

I'm not enjoying this walk. Not one bit. Thanks to Tate.

There's twenty odd students on this trip (some sixth formers, some year elevens), and he's one of them, walking slightly ahead and along the opposite side of the road. He's spent the entirety of this week continuing to ignore and avoid me, and the majority of this trip. But for the past five minutes or so ¬since leaving our side of town behind, I've been acutely aware of him sliding frequent glances my way. He refuses to meet my gaze ¬every time I look over, trying to catch him, he immediately turns away. It's majorly unsettling.

I walk watching my feet.

"This easy beats what poor Steph's stuck doing this beautiful afternoon anyway."

"Yeah?"

"Oh yeah." Lyndsay giggles, "She's helping year eights with their history projects. Can you imagine?"

"Damn, that does sound..." Feeling eyes on me again, my head whips up. "Grim."

Tate doesn't shift his gaze fast enough this time, lingering a moment too long. I see worry creasing his brow, tightening his lips and paling his skin... I see him clench and unclench his hands...

Then, he stops.

...And I get it.

I get it. With the savagery of a lightning strike, I understand.

I'm petrified to the spot.

Lyndsay continues on a few steps before she realises she's lost me. "Mikey?" She pivots around. Her eyes widen. "Oh my...Mikey, you okay? You look like you're going to puke."

I'm not going to puke. I'm too broken for that.

My eyes are fixed on a point just beyond Tate, where the road widens slightly before a blind turn; the place that has featured in every single one of my nightmares —both sleeping and awake —since the age of eleven. I recognise it with such excruciating clarity, I... Nope. I can't breathe. Can't move.

He knew. Tate knew what I was walking into and he just let me.

It takes all I have to force my eyes shut. I press the heels of my hands against them to ensure they stay that way.

The crash site. We're at the crash site.

11

LIKE BEING INSIDE THE SUN

"What's the matter?" There's a gentle tug on my arm, I jerk free of it. "Mikey, you're really freaking me out. What is it?" Lyndsay's sounding increasingly distressed. "Talk to me please."

"Come on." Tate. And he's close. I'm suddenly oh-so acutely aware of just how close he is. It's reassuring and agonising all at once. "Come on, let's go." His voice is cuttingly flat, impassive. Warm fingers wrap around my wrists, easing my hands down from my face.

I'm careful not to look at him. I can't. I go with him, though. Hands remaining on my wrists, he walks backwards, leading me along the road we've just walked, and I let him without protest. I'm not sure my voice would've worked even had I wanted to.

"Where are you going?" I hear Lyndsay shout after us. "What's wrong with him, Mac?"

Then Mr Garrimay: "Boys! Where on earth do you think you're going? Michael, you and Tate need to get back here to the group now!"

Tate makes no reply. I can feel his eyes searing into me. I hold my focus on the zipper of his black coat. The sounds of our YCS party behind me slowly fade and then die away.

"Home, yeah?"

Home. That jolts me. *Home?*

"No." The word comes out sounding like the utterance of a ninety-year-old. "No." The second time is little better.

"Not home?" He stops, releasing me. My skin instantly feels the chill. "Then where?"

Cautiously, I drive my gaze up. I'm not met by the distant, hostile green eyes I've endured since my return. My vision goes kinda fuzzy, my stomach French braids itself, and all of a sudden, I feel very much like I'm capable of throwing up. "The den. Can we go to the den, Tate?"

His frown deepens, confusion mixing in with the concern.

No way has he forgotten. I refuse to believe that. "Our place. By the stream."

Brows lifting, he shakes his head, "The den... it's not there anymore, Mikey."

'Course it's not. The prickle in my eyes becomes unbearable, I daren't blink. Sheets of tarp nailed to old wooden pallets, wasn't built to last. Obviously, it's all long gone. I clear my throat, battling the lump obstructing it. "I don't care."

He studies me. Then nods. Once. Taking position at my side, he starts walking again. I keep pace.

We don't talk.

I'm trapped reliving my worst nightmare. Back in that car. The dark. The cold. Tate bleeding and rasping beside me. Mum screaming. Dad...so quiet. The seat belt biting into my neck. My head humming like it was about to explode. Pleading for an end: For everyone to just shut up; for the pain to leave me be. Doesn't take long for the prickle to win out −I can't not blink forever. Tears fall free and I do nothing to stop them.

Tate doesn't see them anyway. He has his head down, his jaw tense. Not once does he look my way. Doubtless, he's caught up in his own horrifying memory of that winter night. There's little clue on his face as to how he remembers it, but I see not a single tear track down his cheek, nor even threaten too.

Arriving at the site of the den doesn't soothe me as I'd hoped it would. Tate wasn't lying. There's nothing left here. No scrap of fabric, no splinter of wood. Nothing. It's just a small grassy clearing between trees and streambank, indistinguishable from the areas off to either side. In fact, it's only when I see the vast old tree stump, protruding out from the wood line, that I'm convinced we are indeed in the right place. That stump used to be our table. It also once marked a barely-there dirt track which took us the short distance through the close-knit trees directly to Tate's back garden gate, now entirely lost beneath underbrush. My chest aches. Perhaps it was a mistake to come here.

I drop down onto the damp grass, hugging my legs to my chest and propping my chin on my knees.

Tate seats himself in front of me, crossing his legs. He has a small troop of ant-like things doodled over one knee of his jeans. His other features the Bat Signal.

I eye him as he eyes me. For a long while.

"Remember how the den came about?"

His gaze lowers from mine, just a touch. He doesn't answer.

"We were, what? Seven or eight? We got it in our heads we just had to camp here, made all these plans for a campfire and ghost stories and washing in the stream, but we didn't have a tent. So..."

"No."

Oh. "No?"

A small muscle jumps at the side of his mouth and he shakes his head. "My tent. We had my yellow tent. But you, you refused to come in it. Cos of the sun." His lips quirk on one side. Not a smile exactly. Still, a teensy tiny thrill slips through me. "You said it would be too much like being inside the sun. And the sun... the sun kept you awake."

"Shut up. That's not true." I know it is. Jeezus, I was freaking pathetic. "Anyway, then you turned full-on Boy Scout, declaring we build one. Your mum gave us the run of your shed and garage. 'Have at it, boys.' She said, 'But be sure...'"

"'Be sure you're home before dark.'" Tate finishes, the smile wannabe making another appearance.

"Yeah. We worked hard as hell, making this place as camp-outable as we possibly could."

"So many splinters."

"Even down to setting perimeter traps. To keep out all the wolves and bears."

"Mum, she still said no." His lips twitch up further. "We never did get to spend the night here."

"We didn't." I agree. We lapse into silence again. And then, softly: "I did." Don't think I meant to say it aloud. Or maybe I did. I avert my attention to the tree stump

"You did?" Leaning his weight on an arm, he angles himself to reclaim my attention, "what?"

"My last night. When you didn't show."

He's frowning at my chin, his expression regaining an edge of that disquieting intensity. I want his almost-smile back. I shouldn't have let slip.

"I couldn't," he eventually huffs out. He shakes his head. "I'm sorry, I wanted to, but..." His mouth opens and closes several times. Then his face gets complicated. "No. Not true. I didn't want to. I – shit, I didn't want to see you."

My chest compresses, squishing everything within it. Gotta admire his honesty, though. Brutal honesty stated in an emotion-less tone. Surely he can't have meant it to sound so cold.

"I never... never imagined you'd stay out here all night. Middle of bastarding winter. On your own. I just..."

"It's alright." *It's not. It's really not.* Releasing my legs, I set my hands on the ground to either side and make to push myself up.

"Hey." Tate scrabbles gracelessly up to a squat, knees bent toward me. "I know how terrible I'm sounding. Selfish, right? But...Shit, Mikey." He snaps his mouth closed and makes a grunt type sound.

There was a time he'd've thought better than to position himself so vulnerably so near me. I watch him work to steady himself. There was a time I wouldn't have hesitated in giving his knees a solid knock to send him toppling backward, laughing maniacally as his butt slammed the ground.

His eyes locked on mine, tone softer –carefully so –he finally continues, "I didn't know what to...to say to you, how to act. And it hurt. It hurt too much. And you were leaving, and I..." He hitches up a shoulder, dropping it heavily, "fuck! I was the worst friend."

"Yeah." I make my face as blank as I'm able. After the accident, his mum, Laura, called in on me almost every day. She'd bring food and homework, took mum's dog, Roxy (a beagle, long since passed) for walks, and, one time, she gave my mop of hair a cut and tidy in our kitchen. Tate didn't ever come with her. He did come to my parents' funeral, though. And, there, he barely even looked at me. The old hurt bursts wide open. Pretty sure I fail miserably at concealing it. "You actually were."

Relieving my weight from my arms, I lean a little to one side, freeing access to my trouser pocket.

He'd known to meet me here that night. Laura'd given the okay for our late-night goodbye rendezvous. She told me he promised he'd come. I escaped my house, and I waited hours here for him, right up until fifteen minutes before his generously extended curfew. Then, with the aid of a crutch and my Toy Story torch, I negotiated the dirt path and let myself into his back garden. He refused to come to the door. And Laura didn't invite me in as she usually would've –as I could tell she wanted too – only offered me a ride home. I had no intention of going home. *Tate wouldn't seriously let me down. Not tonight.* I'd held so steadfastly to that belief, despite all the signs to the contrary. *He wouldn't let me leave without saying a proper goodbye, no way.*

It'd been a long, cruel night.

His cut scored me just as deep as David's. He, too, turned his back when I needed him most. And for a long time, I nurtured just as much wrath toward him for it.

When did I decide to give him a pass?

The instant I set eyes on him again. I forgave and forgot everything in that single heartbeat.

What's he done to deserve it?

Lyndsay's right: I don't owe him.

I pull my wallet from my pocket and flip it open. "Here." Tate's watching me, somewhat warily, as I slide a finger in behind my bank card and ease out the pristine Pokemon card that lives there. I flick it at him. It hits off of his ant army knee before landing on the moist grass between us, caught between the blades and tilted sideways. The Lucario holo was once Tate's absolute favourite of his card collection. But when Gary Tinwell tore up mine —my Gyarados holo, he gifted it to me. It was a significant sacrifice from him, a big deal, a grand gesture of our friendship, and it meant the world to me. I don't have the words to tell him how I'm feeling right now, and smacking him in the gut probably won't quite suffice. I'm counting on this to clue him in. "Think I'm gonna hang out here for a while longer. You can go home."

He reaches forward, plucking up the card, and his eyebrows steeple. His eyes flit from me to Lucario and back again, something odd going on with his face, as he resettles himself cross-legged on the ground.

I pick at a loose thread on my wallet, pretending with all my might that I really just don't care. Perhaps, if I pull it off convincingly enough, I may just make it true.

To say I'm stunned when he bursts out laughing would be a major understatement. Such a whacked out and wholly inappropriate reaction to the situation, it's a wonder my eyes don't fall out of my skull. I take offense. Or, rather... I'm aware I should. In actuality, I lose full control of my face in a blink, a Team Tate party kicking off in my head.

Because...well.

This, here, is my best friend. This is what I've been longing for from him these past two weeks (or six years; *whatever*): The laugh, so full of the energy and heart I feared lost. The look, like he's finally seeing me again – really seeing me; he's the only one who ever has. This –dismissing all the reasons it really shouldn't be – *this* is pretty freaking glorious to behold.

"What?" I ask, grinning. I'm not quite so far caught up in him, though, to keep the wary, paranoid edge from my voice. He shakes his head. "Tate!"

Another head shake and he futilely rubs his free hand over his mouth before brandishing the card out in front of my face. "Can't believe you – you keep this in your wallet. Fuck."

Oh. Raking my fingers into the grass by my side, I rip up a great fistful by the roots. "I put that in my wallet when you gave it me. It's just been moved across with all my other cards each new wallet, okay? No need to go making me out some soppy weirdo." Obviously, he's blind to the point I thought he'd see so clearly. My bemused kick of glee is extinguished.

His glee, however, flares right up. "You always were a soppy weirdo. Seriously. And, also, by far the most... most hysterical person I've ever met."

It's a torturous realisation: I wasn't ever as important to him as I've believed I was. "I'm not trying to be funny, Tate."

"That's what –shit, that's what makes it so brilliant, Mikey."

"Quit laughing. None of this is funny." If he were to touch me right now, he'd likely burn himself. And his lame-ass attempts to straighten his stupid face only goes to rile me further. Yeah, safe to say his illogical outbursts have rapidly lost all charm. Closing my eyes, I begin counting down from ten. I make it to seven. "I've been so dumb where you're concerned. You're such a massive *fucking* douche. Just go, please."

It's like getting wedgied and doused in ice water and being forced to listen to Bieber all at once when he starts laughing all the harder, practically doubled over with the spasms. "Say...oh, say that. Again." He manages to pant out between convulsions.

I get to my feet. "Forget it. I'll go."

He lunges and snatches hold of my wrist before I can move. I don't look at him.

"Mikey."

"Get off me."

"I'm sorry." Clambering up to stand with me, he holds out the card. He's reigned himself in some, but it's blatant he's still a little too close to the edge. "This is yours. Put it back in your wallet."

"I don't want it."

"Please."

"I don't want it." I make a point of returning my wallet to my pocket. "Now get the *fuck* off of me."

A snort escapes him, and he presses his lips tight like he's inwardly cursing himself for it. And so he should be.

The force I put into freeing my arm has me staggering backward. "Have a nice life."

"Whoa, hey!" He snags my hood, limiting me to one small step. Quick to better secure me by setting his other hand on my shoulder, he whirls me around. I stumble over my own feet and glare at him. "I... I'm wrong to be laughing at you, I do know that." Appears he's speeded well inland of mirth, his expression returned to its solemn home of recent times. "Wrong. All kinds. Well out of order. Don't think I'm mocking you, though. Cos, shit, that's not it. You know me better than to think that's it. Just..." He huffs air out his nostrils, his jaw flexing, "no one's ever been able to make me laugh. Not like you can so easy. And this, this ¬it's been a long time building. You know?"

My stomach plummets, I feel it oozing into my toes. I try to maintain some semblance of control in my voice as I say, "you could have at least come here for a short time that night." I lose it and pause to take a breath. "Answered your door to me at the absolute very least."

His eyes dart away, although only for a fraction of a millisecond. "I've a long list of stuff I regret," he says, locked back on me. "Like you said, I'm a fucking douche." He seems to put a weird emphasis on '*fucking douche*' without actually putting any emphasis on it at all. Or perhaps I imagine it.

I nod. He joins in. We nod at each other for far too long. Like morons. A smirk begins tugging stubbornly at the corners of my lips...

"How's your gran?"

...And then it vanishes.

Tate notices, his brow lowering. "Adele told me. A fall, right?"

"Gran's fine now, yeah. But, um, I saw your family there. At the hospital..."

"Adele told me something about that too."

"They were there to visit you. I figured that much out. Your little sister seemed mighty worried."

"Megan's a worrier. You two would get along great."

I wait. Silence takes over as I stare at him, but he seems content to watch me drown in it.

Until, that is, something he sees on my face throws him giddy once more.

I clench my teeth, eyes lifting skyward.

"For serious, Mikey?" Tate snaps me back. "Straight to the grimmest conclusion? I could only be in hospital cos I'm dying, huh?"

My ears burn.

"I had a fall too." Lifting his coat and shirt, he exposes a long nasty gash —fixed with at least twenty stitches and haloed by a multitude of smaller scrapes and scratches and a bruise so dark and ugly I wince to look at it – running a fair length down his right side. "Down those steps. The stone ones cutting through Hutchings Avenue. Last Tuesday. Some glass lodged in and, uh, came along for the ride."

Tuesday. Just after he'd walked away from me, then. I stare at his wounded torso for way longer than can be considered appropriate. *Always hated those steps.*

Re-covering himself, he flashes a small wry grin. "Ever the fucking dramatic."

"*Fuck* you."

His grin stretches, verging on splitting his face in two. "You've such a face on every time you swear. Know that? Like you're sneezing em out or something." He tries again to return me the card.

I snatch it from him. "Do not!"

Damnit, I owe Grandad the credit for that aberration. Swearing would always earn me a clip around the lug.

12

RAT-A-TAT-TAT. SURPRISE!

There's a knock on my door. Not the front door, but my bedroom door. Two short, light raps.

I still, eyes lifting slowly from my book to stare at it. 7.30 on a Thursday evening. Gran doesn't ever come up the stairs, can't manage them; Sophie no longer bothers knocking; David always knocks in some lame-ass tune; and Mel's out at a spin class or something...

Huh.

Setting my book down on the bedside cabinet, I drop my legs heavily off the side of my bed and drag myself up to sit.

Then it occurs to me: *Might be Tate.*

Tate and I spent an hour and a half at the den this afternoon, talking. It was tough going at times, stilted, and we kept conversation pretty light following the, um... Lucario thing; he kept himself very much in check (which I actually can't decide if I'm glad for or not). While there, I'd felt sure of the promising step taken, but I've had plenty time since to analyse and question every word, nuance and stretch of silence, allowing doubt to rouse my nerves.

A follow up rap kicks my pulse to racing. *Who else could it be?*

I'm across the room in four long strides. "Yeah?" I say as I pull open the door. My face falls. "Lyndsay?"

"Hey." She's rocking a little on her feet, one arm across her chest rubbing up and down her other. "David let me in. Sorry, were you expecting someone else?"

I glance past her, scanning up and down the hall. *Seriously?! David's sending girls up to my room now? Some parental figure he is!* "No. No, I wasn't expecting...anyone. Hi."

"Hi. So, can I come in?"

I take a moment. "Sure. I guess."

I don't move but she squeezes herself in past me. "Thanks."

When I turn, I find her settling comfortably onto my desk chair. "Sooo...hey."

"What happened today, Mikey? I've been worried sick, and you haven't answered your phone all afternoon."

"Right. Yeah." Returning to my bed, I take a rigid seat on its bottom corner. I swallow and avert my gaze. "That place we were, where I left you, that's..." *Urgh,* I'm disgusting, I realise all of a sudden, as I take in −as if with fresh eyes −the dirty clothes strewn all over my floor. Plates, bowls, cups. Crisp packets. My room's a state. *When did that happen?* My voice is thick, "it's where the accident happened."

"Accident?" There's a pause. "What? The one when you were a kid? Oh my gosh!" I dare a glance. Her eyes have grown big as tennis balls. "Oh my gosh, that's awful. Wow. I totally understand." She looks set to come over to me, I shake my head. She straightens her skirt under her then resettles in the chair. "Are you okay?"

"Yeah." I shrug. So messy, my room's *really* freaking shameful. Still need to redecorate too. "I couldn't be there, you know? Just needed to get away. Sorry."

"No. Of course. Of course you did. No need to apologise." Shifting a little in the chair, she casts her eye over all the crap strewn across my desk. It's like she's consciously determined not to notice the pair of boxers and balled up socks heaped on the floor only a few centimetres from her feet. She picks up a blue pen, clicks it on then off and sets it back down. "If...well, if you need the day tomorrow, I can make excuses for you at school?"

"No!" I'm quick to answer, almost set to jolt to my feet to physically restrain her before registering that to be a completely unnecessary and insane reaction. No way am I missing school tomorrow. Nope. I force my shoulders to relax, slumping. "No, I'm good. Just needed some time and space to calm down, that's all."

"So where did you go?"

"We just...we walked." The den's nobody's business.

"We?" She narrows her eyes at me. "You and Mac?"

I nod.

"You guys friends again now then, huh?"

Her tone doesn't sit well with me. "He was in the car with me that night, Lyndsay. It was just as tough on him."

"Oh." She turns, staring at my blank laptop screen, her lips screwing to the side. "I didn't know."

"I know you didn't. It's fine." I sigh, scooting myself across the bed to lean back against the wall. "You really didn't need to come all the way out here to check on me." It's quite a trek from Lyndsay's house. And pretty much all up hill, too.

Her gaze whips back around to me. She's looking kinda wounded. "I tried to ring. Sorry, have I come at a bad time? Were you busy with something?"

I briefly consider lying to her, but it's abundantly clear to anyone with eyes that I've got nothing going on here. "No. No, no. Just I feel bad that you've wasted your time. I'm all good."

"It's not a waste of my time, Mikey. I wanted to see you." She flashes a shy smile, "I like seeing you."

Crap. She keeps coming out with awkward stuff like that, and I've no idea how to respond.

Thankfully, I'm saved from having to on this occasion by the sound of The Rocky Horror Picture Show blasting Time Warp into my room.

My phone's on my desk. Lyndsay glances at the screen which is now alight with the image of me under attack from a wild haired loon with antlers and a bright red nose. "Oh. Who's Jody?"

The ringtone was set on my phone by Jody after she'd forced me to dance the song with her at our year 11 prom last June. She says that the mere thought I could be dancing along again each time she calls amuses her greatly. The pic that flashes up alongside it is from Christmas eve just gone, at Leeson's festive (except, not really) party, taken shortly before she told me she was going for drinks and never came back. This is her returning my Monday call.

"A friend." I shuffle myself across and off the bed.

Trying, and failing, to keep her voice all nonchalant, she pushes, "girlfriend?"

"Not for a long time." I shrug. The phone rings off just as I reach it. "Damnit!"

"Perhaps I should go."

Glancing over, I find her frowning at me, her lips pressed tight. "It's not like that," I blurt. "Nothing at *all* like that."

"You just stayed friends?" She's eyeing me sceptically now.

"Yeah." My gaze keeps flicking to my phone, my fingers itching. "We weren't ever serious. Jody and me, we should never have been anything but friends really. Beauty of hindsight, you know?"

Her expression clears, brightening considerably. "Oh, okay."

What the hell, Mikey? Jeezus! Should have just left her to think what she was thinking. These mixed messages are doing me no good. No good whatsoever. I give my head a stern shake which returns the frown to her brow. "I, um, should probably call her back though. I've been waiting to hear from her."

Something flickers in her eyes, but she says nothing. She stands up.

"Thanks. For calling in."

"No worries." Her gaze lingers on me, seeming indecisive. I can't help but hold my breath as I force myself to maintain the eye contact. She hasn't kissed me since the walk home on Sunday, but she's made it sufficiently clear on a number of occasions that she wants to. Handling her disquieting comments is one thing, handling another advance is quite something else. What would I do with that? She eventually presses her lips and drops her head, moving for the door. Turning as she reaches it, she says, "if you feel like getting out for a while, we're all up at the view. Would be good to see you there."

"Sure. Maybe. I'll think about it."

Lifting her hand in goodbye and flashing a smile, Lyndsay lets herself out, "hope so."

As soon as the door clicks closed, I ring Jody back.

"Hey there, Miktard. How's the South treating ya?"

"Jody, I'm in quite the quandary. Please help."

GRAN'S SCREAMS startle me from sleep. I'm upright in bed before my eyes have even opened, and for the briefest of blessed moments I'm back home, in our Newcastle flat. It's a moment viciously snatched from me the instant my eyelids lift.

I'm not the first downstairs and in Gran's room. Mel's beaten me to it. Dressed in a silk nighty I don't feel right seeing her in, she's hovering just inside the door, seeming unsure of an approach. David's only a few seconds behind, and then Sophie completes the party mere moments later.

"Nanny scared me," Sophie announces, rubbing her eyes and then yawning widely as she plods past us all to plop down on the side of the bed.

Light from the hall streams into the dark room, providing some illumination to the scene.

Gran's stopped screaming, but she's sobbing now, and shaking, clutching her bedcovers up to her neck. "It's hurting him. I can't stand it. I can't. So much pain. Too much pain."

"What's happened, Evelyn? What's hurting who?" Mel asks, her gaze swinging sharply to me when Gran makes no response.

Night terror. Not new. She has runs of them every so often. They started right after Grandad died. I was out with Jody that day, when he collapsed into an agonised fit on the bathroom floor. By the time word got to me, he'd been gone for over three hours. Gran'd suffered through the whole of it with absolutely no support. I think it broke her. I won't ever forgive myself for that.

I sidle past Mel, taking slow steps to the bed and settling myself calmly on the edge by her pillow. She flinches away, her hand flying up to ward me off, like she's about to batter me. "Hey, no. It's okay." I place a hand on her head, stroking her hair soothingly from her face. "It's okay, Gran. I'm here. I'm right here."

"Mikey?"

"Yeah, it's me."

"Mikey? Who're all these other people in me room? They canna be here. I don't want them here. Musna see... Can ye tell em all to go, please, dear love? It's too crowded. I canna breathe."

I turn my attention pointedly to each one of them in turn, lingering longest on Sophie who stares right back at me like it's a contest. I blink first. She grins before turning to crawl further onto the bed.

David finally reacts. "Sophie, come on. Back up to bed, angel. You've school tomorrow."

"But Nanny's upset, Daddy," she replies, holding her position.

Mel takes a couple more steps into the room. Gran whimpers, eyeing her with extreme suspicion. She steps back and holds out her hand. "Bed, Sophie. Now!"

It's with great reluctance that Sophie climbs down from the bed, her petulant lip visible even in this low light.

"I'll take her up and settle her," Mel half-whispers to David.

David nods, moving out of the doorway and into the shadows as Mel ushers their daughter past. Folding his arms, he stares. At me? At Gran? I can't tell.

"Uncle Mikey has school tomorrow too."

"Yes," I hear Mel respond in the same carefully hushed tone, "but Uncle Mikey doesn't have the big spelling test tomorrow, does he?"

"Noooo," Brat-features concedes in a whine. The stairs creak as she stomps up them.

"Gran, can I..."

Gran sucks in a loud sob, David's voice from the darkness whipping up her hand to grab and squeeze my wrist.

"Gran wants you gone too, ya know?" I inform him, meeting and holding Gran's panicky, wide eyes. "I'm good for this."

"You want to talk, Gran? Can I get you anything?" David full-on ignores me, making a slow approach toward the bed.

Slipping her arm behind me and fumbling a moment on the bedside table, Gran draws off a magazine, promptly launching it in David's general direction. I jump, my hand zipping from her brow to my chest. "Get out! Tell him, Mikey, tell him." On this occasion, I'm not feeling even the remotest bit smug over her favouring of me. I hate seeing Gran like this. A small part of me's dying inside.

David stops, staring down at the landed-open glossy, shining in the streak of hallway light, on the carpet a stride off to his left. His finger working to smooth the crease from between his brows, he stifles a yawn to poor effect. "I'm David. David, your grandson. You know me. Take a few deep breaths to collect yourself, and then we can sort through what happened, okay?"

"I don't care!" Gran screeches out over him, her head shaking frantically. "I don't care! Go. Go, go, go."

"You heard her." I try to keep my voice even, calming, but there's surely no way he can miss the bite to my words. Who the hell does this jackass think he is? Freud? "No need for us both to be up. Really. You're not helping."

I'm hyper-aware of his rapid deflation —there's a sudden vast increase to the room's air supply. I fill my lungs as he empties his in a huff, shoving his hands in his dressing gown pockets. "Jenny – next door," he finally addresses me, backing slowly toward the door, "she's a nurse. Let me know if you want her called over."

Turning on his heel, he disappears along the hall, heading for his office rather than the stairs.

I hold out for the sound of the office door snapping shut before forcing a smile to my face and turning back to Gran. "There we go. Just you and me now." Taking my phone from my sweat pants pocket, I tap into my music playlist and scroll down to the one titled 'Gran'. Most times, I've found, these songs are all it takes to soothe her back into sleep. May take a while tonight, she's wound herself up so tight, but I need only to stay with her until they do and then all should be well. "Some Gerry and The Pacemakers to start, yeah? Or Dusty?"

"I've had an accident, Mikey," Gran whispers, leaning into me and looking up, her lip quivering. "I'm sorry, I didna mean to."

"Oh." I lower my phone and work to keep my face from changing. Apparently, this is not a one of those 'most times'. "Okay. It's alright. Don't worry. Tell you what then, Gran, hey," I stand and offer out my hand, "let's go get you cleaned up first. Settle you down in the sitting room with your music. And I'll make you a nice warm mug of milk. Then I'll see to sorting your bed with some fresh sheets, yeah?"

Tension eases from Gran's face, a smile tweaking her lips, and she releases her hold on the duvet. "I'd like those red flowery covers I saw in the linen closet. Ye think I could have those on?"

"Uh, yeah, why not?" I help Gran up. "I'm sure Mel won't mind." *And so what if she does.*

"Morning."

Tate makes no effort to mask his surprise at finding me on his doorstep at a quarter to eight in the morning.

I've had maybe two hours sleep tops since settling Gran in the wee hours of this morning, yet I've awoken feeling refreshed and determined. Everything seems that little bit better than it did yesterday. At some point during my short slumber, or, perhaps, before that, as I sat with Gran enjoying her soft humming along to the songs she holds dear, I made a decision: I'm adopting a more proactive approach. Progress was made yesterday, and no way am I allowing Tate to pull that away from me. I've got my foot in the door (almost literally), and he's not shutting me out again.

I rang the doorbell without the faintest clue if this is still his house. Stood waiting on the doorstep for a full eternity worrying that, even if it is, his dad could be the one to answer. Oh, the relief when the door opened with Tate behind it. Except, well...it's striking me now that his expression isn't exactly encouraging.

"So, I thought we could walk to school together."

Yeah, he's looking pretty damn miffed. "Can't."

"Oh?" My hearty, keyed-up grin's becoming speedily harder to hold on my face.

Tate shakes his head. "Stuff to do before I head in. Dad's giving me a lift."

"Oh." My face muscles ache. "Okay. Well, guess I'll see you..." A sound off to my right snags my attention.

Adele steps out the neighbouring door and pulls it closed after her before her gaze catches on mine. She freezes, hand still on the door latch. Her eyes flick to Tate and my peripheral registers his shrugged response.

"Alston?"

"Saunders," I reply with a curt nod.

"What brings you all the way out here?"

"Just, ya know, delivering the word of God to the unenlightened." Another look is exchanged between her and Tate. This one long, lingering and unreadable. It seems very much like a secret, silent language I'm not privy to, and it starts a significant part of me burning. "See you in school then, Tate, yeah?"

"Hey," he stops me turning with a tap to my elbow, flashing me a small lopsided smile as he steps back from the door. "You can... we – we'll be in the quad at lunch."

The door closing in my face, my grin returns full force. *I have an in!*

"Don't even think about walking with me," Adele's sour tone invades my high.

"Wow. Ouch!" I retort, matching her pace down steps, along path and out gate. "Well, I'll give you a head start to the count of twenty then, I guess. Best walk fast."

I see her roll her eyes right before I close mine and start counting out loud.

13

A FAIL ON SO MANY LEVELS.
AND YET...

"Where do you think you're going?" Lyndsay questions after I start to veer away from her on our way out of fourth period.

This morning has dragged on *forever.* There has never been a longer five minutes than these last five of Media Production, waiting for the bell.

"Oh. Well, I'm not eating in the lunch hall today. Sorry."

"You're not? Where are you going then?"

"I'm, uh, meeting Tate in the Quad."

She frowns. "Why?"

"Cos he invited me to." I hold her stare. At least for a second or two, and then my feet shuffling on the shiny tiled floor drags my gaze down.

"Come on, Lynds," Steph's voice sounds close to my left. "Leave your weird boyfriend to his weirdness. We've got a party to plan."

"Mikey?" Lyndsay pushes.

I turn for the Quad. "I'll catch you out front after last period, okay? I can walk with you guys as far as the park."

~

TATE AND ADELE are already seated at one of the picnic benches when I arrive. There's no one else around because it's frosty as an arctic hell out here.

Only Adele reacts to my approach, eyeing me over her shoulder, her lip curled up all uninviting.

"Howdy."

Tate looks up from the notepad in front of him, his pen stilling, as I drop my bag on the table and slide along the bench opposite him, beside Adele. "Hey." He greets me, releasing the pen onto the page and flipping the pad shut over it. "You came." A small smile flits across his lips. The smile's too brief to decipher whether he's genuinely pleased I'm here, but I'm gonna choose to believe he is.

"Indeed I did. What you up to?"

"Flying kites," Adele deadpans. "You brought yours?"

I ignore her. "A tad brisk out here. You have a particular opposition to the lunch hall?"

Tate shrugs and then, after a notable pause, adds: "Too crowded. Riddled with jerks."

"But hey," Adele weighs in again, "don't let us keep you if that's where you'd prefer to be."

"It's not." I side-eye her, zipping my jacket up as far as it'll go. "I'm good. The bone-deep cold's actually most refreshing."

She snorts, sliding the notepad from Tate around to face her. Flicking through the pages to the one marked with the pen, she flattens it out. I subtly lean, trying to see, but she wraps a protective arm around the pad and hunches over, effectively blocking my view. She uncaps the pen and scribbles something down —a sentence, or maybe two. "Your girlfriend let you off her leash, huh?"

"What's with the secret notes?" They do this a lot, I've noticed. Whenever I spot the two of them together, they seem to have this notebook out between them.

"They're secret," Adele stage whispers, flashing a smirk my way as she re-imprisons the pen within the pages and straightens herself, nudging the pad back toward Tate.

It's so wrong that I wanna hit a girl this much.

"Just to and froing some ideas," Tate vaguely clues me in.

"Ideas? Okay. For what?"

"A... it's a project thing we're working on."

"Yeah?" I prompt.

"Yep," he shuts me down. Peeking in at whatever it was Adele wrote, he reacts with a quick smile and minute headshake. Adele darts me a deliberately provoking glance and waggles her brows.

Well. Rude!

And infantile.

At least, though, Tate has the decency to start looking sort of abashed as I eye-scold him.

"Wind ya neck in, Nebby." Adele shoves my shoulder, harder than could possibly be deemed necessary. "You're not being left out of anything you need to concern yourself with here, okay?"

I put a bit extra distance between us. I've the fleeting urge to reach across the table and make a grab for their 'project' pad, just to spite her. Well, alright, no. It's a little more than fleeting, and it wouldn't be *just* to spite her.

Tate totally picks up on it.

Angling around slightly to his tatty-looking bag beside him on the bench, Tate rips open the zip and shoves the notebook inside, his lip twitching on one side as if to say 'there, all better now', like it's a case of out-of-sight-out-of-mind. Does nothing but peeve me further, to be honest. Should really have acted faster, I realise, as I make a concerted effort to work a sturdy mask of indifference onto my face. He then delves his hand into the bag deep, rummaging beneath the headphones I can see peeping out, and retrieves a rather squashed tin foiled package and a Mars bar.

A substantial oversight on my part all of a sudden becomes abundantly clear.

As Adele conjures an apple, a banana and a snack pack of nuts from someplace about her person I sag. She tears open the small bag of nuts, pouring close on half out into her hand. "Nom, nom. Love me some nuts, I do," she says, straight-faced, before tipping her head back and tossing the lot in.

Tate frees a half of sandwich from the foil and takes a generous bite. Still looking at me, his eyes narrow a bit as he chews. "Not eating?"

"Nah." I shift my weight from one numb butt cheek to the other on the cold, hard bench and drop my head. "I'm good." My stomach rumbles, castigating me. I can practically hear Gran calling me a halfwit.

Yep. It's lunch hour, I've rushed on out here, and I've sorted myself precisely sod all in the way of provisions.

"Oh dude, you're pathetic!" Adele's on to me.

Have to admit, thus far this whole scenario is so entirely not meeting my expectations.

"Mikey, here." The silver package is finger-shoved a quarter way toward me. "Yours if you want it."

My gaze flicks up to Tate then down to the half sandwich offered to me. My stomach flutters and turns over queasily all at once. It's squished and unappetising. But I want it. Not just because I'm now realising I'm starving. The gesture has me thinking of the picnics we ate on the tree stump at the den, splitting the food from his house and the food from mine equally between us right down to counting out the grapes. "What is it?"

I glance up at him again when he doesn't respond to find him frowning at me. I frown back.

"It's a sandwich, genius," Adele says, chewing loudly. Tate's frown slides to her. "What's the filling today, Tate?"

"Oh. Cheese. Spam. Brown sauce."

Okay, sounds no more appetising than it looks. *Bleugh!* I reach out and draw it to me, flashing him a mini but undoubtedly stupid grin. "Thanks."

It's a stiff silence we eat in. Adele makes a couple of comments about how low the atmosphere is today compared to usual until Tate gives her a stern look and she shuts up. I attempt to start a conversation about how underappreciated spam actually is and am completely ignored. Tate just munches, glancing between Adele and me with a shallow crease to his brow.

Twenty minutes later, I've reached a point of uncomfortable enough to consider excusing myself. Adele gives me pause, though.

"Well," she says, thumping both palms off the table and swinging her legs over the bench. Snatching up and shouldering her small devil-red backpack, she stands. "As much fun as this *isn't*, I'm gonna go. Elsewhere. See what Ellory's up to or something."

I watch Tate as he tracks Adele round the table to his side. She lowers her face to his, her index and thumb pinching his cheek, and lands a quick kiss to his forehead. Releasing him and backing a small way away but holding his focus, she must whisper something I don't catch cos Tate nods once and holds up seven fingers.

I stab a short, sharp glare into her back as she passes by me without a glance. A moment later, I hear one of the double doors creak open, but I'm fixed back on Tate.

Something that hasn't even entered my mind up until now is suddenly swarming it. I'm sick a little bit in my mouth, the thought is so disturbing.

When the door skrees and clicks closed, Tate's attention returns to me. I pick up on a certain guardedness that's entered into the way he's looking at me. Like a less intense version of the way he regarded me up until only yesterday. I don't like it one bit.

"Want to go halfies on my Mars?" He eventually slices the tension. "Or you still find them gaggy?"

"Still repulsive," I say, shaking my head with some regret. His lips don't so much as twitch, but I'm almost certain I see a glint of amusement interfere with the unsettling wariness in his green eyes. He always did find it odd that I could be so opposed to what he considered to be the chocolaty creation of angels. I'm not sure what it is exactly, they just make my stomach heave. The one time he convinced me to try one, I'd thrown it straight back up all over his bed. "Thanks for the sandwich though."

"No problem."

"So, are you and Adele, like...romantically involved?" I blurt before the silence has chance to regain control.

He continues to stare at me, his brow lowering. His lips part a fair while before he asks, "what?"

My cheeks warm, but I've started so I'll finish. "You and Adele. Couple?"

His eyes flash wide, and then he's laughing at me. *Again.*

"Jeezus, Tate!" I admonish weakly, my face scrunching and flushed. I'm careful not to swear.

"You not heard?"

"Heard?"

"Thought for sure you'd... Never mind." He sobers up with such abruptness, I'm utterly thrown off kilter.

"Huh?"

"No. Fuck no, nothing like that there, Mikey."

"Huh."

The relief that sweeps me is completely unreasonable. I'm quick to drop my head, hiding my face. I guess I...

I don't know.

Well, okay, I kinda do.

I'm finding it hard enough accepting that in my absence Adele's wheedled her way in from the fringe and taken my place. It's tough seeing them with their private notebook and silent exchanges, aware that I'm excluded. Being the fringer in her stead gnaws at me. To think that she's secured herself a position closer to him than I could ever hope to compete with, I just... yeah, no. Nope. The news that that's not the case, it feels good.

The portion of table in front of me thoroughly cleared of crumbs, I clear my throat and raise my eyes. "So. I was thinking maybe, if you're not busy, we could hang out tonight? Be good to go for a skate, yeah?"

His expression shows not one single dot of enthusiasm for the idea. Discouraging. I thought for sure the suggestion of skating would go some way towards repairing our bond. Opening his chocolate bar, he bites, chews and swallows before responding, "I don't anymore. Skate, that is."

What?!

"Uh, what?" I feel like I've just caught my mum out as the tooth fairy all over again. He surely has to be kidding. Though he really doesn't look like he is. Tate taught me how to skate. He would joke that he'd worn skates before shoes. Rarely was he ever without wheels on his feet. Hard pushed to get them off him for bed. This is possibly the biggest blow he's delivered me thus far. "Why?"

His eyes darting away and then back to me, he shrugs and takes another bite. I wait, but on emptying his mouth he does nothing more than immediately refill it.

I draw in a long breath in an effort to compose myself. "Right, well, we could spend some time at the den then. Or go for a drink or something?" I refuse to be knocked off course.

Jaw still working steadily on chocolate and caramel and nougat, Tate regards me contemplatively. But then his gaze lifts past me, chewing paused, and he juts his chin toward the double doors at my back.

I swivel around to find Lyndsay waving out the door's window at me. Sighing, I lift my hand. I mean the motion as nothing more than an acknowledgement of her but, her smile widening and her thumb giving me the *okay*, she's apparently taking it as a 'wait there, I'll be right with you'.

"Guess that's your cue."

I turn back to Tate. "Tonight, then?"

He swallows and glances down at the small remaining chunk of Mars bar in his hand. Pressing his lips, he shakes his head. "Can't."

"Tomorrow?"

Another rejection.

I hear the door behind me opening. *Chrissake!*

"Right." Snagging up my bag, I slide off the edge of the bench to my feet. "Got it." *Loud and clear.* Tate huffs out a sigh. Of relief? Probably. My grip on my bag strap tightens and I briefly press closed my eyes. He's in for more disappointment then, cos, see, this is not me giving up. This is simply me accepting I need to restrategize. "I'll see you in History."

Lyndsay's halfway out the door. She's stopped as I've made the move from the table. "Miss Shaw's asked me to grab some forms from reception. Come with?"

"Sure." I shrug stiffly.

"Mikey?" I'm halted two steps away. I don't turn around. There's movement at my back and, a moment later, Tate's rounded the table to stand in front of me. "Sunday."

I slacken the vice grip on my bag strap. "Sunday?"

"Afternoon." He nods. "Dad's taking Megan to the cinema. Call round after one. If you want."

14

IT'S ALL ABOUT BALANCE

*O*n arriving in Friday afternoon to find the house empty, a note attached to the fridge informing me David, Mel and Gran were collecting Sophie from school and heading through Mel's parents', I ended up spending a couple of hours at the View. It was a pretty decent evening.

So today, when Mel declared that she and Sophie were taking Gran out again for the day, I elected to fill in that empty time up at the three-sided shed as well. Sure as hell beat spending the afternoon in with David, watching the clock move one tick forward and two ticks back.

It's now almost 4pm and the place is crammed, by far the busiest I've seen it. I'm well-positioned; sat just enough under the roof to benefit from the shelter, yet close enough to the open side for the fresh air and the wide vista of Yoverton town.

For the past half hour, however, my back's been turned to the view.

"Why does Alex keep looking at me like he wants to murder me?" I ask, keeping my eyes trained on faux-hawk as I turn my head to Lyndsay who's sat in the chair close on my right.

Alex arrived with Steph a short while ago and he seems to be making a very deliberate point of cold-shouldering me. It has me seriously on edge.

"Oh, ignore him." Lyndsay flaps a dismissive hand, taking a quick drink from her toxic-blue alcopop. "Alex is just the sulky type. Broody, you know?"

As if to disprove her point, an instant after she's voiced the last word, we're both jolted by the sound of his hearty guffaw.

He's grabbed Callum into a headlock and is spinning around. Steph steps up and lands an impressive sounding slap to the back of his head which sets him to laughing all the harder.

One brow lifting, my gaze slides to Lyndsay. She shrugs, flashing a sheepish smile, and sups another mouthful.

I'm abstaining from the alcohol today. Aside from the fact drinking through the day time strikes me as kinda wrong, I went a smidge over board −by my tight standards −last night and I'm secretly suffering for it. I've got a four pack of Dr Pepper with me and I'm now on my third can. Lyndsay had a couple too many as well yesterday, and I'm not especially a fan of this hair-of-the-dog approach she's chosen to take −drink boosts her courage. She caught me off-guard with another kiss as I accompanied her home last night. I can only hope my clear head will aid me in dodging a third such advance today.

"Come on, Lynds. What have I done to upset the guy?"

"Well..." She draws the word out for a really long time. And then she shrugs. "It's probably cos of Mac."

I frown. "O. Kay." My eyes dart across the room, to where Alex is now bear hugging Steph so her feet are off the floor and is also − it appears to me −chowing down on her neck. "Something to do with Tinwell's rumour? The one no one bought into anyway?"

"What's this?" Callum drops down onto the concrete floor by Lyndsay's feet, crossing his legs. "We talking the great Craig and Mac scandal?"

The warning look she flashes him goes unnoticed, so I push the advantage. "Yep."

"Thing that gets me most about that is how brutally detailed

Tinwell's account was, right? Like, seriously, he for sure must have watched real close for a looooong while to see all the handsiness and grinding and panting he reported. *That's* what I find most disturbing, if you get what I'm saying." He chuckles. Until Lyndsay shoves his head and he startles around to her. "Hey! Oh. He didn't know?"

"Idiot!"

I'm rigid in my seat.

Expression turning downcast, he sighs. "So what if it is true though, you know? I mean, its no big deal to me."

"Me either." Lyndsay angles her legs away from Callum, finishes off her bottle, and slides a wary glance toward Alex. She pats my shoulder. "Just leave it be, Mikey, 'kay?"

I nod my agreement. Or, at least, I think I do.

FIRST THING I NOTICE, as Tate lets me in and leads me through his house, is how little the inside has changed. The place instantly wraps around me like a welcoming hug. Second is how worn it's all looking; I'd hazard a guess that the cream walls of the hallway and staircase haven't been repainted in the time I've been gone, and the soft brown carpet is really starting to show its age. A smile tugs as I spot the chip to the skirting board five stairs up –caused by Tate dropping and smashing a monstrous glass mixing bowl full of strawberry Angel Delight. Third thing is that Tate has a doorbell fitted to his bedroom doorframe. That strikes me as bizarre.

"What's with this?" I can't not press it. The little LED above the button flashes blue, but I hear no corresponding ring.

Tate looks uncomfortable. He has done since he opened the front door to me. Shrugging, he swings the door to his bedroom open and gestures me in. "Joke present. No batteries."

I frown at him as I step by but make no comment. I stop just inside the door, taking in his room. Now this has changed some. I'm all of a sudden feeling kinda bereft.

No more Spiderman wallpaper, in its place there's one dark

blue wall and three white. They look bare; all his posters are gone, and his penned sketches have been thinned down to four, framed instead of blu-tacked. The big Spiderman figure that once took pride of place on his window sill has been exchanged for a cactus plant. A double bed covered in a navy checked bed spread is set against the wall where his single bunk beds used to be, and a desk supporting a mammoth computer with three monitors takes up practically the entirety of the wall I remember as being shelves for his DVD collection. The bookcase full of his comics and Manga remains though, *thankfully*. As does his rickety chest of drawers covered in superhero stickers, except a pair of well-worn skates no longer reside on its top.

My skates are downstairs, by the front door. I arrived here in them harbouring the slightest spark of hope that, in seeing them, his passion would be reawakened. He didn't even spare them a glance.

"It – it's supposed to give a shock when pressed," Tate says, following in behind me and pulling the door closed. He takes the big, black leather swivel chair by the desk and I stand gawkily, unsure what to do. Tate's room isn't huge and, between desk and bed, there's only a narrow stretch of floor space and no other chairs. He juts his chin toward the bed. "This is weird. Having you back in here."

I nod, perching myself on the foot of his mattress. "That it is." Shirking out of my jacket, I let it drop down behind me. Tate swivels his chair a touch so he's facing me and flashes an awkward smile. He's fidgety and antsy. As am I. It's *so* frustratingly weird. My gaze again roams his room, picking out the familiar from the new –the few reassuring stamps of my best friend from those significant chunks that mark him out as something of a stranger. His drawings are awesome: A prowling black panther; a wide-branched tree made up of words that I can't read at this distance; a forbidding pirate ship cutting through waves; and a hand, fingers cupping, finely detailed. He's improved. These, obviously the favourites of his works. Too few, though. I slide to a rest on the fat pillows at the head of his crazy-neat bed. "Where am I gonna kip now on our sleepovers?"

Oh sweet freaking jeezus. My face heats. Tate doesn't respond. *What the hell kinda dumbass thing was that to say?!* Slowly lifting and turning my head back to him, I'm met with a perplexed frown.

"Sorry, what?"

"Never mind."

Head tilting a little, he continues staring at me.

"So." I clear my throat. "Your dad's took Megan to the cinema, yeah? Where's Laura today?"

He tenses, his face scrunching up further. Seems I've wrong footed again. Somehow. This one I can't fathom. I bite my lip, waiting, as he lifts a hand to rub the back of his neck.

"Mum's..." With a small shoulder bop, he huffs out a breath and drops his hand down to his lap. "Not sure what Mum's up to."

"Huh," I say, no less confused and a fraction more uneasy. The issue's with Laura? *Why?* This is getting off to a truly superb start. Wonder how long I have before he remembers he's supposed to be doing something else super important and asks me to leave. "What you got in mind for us this afternoon then?" If he does want to opt out, the opening for him's right there: *'Actually, Mikey, I'm sorry but...'*

"Well..." he starts in. I hold my breath and steel myself. Instead of continuing, though, he gets to his feet and crosses the room to his built-in closet. Opening the door, he crouches down, fumbling around the floor inside. I can't see what he's doing. When he straightens, closes the door and turns, he has his History textbook in hand, held up toward me. "Essay?"

I'm horrified. My mouth drops open. Worse than making up an excuse to free himself of me, appears he intends to avoid the dirty work by forcing me to leave of my own volition. "You have got to be kidding!"

In a blink, Tate's straight face falls apart, a grin cracking wide.

Air expels from me in a rush of relief, my body zinging. "Jeezus, Tate, phew! You really had me going..."

"No, no, no," he cuts me off, shaking his head as he works to pull his face back into line. The book thumps down onto the bed beside me. "I'm entirely serious."

"Give over. What?"

"Come on, Mikey." He resettles in his seat, propping his elbows on his knees and leaning in toward me. "We both have it to do. Gotta be better working through it together –helping each other – than doing it alone, right?"

"We have two weeks."

"Exactly."

He's misheard my point. "I haven't got any of my stuff with me."

"You've started already?"

"No. Because we have two weeks."

Dropping his head, I hear a chuckle escape him. He returns his attention to me, amusement still bright. "My textbook's there. Welcome to my computer. Pens and paper. We're all set."

I groan into my hands. Perhaps *I* have something else super important I should be doing elsewhere... But, hold up, no. No way. That's what he's shooting for, and he's playing a blinder, for sure, but I refuse to forfeit. I straighten up, slapping my thighs, "fine. Russian Revolution. Bring it."

Once started, however, my misgivings fizzle away pretty damn fast. As does much of the tension.

Okay, so it's not the most fun afternoon I've ever had, granted. A far stretch from how I expected the day to go. And I wouldn't say it becomes *comfortable* exactly – not in the easy to wear old jumper kinda way. We don't talk much as we work; Tate proves himself a master at blocking out any and all distractions. And when we escape to the kitchen, settling at the table with drinks and snacks, he steers me clear of every attempt to reminisce on our shared past, the stuff that bonds us, the reminders I'm surrounded by.

But I do make some good headway with the project I'd other-wise likely have ignored until the night before its due date, put decent effort into it too. We then chat about his gaming interests and my Northern friends, share a tube of Pringles and a bottle of Fanta, and I talk some about Gran – the good bits. He's laughed. Twice. It's more of a reassuringly tangible *relaxed* vibe that we achieve between us, getting to know each other anew. And discovering I still like him, still enjoy his company, brings me a small step or two closer to happy than I've been for a long time. Even with the tedious study and tricky restrictions to conversation and occasional treacle-thick lulls, there's actually nowhere else I'd rather be.

Setting my empty glass down on a coaster, I look across the small pine table at him, watch him disappear several crisps into his mouth at once, his jaw flexing as he crunches, and flash a smile when he catches me out.

"What happened to New Zealand, Tate?" I ask, recovering myself. Although by far not the most pressing question I have for him, I am curious. Feels a safe enough topic. "Why didn't you go?"

His munching stops, expression becoming one of utter confusion, like my words aren't computing. My nerves flutter in the face of another accidental misstep.

"You... weren't set to move to New Zealand?" Perhaps Melissa seriously did just fabricate that news for her own designs. She claimed to have heard it directly from Mai Saunders –Adele's mum. They'd worked together then. Apparently, Mai had gushed about her neighbours' imminent departure, delighted her daughter would finally be freed of that troublesome boy's influence. Mel has more cunning and imagination than I credit her with if that was all nothing more than a ploy.

But then Tate's brows lift, face smoothing. The munching resumes. "Just. Didn't work out," he says with a shrug once his mouth's emptied. "Dad had a job offer –a good one. But he decided, in the end, it was, uh, too much of an upheaval. For us all. And Mum really didn't want to go."

"Did you want to go?"

Drawing the Pringles to him, he squeezes a hand in. "Yeah."

"Oh." That stings for some reason I can't even begin to justify. "And now? You still wish you'd gone?"

One corner of his lip twitches down. "Sometimes." He wriggles his hand free of the tube, a substantial stack of crisps pinched precariously between two fingers and his thumb. "Sometimes... I just think starting fresh... it would have been the best thing for us. But." His head seems to go far, far away for a moment. Returning with a hard press of his lips, he sets about separating his crisps into three separate piles then reverting them back into one. "Then again, maybe it wouldn't."

I don't know how to respond, so I don't. Slouching back in my chair, I watch his game of Pringle Pile-up.

"What about you?" He asks just as the silence presses in again.

"Me? What about me?"

"You had your fresh start. How is it being back home again?"

There's that word again: *Home.* "I'm not home, Tate." I throw a quick glance around the snug kitchen: Same brown counters; same yellow and blue tiles; same scuffed and shabby table. I'm more home here in this room than I've felt anywhere in weeks. "It sucks."

Tate's eyes are probing me. His expression's solemn and I regret the turn I've caused this conversation to take.

"Time to get back to it, yeah?" He says, standing. "Final stretch."

"Hey." I give him pause as he's about to turn. He frowns at me. "If we were to rebuild the den, that would go a long way to settling me, I think."

I've took a bit of a risk. His eyes narrow but the grin I sincerely hoped for hints on his face. "Rebuild the den?"

"Yep. And you could also help redecorate my room. It's a disaster."

"Oh, is it?"

"You've no idea," I nod. "Your art wall's gone, painted over. I want a new one."

"Well. If that's what it's gonna take," his grin makes a more pronounced appearance, "then that's what we'll do, Mikey. First, though, the books are calling. Race you to the next five hundred words?"

I feel somewhat giddy following him back through the house and up the stairs.

Plans.

We have plans.

FOR THE NEXT WEEK, I sit opposite Tate every Study period and beside him in History, though we get very little chance to talk (what with him being ever such the diligent student and all). He refuses to walk with me to and from school, but I do eat lunch with him every other day. If the choice were mine I'd eat with him every day (even despite Adele's acidic presence), but it's not. Tate's hell-bent on me keeping a balance. He says it's unfair of me to cut out Lyndsay and co. in favour of him when they've made such an effort to welcome me into their group. And I get what he's saying. I totally do. My problem is that I don't much enjoy those days I'm eating with them in the lunch hall and not with him in the Quad.

Lyndsay's noticed. She's smiling a whole lot less lately.

15

VIOLATED LIPS

othinGintheVersE:
You're stupendously awful at this, Mikey.

Tate's big-time into gaming these days. So, of course, I've set myself up a Steam account and purchased the game he's currently favouriting. Not as creeptastic as it sounds, I swear; I'm simply interested in better understanding his fascination with it. By all accounts, this is what's replaced skating in his life and I need to figure out how it could possibly even come close to comparing. I've had to make serious sacrifices for this: First, asking David for the money to buy the game. My job hunt has now started in earnest. Second, pleading with Sophie for the time on her PC in the sitting room cos my laptop's not powerful enough to run it.

NothinGintheVersE:
Where are you going?
mıK3y_A:
I don't freaking know! Where am I supposed to be going?
NothinGintheVersE:
Not into the wall. Turn around.

For the past two evenings, Tate's been tutoring me on the gameplay but, yep, I'm most definitely not a natural. It's hella infuriating. I absolutely am not going to admit to him I've been on it pretty much since the moment I got in from school today, getting some practice in before he logged on −gained me zero improvement.

mɪK3y_A:
Love to. It won't let me.

I keep reminding myself that the first few times he took me out skating, I'd hated that too. I'll get my head around this soon, I'm sure...

NothinGintheVersE:
And you've killed yourself again. Wow.
mɪK3y_A:
DAMNIT!

...*Possibly.* Least it's facilitating extra quality chat time.

As I wait to respawn, I figure now's as good a time as any to ask what I've been itching to this past hour. I flex my fingers a moment before I start typing.

mɪK3y_A:
So, hey, I'm going to the view after school tomorrow for a bit.
You fancy it?

I hold my breath while I wait for him to respond, but my chest starts to ache and he's giving me nothing.

mɪK3y_A:
It'll be quiet. Won't be staying too long.

I know Alex won't be there −he, Callum and a couple of other guys are headed over to the fancy side of town for a footie game with his brother, Craig. Likely only gonna be a handful of us up at the shed. Perfect opportunity to reintroduce Tate into a bit of social activity with his peers. It'll do him good.

mɪK3y_A:
Come on, Tate?

And I'm back in the game.

NothinGintheVersE:
Location?

mɪK3y_A:
That stupid warehouse thing.
So, the view tomorrow, yes?
NothinGintheVersE:
No.
Take cover. I'm coming to you.

Well, there it is. I slump. It's the answer I fully expected, but I'm still disappointed.

mɪK3y_A:
Why not?
NothinGintheVersE:
Come out the back. I'm behind the truck.
mɪK3y_A:
On my way.
Seriously, though, it won't kill you to spend a bit time outside. You may even surprise yourself and have fun.

I make it out the back, as instructed. Tate shoots me in the head.

mɪK3y_A:
WTH?!

He then logs out.

∼

"You're coming to the party, right?" Lyndsay asks, subtly (only, not so much) skooching closer to me on the bench. "Steph's parties are legendary. You really can't miss out."

It's a magnificent late-winter Wednesday afternoon. Yeah, it's still super chilly, but the sun's shining, the sky's a striking blue and there's not a cloud in sight. At Lyndsay's suggestion, her, Steph, Callum, Alex and I are eating lunch outside, in the Quad. 'It's far too beautiful to be stuck inside,' she'd said, 'let's have us some rare vitamin D'. Tate and Adele are settled only two tables away, that blasted notebook out between them again (I remain blind to its contents. It no longer makes an appearance on those days I sit

with them) and so, I'm a teensy tiny bit distracted from my immediate company. "What?"

She huffs. "Steph's party, Mikey. Saturday. You coming?"

"Oh. Yeah. I said I would, didn't I? For a bit."

"Good." She moves in even closer, her arm pressing against
mine. "That's good. I'm so looking forward to it, you know? Think
we're totally in need of it."

"Mmm," I say, with only the mildest comprehension of what
she's said, "totally." Tate's just caught my eye and then swiftly
averted his gaze. It's the ninth time he's done that in seven
minutes. I'm getting kinda annoyed he hasn't come over yet...Well,
no, I realise there's very little chance of him making that move.
But he could've motioned me across to him. He's not mad at me
for last night, surely...?

Lyndsay's hand settles on my knee, jolting me back to our
table, "Mikey, Steph's asking if you have any particular drink
requests?"

"Err..." My attention slips to Steph, who's staring at me like I'm
some bizarre oddity. "No. Thanks." I hear Adele giggling and it's a
tough call not to turn but I manage. "I'm good with anything."

"Yuh-huh," Steph says, rolling her eyes across to Callum. "Your
brother still okay to get stuff?"

"Of course." Callum nods, side-eying me and smiling at Lyndsay. "Though not stupid-huge amounts. Someone else will need to
pick up stuff too."

"Urgh, I hate small town living!" Steph whines dramatically,
flapping her hands in the air. "We need a trip through Exeter or
something. I can easy get served myself outside of this pithole."

Now Tate chuckles and there's the sound of a soft slap.

"I'm through Craig's tonight," Alex chips in. "That place by
him —Shaunacie's —they serve me. Get me some money and I'll
call in."

"Anybody object to me inviting Adele?" I blurt.

Obviously, I don't actually mean Adele. But Lyndsay's clued me
in to the possibility of an adverse reaction from Alex had I said

Tate. I'm figuring if I get an in for Adele then I have an in for talking Tate around. Okay, so yesterday's effort with him may not have gone down too well, but it's a fresh day and a fresh opportunity. I'm of the mind persistence is key.

"Who?" Steph frowns.

My eyes dart two tables over. I can sense Alex's glower without turning to look his way. Lyndsay sighs heavily. Fixing on her, I get the distinct impression she set a trap here, one she devoutly hoped I wouldn't fall into, and I've failed her. I flash her a weak smile before rising from the bench. "More the merrier, right?"

"Now, there's the spirit!" Steph gives me the go.

I approach Tate and Adele's table and Tate shakes his head at me. My pulse gallops into chaos. I take a seat by Adele. *Positive approach. Positive approach.*

"What the fuckity crap, Alston!" She snarls at me. "Today's not your day."

"Consider it a treat," I retort, my attention focused on Tate.

"I'm getting poison eyed by your girl, Mikey. You should go back to your table."

Screw that. They can cope without me perfectly well for a minute or five. "I'm here to cordially invite you. Both of you," I add with some reluctance. "To the party of the century. Steph Willis' house. Saturday night. In?"

"Oh, boy! Really? I can hardly believe it," Adele gushes with such saccharine sweet sarcasm my teeth ache. "For realsies, Mikey? Really for realsies?"

My lip curling, I blank her. "What d'ya think, Tate? Up for it?" *Please,* I don't add.

His expression's not encouraging.

I wait with barely concealed agitation through a brief silent exchange of glances between him and Adele. Adele grabs the notebook, scribbles something down and shoves it at him. He reads it, and then, without a word or gesture, or even a look my way, he gets to his feet and shoulders his bag. His face resembles an imminent storm.

"Tate? What the hell did you write, Saunders?" I snap to Adele.

"Not what I wrote, doofus. It's all on you." She, too, is eyeing Tate with obvious concern, though hers isn't mixed with quite as much bewilderment. She reaches again for the notebook, but Tate snatches it up from under her fingertips.

"I can't do this," he says before striding for the alley between Sixth Form and Music.

"Leave it!" Adele orders as I jump up.

No. Not a damn chance. I'm not crashing straight back down to square one. Persistence. Is. Key!

"Hey, Tate!" I chase him. Catching up at the far end of the narrow walkway, a few steps from where it opens out onto the car park, I grab his arm and blast him, "can't do what?"

"Just don't know when to quit, Mikey, do you?" He hisses the words through clenched teeth. Turning to me, I'm not hit by the soul-shattering attack of anger I realise I've tensed for. It's there, I can see it simmering in his eyes, thinly veiled, and in the tight set of his jaw. Mostly, though, mostly he's looking and sounding... weary.

"Can't do what?" I repeat, dropping my hold on his arm.

He presses his eyes closed a moment, shaking his head. The muscle in his jaw jumps.

"You insist on me keeping a wider group of friends. Why is it so unreasonable for me to push the same for you? It's a small house party, Tate, it's..."

"I'm not going to the party. I'm not going to the View. Fuck. There's so much –*too* much you don't get."

"Then explain. Please, I beg you. Cos the way I'm seeing it, you're shutting yourself off from everyone over some crap a moron spouted about you and that's just dumb. It might be true, it might not be, but any..."

"Fuck sake, Mikey! You're so far off base!" His anger has now exploded free of its flimsy cage. He steps in to me, green eyes harsh. I'm probably supposed to be taking a step back, but I don't. My feet are rooted. The heat pouring off of him engulfs me, but

I'm fairly damn incensed myself at this point. Slow and deliberate, he snarls, "what people think. What they say. I. Couldn't. Give. A. Shit. I know who I am. I'm okay with who I am. Perhaps it's time you work out who the hell you are. Cos, seriously, this people-pleasing-sucktard thing you're playing at right now, it's really... *really*. Fucking. Cringey."

His words spear through me deep, brutal. But my response is something else entirely more damaging.

One short move forward, closing the distance between us...

Pressing myself tight against him...

I kiss him.

My mind empties. There's no before, no after. Only this gunshot moment: My lips on his, then the smooth skin of his neck and the silky feel of his hair as I draw him nearer. Possessed and surrendering to it, I probe his lips with my tongue. The thrill is wild to the point of dangerous.

And he kisses me back. For a blissful pounding beat, his lips part and he kisses me back. That light skimming touch of his tongue on mine is *everything*. I'm set to implode.

Then he stops, tenses, pushes me away. With force.

Meeting his wide-eyed, horror struck glare, the panic button's hammered and my insides slam into immediate shut down. "What...? Shit, Mikey, why did you do that?"

There's the question. I take a second –or an eternity – trying to figure out the answer. He waits. "You...uh, you were staring at my mouth. You always stare at my mouth. And...I just...I..."

"You kissed me because I... cos I looked at your mouth? Brilliant." He's not at all amused by my absurdity on this occasion. The air's turned so lumpy, I'm struggling to draw breath. His eyes lift to look past me, "fucking brilliant."

Tate walks away from me before I have chance to turn. When I do turn, I see...

"Alex."

He's statue still, slack jawed and nostril flared at the opening of the alley from the Quad. "What the...?!"

I plummet into a pit of absolute utter despair.

~

I DON'T GO to the View after school. I cut my school day short at lunch time, fleeing through the car park.

Now shut in my room, curtains closed, duvet swaddled around me, I'm riding the afternoon on alternating waves of hysteria and self-pity, my brain continuously tripping and resetting over one excruciating point: That kiss had felt so *right*. In that one bright flicker, I'd felt more alive than I ever thought possible. Real and euphoric and... well, aroused.

Urgh, I'm so freaking messed up!

I violated my best friend's lips. What on God's green earth possessed me?! There's no coming back from that. All I can see is that look on his face when he'd pushed me away. It's slaughtering me over and over.

I start up my laptop and log into Steam. No intention of playing the stupid game, just kinda desperately hoping for the chance to talk to Tate, explain. But staring at the screen has me realising I have no idea what I could even say, and I shut it back down.

Doesn't matter anyway. Tate's not online. Or if he is, he's blocked me.

I have his number. I could try calling him. Or send a text. But, again, to say what?

In one deviant flash of extreme bravado, I almost convince myself to go out. Whether to call in on Tate —perhaps, face to face with him, something'll click —or to find Alex and bluff my way out of the threatening scandal, I'm not sure, but I make it no further than my bedroom door in any case. I don't even go so far as releasing the duvet from my shoulders.

My phone buzzes several times, the frequency picking up as the afternoon draws into evening. All Lyndsay. The fragment of my brain stubbornly insistent on positivity tries convincing me she's only concerned about my View no-show, but that fragment's foolish and I discount it. She'll have heard. I don't read her texts or listen to her voicemail.

～

I SKIP school the next day. I ignore four calls and eight texts from Lyndsay. A call from Steph too. And, also, a text from Alex. But when a text comes through from an unknown number, my curiosity's piqued enough to at least read it.

Dunno what you've done, Alston, but you're fucking gonna fix it! Tate's a wreck.

Adele.

I didn't think it possible to feel worse.

～

I FULLY INTENDED to stay off school Friday too, even knowing David was taking the day off and would be on my back all day, but Lyndsay calls around bright and early, and David lets her up to my room.

"You're a state, Mikey. Get in the shower," she greets me when I open my bedroom door to her.

I blush scarlet: I'm wearing only my tatty grey sweatpants and a tee that hasn't properly fitted me for about four years. "What... what are you doing here?"

"Our History assignments due. You can't skip again. Done it, right?"

"Uh, yeah." I nod. With Tate, over the course of two blissful Sunday afternoons. I'm immensely proud of it.

"All sorted then. Come on, we'll walk together. Though not like that." Her eyes slowly roam the length of me and, I swear, a flame sparks on the tip of my ear. She smirks like she's aware of it. "You're looking rough."

Lyndsay's looking as well presented this morning as she did on

139

our date (though with a more casual tone). And she's rocking this bossy self-assured vibe that I'm really quite unsettled by.

I don't get it. Why is she here? Why is she not going all psycho bitch on me?

"I'm... sick. I'm staying home today."

"Nope. You have half an hour." She squeezes past me, into the room, and I turn to find her settling into my desk chair again. "I'll wait for you here. Now go shower."

Could it be that Alex has stayed quiet, and the kiss he witnessed isn't the big scandal I've been imagining it to be?

The damage I've caused between Tate and I remains critical, of course, but maybe –just maybe –I'm not totally ruined.

KILL ME. KILL ME NOW

I'm totally ruined.

Usually, I make it in the school gates unchecked, but not this morning. There's eyes on me every which way. And though I can't hear the whispered words, I'm acutely aware of their existence in the air around me.

"Ignore them," Lyndsay mollifies, squeezing my elbow.

"You know, don't you?" I turn to her.

She presses her lips into a tight line. "It's fine, Mikey."

Fine? "Is it? How? How is it *fine?*"

"No one's blaming you."

"Uh..." I freeze, my brows pulling so tight together, they're practically crossing over, "what...? What's Alex said, Lyndsay?"

Stopping a step ahead, she turns but her eyes flit around me, carefully avoiding mine. "Don't worry about it. Honestly. You're good."

Her caginess won't wash here. I've asked a direct question, I'd very much appreciate a direct answer. Now. Before I walk into lord knows what. Terror is rising. "Tell me what you've heard. Please?"

"That Mac kissed you," she eventually admits, her words tumbling out in a rush, "and you freaked out."

Oh. Crap. My head starts shaking. "No."

"Listen." She juts her head toward the school gates looming menacingly too close up ahead and, linking her arm through mine, starts walking again. My legs sluggishly follow her lead. "It'll die down soon enough. Just...don't let it get to you, okay? Don't let the idiots get under your skin."

My stomach's writhing too much for me to concoct an answer.

The first person I lock on as I'm half-dragged through the main entrance is Alex. I guess it's somewhat unlikely he's been stood by student services explicitly to catch me, but the sneery look he fixes me with is all the excuse I need to scurry away. I manipulate my arm free of Lyndsay.

"Oh, come on, Mikey. Where you going?"

"Toilet?" I don't hold out for her okay, I'm headed for the little-used side corridor leading to the Geography classrooms.

"It's not you, Alex," I hear Lyndsay say behind me. "He's still sort of whacked out about it all."

No sooner have I turned the corner, however, than I'm side-barrelled and slammed against the wall.

"I'm gonna castrate you." Adele gets her face right up in mine. "Slowly."

"Good," I wheeze, turning my head for breathing space.

"Tate's not telling me anything. Not that he needs to for me to know these rumours are a stinking pile of bullshit. Start talking, Alston, or I swear I'm sending you into a whole world of agonising pain."

"I. Kissed. Him." The words don't come out easy but −damn − once free, they're a burden lifted. Adele's weight, however, presses all the heavier on my chest, her hand cupping a tad too roughly around my delicate man parts. I rush on, "it was all me. He pushed me away. Alex saw."

A sharp crack assaults my ears and my head bounces off the wall. Teeth snapping into my tongue, my cheek has been set ablaze. There's a dazed delay on me registering she's slapped me. I blink the tears from my eyes. "You wanna be thankful I didn't twist and pull with my other hand cos, maaan, was I tempted! Why? Why would you do that?"

I manoeuvre my hand free from its prison between us to press against my cheek, as if it has some dock leaf type power to soothe the sting, and swallow hard. She doesn't spare me the time to answer though.

"You know they're spinning it like he launched himself on you? Gary Tinwell's having a blast with his '*I told you so*'s." Straightening herself, she yields enough space for me to drag in a full breath, but not enough for me to escape her. "He's been through so much already, he doesn't need this, Alston. He doesn't damn well deserve this!"

"I know, I... I don't know. Just." I shrug. "It wasn't... supposed to happen."

"Yeah. Well." Her hand lifts from my groin, a finger jabbing into my chest. "You want to make it right."

"I will. I'll clear this up, sort it out." I nod. No idea how I'm gonna pull that off. "Where is he? I'll talk to him."

"You'll keep well away from him. He stormed out halfway through second period yesterday apparently, hasn't replied to my texts since and his dad says he doesn't want to see anyone. Not even me. You'll clear his name and then you'll stay away, right?" I don't respond so she jabs me again in the chest, harder, "right?"

"Get your hands off him!"

The intrusion of Lyndsay's voice, shrill with indignation, has me grimacing more than the pain to my chest.

Adele turns to her. I do not. "Chill out, lovey. I'm not after your mister." Eyes returning to mine, she backs away with deliberate slowness, "knew you'd be trouble. You're such an epic screw up."

"You alright?" Lyndsay rushes up to me as Adele pivots on her heel and saunters away along the corridor. "What'd the sour-faced mare say?"

"Nothing. I'm..." '*Good*' won't come out. I sag against the wall, "a terrible person."

"Oh, shut up! You are not. Come on, it's time for learning."

Taking my hand, she tugs, prompting me up. "Seriously, just ride it out."

It takes less than first period for me to discern that Alex took full advantage of my absence yesterday to spin the tale he saw Tate jump my bones and me throw him off. The word has spread far and fast. Excessively more difficult to get a handle on is an approach to combat and extinguish it.

Admitting the truth to Adele is one thing, but it's most certainly not an admittance I'm brave enough to lay bare to the entire student body.

How the hell do I set the record straight and cinch vindication for Tate without incriminating myself beyond recovery?

As soon as the bell sounds at the end of class, I'm off in search of Alex. Doesn't take long.

"Hey." I spot him lingering just a few doors down the corridor. He turns and raises one brow. I approach with a steely gaze and a distinct measure of reluctance in my gut. Stopping close but outside of easy reach from him (no clue of the reaction I should expect here), I make every effort to ensure my voice comes out steady. "You've got to put a stop to this. What you think you saw, you didn't." I have minimal success. "Nothing like. I swear."

"Relax, Mikey. There's no heat on you." Pushing up off the wall, he smirks, and it's in a way that tells me oh-so-clearly that he knows *exactly* what he saw. "I've done you a solid. Seriously."

My whole body tenses. "A solid? How can you even claim that?" Jeezus, I'm under no illusion he's twisted his account for my benefit. In his head, this isn't likely about me in the least. This is very much all about his brother. This is about untainting Craig's name by damning Tate as some kind of sexual predator. "You're wrong. Please. Tate's done nothing."

He huffs out a hard laugh designed to make my plea seem stupid. "No. You're wrong. McAllister's done plenty. The more distance you set from him, the better off you'll be." With that, he winks at me and walks away. "Trust me."

"ALEX!"

"Ah, Michaela, you're back!" Gary's voice booms behind me, jolting me into biting my tongue again. I turn to stone and he laughs, drawing up beside me. "Told ya you had a real shot with your boy, didn't I? I'm so happy for the pair of you. No. Wait. My bad, not happy...Disgusted, I mean disgusted."

"Get back to your cave, Gary," I mumble, failing to inject the intended heat. I get my feet moving. "Dunno what you're talking about."

"'Course ya do, princess!" He keeps pace. "Poor Alex. He's who I'm feeling for. Scarred for life. Never will that image leave his head. I should know; I've been there." Performing a theatrical shudder that pulses a genuine one through me, he pounds my shoulder, knocking me a stumbling step sideward. "Nasty! Yet even after this, he won't believe me about his bro. And, mind, Craig wasn't freaking out over Mac's *assault*, I can tell ya. Least, not until he saw me."

I speed up. "I'm not listening. Swallow your tongue."

"Hey, you liked it too, didn't ya? Got you *hard*? Your little tinkle ready to spurt her excitement juice?" He hasn't matched my quickened step, he's just raised his voice. "How's your sweet little Lyndsay taking...?"

"Nothing happened!" I shriek, *way* too much heat flooding my voice. "Tate didn't jump me. It's a depraved work of fiction. So shut your foul, hateful mouth and leave me be, or..." *Or...?* I've got nothing. Hurrying to the nearest door, I dart through, slam it shut and press myself against it.

"Pathetic!" Gary bangs once, the force vibrating the door. Then, slowly, his disturbing chuckle fades away as he moves off.

"Is there a problem?" A gruff voice snaps my attention to the right where I find Mr Bell sat behind his desk, frowning at me. I've shut myself in my Maths classroom. *Awesome.* "You're not due with me until fourth. Lost again, Mr Alston?"

"Yes, Sir. Exceptionally lost. Always," I reply truthfully as I twist the doorknob at my back. Moving free of the door, I slip out, "Sorry."

Spying Lyndsay back along the corridor, looking confused outside of my first period English room, I trudge over.

～

NEEDLESS TO SAY, fourth Maths with Gary is excruciating. Every word he has to say is unpleasant, directed at me, and said unnecessarily loud. Mr Bell —as is his norm —pretends obliviousness while the class around me titters and whispers none-too-quietly. My efforts at defence just seem to worsen the issue.

"You're only fuelling the fire," Callum cautions me with a sage nod when I further attempt to refute Tate's guilt at lunch. "Folk'll get bored faster if you give them no reaction."

Beside me, Lyndsay's chewing on her lip, staying determinedly quiet. She's spent every single minute she could possibly manage by my side this morning, and I'm guessing she's beyond sick of hearing me out, sick of hearing herself sounding like a broken record.

There's a heavy truth to their words, I know there is.

This denial approach I'm taking has been tread before by Craig to little success, and he was up against Gary —the renowned crap-creator king. There possibly wasn't even an actual dot of truth to what he was fighting against.

My protestations are making no impact whatsoever in halting the tongues set wagging by Alex. He's without a reputation for gossip mongering, and he's made it very clear a retraction of his account is not on the cards.

But, see, thing is... not only have I destroyed what Tate and I had been steadily building, I've managed to stomp him down deep in the mud, Adele is promising my untimely death, and if I don't at least try to pull him out and clean him off here, my self-loathing may very well end me before she can. Taking their smart advice'd be like accepting the misdirected consequences of my thoughtless actions. Can't do that.

I open my mouth but Callum cuts me short. "We get it, man,

okay? But, here's the thing, if honest-to-God nothing actually happened, then why'd you cut out on Wednesday? And stay gone yesterday? And ignore your phone? And be acting all deranged as hell today?"

Lyndsay winces and nods.

"I, uh..."

"Oh, who cares?" Steph rudely buts in —my saviour. She slams her lime green boots down on the chair beside her and points a finger at herself, "Not this girl. We've more important things to discuss. Like my party. It's tomorrow night, people! Let's go through what supplies we have, should we?"

Wishing I'd stayed home and dumb today, I sink down in my chair.

17

BAD BROTHERING

"MIKEY!"

David's loud bellow startles me awake. What time is it? Late afternoon I'd guess; I'm feeling that grogginess that comes from way too much sleep. Not feeling a smidge of the refreshment that follows a decent sleep though.

"DOWNSTAIRS NOW, MIKEY!" Dave hollers again. "RIGHT. NOW!"

I turn in bed, putting my back to the door, and pull my duvet up over my head. *No, David, not today.*

There's a few minutes of silence. My eyes drift back closed. But, then, stomping feet on the stairs sharp vaults me upright with an almighty curse.

Unfortunately, David makes it into my room before I make it out. He switches on the light and my retinas are set to burning. My hands swoop up to cover.

"Screw you, David. You can't just walk in here!"

"Think you'll find I just have. Get dressed."

"What? No."

"It's four in the afternoon. You've been shut up in here since four yesterday aft..."

"Not true."

"Yes. It is."

"Nope. I spent a bit quality time with Gran doing a Cinderella jigsaw until Sophie trounced in and took over. It was much closer to half four."

He's rolled his eyes, I'm certain of it. "And just how do you think Gran feels seeing you like this, huh?"

Oh, the low blow. Why must he always play that? I sigh, pressing my fingertips into my eye sockets. "Gran's not seeing me like this. That's very much the bonus of me being up here. If I'm to do what you're suggesting though, well, then she will be subjected to seeing me like this, and −for sure −that would be really crappy."

"Uh-huh. You're going to spend the remainder of this day productively. Now, put on some clothes and get out of this pit."

"You get out of this pit. I'm staying in it." I drop my hands and flop back onto my bed. "And if I should decide to stay in it forever, I don't see how that's any business of yours. Buh-bye."

"Michael..."

"Mikey."

"*Michael,* enough is enough. Sulk time is over, and I will drag you out if necessary."

"Jeezus, what's the issue? It's not like I'm needed for anything. I'm keeping out of your way, just freaking enjoy it while it lasts."

"You profess your maturity and capability and then behave in a way my six-year-old daughter would be ashamed to, that's the issue." I hear him move further into the room and a bizarre noise bursts free of my throat. "I'm not demanding you tell me what's going on with you, I know you won't. But you are getting up now and you are re-joining the living world. There's food on the table, I insist you eat with us."

"I insist you leave and close the door behind you," I retort, slamming my fisted hands down on the bed either side of me. "I'm not hungry."

He mutters something on a long sigh. I sense him looming over me. "Dragging it is then."

A hand encircles my wrist, another locking around my ankle. I squeal (yes, *squeal*), and writhe myself free to the result of tumbling to the floor with a resounding *thunk*!

"Dare touch me again," I spit, scrabbling to get my feet under me. "Dare!"

"Oh, good," David claps his hands, looking pompously triumphant. "You're up."

"You want me out in the living world? Well, alright then," I hurl at him belligerently. "I'll go out. There's a party. Unsupervised. Lotsa alcohol. Likely drugs too. I may not make it home tonight, so don't wait up. Happy?"

His coffee dark eyes lock on my own, mouth a matching straight, tight line. "Okay," he nods. "That works for me."

"So glad." With a wide sweeping gesture, I show him to the door. "I'll pass on the safe-sex talk and so we're done here, I believe."

"Joining us to eat first?"

"No." I snatch up clothes at random from the floor. Noticing David's making no moves to leave, I lob a hoody at him. It flumps off his shin before dropping to his feet.

Lips crooking up, he glances down and rubs a hand along his jaw. "Drinking on an empty stomach then, huh? Smart. I'll leave a plate on the bench in case you decide at any point to engage your brain."

"I won't."

Striding to the door, he throws a final smirk over his shoulder as he steps out, "at least try to have fun. The safe kind of fun −I should hope you know what that entails without me telling you. Don't get too drunk. And be home by two please."

I pelt a sock his way but the door shuts before it reaches target. *Oh, goddamn the lanky heaping, stinking crap pile!* What the hell sort of reaction was that?! I hadn't really been planning on going to the party. Thought to go for a skate, perhaps past Tate's house once or thrice, while away some time at the den maybe, before sneaking back in to my room and under my duvet. But −bollocks to him −now he's left me no choice. I've a sudden and unreasonably overwhelming compulsion: Steph's party will be graced with my presence after all. I'm going to have a downright miserable time, determinedly stay out until dawn, and drink myself stupid drunk. If I should throw up all over the beige carpet on my eventual return, then so be it.

Challenge accepted, dear brother mine.

Dropping the clothes in my arms, I hunt out better from my drawers and go shower.

Oh, it's on!

 ∼

"YOU'RE EARLY!" Lyndsay exclaims with a grin on opening her door to me. "I thought for sure you'd be standing me up tonight, what with you ignoring my texts and everything, yet −wow −here you are, almost three hours early."

"Sorry." I shove my hands deeper into my jacket pockets. Is she mad? She doesn't look mad. "Should I, uh...come back later?" Furiously hoping she says 'no'. It's raining, and I'm drenched. I'm also seriously at risk of losing my nerve on this.

"No, no, don't be silly," she casts a wave of relief over me. "Come in. Mum and Dad are going out shortly, and I've some pre-party drinks we can get in the mood with."

"Awesome," I say without a trace of sarcasm. Sooner I can get started the better, so far as I see. She stands aside, and I step in by her with a smile.

"Pass your coat here, I'll stick it on the radiator."

Wrestling myself free of it, I hand the dripping jacket over, "thanks." Then I tug off my trainers and she's quick to snatch them up too, tucking them in underneath the radiator. "Thanks," I say again.

First time I've been inside Lyndsay's house, and it's exactly how

I imagined it to be: Cosy-small, elegant and immaculate. There's a strong feminine influence to the décor.

She doesn't lead me up the stairs to her room, for which I'm super thankful —she may have been in mine, but I'm so not ready for the intimacy and associated pressure of us spending time alone together in hers. That's the one element of David's challenge I fully intend to let him off on.

She instead, however, takes me through to her kitchen, "Mum, Dad, this is Mikey."

Knee-jerk reaction: Abort. ABORT!

Oh, curses to me for relinquishing my jacket and shoes.

18

I CLAIMED HIM FIRST!

"*I*'m not gonna talk about Tate tonight. Not at all. Not even gonna think about him. He's outta my head. For the whole duration of this party."

"Yeah," Lyndsay lets out a giddy little laugh and reaches across the precariously burdened drinks table between us to slap me cutely on the shoulder. "You've said, like, a dozen times already."

I frown at her until it registers that my hand is suddenly soaking wet. Glancing down, I find my cup is fountaining, well beyond its full capacity. I set down the bottle of coke. It's okay, cos I went overboard on the rum too, so I figure it's surely balanced out now. Rum is good, I've determined; goes down far more agreeably than beer, ale or cider. "Well, I really mean it. I'm not thinking about any of it. I forbid myself."

"Mmm, and you're doing great with it. Really," she responds with a level of sarcasm that doesn't pass me by. Polishing off her bottle, she sets it down on the edge of the table. She doesn't pick up a fresh one. At hers, she was matching me drink for drink. But since arriving at Steph's, the inexplicable recovery of her sensible drinking head is kinda peeing me off. "What? You're drinking

153

enough for the both of us, Mikey!" She laughs. "I think it wise we look for somewhere to sit for a bit, okay?"

Lifting my cup, I take a big drink to lower the volume, but much of it streams down my chin as I nod.

We've been at the party now for...some time, Steph's house has *wayyy* too many people in it (only a handful of faces I recognise), the volume of the music has been steadily notching up toward abhorrent, and the drinks table is being built up as quickly as it's depleting.

I don't know exactly when the world started its slow spin around me, but as Lyndsay takes my hand, guiding me from the kitchen to the front room, I miscalculate the two steps between the rooms and career wildly into her, liquid sploshing over my already sticky hand.

"Whoa!" She's swift to steady herself against the wall, flattening her back to it, and I topple to pin her there, the floor beneath my feet continuing to list. "Smooth," she says into my ear, all breathy. It's possible I'm crushing her lungs, but she makes no complaint.

"You always smell so amazing." The thought blurts out my mouth, loud. "Coconutty. Like a tropical holiday." Her eyes flash wide along with her grin, and it suddenly dawns on me that I don't, perhaps, say nice things to her anywhere near as often as she deserves. I feel bad for that. "You're lovely, you know that right? You really are. And your freckles are just...precious."

She makes no reply, simply continues to smile and hold my eye. Her tongue peeks out, smoothing over her bottom lip. And it's at this point I regain confidence in my stability.

"Callum headed out this way before, didn't he?" I nod, answering myself, as I clumsily initiate extraction. "Let's go hunt him. Come on."

She mutters something, drowned out by the pounding music. Then, straightening up off the wall, she regrips my hand tight and starts manoeuvring us through the unobliging throng of strangers blocking the front door. We upset quite a few of them and my t-shirt falls casualty to an abundance more spillage.

"Oh my actual...Phew!" Lyndsay says, slamming the door behind me as we finally break free.

The blissful cessation of head-pounding noise hits me first.

Then, the sharp slap of fresh, icy night air knocks me stupid.

"Hey! Hey, Mikey, you okay?" Her face floats in close to mine.

"Good," I nod −big mistake, "yep." Gravity wins the battle I didn't prepare for and I slam to the ground. My valiant efforts to save the enduring contents of my cup fail miserably and I watch the last of it puddle and trickle away across the paving. "Feeling peachy." I hold up the emptied cup. "May need a refill though."

She holds her hand out to me. "Really don't think you do, sweetie. Not quite yet anyway."

"Look after that for me then, will you?" I say, forcing my cup into her proffered hand. I've a hazy awareness of a dull throbbing pain across my backside, also of dampness seeping through my jeans. It stopped raining at some point while I was in Lyndsay's, but the world remains soggy. I don't mind. I want to lie down.

"No, no, no!" She crouches in front of me, tossing the cup to one side.

"Hey!"

"Sit up." Her hands press each side of my face. They're too warm, like inside-the-house level sweltering. "We'll go find the others, okay? Come on."

"Okay." I'm quite the hindrance but she's persistent. Eventually, she has me on my feet. And I'm feeling glorious again. "You lead, I'll follow."

"How about we walk side by side and you put your arm around me to use me like a crutch?"

"Sure, that works."

She nuzzles in close as we walk, and shivers. I have a sneaky suspicion her suggestion is as much about her as it is aiding me. Donning our jackets would have been a smart move, it occurs to me. But they've been confiscated, held in an unknown secure location by Steph to ensure our stay. I press us in closer together, licensing her to warmpire away. She seems content with that.

We don't need to go far and, mercifully, not back inside. I spot Steph and Callum sat with Ashleigh on the swing seat across the far end of the lawn as soon as we pass through the side gate, into the back garden.

"Hey!" I release Lyndsay to raise both arms high and wave. The large and pretty garden, lit up with twinkling fairy lights, is barely less crowded than the house. "Hey, there you are! Look, there they are."

"You can put your hands down now, Mikey. They've seen us," Lyndsay mutters close to my ear. Callum's up and quickstepping his way over. I flump my arms down, returning one to Lyndsay's shoulder. "How long you guys been hiding out here?" She asks as he joins us.

"Not long. Steph freaked at finding three used condoms in her mum's room." He's eyeing me curiously. I hold up a hand to assure him they most certainly weren't mine. "Says a lot when Little Miss Wild, herself, admits this is too crazy, right?"

"Wow, and eww! I warned her to be careful who she told. We saw a guy trying to jump his bike onto the coffee table. It's mental."

"You alright, man?" He asks. He means me.

"Oh, I'm..."

"Mikey's very, very drunk," Lyndsay cuts me off. "Overdosed on the party spirit." I'm not a fan of her patronising tone. "He needs to sit down for a while, maybe drink some water."

"No," I contest, only the word comes out all stretched and stupid sounding. Does me no favours in the least. So I try again, drawing myself up ruler straight, "no, actually. All is well with Mikey. Feeling pretty damn magnificent, actually." Nailed it.

Callum snorts, shaking his head. "Think he may also need a bucket sometime real soon." I'm only made aware I've mayhaps been standing somewhat short of ruler straight when he takes up a position as my second crutch. Unprepared for his efforts to move me forward, I have him staggering. "Oof! Man, you're heavier than you look."

My feet remain anchored to the spot. The sight of Alex has arrested my full attention.

A few feet away from the swing seat, he's perched on the low wall surrounding a flower bed, beside a guy in a beany hat who I don't recognise. He's not looking at me, but ¬positive I've caught his eyeballs scrolling my way as I've stared ¬it's like he's making a very deliberate attempt not to. And that infuriates me.

"Hey, Faux-hawk!" I call, my voice a tad louder than necessary and holding a minor hysterical note that should definitely not be there. "Why so rude, dude?"

His neighbour looks over. Alex does not. In fact, he turns to look more so in the opposite direction.

Oh, how the righteous indignation surges. "Oi!"

Lyndsay's hand presses into my chest. "No."

But yes. Absolutely yes.

Outrage is streaming from my every pore

Loosing myself with some difficulty and cursing and undue concern from my props, I start a purposeful and confident stride toward him.

"Don't, Mikey," Lyndsay orders, catching and losing a hold of my shirt. "Crap."

Callum trails me a step behind. "What you thinking here, man?"

I'm thinking I put up with the insulting filthy looks from Alex for too damn long, let him get away with his lie, the lurking and the taunting in true spineless form. I'm thinking it ends now. I'm super juiced up, and I'm feeling scrappy. The prick has destroyed me, and no way does he get to now simply blank me out!

"Oh Lordy, he's ending up in the bushes," Steph chortles, leaning forward, as I pass her.

I don't. Not even close, so *har-dee-har*. I make it to exactly where I intended to. "You're such a ma-hoo-sive helmet. You know that, right?"

Alex is finally forced to acknowledge me. Brows raised, he gives me the slow, scathing once over. "Not now, mate. Run along."

"No," I fire back, shaking my head hard for emphasis (and, urgh, immediately regretting doing so). "You don't get to call the shots here, *mate.*" Sensing I'm being probed, I dart a glance to his beany-wearing buddy. And then swiftly do a double take. Because, *bright devil-stoked hellfire,* the chewing-broken-glass expression with which the guy's regarding me is so perfectly played on his perfectly chiselled Adonis face it's freaking obscene! But I don't stay distracted for long. Widening my stance, I fold my arms, "I do. And we're talking this out. Now."

"Ooooh!" Steph trills behind me. "Look at Mikey being all alpha, Lynds. Juicy."

"No, Steph," Lyndsay rebuffs. "Mikey, this isn't smart."

Alex trades a glance with Thor and then drops his head back to cloud an exasperated sigh into the dark sky. "Listen to your girl-friend. You're tanked. Get lost. Go home. Seriously, before you say something you regret."

That's all it takes.

Unbidden, words spill from my mouth into the moist, cold night air; all the trapped words weighing me down and pleading for escape rush up my throat and off my tongue. There's no stopping them. "I don't give a toss about your cousin − brother − half-brother − whatever the hell he is. Not one eensy-weensy tiny little part of me cares to be used in exonerating him to the detriment of Tate." Shoddy articulation devastates my delivery but I soldier on past it without pause, ignoring Thor's rising brows and Alex's infinitesimal headshake, "I know very well that you know what you saw − you know what really went down. And you think you have a hold on me cos you think I'm ashamed. Well, no more, Alexander. No. More. I'm gonna pee all over your twisted, black fib, making you look the fool and Craig as suspect as ever."

"Shut up!" The command in his voice is formidable, and the look on his face is one I entirely don't trust. *Danger! Danger!* A soli-tary, non-alcohol drenched neuron begins to wail. The guy could floor me with ease even if I wasn't under the influence. And, boy, has my dizziness returned with a vengeance. But my mouth is dead-set on rebelling.

"No, please, go on," Steph redundantly prods.

"It was my mouth attacking his. *Mine.* And here's something else for you: I liked it. In that moment before *he* threw *me* off, I was really *f...*"

"Mikey!" It's this scandalised exclamation at my back that cuts short my flow. I swerve around. Lyndsay's staring wide-eyed at me. "Mikey?"

She seems to be waiting on me to make some kind of stammering explanation or retraction, but since I'm truly neither embarrassed nor ashamed, that's just not gonna happen.

"Yeah." I hold her stare and bunch my shoulders toward my ears, hands lifting palm up. Callum's close by her side, gaping, and beyond them, Steph and Ashleigh have stood and moved in nearer to better see. But theirs are not the only eyes lasering me. I'm quite the spectacle. It's a horrendous point to be surprise-attacked by the chuckles, my face contorts into an awkward grimace to cover. I release my shoulders. "Look, Lynds, it's not that I don't like you, okay? Your smile is delightful, you smell yum and you're very wonderful. No word of a lie. It's just that... well, I've come to suspect I may be somewhat extremely, terribly...gay."

A tight and tentative giggle escapes her, dying a quick death as she accepts I'm not kidding. "You and Mac?" She snarls indelicately. "Of course. Shit!"

It's the first time I've ever heard her swear. Sounds so wrong. My face scrunches up further, "I hate that you call him Mac, you know?" Might as well have it all out there.

I miss her response, snagging on sharp movement in my peripheral. Alex is all of a sudden mighty close, his hands fisted at his sides. I'm not so far gone I've lost *all* sense of self-preservation: I reflexively cower away, my hands lifting to shield.

But the blow doesn't come from his side. No, never the enemy seen. It comes from behind, pounding my temple, and I'm pitched ground-ward, the stars plummeting with me to circle my head. Grass fills my mouth and tickles my nose.

"Craig, no!" Alex's voice penetrates through my sicky daze, booming. "Leave him."

Ah, Craig.

Wait. What? I rock my head to the side freeing my face. *Craig?*

"What's he on about, bruv?" His voice, low and husky, hums with a menacing undercurrent. "Little scrote. Running your mouth off about me. You don't even know me."

Chiselled features is Craig? Well. Damn.

All I can see of him from this lowest of viewpoints is his heavy black boots. With a groan, I make the mistake of moving, and in response those boots step in closer to my face. I press my eyes tight.

"He's not worth it," Alex bellows. "Believe me. Let it go."

There's the distinct sound of a scuffle directly above me. Atmospheric voltage swelling, an awareness of the commotion surrounding me crushes like a sack of bricks. Jeezus, it's loud. I decide it best to stay prone. At least until all signs of peril have passed.

Then hands seize my shoulders and yank me forcefully up. I'm dragged, stumbling and struggling and pleading incoherently for mercy, several thousand harrowing paces before being whirled around with enough clout to make me yelp. "Please don't pulverise me!"

"You are a special kind of stupid, Alston!" Adele's voice snaps my eyes open.

"Oh. Oh, my days! Never thought I'd be pleased to see you!" I breathe. Spying an open bottle of beer peeking out of her hoody pocket, I nab it and glug it down my throat like medicine. Tastes just as foul as medicine too, but I need it – need my edge back. "What are you doing here?"

"You invited me, cretin."

"Oh! Is...?"

"No." She snatches the bottle back.

"Oh."

"What, in the name of the stars, have you done?"

"Cleared up my mess. Like I promised I would."

"Yeah?"

"Yeah."

She lifts her gaze from me and sweeps it around us, the tilt of her chin imperious.

"It...didn't go entirely to plan," I concede, shooting a quick glance back for Craig. I don't see him. "I think my brain's bruised. But it's all out there now, right? In the open. Pretty sure word won't take long to spread. And then, oh," I realise something quite disturbing, "then I'll be the one known as the frenzied homosexual predator."

"I'd be doing the world a great service were I to just knock your teeth out. Maybe I should have just left you to Craig."

I frown at her, my hand darting again for the bottle. She rips it away from me the instant my fingertips graze the neck. "I detest you. You get that, yeah?"

"Oh, Mikey dear, on that we are most understood."

"No, but seriously though," I push on, abruptly discovering I'm not yet done with my unburdening of words. "It's cos you're my competition, see. That's what you are now. I didn't like you before, don't get me wrong, but you never even *mattered* before. Now you do, and your sheer existence offends me."

"Lovely. Ever the charmer."

"Cos Tate promised me ¬*promised* me that I would always be his best friend. But I come back and you've thieved him. And that, well...that sucks donkeyballs, Saunders. Gigantic, hairy, sweaty donkeyballs. Cos he's mine, you know?"

"You aware how childish you sound? Christ! Shut up. Right now."

"Let him continue!" Steph pipes up. *How the hell long has she been there?* "This is epic."

"I claimed him when I was six," I say over the top of them both. "Mine. And here's a little secret I want to share with you, just you." Lowering my voice to a whisper, I bend into her, "just so..." A frosty-cold hand's clamped over my mouth.

"Nope. No more." Adele glares at me, her fingers and thumb gouging my cheeks. "As much as I hate having to, I'm taking you home."

I try to shake my head but there's no give. It's not dawn yet. I have a mission, and David doesn't need to know I'm not having the most miserable time.

Steph comes to my aid, stepping in and linking her arm through mine. "Shoo!" She tugs on Adele's wrist. "No killjoys at my party. Shoo, shoo!"

I'm released. Adele yanks herself free of Steph's scarlet clawed grasp and moves back, narrow-eyeing me dangerously. "This isn't a bit amusement for your benefit, bitch."

"And, yet, I'm still choosing to benefit from this bit amusement," Steph retorts. "My party, my prerogative, *bitch*. Come along, Mikey." She lays her head against my shoulder, hugging my arm to her chest. "You don't need all this negativity pelted at you on your grand outing from the closet. What you do need is another drink, yeah?"

"Yes!"

"NO!" Adele lunges for me. She doesn't get me. I spin toward the house, whirling Steph around – laughing maniacally – with me. By a whisker, Ashleigh dodges a head-on collision. "Mikey, don't you dare!"

"I do dare. I totally do."

"Hell yeah, he does," Steph agrees, seizing Ashleigh's hand and frogmarching the both of us back across the lawn. My gaze roams. I pass two girls I recognise from my maths class, then Robbie and Liam from homeroom, and spy Adele's large blue-haired friend lounging against the side of the shed. Alex and Craig are nowhere to be seen, though. Lyndsay neither, nor Callum. I hone in on the back door, speeding up and taking lead of the charge. "Yey!" Steph trills. "Now this is a Mikey I can get on board with. Be gone from my land, sour wench!"

19

AND WITH DAWN COMES DISGRACE

*H*ead's pounding. Stomach's antsy. Mouth's desert dry. I need water. Gallons of water. The entirety of my body's moisture, it would seem, has been lost in sweat; I'm roasting in my own juices.

Jeezus! Far too freaking hot.

As soon as I attempt to roll over I realise why: *I'm not in the bed alone.* My back's pressed tight against a solid, heat-radiating mass. Deep, even breaths that are not my own invade my sluggish consciousness and I seize up, eyes point blank refusing to open.

I'm flummoxed.

Last I remember of the party, I was...

Think, Brain, think.

It's like venturing through a thicket of thorns. Nausea storms my stomach. I catch at shredded fragments: With Lyndsay, having a most merry time... A tall guy, angry blue eyes set in an otherwise fuzzy face... Lyndsay disappearing on me... Adele. *Adele was there?*... Steph hugging me. Steph declaring herself my biggest fan. Steph biting my earlobe and pinching my arse...

The body moves. I sever contact. My eyes finally snap open, and a swarm of wasps viciously attack my eyeballs. Never have I ever felt so legitimately close to death. My arm darts up to cradle my broken, broken head. "Steph?" I croak.

In response, I get a groan, and unless mornings are most especially rough on Steph, it sure as day isn't her beside me. Far from relieved, alarm bells siren.

What the hell did I do last night to land myself in bed with another guy? Who the crapping hell is it?! My bed I'm in, at least. Fairly certain I feel my boxers on and covering what they're made to, as well. No shirt, though. I never sleep without a shirt. Is he in any way clothed? Don't know, not checking... *Oh, Jeezus!* I better not have woken Gran on my way in. Did I encounter David? How did that go down? Nope, not important right now. One thing at a time, I can deal with only one thing at a time. Or perhaps not even that.

Slow and careful, I roll my head to the side, and blink.

I'm confronted with a dark head. It's a dark head I've become extensively acquainted with these past few weeks. I didn't think it possible for my mouth to dry out further, I'm proven wrong.

Could we have...? No. Not a chance. No way. I'd have remembered *that*. Besides, he's mostly on top of the duvet and appears fully dressed. Hasn't even took his socks off.

I, all of a sudden, become far too aware of my own condition: Practically naked and likely smelling as bad as I feel. Need to get to the bathroom, ASAP. I begin a cautious sidle for the bed's edge.

Before making it out, however, the head turns. Heavy-lidded green eyes fix on me, anchoring me in place.

"Hey," Tate says through a stifled yawn. "Feeling rough?"

I manage a nod. I think.

Awkwardly propped, one leg hanging down the side of the bed, I just stare at him. And he stares back at me. For a long time. Ample long enough for me to wither and die.

Then, eyes narrowing, he says, "you don't remember." Not a question.

I'm right on the verge of another assenting nod when, out of nowhere, I do. I *do* remember. The significant episode of the previous night blasts into my head with such gut-pummelling clarity, a splurge of vomit rushes my mouth. I gag it back down.

"I'm appointing myself your first official fag-hag." Steph declared, laughing. "Hold on tight cos your ride's about to get wild."

We were in her kitchen. I was resting, sprawled across the floor with my back propped up against a cupboard, while she mixed us some drinks.

"Stop making a joke of it, Stephanie. It's not a joke. It's serious. Super serious. This revelation of mine, it's life changing. I'm feeling liberated and I refuse to be mocked."

"Hey. Hey, hey, *hey*. Who's mocking you? Not me. I'm celebrating with you, dafty. We're celebrating the wonderful arse off this thing! Now, here, drink." Squatting down in front of me, she shoved a cup in my hand.

"Well. Okay. That's alright then." Whatever it was she'd concocted, it tasted damn vile. The tiniest of sips made me wretch. I set the cup down on the floor beside me.

"I'm the most awesome Wing Woman, I kid you not. We'll have you a boyfriend in no time. Exciting, right?"

"No. No thank you."

"Oh, Mikey, darling," she sighed with no small dose of exasperation. "This thing you have going on with Mac, it's unhealthy. You need to spread your wings and let go. Look further afield. There's so much better out there for..."

"Me and Mac – I mean, Tate, we're not unhealthy!" I cut her off. "How are we?"

"You've built him up on this sky-scraping pedestal, sweetiepie, and for a start, he really doesn't deserve to be there. Secondly, wanting more from your hero, it only ever leads to disappointment, you know?"

"Shut up! You don't know him at all, clearly. But I. Do. It's not hero worship, so don't you even be thinking that, okay? Okay, so maybe it was before, a little bit, when we were kids – he was crazy impressive. But now, now it's more. I feel more. And it's absolutely, positively, unquestionably *real*."

"Wowzers! Sheesh, you've got it worse than I thought. Okay then." She dropped down beside me. "So whatcha gonna do about it, babes?"

"What do you mean?"

"You want to just continue chasing up his heels like his devoted pet pup, do ya?"

I shook my head, frowning at her. "I'm telling him."

"When?"

"Now." I scrabbled to get upright. "Right now."

"Ohmagod, you're not serious?"

"I'm totally serious. This is happening."

"YES!" Steph sprang back up to her feet and helped me steady on mine. "You are killing it tonight, Mikey Alston! You're an inspiration." She pushed her drink onto me. "Quick drink for extra courage. Then we'll go get you your man."

I took the cup and I swigged a mightily unwise mouthful. My throat burned, my eyes watered. "You're not invited. I need to do this alone. I'm going to his house and I'm telling him that I know who I am, and that I'm okay with who I am." Raising the cup high above my head, I then shouted: "This is me, people, out and proud! And I'm telling him that I want him! Want him in a more than best friends kinda way! In a sexy kinda way!"

Oh. Cruel. Merciless. Lucifer. I'm no longer breathing and I'm in a tremendous amount of pain.

Moments earlier, I was dying. Then I died. Now, I am most assuredly dead and trapped for all eternity in the deepest depths of the devil's fiery pit.

"Don't freak out, Mikey." Tate shifts fully onto his side, better facing me. He props himself up on his elbow. "You're turning blue. Take a breath."

I don't willingly obey him, but my body caves. Air floods my dumb, wretched lungs.

"Good. Didn't want to call your brother in."

Lifting my dangling leg back onto the bed, I tuck the whole of me up to the neck in under the protection of the duvet. "I found you last night then, huh?"

"Not – not exactly. Adele found you. On her way home. You were... sleeping against the lamppost at the end of our street. She couldn't get you up. Came for me."

"Oh." I allow for a small measure of relief.

"Oh indeed." His expression turns grave, and my insides clench right back up. "That state you were in, Mikey: Stupid. Scary stupid. Took an age to rouse you; clothes soaked through; couldn't walk. Almost got you a fucking ambulance. 'Til you puked – all over yourself, perked up some." His flat tone makes his hard words all the more damaging. He pushes himself up to sit. A corner of his mouth kicks up in a wrenching non-smile. "Sure had a shit-tonne to say, too. A shit-tonne you're probably going to regret saying."

Can't drop my head fast enough to hide the devastation that sweeps my face. *I told him. I told him exactly what I set out to.* "Oh."

"And Adele filled me in on your party performance."

"Oh." He's far better informed than I am at this point then.

The night's coming back to me. Awful bit by awful bit, fragments are freeing themselves and piecing together. Huge blank spaces still remain though. I dread them being filled, and I'm most certainly not asking him for prompts. I remember plenty enough to know that this big picture is one I really don't want to see.

"Mikey?"

"I don't get it, then. Why are you here? Why'd you stay?" My gaze remains fixed on the dragon doodle adorning the right thigh of his grey sweatpants. From this angle, with the way his leg's bent, it appears to be spurting fire at his crotch. "There's no fixing anything now. I've achieved complete self-sabotage. Left nothing to salvage. You've an abundance of reasons to be pissy with me, to freeze me out."

"Mikey. Look at me."

Nope. No can do. The dragon's blurring, morphing into a smudgy outline of an upside-down Italy.

A warm finger steals in under my chin, its touch jarring me, and nudges.

I shake my head. A single tear tracks across my temple and into my hair, because of course I'm capable of being more pathetic. I set my jaw, determined to hold off any more of them.

With a sigh, Tate sets his whole hand under my chin. I try to pull away but his fingers and thumb press into my cheeks and he drives my face up. "No going back in the closet, you realise that, right? Locked and bolted that door behind you." He's leaning in toward me, his face invasively close.

I let out a choked laugh. "Guess I've well and truly annihilated my people-pleasing-sucktard label, huh?" It's hard to avoid his pointed gaze with him controlling my jaw, but I do my damnedest. Tracing his jawline, his nose, his mouth, however, proves no less discomforting. "This place really isn't working out for me, Tate. I want to go home. Back to Newcastle."

"Runaway, you mean." He dips his head, chasing my eyes.

I flinch. Then I nod. Yet even in doing so, I acknowledge it a lie. Because right in this moment, here, I'm painfully aware of wanting nothing other than to relax into his touch. "I don't know what I'm doing, where I fit. I'm miserable. All the time. It's like I'm drowning, you know, just...pressure. But last night – last night I felt good. The release, it felt so good. I took control of my own life and it was a rush." I take a breath. "I wasn't *in* control of anything really, though, was I? Far from. And now, what? I'm even more tragic than ever."

As if reading my mind, Tate eases off his grip and smooths his thumb once across my cheek. The light motion disentangles another small part of the night, tattered and murky. He was sweeping wet hair away from my eyes – or picking debris from it – probably a little bit of both – and talking to me. I don't recall what he was saying, because I was talking over him. Can't get a fix on what I was saying either, although I've a fair idea what tack it took. His face was just as close to mine as it is now, and I was running over its fine features in much this same way. He was frowning, and then he grinned. A wild, errant grin stole across his face; one of those sudden and brilliant transformations he floors me with. What brought it out, another unknown. It didn't stay long. Coming through stronger than the image is the feeling: The overpowering desire to pounce, cover his mouth with my own, and taste him again. The staggering kick of being absolutely on board with owning that desire. The all-consuming need for him to okay it.

My heart spasms. "Everything I said, though, I meant. All of it."

"Yeah." His jaw tenses, brow lowering. "I know." He releases his hold on me, pulling away to lean back against the headrest. I mourn the loss. "But..." He heaves out a sigh. "Nothing's going to happen between us, Mikey. Not in the way you want."

I didn't think I'd been seriously holding any real expectation of a promising outcome from this, but the sharp lance of despair that ruptures the centre line of my torso at his plain-stated rejection vehemently suggests otherwise. "You're not...?"

"I'm not prepared to fuck my best friend, Mikey, no." He rubs salt into the wound.

Clutching onto the only positive he's given me this entire conversation, I desperately try to shove all my feelings back down deep inside myself. I need them locked up and left to rot. "I'm still your best friend?"

He cuts his eyes away, straightening up and then skooching his way toward the end of my bed. "I best go. Get home. Dad'll be wondering."

I nod only because my brain can't come up with anything else to do. Eager to get away, of course he is. I've widened the chasm between us even further, snapped the bridge too. He's looked out for me, sure, but it's likely pity that drove him there. No disguising the vast divide.

"I were you," he continues, standing, "I'd stay put a while. Adele bunked with little Sophie last night. Prefer she didn't get a –

a murder charge set against her. Maybe best to avoid your brother, too."

I nod again but I don't care. I don't care about either of them. "What about Gran?"

"What?"

"Did I disturb Gran last night? Will she be upset?"

"Ah." His face softens though his tone remains the same, "no. We didn't see your gran. Think you're safe there. Think she slept through."

"Good." I close my eyes.

"Hey, drunken stupidity aside, Mikey, you put yourself out there. Don't beat yourself up for that. Was pretty fucking brave. You can ride out the shit storm. You'll be alright."

"Yeah," I say with no conviction whatsoever. It wasn't brave. I'm not brave. The sooner I can make the world go away, the better. "Thanks. For getting me home."

I hear the door open.

"Sleep off the hangover. See you in school tomorrow."

As soon as it clicks closed after him, I bury myself in the duvet.

20

NO THANKS, MONDAY. NOT INTERESTED

*G*ran's had another disturbed night. I've been out of bed with her since 4am. Not that it especially matters, I wasn't sleeping anyway.

The kettle's just boiled for me making us both a cuppa when the doorbell rings.

I'm not answering. Seeing anyone from the outside world is not in my plans for the day. Sophie left for school moments ago and Mel's heading straight for her salon after drop off. David's already shut himself in his office. I have Gran to myself and today is a day for nothing other than crappy TV, biscuits with a brew and some sofa napping.

When the ringing and rapping at the front door builds into something of a cacophony, however, and I hear Gran mumbling her way along the hall, I have a rapid change of mind.

"Well, that's not right." Dressed in only her white cotton night-gown, Gran's stood eyeing up the door like she can't make sense of what it is.

Riiing. Rap, rap, rap.

"Hey," I move up beside her. "It's okay, I've got this."

"Who changed it?" She asks, still staring ahead. "It was blue. I liked it better blue, didna you, dear love?"

Riiiinngg.

I'm puzzled for only a beat. "I did, Gran. I definitely did." Taking gentle hold of her elbow, I guide her to the side. "I'll just get rid of whoever this joker is, and then I'll finish making our tea, okay?"

"Ask him about the door, won't ye? We want our old un put back. Get him telt."

"You should probably go get your robe on. You'll catch a chill."

"Yes, yes." She takes one small step back but moves away no further.

I sigh. Unlatching the door, I open it a narrow slither.

I'm not exactly sure who I expected to find on the other side, but Tate and Adele aren't it. My heart plummets. "What you...?"

"Canna be gannin' round changin' folks' doors willy nilly!" Gran shrills over me, painfully close to my ear.

At the exact same time, Adele shoulder barges the door, swinging it wide. "Time to reap what you have sown, Alston!" Her hands intercept mine on their dash for my ears, and she yanks me stumbling forward through the doorway. "Let's go."

I've barely had chance to catch my balance, never mind initiate my resistance, when something long, thin and pink whizzes past me to thunk Adele on the head. "Get your nasty hands off of my boy, ye filthy wretch, you!"

"OW!" Adele drops me like a hot potato, her hands darting up to shield as Gran rounds me, swinging what I now recognise as Sophie's umbrella up high in preparation for a better second blow. "The hell, lady?"

"Ye canna have him!"

"Sorry, Evelyn. We're sorry." Tate swoops in, pushing Adele behind him and holding a placating hand out toward Gran, his eyes huge, as I shoot a blocking arm out across her, reaching up with my other to disarm her.

I lock her attention in on me. "I'm okay, Gran." She allows me to drag her weapon down to her side, but she doesn't willingly relinquish it. "They're friends. It was just a game."

"What on earth's going on out here?" David intrudes on the ruckus, coming up behind me.

I ignore him, pulling Gran into a hug and stroking her back in an effort to calm her. She's shaking. I let her be with the umbrella, she's clutching it so tight. I'm fairly confident she intends no further wounding with it. "It was just a very stupid game. I'm fine."

"Mikey? Shouldn't you be on your way to school already?"

"That's why we're here, Mr A," Adele's straight in to reply, rubbing her head and scowling at me. "We knew he'd be wanting to skive today, so we've come to remove that option from him."

"Love you," I whisper into Gran's ear as I match Adele's scowl and raise her the finger.

David puffs out an inconvenienced sigh and I adamantly blank his chafing scrutiny. "I see."

Tate's staying quiet, making my effort to ignore him too that much tougher. I risk the swiftest of glances. He catches me on it. His expression's unreadable, and I'm knotted all the tighter because of it. "I'm not going in today."

"You're wrong, little brother," David says. He attempts to manipulate Gran free of me. "Come on in, Gran. Shouldn't be out here in just your nightie."

"Ye canna trust em, Mikey." Gran seizes a fistful of my t-shirt. "That un, there," – the umbrella comes up again, prodding the air with menace, and Adele flinches away – "she has a deceitful face."

"Ha. No offense taken," I hear Adele mutter under her breath as she works fast to assume an unruffled air.

David plucks the umbrella neatly from Gran's hand. "No need for that. In, and we'll find you something to watch. Your boy has school to get to."

That's right, David, go plonk her in front of the TV then disappear into your office for the day.

"Go on in." I pat her hand before reluctantly easing it free of my chest. "I'm going nowhere, don't worry. Just give me a minute and I'll join you."

"I'll leave him to you two." David's leading Gran inside. "Best of luck." As he pushes the door toward closing behind them, I hasten to slam my hand against it, stopping it short. I slip my foot in the gap as extra precaution. Not putting it past him to lock me out, and I'm only wearing the tee and sweatpants I put on for bed. No shoes, haven't brushed my teeth or hair, and really don't much fancy knocking on the neighbours to gain access through the back. There's a moment of force against me, then it gives. "You're ridiculous!"

"Your gran adores me, I think," Adele deadpans once we hear the snick of an interior door shutting.

I bristle, "I'm not apologising for her, you totally deserved that."

She rolls her eyes. "Just get your arse into gear. You've made us late enough already."

"You've made yourselves late on a wasted effort. Please, don't let me keep you."

"You can't hide, Mikey." My eyes unwittingly flick to Tate, startled by his voice. Not that I'd come even close to forgetting he's stood right there, a mere few feet before me, staring. I'm quick to look away, but not quick enough. The look he's fixing me with makes me want to bury myself, never to be seen again. And that's surely what he must want – for me to disappear, to be unburdened of me. I'm making zero sense of him being here, pushing.

"I never wanted to do Sixth Form in the first place," I say, refocusing intently on Adele. She's easy to stink-eye. "So it's no big deal."

"Gah! You really *are* ridiculous. But whatevs. We tried, we failed." She slaps Tate's arm; he turns to her. I take the opportunity to push the door wide and angle myself for heading back in. "Leave him to wallow. Come on."

"No." A hand crashes down on my shoulder, gripping tight and tugging for me to turn back around. I bite into my lip as the rough touch ripples through the whole of me. "You're not dropping out over this."

I should rip myself free, but I don't. I've frozen. I do, however, continue to determinedly not look at him, my gaze directed into the empty hallway. *Where's Gran been shut away? In her bedroom or in the sitting room?*

"Believe me, I've no idea why he's bothering with you either," Adele grumbles, as if reading my mind.

I finally manage to rouse myself into pulling away, practically throwing myself through the doorway. "I need today," I snap, taking hold of the door handle. "Gran needs me today. Get lost." The door slams on my last word and I collapse against it.

"Mikey," Tate calls, sounding peeved. He accompanies it with a sturdy thunk that travels through the thick wood and reverberates down my spine. I squeeze my eyes closed and start counting in my head, *One-elephant-two-elephant-three-elephant...* "Fuck sake!"

Starting my count afresh, I go up to sixty before I open my eyes. A full, uninterrupted minute. A darting peek out the spyhole confirms their withdrawal.

Win to me, I guess.

I expel the breath I feel like I've held since finding them on my doorstep. It's a relief. Though not one I'm able to take much pleasure in.

The day does not improve any from that point onwards.

Gran refuses to settle, veering from restless and irritable to lost and panicky then back again too fast to track. And, as if aware of and intent on deliberately disproving my suspicion, David is incessantly meddlesome, quite the damned vexing nuisance.

By the time Mel arrives home with Sophie, I'm in my room staring longingly at my skates from my duvet cocoon.

HANGING BY A THREAD

"The hell?!" I sputter, instantly alert and upright.

Barely five minutes since I achieved sleep, I've been brutally awoken by an icy dousing of water over my head.

"Wakey, wakey, sunshine!" Adele laughs with cruel glee, stood over me brandishing the now-empty mug.

A towel's thrust toward me. "Here."

Turning, I see Tate perched on the foot of my bed. *Damnit, David!* I drop my gaze as I take the towel from his outstretched hand. "Was there really any need?"

"Nope," Adele crows. "None whatsoever."

I flop back down only to immediately bolt up again, my groan switching up to a yelp. My pillow's like cushiony snow. "Get out!"

"No can do, Mikey-moo. David's given us permission to drag you kicking and screaming if need be. You're coming to school."

"Why? Why does it matter?" I'm shivering something chronic now, as drips from my drenched hair soak into my t-shirt. "Why would either of you even care?"

"Oh, I don't care. Not one iota. I'm here purely to torture you. And cos Tate asked me so nicely. Bugger if I know why he gives a damn. I mean, you've totally screw..."

"You're being a coward," Tate cuts her off.

Shaking out the towel, I throw it over my head to save myself from looking at him. "So." A coward is who I am, I've come to terms with that, I'm good with embracing that. "Leave me alone."

"Adele, give us a minute? Wait outside?"

I hear a huff, and it's followed by a long minute of silence. I scrub at my hair to distract from peeking at what's going on. I don't want Adele to leave me alone with Tate. I don't want either of them here. They need to go and need to stay gone. Tate and I have no future, I get that now, and I have to give him up, move on.

"Ready and out in ten, Alston. You're not making us late again." Adele's voice makes me flinch.

The moment I hear the door click, the tension in the room becomes stifling. There's sounds of movement. I clench my fingers into my hair through the towel, so tightly I can feel clumps being pulled out by the roots. It's a comforting pain. The scent of mint & tea tree ghosting around me, I'm hyper aware of Tate's close proximity. Don't need to look to know he's right there, perched on the bed beside me.

The towel's lifted from my face and, taken unawares, my eyes are caught by his. "What's your plan then?"

I stare at him, blankly, putting everything I have into holding myself rigid.

"Dropping out of school, right? Then what?"

I do have a plan, actually. The bare bones of one, anyway. I've not been completely idle in my misery. I'm going to refocus on Gran, on her needs, and in doing so, she'll come to realise that being here is absolutely *not* what she needs. I'm going to extend the olive branch to Suzy, Jean and Hannah. They're surely missing us by now, be far more open to accept the mistake of our situation. Then we'll get to return home, pick up our lives where we left off and mark up this disastrous episode as nothing more than an unpleasant blip on our timelines. I need to work on the specifics, sure, and it's a plan that'll take time, but I'll have more than enough of that from here on out. "I'm looking for work. Have an interview on Thursday."

"Yeah? Where at?"

"Citreena's Bistro." Clearing tables. Pot washing. Floor mopping. Twelve hours a week. But those details are none of his business. "Earning money for my time. Beats YCS."

"Huh," he says after a long moment of unsettling study. His jaw ticks. "Well, good for you." He stands. "Best of luck."

Really?! That's it? I yank the towel from my head and throw it to the floor by his feet. "You've got me so messed up! What the hell's the point to this? Why are you here?"

"I don't want you to drop out of school, Mikey. Not over this. Nothing's really changed. Nothing *has* to change. But I can't..."

"*EVERYTHING's* changed!" I explode over him, throwing my arms wide to encompass the whole wide world. "How can you say that? Jeezus! My life has changed so much, so damn fast, I'm about three hundred miles behind with no chance of ever catching up. And I don't even want to catch up, cos I freaking hate the direction it's taken. Nothing's how it should be. Nothing's right."

"O. Kay." Settling back on the edge of the bed as I slam my hands down into the duvet to either side of me, he sighs and shakes his head. "Think, perhaps, you're... blowing this out of all proportion?" Well, that response infuriates me. "So you're gay. So what. People know. So what. It's no big deal. You've nothing to be ashamed of, Mikey."

Right, yeah, no biggy. And my newly-realised and publicly declared 'thing' for you, Tate, that's so inconsequential it doesn't even rate a mention, eh? I bite into my bottom lip until I feel close to breaking skin. "You are *such* a hypocrite!"

"W– uh, what?"

"On my case for hiding, for skipping out on school. You hide from *everyone!* You're AWOL from school almost as often as you're there. But, hey, I'm sure my issues don't even compare to yours, right? I'm just being neurotic and dramatic – typical Mikey!"

He's on his feet again, hands clenched at his sides, eyes boring into my face. "Like I said, I don't want... don't want you dropping out. You – no matter how much I pushed, you didn't give up on me. And, fuck, I'm glad. I'm fucking glad you didn't, okay? Now it's my turn. You're my friend, you mean a lot to me, and I'm here for you." He leaves no pause for a response before storming from my room and slamming my door hard enough to make things rattle.

Fortunate. I've no response to give.

～

WEDNESDAY, I'm trudging my way toward YCS.

It's like my first day all over again: The nerves, the reluctance, the absolute certainty of impending unpleasantness. Except, today's worse. Far worse. And, also, today I have Tate at my side.

He called for me alone this morning. Waited at the door until I came down. I noted distinct surprise on his face when I appeared dressed and ready to go. Won me an approving nod and a dashing grin. That reaction, alongside Adele's absence, gave me a short, sharp shot of cheer to propel me on my way.

Now, though, he has his eyes fixed dead ahead, headphones in place over his ears, and we're walking in silence.

He seems content in it, glancing across every so often to flash me a quick smile.

But I'm not.

We pass by the corner shop that claimed all our pocket monies, where Tate had cheekily endeared himself to the owner, Mrs Branswith, to score us both a free lolly from her every time we called in. The old loon still runs the place, I spy her behind the counter, but Tate doesn't so much as peek inside today. On we go down the steep bank Tate would skate with such effortless skill, I'd been fooled into believing it an easy feat only to skid most ungracefully and painfully after him on my backside. He catches me in rubbing at my spine but shows no sign he's registered the significance.

I'm in major need of conversation; small talk – light chit chat – *anything* to distract me from the hell I'm heading into here, to calm my nerves, to reassure me things really can be okay between the two of us. I continue to have difficulty looking at him, I need for him to give me something to build on.

Along by the leisure centre, our old cub scout base, and past the play park, we turn on to colourful Hutchings Avenue. Somerton Primary comes into view at the row's far end. His steady step doesn't falter.

So much history tying the two of us, all around, and it hurts like alcohol to an open wound that he's blanking all of it.

Friends.

He said, yesterday, that he's glad for my persistence with him, said he's here for me.

Part of me refuses to buy that there's anything more than pity behind his words – I'm well aware of just how damned pitiful I am, and pity is not a long enough standing foundation on which for me to lay down a whole lot of hope.

Even if, however, genuine sentiment does power his reach out, there's a fear that the ground beneath us has become too fragile to hold.

We'd barely found legs on reforming our friendship when only his stubborn attitude problem obstructed our way. A problem that remains very much in play. Now, though, added in: I know how much more I want from him, and he knows it too. I've put it out there into the world, as impossible to ignore as it is to retract.

This – whatever it is he's offering – is better than nothing at all with him, perhaps, but further down the line...?

We're not ever going to reach that place I want us to, that's one thing he's made very clear. Maybe – just maybe, I'm being foolish and weak (again) in hanging from this thin thread he's thrown out to me, and the smart move would truly be to let go.

I've overthought this to death all night and my head's still none-the-clearer on it. It has me exhausted. But it's unrelenting.

Friends.

Do we have any real chance of working on over this and forwards, no matter his good intentions and my desperate hopefulness, when I'm feeling so tormented with anxiety and insecurity in his company?

How am I supposed to act now around him?

Hell, how am I supposed to act now full stop?

The tension I'm carrying is making each step that bit harder than the last.

I've had my phone off until this morning. When I turned it back on, aside from two texts from Tate warning of his impending early calls, Steph's the only other who's tried to contact me these past few days, pleading for all the juicy details of my *'Grand Romantic Confessional'*. She's gonna be on my case today, probing, but she also may very well be the only one I'm guaranteed any kind of support from. Gary was one very noticeable absentee of Steph's big party and, for this, I'm abundantly thankful; I daren't even imagine the horror if he had been there. I performed for a significant audience that night, though, and word will of course have reached him by now. There'll be no slithering by him unscathed. Still, he's far from my biggest concern. It's facing Alex that terrifies me most. And Lyndsay. Crap. *"It's not that I don't like you... I've come to suspect I may be somewhat extremely, terribly gay."* The more I've pictured her face in that moment, the more I feel like a despicably cruel douche. There's no excusing the callous way I treated her. 'Sorry', I'm certain, just ain't gonna cut it.

Reaching the bottom stone step of the narrow flight cutting Hutchings Avenue in half, I pull to a blunt stop. Can't will myself to move further. These steps used to unnerve me – too steep, too tight and gloomy a space. These steps also sliced up Tate's body and landed him in hospital. These steps feel like the last barrier I have separating me from YCS. I've no trouble backing the hell off away from them.

Tate reaches the top before he turns and frowns at me.

"This is a mistake," I grit out, "I'm making a huge mistake."

His brow lifts, lips pressing tight. Without a single word, he picks his careful way back down and grabs hold of my hand.

He leads; I follow.

22

CAN'T WORK WITH NEON

"She is not eating with us!" Adele bolts up from the bench as soon as she catches sight of Steph trailing me across the quad.

Tate's head whips up. He glances first to Adele, then beyond her to me. The beginnings of a smile tick one corner of his mouth until his gaze travels on to Steph, and it vanishes beneath a frown. Not reassuring.

"'Scuse me?" Steph strikes back, sounding amused. "Rude much?"

"Alston, no."

"Shut up, Saunders. You're okay with Steph, right, Tate?" I *think* I see him shrug before he drops his head back down to the half-eaten sandwich in his hand.

His attempt at subtlety is unsuccessful as he slides that damned notebook of his off the table, into his lap. My steps slow. This isn't going quite so well as I'd tried deluding myself it might when Steph invited herself along. She's leapt to my aid with Gary twice this morning, though. Unasked for, but still...I figure I do kinda owe her, and having lunch with us, it's a small thing. Or so I thought.

Steph strides right on past me. "I'll sit myself here," she says, sliding onto the bench at the next table along from ours. "Alone. Not eating with you. How's that for problem solving, huh?" Smirking, she swings her bag from her shoulder to the table and unzips it.

I slide into my spot beside Adele. She skooches away from me, as she makes a point of doing every time.

Head remaining lowered, Tate lifts his eyes to me. His look says a lot more than I'm able to read but, loud and clear, I get that he's not happy. He flicks to Adele then turns to Steph, "Stephanie."

"Mac." She inclines her head. Eyes darting my way, she corrects herself, "Tate."

"Way to ruin lunch hour," Adele grumbles, slumping back down on the bench. "Dickface."

"So, Tate," Steph starts as she pulls a bottle of water from her bag. Something in the curve of her lips gives me a bad, bad feeling. She unscrews the lid and takes a sip continuing, "you blew our Mikey off, huh? And not in the fun way."

Yep. This was definitely a mistake. "Steph," I warn, shaking my head.

A sound of disgust erupts from Adele's throat.

"Gotta say, I'm disappointed," she pushes on. "Had such high hopes for you two."

"Steph!" I try again with more conviction (read: Desperation).

"No chance for him at all, no?" Side-eyeing me, she drives the blade home with an eyebrow waggle and I wish her dead: "Cos, you know, you guys actually look pretty darn cute together." Think I much preferred when she barely registered me.

Tate considers her for a long and painful moment, her head almost consumed by her bag as she delves in to rummage. He waits for her to resurface before he responds. "Not talking about it."

"Getting no juice from you either then?" She sighs, shrugs, then stretches her leg out to tap her boot off my shin, "Ah, well, not all's bad come of it, Mikey, babes. Other fine fish in the sea, yeah? And you're my party VIP now. Number one on my guest list. Though, sadly, next one might not be for a while. Mum's grounded me for, like, a month!" Retrieving a Tupperware box, she zips up her bag and swipes it to the ground. "It's my seventeenth two weeks tomorrow and she's not even giving me a pass for that. I mean, too harsh, right? Way too harsh. How am I even...?"

"Oh, for the love of all that is good!" Adele interrupts, throwing her hands skywards. "Do you ever take a breath?"

Steph stares at her, blinks, and then she cracks into laughter. "Wowzers, that stick must really be rammed right up there, huh?" Prising the lid off her pack lunch box, she cocks her head, "I'm making conversation, sweetie. Or is that something not done at this table?"

"Conversation tends to involve two or more participants. No one else is getting a word in."

"Should pull that stick out, Adele," I decide to chime in. "It's rotted through." So what if I agree with her on this? Not a chance am I admitting it.

Adele transfers her scowl to me. "Ooh, ow, the burn. My, how it stings!" She rolls her eyes. "The party was lame; Alston made a gigantic tit of himself – nothing new or entertaining there; and he's blubbered about it none stop since. Your voice," her finger points to Steph, "makes me wanna hit something almost as much as his face," the finger swings toward me, "does. So, now, can we please take a break from Steph's world for a...*forever*? That would be super."

"Bitch," I mutter out the side of my mouth.

Tate groans. "Adele, stop."

"What?" Her narrowed eyes whip across to him.

"I'm making an effort here," Steph says with deliberate conde-scension, stabbing a fork repeatedly into her leafy-green salad lunch. She looks as turned off by it as I am. "Least you can do is the same. For Mikey's sake."

"I do nothing for Mikey's sake," Adele snarls. She starts collecting up her things from the table and shoving them into her patchwork bag. Tapping Tate on the hand, she stands up, "coming?"

His eyes dart from her to me and back again, then he shakes his head. My heart skips a beat.

"Sure?"

"I'm good."

She hesitates, seeming about ready to drop back to the bench in defeat.

Tate's lip ticks up. "Go."

Tension seeps from my muscles and a relieved sigh escapes me. I flash Adele a snarky grin.

"Suit yourself," she huffs.

"Oh, honestly!" Steph giggles.

Shouldering her bag, Adele stalks away.

Perhaps she's the issue, I muse, turning to glare after her. Perhaps it's her sour influence that's to blame for Tate's drastic attitude shift. She has something on him I don't, that much is obvious. Could she really have secured enough control over him to chip him away to ruin? I despise that there's a definite possibility she has, no matter how on board I am with blaming her. But, whatever. She's left, and he's stayed – with me. I watch her pass through the doors into school. "Good riddance."

"Absolutely!" Steph says, drawing my attention back to the table.

Tate's screwing up the tinfoil wrap from his sandwich. I smile at him and he returns it.

The doors have barely snicked shut behind Adele, however, when I hear them flung wide again. "Well, isn't this cosy?" Lyndsay's voice jolts me. I tense.

"Poop." Shovelling a forkful of leaves into her mouth, Steph clips the lid back on the box before standing. "Let's not, Lynds, please?"

Tate's expression's darkened, looking beyond my rigid shoulder. He glances off toward the alleyway before dropping his head.

"I can't believe you! He made a fool out of me and here you are..."

"You made a fool of yourself," Steph cuts her short, tone sharp.

185

I track her around her table. She plants herself in front of Lyndsay, facing off western-showdown style, and folds her arms. "Anyone with eyes could see he wasn't really into you; he just didn't have the balls to set you straight." Amusement quirks her mouth on the word *straight*.

Lyndsay sets her jaw hard, lips pursing to the side. Her eyes start a rapid blink. My gaze snaps away.

I fix on Callum, who's hovering at Lyndsay's back. I flash a tight, *so-this-is-awkward* tester smile, but he refuses to meet my eye.

"Some friend you are."

"I'm sorry," Steph softens, "I'm not trying to hurt you. Seriously. I love you to pieces, girl." Dropping her arms to her sides, she takes a step forward. "You've got such lousy taste in guys, though, sweetie. And you can be so dense sometimes, it's unreal. Take Callum." She flicks a hand toward him. He pales, eyes widening, but his silent plea goes unheeded. "This guy worships the very ground you walk on. But he doesn't stand a chance, does he?"

Callum combusts into flames. Neither girl appears to notice.

Steph continues, "'cos you're off wasting your attentions on absolute hopeless cases." Her hand flicks in my direction. *Ouch!* "No offense," she tacks on.

"Right."

My voice breaks Lyndsay's resolve to blank out my existence. She narrows in on me, her face disconcertingly flush. I swallow. "If you weren't interested, it'd have been kinder of you to just *SAY!*"

I hear Tate shift on his bench, and then he's sliding in beside me. Automatically, I dart a glance his way.

"You're a jerk. And a joke," Lyndsay chokes out. "You and him deserve each other." Swirling on her heel, she storms back into the building.

"I'm sorry," I manage too late.

Steph's quick to grab up her bag, box and bottle from the table and follow after. "Come on, Lynds! The boy's not worth us fighting over! Don't be like this."

Callum lingers. His embarrassment blazing just as fiercely as my guilt, he stares at his feet.

"Hey, Callum?" I can think of nothing else to say.

The guy still refuses to look at me. "Whatever." Pushing his glasses up his nose, he shakes his head, turns and skulks inside.

Tipping my head back, I smack both hands over my face and scrub. A light drizzle starts. *Perfect.*

"She'll come around, Mikey," Tate says over my savage blitz of expletives. He takes a hold of my arms and drags them down.

I find I can't take his touch right now, nor his concerned probing study of my face. They're fuelling my self-reproach. I free myself of them, lurching to my feet. "Don't see why she should."

I ALMOST PULL off a full day of avoiding Alex. Almost.

Calling in to the library before last period, I stupidly figured that taking the work station in the far back corner, tucked in snug behind the shelves of Business and Economy books, would work to my benefit, keep me hidden. But, no. In actual fact, all that I've done is enable Alex to trap me.

"Gary's already exceeded the gay-bashing quota for today," I say, cramming my books back into my bag. "Thanks all the same."

He pulls out the chair beside me and sits, his lip curled, "I'm not a homophobe, moron." Swiping the Understanding Dementia book from my hands, he starts idly flicking through. I grit my teeth. "Each to their own, live and let live and all that."

"So, what? Just been itching to catch me for a bit chin wag, huh? Or are you about to apologise?"

"And what, pray tell, do I have to apologise for?" He pretends study of the random page he's opened to.

"For your brother." I don't remember much of Craig from the party, only that his face stunned me. And then his fist did.

Slapping the book shut, he tosses it onto my bag and rolls his eyes. "Get used to taking blows, mate, hanging around McAllister."

My brows shoot up. I cram the book into my bag and pay extra special attention on pulling the zip around to ensure my eyes don't stray across the room. Is he aware Tate's behind him, just beyond the Drama and Music section, scanning the Science shelves? The zip catches and sticks, I tug at it to no avail. "A threat? You're threatening me?"

"No." He grins. It's unpleasant.

That was definitely a threat.

"Tate's not to blame for Craig leaving school."

"That's what he's told you, is it? He's lying."

I shake my head. "If it's on anyone, it's on Gary. He spread the..."

"Shite all to do with Tosser Tinwell!" He erupts, his eyes burning my face off.

I jerk at the zip so hard the seam rips. "What was it Tate did then?"

He continues laser-eyeing me, cocking his head to one side.

I so totally do not have the patience for partaking in this head game of his. "What is it you want from me, Alex?"

"You can't trust him. The guy's a screwed-up loser, and he'll screw you up too if you let him."

I snort. Then, shouldering my half-open bag, I stand.

"I've warned you," Alex says, standing too. "You choose to ignore it, that's on you." He turns and starts walking away. "Prick."

"He's not an addict!"

"I never once said he was," Alex throws back without a glance. He does, however, cast a pointed look toward the area I know Tate's occupying before he turns in the opposite direction, for the library's exit.

TIME OUT

"Go upstairs and fetch Suzy down for me, dear love, would ye? Been ages since she called in. Think she's mad at me."
I've been in from school less than two hours and it's the fourth time she's asked me this. Except the second time it was Jean's company she requested.

"Suzy's at work, Gran. Sorry," I reply in a small voice.

Tried explaining it to her, she's just not getting it. Tried calling Suzy so they could at least talk, but Suzy didn't pick up. Jean didn't either. And Gran launched my phone across the room, screaming at me for thinking her stupid before I could try Hannah.

"Did she say when she'd be home? Should I make her up some tea?"

"It'll be very late. She said not to wait up."

"Oh."

Five minutes ago, she was asking me when we could expect Elaine (my mum; her daughter) home. Said she'd be grounded again if she didn't show her face before dark.

I feel like crying.

Mel *is* crying. She fled to the back garden almost the instant I walked in. Gran's spent the afternoon hysterically ordering her out of the house. Two cups and a plate have been smashed. All because Mel stopped Gran putting her mug in the microwave with the teaspoon still in it.

"Homework, Mikey." David enters the room through the door from the kitchen. He's been out talking to Mel since he arrived in from his busy day of meetings twenty minutes ago. His face is grim. Still, he manages a smile for Gran. More than I can do right now. "Go on. Upstairs."

"So Suzy is in?" Gran accuses, shoving off the sofa to her feet. "Ye lied to me, boy?"

I'm disgusted by the surge of relief that courses through me as David shoos me out. More so that I barely even hesitate in taking him up on the rescue. I retrieve my phone from the floor by the coffee table before hurrying to the door leading out into the hall. "Sorry, Gran." I'm such a colossal let down. "I'll be back soon, okay?"

David winks at me and my stomach sours.

I do have homework. Loads. But my heads not in a place to be tackling any of it today. Instead, I skate up, pull on my hoody and head out.

IT'S HARD GOING, following the wide dirt track alongside the stream to the den in skates. Doesn't at all help that the sky's already darkening into night. Nor that there's a harsh wind blowing against me. I didn't think this through. I push on regardless, though. At least it's dry.

Spying a bright beam of light up ahead, my steps slow. *Torchlight? At the Den?* I pick up the pace.

"Tate?" The wind catches my voice.

He's sat, cross-legged, atop our tree stump table. The light's coming from the rather fetching headlamp he's sporting. Head bowed, he remains fully immersed in the comic book open on his lap, unaware of me.

Snagging a tree root with one hand and a fistful of the long grass with the other, I toe my way up the short, steep bank separating the path from our little clearing. This move startles him.

He scrambles to his feet in a frenzy, his comic falling to the ground.

"Hey, whoa!" I make it up and straighten. "It's me. Only me."

"Mikey? Fuck!" I can't help but laugh as he takes several deep breaths in an effort to soothe himself back down. "You scared the fucking shit out of me."

Picking up his comic (*an Avengers*), he resettles himself on the stump and motions me forward. "What you doing out here?"

I straddle one of the stumps two upraised roots – always my seat at this table – and face him. "Not sure," I shrug, adjusting my position. Damp's already seeping through the arse of my jeans, the bark rough and bumpy beneath me. "Just didn't have anywhere else to go, I guess. You?"

With a heavy sigh, he sets the comic down beside his leg and leans forward, resting his elbows on his knees, and the torch light blasts my eyes. I balk, my hand flying up to protect. He's quick to remove the headband, flashing me an apologetic grimace, then sets it down on the stump between us. "Truth?" The upward beam creates an eerie play of light and shadow on his face. On mine too, I imagine. "I come here a lot. Whenever I need to get away. Clear my head."

"Huh." I don't know why that surprises me so much. It is, after all, *the* perfect time-out spot only a stone's throw from his back garden. I'm discomforted by the sudden feeling I'm intruding. I run my wheels back and forth across the bumpy ground each side of the root. "You want me to leave you alone?"

He shakes his head. "Actually, thought you'd... expected you to show up here again long before now." A smile flits over his lips, raising goose bumps on my skin in all the places the wind's chill hasn't already and stilling my feet. "You okay?"

"Not so much."

"School wasn't that bad, was it?" He frowns.

I wrap my arms tighter around myself and shrug, "no." It really wasn't. Sure, there'd been plenty moments I wanted to crawl beneath a table and hide, but in comparison to my imaginings of the past few days, school was a veritable breeze. He'd been there with me for as much of the day as he could – lunch and breaks, the two lessons we had together, even meeting me outside a couple of classes to walk with me to my next. And he had almost as many jibes directed his way as was mine. The way he let them ping right on off of him without so much as a wince greatly aided me in armouring up through it.

"Your interview tomorrow, right? Nervous?"

"No."

"Liar," he accuses, seeing through me.

"Yeah, okay, I'm a little nervous," I concede. "But it's no big deal. It's a job cleaning dishes and tables, not my one big shot at a dream career."

Tate continues studying me with patient expectation. Pretty certain I can't talk about Gran without breaking down, though, and I refuse to do that. I let my eyes stray, scanning the darkness beyond the torchlight. "Is it totally lame that I want to rebuild this place?"

"A little," he responds. My gaze whips back to find him restraining a roguish smirk. "Not totally."

I slap his knee and he lets the smirk go, a light chuckle escaping with it. Tingling, I feign a scowl.

This is how it should have been that night before I left. This is all I'd wanted from him. Just to have him here with me, reassuring me that no matter how crappy and dismal life gets, I'm not going it alone. Why couldn't he have given me this?

"Worries me, though," he says a few moments later, breaking the soft silence and snapping me out of my head.

"What?" The way he's considering me, I almost believe he's tracked my thoughts. "What do you mean?"

"Your reasons."

I'm confused.

"For rebuilding."

I'm no less confused. "I've so many memories here, with you, almost all of them good. This place just looks sad now, all bare and neglected."

My answer appears to be a bad one. His next words come slowly. "This place is... it's all about who we were, Mikey, you know?"

"Yeah," I venture, drawing the word out. "Fun times. Simple times, when the world made sense. When I wasn't a seventeen-year-old gay orphan, and you weren't... hell, I don't even know what!"

"Sixteen," he slips into my pause. I raise a quizzical brow and a trace of his teasing smirk returns, "I'm still sixteen. For another two months."

Huffing out a breath, I flash him an *alright-smart-arse* look, "Fine. A sixteen-year-old unfathomable recluse."

"And that's my point," he goes on, eyes raking over me. "Those kids are long gone. There's no bringing them back."

I give my head a slow shake. "I'm not..."

"I think you are," he counters me with a sad nod. "I think you're clutching on so tight to – to everything we used to be, cos you know, deep down, there's not enough of us now to work on."

My head keeps right on shaking. "So, we're not going to be okay, that's what you're saying?"

Pressing his lips, he throws a swift glance up at the charcoal sky. He says nothing. I see his fingers tighten their grip on his knees.

"Is it really so terrible that I want to claim back something good for myself?" I stare at his knees and the indistinct shapes drawn over them, peeking out between his fingers. "I can't just write off our entire history, Tate. Blank it out. I won't." A lump's formed in my throat. I pick at the bark between my legs. "It matters too much to me."

"Okay, I get that. I do." He leans in further, his face moving in closer, his eyes chasing mine. The torch shifts as he does, its light aiming more fully on me. I flinch away. "But you need to accept that it *is* history." He covers my hands with his, just lays them there. "It's in the past. You have to move forward."

I'm not thinking when I flip my hands palm up beneath his and clutch. I stare at our entwined fingers with detached curiosity. He's messing with my head, drawing closer while his words pull us apart, as if I'm not messed up enough already. "Without you?"

He allows me only a moment before he withdraws from my hold. He doesn't move away but ducks his head, running his fingers through the dark hair at the nape of his neck as his gaze runs over my lips. "Sorry?"

I want to reach out and touch that hair, card my fingers through it, guide him in until my lips can press against his. "Moving forward." Unintended emotion taints my voice, betraying me. I swallow, trying to soothe away the expanding obstruction in my throat. *Gotta keep it together here, Mikey.* "Without you, right?"

"I don't..." His hands drop back to his legs and he shrugs. He appears to be struggling with words. Then, with an almighty exhale, he looks up and works an unconvincing half-smile onto his face. "I'm here with you now. Plan to be tomorrow, too. I'll call over for you again, we can walk in together if you want?"

I make no response.

He continues, "and next week, it's half-term. Still want help with your room?"

His propositions fail to invoke the boost they should. I'm hearing what he's not saying: *Our friendship has a deadline.* My most immediate reaction to this is blood-chilling alarm; my suspicions of his impending demise re-flaring. But it's grip is brief, rational thinking swiftly snuffing the life from it. A week, then, that's really as far as he can count on his sense of obligation holding out?

"Don't have paint. No brushes or rollers or dust sheets either. Nothing."

"Leave all that to me. Just pick a colour."

I frown at him.

"Got a contact," he shrugs. One brow lifting, his lips quirk up, the smile dim but far closer to genuine than his last. "Ask no questions, I'll tell no lies."

"Adele's dad's still a painter-decorator then."

"Damn!" His smile brightens several notches, a soft chuckle accompanying it. "Called it in one."

It's through no volition on my part that my mouth copies his.

"So, Sunday then? At one?" He taps my leg as I turn my face away, my gaze again roaming the dark space around us.

I should say no. I should heed his advice, call quits on us now. We're going nowhere; hard though it is to admit, I do know this. But...

Another soft tap to my thigh draws me back to him. "Green."

"Green?"

"Yep," I confirm with a sure nod, locking onto his eyes. "Leaf-green."

...Screw my near-future self. He'll have to deal, cos present-me just ain't ready to yet.

24

FUN PLANS AND FOUL PLAY

*I*t's hard work, this decorating lark. I was ready to give up on the idea before we'd even finished shifting out all the furniture in preparation of getting started. But come Thursday afternoon, we have it almost completed.

All ship paraphernalia has been removed. Three coats of green paint have been applied to two facing walls – the one at the head of my bed and the one behind my desk – covering over the hideous blue-striped wallpaper. The window wall, the door wall and the ceiling, we've given a fresh coat of white. The wardrobe and chest of drawers have been sanded down, ridded of all pretentious gold-leaf detailing, and repainted white, gold door and drawer knobs replaced with chrome ones. We've re-glossed the skirting board and doorframe, replaced the heavy blue curtains with the black ones I had hung in my room at Gran's flat, and put up two shelves above my desk. Even the beige carpet has had a thorough cleaning.

I'm ready to drop.

Tate's definitely been the lead on this operation, and he's cut me no slack. Slave driver. As with our essay writing, when working, we've *worked*. He's insisted on music, turned up absurdly loud to 'help with motivation', and keyed his full concentration to task.

But at least his damned headphones haven't made an appearance. He's given total control of the playlist to me, made no comment on my questionable taste nor griefed me for my tuneless singing. And, honestly, there's something shamefully satisfying in watching him toil up a determined sweat. He has been most generous with breaks too. At break times, the music goes off and we take a breather from the room for a while. We eat, drink, talk. Sometimes stay in, sometimes go out. He's teased me often and we've laughed a lot.

As much as I've kinda been dreading this little project of ours coming to it's inevitable end, I rejoiced when, returning to the room with the cleaned-off brushes, Tate declared it time to clock off for today. All that really remains to be done is retrieving and sorting through my boxes of old stuff from the garage. Given Tate's openly dismissive attitude to our past, I've deliberately left this until last as I'm anxious of his reaction when I protest letting any of it go. I'm more than happy to put it off for that bit longer.

I could do this final part alone, of course, but not a chance that's happening. I'm secretly, fervently hoping I can convince him to hang around, spare me a few extra days, and take to the blank canvas of the door wall with his sharpies. My room won't ever feel complete without his artistic touch.

Washed up, we're now on our way out, heading into town, calling at Citreena's Bistro for my employee perk of free coffee (of course I got the job, I wasn't ever in any real doubt...).

We've just reached the bottom of the stairs when bouncy footsteps closing in behind whips me round.

If the icing on the cake of this week is the complete absence of Adele from it, Sophie's frequent interruptions are the chips of eggshell tainting the otherwise superb sponge.

"Jeezus, kid! What now?"

She completely ignores me. Prancing right on by me, she tugs on Tate's sleeve before planting herself in front of him and waving like a dork.

"Hey, Soph." He easily finds a smile for her. "What's up?"

"Are you going home?" She asks, her words accentuated with a finger jab to Tate's chest and a thumb thrust toward the door.

"No," I answer for him.

She shoots me a haughty death glare. "Was I talking to you?"

Tate works his jaw, chewing on his amusement. "Not my home time yet," he says, snapping her attention back to him with a whip of her hair. "I'm going for a coffee with – with your uncle Mikey. Want to come?"

I mentally rip his tongue out of his beguiling mouth as I shake my head, glowering. She manages to wheedle her way into freaking everything and he needs to quit encouraging her!

"I don't like coffee," Sophie replies, screwing her face up. "I wanted to go play with Megan."

Yeah, turns out Sophie and Megan are friends. 'Not best friends,' she'd been quick to clarify, 'cos I am one whole year biggerer than she is, and she can't even count up to 100 yet'. But they've visited each other's houses for play dates and Sophie has an invite for Megan's birthday party three weeks from now. I can't figure out how I feel about it. Should I be glad for the second cycle of Alston-McAllister friendship? Or miffed that, all this time, there's been contact between our two families and I've been kept in the dark?

"Aww sorry, Meg isn't – she's still away on holiday. Not back 'til Saturday," Tate tells her, not for the first time. Her face falls and, staring up at him, I believe she's working up some tears. "Tell you what, I'll ask my mummy to talk to your mummy. Sort out a meet when she's home. Okay?"

"Kay-kay!" She snatches him up on the offer with an instant wide grin and an emphatic nod. Then, giving her hair another flick, she flounces around us and back up the stairs.

I watch after her.

Tate shoves my arm, knocking my balance a step sideways. "She's a good kid, Mikey. Shouldn't be so fucking hard on her all the time."

I flush as I realise the scowl creasing my face. Shrugging, I make for the door. "Come along. I'll treat you to a cookie with your coffee."

We've made it only as far as the corner shop when we're intercepted by Steph. She bounds out the shop's door and blocks our path. "Christ, sweetie, am I glad to see you!" Launching herself at me, her arms fasten tightly around my neck. Her bag of sweets (or whatever) slaps off my back. "You've gotta save me, guys, please."

I side-eye Tate. He frowns, bouncing his shoulders in a *no-clue* kinda way.

"Good to see you too, Steph," I croak out, puffing her wild red hair away from my face as I try – and fail – to ease her off of me. "Something wrong?"

"I'm *BORED*, Mikey," she says, rocking me from side-to-side with her. "This holiday has been *sooo* boring! You have to come to the View with me. Now."

"Uhh..." I glance again to Tate. His frown's deepened, he's looking a little bewildered and a whole lot uneasy. "We actually have other plans, sorry. But, hey, aren't you supposed to be grounded?"

She finally lets me go, skipping a step back. "Mum got sick of my whining, she totally caved. Always does. Lyndsay's still in a sulk, though, and Ashleigh's away at her Dad's. Don't know where Alex is at. I'm stuck with only Callum and – don't get me wrong, he's a sweetheart, but – he's super dull. You can spare me an hour, right babes? Please?"

There's something going on in her crazy eyes that I'm not trusting at all. Turning my head and cocking a brow, I silently pass the decision over to Tate.

He doesn't get chance to make it.

"Well, boys, asking nicely isn't doing it," Steph declares, smirking as she snatches up both of Tate's wrists and tugs hard. Unprepared, he's lurched stumbling forward with a grunt and a curse. Her white carrier bag swings violently between them. "Leaves me with little choice but to drag you there, I'm afraid."

He puts up surprisingly little resistance when Steph begins walking backwards, pulling him along with her.

"Tate?" I'm blasted with a look from him that's all parts objection. His hands are fisted above Steph's purple clawed shackles. He could easy break himself free of her, the set of his jaw shows that he blatantly wants to, yet he makes no attempt. "We'll just go for an hour, okay?" I wince apologetically.

"Oh, would you look at that." Steph giggles, speeding her backward trot. "Where Tate goes, Mikey follows. Who'da thunk it?"

And so, we find ourselves at the View.

Steph maintained her firm grip on Tate our entire trip here, sensing the flight risk, and she seemed entirely unconcerned with having the silence all to herself to fill.

A hush fell as Tate was led into the rickety three-sided shed, a sharp reminder of his well-established outcast status. For all that Steph had claimed Callum as her only available source of company, I made count of at least a further ten heads, all turned to eye up the unexpected arrival.

"Bunch of nobodies," Steph responded to my pointed look before clapping her hands and raising her voice: "Now, now, guys and gals, remember your manners. Rude to stare."

On his release, Tate immediately settled in a chair placed just within the shelter, positioning himself to look out over the spread of Yoverton down below. I took the seat beside him. Steph claimed the seat beside me.

Less than five minutes we've been sat, Steph ranting about the ridiculousness of YCS's dress code, when a shadow falls over me.

"Steph, you're on Callum's team. Girls, we're a player short. Which one of you's stepping up?"

Steph almost called it right: Most of the kids here this afternoon are *'a bunch of nobodies'* – faces from other year groups that I don't especially recognise. But not entirely: There is one very notable *somebody* in attendance aside from Callum. And he's a somebody I'd have greatly appreciated the heads up on.

I drag my eyes slowly up to Gary's plump-cheeked, sneering face. "What?"

"Footy, Michaela. Five-a-side. It's you or your bum-chum. Decide."

"Shut up, Tinwell!" Steph berates, standing. She holds her hand out to me, "come on, Mikey, help us out."

"Ah." I look to Tate only to discover he's conjured up some in-ear buds from somewhere and has them firmly implanted in his ear canals. He's staring out across the town, appearing for all the world utterly oblivious to the goings on at his side. The sudden flare of irritation through me comes as something of a surprise. "Okay then, fine," I grit out, taking Steph's hand and pushing to my feet.

He could at least try, I fume, *wouldn't freaking kill him!* This ain't how I saw us spending the afternoon either, but here we are. It's not like we'll even be staying long anyway. Considering he's the one dead set on me mixing, sharing my time, it's pretty damn lousy that he rigidly abstains from the slightest effort to do likewise. Hypocritical.

And always with the goddamn headphones! I don't even know what type of music it is that he's into; he doesn't ever sing or hum or bop along. It's odd, and I'm beginning to suspect they're just another device he employs – much like the private lunchbreaks and note-writing with Adele, and the unfavourable reputation he's nurtured – to further alienate himself from his peers.

"Callum's side for you too, Pansy-pants," Gary sniggers as he saunters away.

Trailing Steph as she follows Gary, I move out of the shed onto the flat makeshift pitch just off to the left of it. We team up.

Callum calls Steph and me over to him. A gangly year eleven boy with hair a brighter red than Steph's, referred to only by his nickname 'Squirrel', and a small, sullen-faced year ten girl called Rosa make up our five.

Across the far side of the grassy stretch, Gary's huddled up with two fellow year twelvers – a brutishly built boy and a girl I can best describe as spiky-looking – and two far younger kids, one of whom I believe to be his brother. They appear to be amped-up beyond what this kick about calls for.

"Squirrel, you're in defence with Steph," Callum orders as he stashes his glasses with his jacket down by the shed wall and pulls on a beany hat. "Rosa, goal; I'm centre; Mikey, up front."

Giving him a thumbs up, I reluctantly pull off my jacket and toss it down by his.

I dislike football. Not because I'm no good at it. The co-ordination and foot control I've developed in my years of skating come into play rather well for me out on the field. My stamina's pretty awesome too. But I don't ever watch football and rarely ever play it because I just don't enjoy it. It's dull. Remaining sat beside Tate, stewing at him, whilst he continues to blank me and the rest of the living world, though, that strikes me as far less appealing.

Casting a glance back toward the shed as I jog into position, I'm a little startled to see that Tate, his seat placed just barely within the shelter, has a pretty decent view over the pitch. Wishful thinking, perhaps, but I'm almost certain he's budged himself forward. *Deliberately to watch?* I wave. But, no, his head's turned away.

The game kicks off without preamble.

Around the ten-minute mark, I'm crashing to the ground.

Running for the ball, my attention divided between it and Tate, I collided with Callum.

It's Gary and his filthiest of filthy tackles that's felled me, though. He's kicked my already unsteady legs out from under me and barrelled right on through into Callum. "Kiss the dirt, losers!"

I land hard and Callum collapses on top of me, crushing the air from my lungs. His elbow slams into my nose with a sickening crack.

25

MAGIC HANDS WITH A LITTLE
SOMETHING SPECIAL

There's an eruption of noise; shouts and pounding feet. I can't focus on any of it.

Tears and blood cascade down my face. The pain is excruciating.

Eyes wide with alarm, Callum frantically sets about extricating himself from me. "Shit, man! I'm so sorry!" He struggles to disentangle his legs and get them steady enough to take his weight off of me.

I groan, my one unpinned hand moving to tentatively cup around the smashed up centrepiece of my face. The blood is slick, streaming into my mouth, down my chin. It's all I can taste and smell and think about. My stomach clenches and, retching, I attempt to roll on to my side, push Callum off, but I've no wriggle room.

"Oh crap. Hold up, Mikey, I'm..." Callum's words are severed when, out of nowhere, an arm encircles his neck and wrenches him up.

He comes crashing back down off to my right a mere second later with a winded "*oof!*" and I scrabble to my knees, a hand still covering my face, as Tate comes into focus, bearing down on him.

"THE FUCK D'YOU THINK YOU'RE DOING?!" He rages. "Tate?"

Setting his forearm across Callum's collarbone as he draws his other arm back, hand fisted and threatening, he doesn't appear to hear me. "FUCKING LAYING INTO HIM, I'LL FUCKING GIVE YOU SOME BACK!" Before I even register what I'm seeing, the blow lands hard on Callum. I don't know where. A second and third follow in quick succession.

Callum whimpers. Someone else screams. The shouting soars in volume.

"TATE!" It's enough to rip my head far clear of my own agony. I lunge at him, securing both arms tight around his waist, and tug. "Whoa, Tate!"

He fights against my hold. And for one horrifying moment, I think he's about to turn on me. But then, swerving around, he sees me. He becomes a statue. With a fair bit of straining, he allows me to haul him free of Callum.

Callum throws himself sideways and curls into a ball, moaning.

"What the actual hell, Mac?!" Steph shrills, towering over us before dropping to her knees at Callum's curved back. "You fucking psycho!"

Behind her, Gary laughs. "Now there's the mental thug we all know and despise!"

Tate ignores them. He's breathing hard, his body still held taut against mine. My breathing's just as rough. I cautiously ease my arms from his waist, pulling away. He instantly falls back onto his arse, fixing on me. I can't meet his eyes, can't pull away from the bloody smear my hand's created across the front of his grey jacket, but I'm hyper-alert to him taking in my bloodied face, my expression, the whole awful situation. "Shit!" He lifts his hand toward me, as if to touch my face, hesitates, drops it back down to the grass. "Shit, shit, shit!"

My nose has started throbbing again with a vengeance.

"This turn you on, Michaela, eh?" Gary pipes up again. "Lover boy flipping out, all crazed alpha? Cumming in your panties right about now, I bet."

Tate gives not one flicker of reaction, remaining utterly horror-struck. I, on the other hand, bolt to my feet. "You!"

"Mikey." Tate snaps into gear, jumping up barely two paces after me. He grabs my arm. "Mikey, I'm sorry. I thought that he... I..." He draws in a ragged breath. I whirl around to him but he's already let me go, his eyes flicking away to the side, where Callum's huddled. Reaching a hand into his jeans pocket, he retrieves a pocket pack of Kleenex and holds them out to me. His shoulders sag the moment I take the tissues from him. "I need to go."

"What?"

Shaking his head, he hangs it low and starts walking away. Red stains his shoulder blade, too, from my face pressing against him as I attempted to force him back. His pace picks up to almost a sprint before he even makes it across the grass flat to the head of the path.

Had he missed Gary's tackle, I get how it could have looked to him from his position. But still...

And now he's just leaving me here?!

I waste vital seconds trying to process before I give chase, "Wait! What?"

I hear Steph, behind me, fussing over Callum: "We should get you home. Can you stand?"

"I'll give you fudge-packers this, yous sure know how to put on a good show," Gary continues to taunt, but he's now flung miles from my mind.

There's a chorus of murmurs and mutters amongst the others. I shut them out too.

Every impact my feet make with the ground shoots pain through my face. It's a struggle to breath.

By the time I reach the start of the trail leading down, Tate's built up a significant distance between us. I feel lightheaded and queasy. "TATE!" I screech. He spares me no acknowledgement.

Jerking to a halt, I watch his swift descent. He's well past the slope's halfway mark before his speed begins to slow.

I frown down at the tissues in my hand, a drop of blood splotching their plastic wrap, then toss a glance over my shoulder at the small crowd of whispering onlookers. When I turn attention back to the path a few seconds later, I find the picture slightly changed.

Tate's eased to a walk, his hands deep in his jacket pockets, his posture still slumped, and he's no longer a solitary figure on the path. Two others have joined him on it, ambling up the hill toward him.

One I recognise instantly as Alex – the broad shoulders, the stupid hair, the cocky swagger. The other – a hood up over his head, his strut far more reserved – takes me a couple of beats longer to pinpoint...

Craig.

I witness the moment the two notice Tate: Heads lifting, locking in, their steps falter. Craig's hood comes down.

Jeezus! Even at this distance, with me completely sober (if a little knocked bereft of my full senses), the guy's looking too damn perfect. His hair's a lighter shade of blonde than Alex's, shorn short. His face, an ideal blend of rugged and pretty. He makes my chest feel tight and my gut heavy. It's not a pleasant sensation.

Alex leans into Craig and words that don't reach me are exchanged between them, hands gesticulating wildly.

I blink to Tate. He's continuing steadily on. I don't see how he could possibly be unaware of the pair's approach, but he gives no tell-tale signs to the contrary. I remain fixed on him as the gap separating them closes.

They're within throwing distance of each other when I finally catch the break in his step. His posture shifts, shoulders straightening, and he draws out his hands from his pockets. Then he pushes right on forward, his head bowing back down.

I hold my breath as Craig stops, and then Alex. They're blocking his way. Alex has made his opinion of Tate crystal clear.

Craig's opinion of him, from what I've gathered, is a whole other level lower again. My heart begins racing in apprehension of yet more messy fallout.

But Tate doesn't appear to permit them any further reaction.

Moving off the path, into the long grass, he passes around them as if they're nothing more significant than boulders interrupting his course.

Craig turns, tracking him. I think he's talking but I can't be sure. If he is, he certainly doesn't seem to be getting any response.

As Tate rejoins the path some way beyond them, Alex starts to tug at his brother's arm, prompting him on.

It's not until Tate's turned off the path at its end, though, with not one single backward glance cast, that Craig finally unpins his eyes from him and matches pace with Alex.

Pressing three tissues beneath my nose, I collect my jacket from the side of the shed and disappear around the back. I risk the steeper, un-pathed route down the slope.

"YOUR FACE MAKES MY EYES HURT," Sophie informs me. She's perched on the arm of the chair to my right, swinging her legs and examining me through slits. "It's not pretty."

"Don't look at me then."

My nose isn't broken, I've been assured. It'd stopped bleeding by the time I arrived in on Thursday afternoon, but Mel had pitched a fit at the gory sight of me, whisking me over to visit the nurse next door to have it checked. While she sat with a coffee, Jenny cleaned and fixed me up; forcing an icepack and painkillers upon me before allowing me leave of her kitchen. Really nice lady, actually.

Sophie's not wrong, though, I'm certainly quite hideous: My nose at least twice its usual size and my eyes rimmed thick with all the colours of a dismal rainbow.

Callum messaged me over Facebook yesterday, apologising. It's not in any way his fault, I reassured him, and in turn, I apologised to him on Tate's behalf. I didn't quite buy into his acceptance. Steph messaged me as well, saying she hoped I now saw sense. I've left that one marked as 'unread'.

Sophie raspberries out a long sigh. "Are you nearly done yet?"

It's now late Saturday afternoon and I'm sat at the computer in the sitting room, logged into steam and building a virtual prison. I have been for approximately three hours. Sophie's been whining at my side for the past one and a half. "Nope," I reply.

Tate didn't call around yesterday, and he hasn't today either. Okay, so, the rain's been pelting down relentlessly and the sky's looking ripe for a storm, I'd probably be set to readily forgive his no show were it any other such crappy day. But after Thursday's episode, it has me wound up super tight. I've heard nothing from him. He's not picking up his phone... not that he ever does, but my five texts yesterday and three today have also gone ignored. He hasn't responded to my short *'Hey, how's things?'* email either or logged onto steam in all my time of waiting thus far, and beyond those two avenues, his virtual presence is non-existent.

"Uncle Mikey, it is actually my 'puter you know?" The brat persists.

"Go do something else for a bit."

"There's nothing else *to* do. Everything's so *booorring!* I just want to go on Cbeebies."

"Fine," I snap, closing down my pages and shoving the chair back from the desk. "All yours."

I'm wasting my time anyway. He's probably blocked me on steam. I should probably just – as Steph said – see sense; accept that the deadline he set on our friendship has been pulled forward...for reasons I may not ever fully understand.

As Sophie launches herself into my place the very instant my bum lifts from it, I cross the room to the large bay window and nudge a gap between the closed curtains to peer out.

The sky's still ominous and the rain's still falling, but it doesn't look anywhere near so bad as it did half an hour ago. *Possibly.*

"Hey, Soph," I say, turning. She's leaning so far forward, her nose is practically touching the monitor. "Megan's back from her holiday today, right?"

"Um..." Her eyes remaining fixed to the screen, she screws her mouth to one side and bops her shoulders, "yep?"

"I could walk you over to call on her, if you fancy it?"

"Really?" She jumps from the chair with such sudden gusto, she knocks it shooting back into the sideboard. The mouse tumbles from the desktop to swing mid-air by its wire. Not bothering to wait for my confirmation, she rushes for the door, "I just need to get my wellies and my 'brella. Tell daddy!"

Kid has a use after all.

"Did you know," Sophie interrupts the brief stretch of silence I'd only just begun to appreciate, "that Cbeebies has two shows what learn you how to talk with your hands?"

"I did not," I sigh.

"Yep." She nods. We're a couple of minutes away from the McAllister's house and she's walking slowly beside me, clutching my hand as she plods from puddle to puddle. Her pink umbrella's folded down and tucked into the belt of her spotty raincoat like a sheathed sword. She doesn't even care if the rain wets her pigtails, she's told me. Twice. "Something Special is my favouritist. Mr Tumble is so funny! And there's Magic Hands too. They do rhymes, all the words with their hands."

"Great."

"Watch this." Dropping her hold on me, she stops and puts her index fingers side-by-side, pointing down to the ground. She kicks one out and then brings her hands together, drawing opposing crescents through the air to make a full circle. Giggling, she repeats the motions while looking expectantly up at me. I stare blankly at her. "Wanna clue? Kay-kay. One hit you in the face." I continue to be clueless and she rolls her eyes up to the sky, clicking her tongue. "Football. It means football. Look." She goes through it a third time: "Foot. Ball."

"Right." I don't bother with correcting her that my face was actually hit by an elbow. Who knows what that might launch her off on. "Very clever. Now keep moving, or else it'll be your bedtime before we even get there."

She hurries the few steps to catch up, reclaiming my hand. "I do lots of watching and practicing. That's important if I'm gonna get good. Megan's good – for a little kid." The girl talks for the sake of talking, just loves the sound of her own voice. "It's hard work cos 'membering can be tricksy."

"I bet."

"You can watch with me if you want."

"Watch kids' TV? Uh, thanks but I think I'd rather get hit in the face again."

"Oh, Uncle Mikey!" Holding back a step, jerking my arm, she bends her knees and pounces forward. "You can be so silly sometimes."

Sophie continues on with her jabbering the entire rest of the way to Tate's house. And it takes far longer than the two minutes it should have cos walking and talking at the same time is apparently something she's not been practising nearly enough.

I stop at the gate, push it open and sweep out my hand, motioning her through. "After you."

She's fallen very silent, very sudden. I turn to find her staring up at the house and chewing at her bottom lip.

"Come on, Soph. You'll leave yourself no time for play if you don't get a wriggle on." I sweep my arm again, but she shakes her head. "What? You don't want to play with Megan now?"

Despite responding with a vigorous nod, she still doesn't make a move.

"Fine. Suit yourself," I sigh, passing through the gate and letting it swing shut with a whine behind me.

"But, Uncle Mikey!" Sophie whisper-shouts at my back as I start up the garden path. Still stood out on the street, her eyeballs are darting from side to side as if we're up to something shady here and she's terrified we're about to be caught out. "This isn't where Megan lives."

"What?"

"We're at the wrong house!" She persists with the whisper-shouting.

I step up onto the doorstep, my eyes raking over the front door – a green door I could never in a million years mistake – and I sigh, raising a hand and ringing the bell before turning my head to frown at her. "You just gonna stay out there then, are you?"

Sophie's eyes have grown huge, "I don't think you should have rung..." Her last word is cut off as the door's swung wide.

I whip back around, sending droplets of rain water flying from my sodden hair.

Mr McAllister fills the entrance, glowering.

26

DIFFICULT

I feel myself shrinking at an alarming rate as Graham stares me down. Think it's safe to assume that distance has failed abysmally to make his heart grow any fonder.

But then his stormy grey eyes slide on past me, to Sophie, and the menace in them is swiftly powered down. He flashes her a smile (or, at least, something I imagine he intends to be one) as he addresses me. "He's busy."

"Oh. Okay." I swallow, moving back off the doorstep – just out of his arms reach. "Could you perhaps, um, please ask him if he'd come down for just a minute? Just for a quick word?"

"You've already taken up his full week, boy. Had plenty time to get all your words said."

"Right, sure. But if you..."

"He doesn't need the distraction today. Tomorrow neither. You can hold on to your word 'til school, Monday."

"What about Megan?" I blurt out before he has chance to shut me out. "Sophie was hoping to play with Megan for a little while."

The tight grimace-y smile returns to his furry face. "I'm sorry, kid," he calls to Sophie, "Megan's not here right now."

Sophie makes no response. I cast a glance over my shoulder

and find her half hidden behind the hedge, peering around. First I've seen her behave timid.

"Hey, Graham?" An all too familiar girl voice suddenly chisels in, scratching my eardrums. "Tate's needing a new battery for his... Alston?" Adele appears at Graham's shoulder, her brows arching high as her dark eyes scour over me. "What do you want?"

Busy? Right. Too busy for me, but not for her. That's painful.

"Will you at least tell him I called please?" I ask Graham.

With a non-committal grunt, he slams the door in my face.

Trudging down the path, toward the gate, I'm near enough launched into space when Sophie lets out an almighty squeal and bolts past the gate, along the street.

"Sophie!" I shout, hurling myself in pursuit, at the same time someone else exclaims: "Oh my goodness!"

I vault the gate and then slam to a standstill.

Stood beside a red Ford parked on the roadside a few paces further along the street, Laura McAllister's gaze jolts up from Sophie and Megan embracing in front of her, pinning me. "Mikey?"

For a long moment, I can do no more than stare at her; at the strangeness of her in a prim suit – all clean lines and muted tones.

But then, stepping forward, a grin takes over her face and, jeezus! It's a grin of rainbow pancakes and pasta art and crazy dancing, and it soothes like balm.

Sophie's whipped out her umbrella and she and Megan are huddling close under it gossiping conspiratorially beside the Ford as Laura passes by them.

"Little Mikey Alston, gracious me. Look at you now, sweet-heart, quite the strapping young man." She's kind enough not to linger too long on my gargoyle-esque hooter. "How are you?"

Thoroughly wet and miserable. I flush, my tongue all tied up.

Stopping a small step in front of me, she runs her warm green eyes – a near-perfect match for Tate's – over the whole of me, and it's everything I remember it being and everything I hadn't even realised until now I sorely needed. But then she glances beyond me, to the house at my back, and her smile falters. Slight though the change is, I catch it. "You're here for Tate?"

I nod. "But he's... Graham says he's busy."

Her smile drops altogether. "The two of you – you're friends again though, right?"

The girls break down into a fit of boisterous giggles, Sophie's umbrella sent to jiggling through the air.

"Yeah. I mean, uh..." *What's he been saying about me?*

"Something's happened?"

The perplexed crease to her brow has me uncertain how best to proceed here. I've no idea how much she knows. "Nothing. No, we're good. Just he... I was hoping he'd help me with my room again today. No biggy, though. It wasn't a definite plan. Guess I can..."

"He's not responsible for...?" And now she calls attention to my nose, her finger motioning toward it. Her tone's soft and cautious, "is he?"

"No," I'm lightning fast to assure her. She looks genuinely relived. "No, no. It's nothing." Self-consciously, I drop my head. "Nothing to do with Tate." *Callum's bruised ribs, on the other hand...*

"Look, honey." Stepping in closer still, she takes my hand in both of hers. "My boy can be difficult, I know. But you understand why, right?"

I stiffen.

Her brows dip further, the crease deepening, and her study of my face intensifies. "Oh." She forces the bright curve back to her lips, though this time it falls far short of her eyes and lacks all its therapeutic properties. "Please give him time, Mikey, okay? Don't give up on him, no matter how impossible he gets. You're good for him – always have been – and, whether he realises it or not, he needs you."

"I..." I've got nothing.

Her gaze probing me a moment longer, she pulls me in close and hugs me tight. Bewildered though I am, I breathe her in and savour the reassuringly *right* spicy cinnamon blast. "I'll speak to him for you," she whispers in my ear before releasing me. "It's so wonderful to see you, Mikey. I'm sorry, hopefully we'll find time for a proper catch up very soon, but we best get in. Megan," she calls out, "come along, sweet pea. Sophie, you best hurry home with your uncle. Storm's not far off now and I'm betting it's a corker."

"Awww!" Both girls grumble, neither moving.

Laura turns to them, hands on her hips, "Both do as I've asked right now, and I'll arrange for Sophie to come for tea after school on Monday, deal?"

"Deal!" Megan agrees, skipping to Laura's side, as Sophie moves to mine and says: "That would be very lovely, thank you."

Despite Sophie's insistent tug on my hand, it's several stretched minutes after Laura's moved on by me with a pat to my shoulder, through the squeaky gate and into the house, that I'm able to coax myself to start walking away.

JUST JODY. JUST ONCE

*T*here was a spectacular storm on Saturday night. It kicked off around an hour after Sophie and I arrived safely back at the house. I sat on the front doorstep for nigh on three hours watching it.

Radio silence from Tate continued through Sunday. I deliberately whiled away the bright post-storm morning out of the house, aimlessly skating the streets, my phone left in my room. The afternoon, I filled in with Gran. We played a few creative games of Sonic the Hedgehog chess, listened through her playlist as we pottered about in the garden, and then I made us some beans on toast for tea. My phone remained in my room. I settled myself in for an early night and, when I couldn't sleep, I forced my overactive mind into some productive revision.

Tate doesn't call around for me on Monday morning. I wait in the house until 8.40 before admitting it a lost cause and setting out alone.

Lyndsay hijacks me before I even make it through the school gates.

The moment she sees me approaching along the drive, she jumps up from the bench – the very same one on which I first saw

Tate again – and quicksteps toward me. "Mikey! Can we talk for a minute, please?" Her expression isn't an overtly angry one, but that doesn't stop my nerves from fluttering. Plus, also, we've only a minute or two before the bell sounds and we'll be marked down as late.

I make a point of checking the time on my phone before forcing out a very unsure, "suurrre?"

Flashing a miniature smile, she stops and indicates for me to follow her back to the bench.

"Steph says," she starts the instant I settle down beside her. "That if I really care about you, I should support you in accepting who you are." Looking mighty uncomfortable, her fingers fiddling with a toggle button of her pretty pink duffle coat, she's picking her words with obvious care. I clamp my tongue between my teeth, smart enough to know not to interrupt yet. "Deep stuff, coming from her, and she's right, I know that. And I do care about you, Mikey. But she's making out like it's such an easy thing to do. It's not." She takes a breath, inspecting the state of my face with only the slightest pinch to her brow. No doubt she's been fully filled in on what went down last week. "I just feel so stupid. I feel like I should have known. Steph's right about that too – I'm dense."

"Hey, no," I venture cautiously when she drops her gaze, screwing her lips to one side. "How could you possibly have known when I didn't?"

"Thing is, it's not the first time this has happened to me." Her admittance is made in a mumbled voice I just barely catch. "Déjà vu."

I raise my eyebrows questioningly, "sorry?"

She shakes her head then puffs out a grim laugh, looking out into the trees. "Me and Ma – *Tate* share very much the same taste in guys, apparently. Only he has far more success with them than I do, what with him being, you know, the right gender for *their* taste and all."

My brows plunge low and I shift uncomfortably in my seat.

When I say nothing, she darts a glance at me and then fixes back on the trees with a sigh. "I had a huge thing for Craig. I wasn't alone in that, obviously. You've seen him. But my crush was much more than a – a shallow appreciation. He was always really sweet with me, and – dumb me – I convinced myself I had an honest-to-God shot at something with him."

The incoming foot traffic along the drive has all but died and I know the bell will have already sounded. We're officially late. I no longer care. This feels important.

She continues, "when Tinwell started up that rumour, I defended him against it, and it was my shoulder he cried on when it spread and things got messy. He kissed me. A few times. Never said we were together but I kind of got to figuring we were. Then Tate showed up back at school, all screwy in the head, lashed out at Craig and Craig up and disappeared. He cut me out entirely. I felt used, and now I'm feeling like you've used me too. Not only does it hurt, Mikey, it's humiliating."

"I didn't intentionally use you, Lynds. I hate that I've hurt you." I reach tentatively for her hand but she pulls it away, flashing me a small, sad smile. I'd perhaps never have realised the soft spot Lyndsay's carved for herself within me had I not shoved her from it, leaving it empty and forlorn. "I'm sorry."

"Yeah. Well."

A heavy hush falls, and as she tracks the flight of a tiny sparrow from one branch to another, I process the insinuation of her words.

"So you think something actually did happen, then? Between Craig and Tate?"

Measured up against Craig, I do not fare well. Just knowing the rumour without any belief in it had been enough to make the mere sight of him hugely unsettling. With an attachment of credibility, well... Brutal. I've been consoling myself that probably, in actual fact, Tate isn't even gay. If he is, and – worse – his ex is a guy like Craig, then his rejection of me becomes a whole lot harder to swallow.

"I don't know!" Lyndsay's eyes slam into me. "Honestly, I really don't want to discuss Tate with you right now, Mikey, okay?"

Guilt twists my gut, vaulting me out of my murky thoughts. "Right."

A long moment of hush weighs down on us again before she says, "my cousin's gay too, you know? Derek."

I determinedly focus in on what she's saying.

"He came out two years ago. Mum banned him from the house, forbade me from seeing him."

"Your mum...? Really?" I sound more surprised than I am. Her mum left a rather bitter impression on me in our brief meeting before Steph's party, all pursed lips and waspish assessment.

But, still, *harsh*! "So she doesn't know you go to his gigs?"

She shakes her head and then drops her gaze to her fidgeting fingers. "I'm sort of starting to wonder if it's, like, the effect I have on guys or something. Not that I ever... had a thing for Derek, that would just be so seriously wrong," she shudders. "But you get what I mean, right? I care about a guy and..."

"It's not you," I interrupt her. "Nothing at all to do with you."

"Of course I know it's dumb. I know it doesn't work that way. But the thought's dug deep inside my head, I can't shake it."

"I'm such a humongous jackass!"

"Yeah. That you are," she says, a strange, soft giggle escaping her, short lived. Her blue eyes lift to me, head tilted. "You really didn't know you were gay?"

"Nope," I shrug one shoulder. "Well, I mean, I guess part of me probably kinda did. Not like I turned gay overnight or anything, right? It's just a thing I didn't ever think too hard on, I guess, like it just never felt...all that important. Until now."

"With you, I figured your awkwardness was just down to nerves. Inexperience."

"I'm not a virgin!" I feel the need to defend myself. Against what, I'm not sure. I immediately bite down on my tongue.

"Oh." Her brows have shot up way high in pride-wounding surprise. "Guy or girl?"

"Girl." *Obviously.* I roll my eyes and she almost allows a grin to break. "Just Jody. Just once." And it was not the most magical of experiences ever. It was in Jody's room while her parents were downstairs, watching TV. We had to keep really quiet and neither of us had a clue what we were doing. We got naked and fumbled with each other's bits awhile. Took almost a full ten minutes to get the condom on, a rigmarole that had me go floppy, forcing me to work myself up again. Once inside, four jerky pumps in, I was done and she was frustrated. "She finished with me the next day."

"No way!"

"Yep." I remember realising that I should be upset over her, forcing myself to feel the sting of her brushoff: *I'd given her my first time, we were supposed to have been brought closer together!* I sent her a number of spite-fuelled rage texts and unfriended her on Facebook. She cornered me mid-shift at the supermarket, told me to quit taking the oestrogen tablets and to get over myself. Two days later we were friends again, acting like our brief relationship was a thing that hadn't ever happened, and we've not spoken of the disastrous affair since. "It's like I told you, me and Jody shouldn't ever have been anything more than friends."

"Same can be said for you and me, huh?" She nudges my arm with her elbow.

I match her guarded smile, "I'd very much like for us to be friends."

"I'm willing to try if you're willing to be patient."

"Deal."

We sit and talk for a few minutes longer, about nothing of any consequence. It's nice; a relief to have Lyndsay back on side, her lovely smile fills a small hole in me. I let her be the one to call the close on our time.

She stands, stroking her hands down the front of her coat. "We should head in, we'll be in trouble."

"I guess so."

"Thanks for talking to me, Mikey."

"No. Thank you for asking me to."

She holds her hand out toward me. I take it.

"You're a truly beautiful person, Lynds. You're gonna make someone very happy one day."

"Uck! Seriously?" She giggles, pulling me to my feet. "Too sappy and cliché, too soon."

"Shut up."

~

ATTEMPTING to keep up with Tate's unstable mood fluctuations is zapping way too much of my energy, I've decided.

So, when he takes up his usual seat across from me in Study, my reception of him is dosed with a little more exasperation than enthusiasm.

Though, try as I might, there's no stopping the tingles that jolt out from my chest through the whole of me as his eyes fix on mine.

He offers nothing in the way of an *'I'm sorry for schitzing out on your innocent friend on Thursday, I think I got the wrong end of the stick'*; nor *'and sorry I fled right after, leaving you bleeding and stunned. How is your nose?'*; nor *'sorry I've since ignored you completely and let my dad slam the door in your face'*. Not a hint of an *'I'm sorry I'm behaving so needlessly difficult, leaving you with no clue as to where you stand with me'* either.

Pulling his bag up onto the table and rifling through while his gaze remains locked on me, what he leads with instead is: "You and Lyndsay made up now?"

I hold my frown in place.

"Saw the two of you chatting this morning. She looked happy."

So he must have been late in today too, then.

One at a time, he pulls out two textbooks and a pad of lined paper without looking down, and then I track his bag's move to the floor by his feet. He's left it open and I spy the *secret* notebook peeking out. "Not that happy," I shrug. "I'm still gay."

"Ah," he says with a light chuckle. "Friends though?"

I return my eyes to his, narrowing them, "possibly. Why?"

"Nothing. No, it's good. I'm glad you've worked things out with her." Then, with a weird half-smile crooking his lips, he opens up his paper-pad and a psychology textbook, pulling a pen from his jeans pocket, and promptly switches off from me to work.

"Well. Glad you're glad." I mutter, frowning at him a few minutes longer to no effect. My attention slides back to his bag – and the notebook calling out to me from it.

A ONE-WAY TRIP ACROSS BARRIERS

'*Dad's on my case again -big time, making the threats of what'll happen if I fall behind in my studies. Need to stay in tonight and hit the books so he doesn't hit the roof.'*

Tate's handwriting is easily identifiable: Slanted and loopy and expressive.

Adele's hand is far cutesier than expected, missing only the hearts over the I's.

'Oh, what a surprise. Cancelling on me. Again. Did not see that coming.'
T: You know how he gets.
A: I know he works as a very handy excuse for you.
T: You won't miss me.
A: 'Course I will.
T: I'm hardly the life and soul, Ads.
A: You totally rock my world.
T: Still no.
A: Miserable bastard!
-

A: Jackson asked me out.
T: And that's made you glum because...?
A: The wankshaft did it via text.

T: Shit! You've castrated him, haven't you?

A: In my head, several times, yes.

-

T: Mine tonight?

A: Unless something better comes up, I suppose.

T: Wow. Cheers. I'll hold off on getting the pizza then. Just in case.

A: You do that.

-

A: Missed you yesterday. Leave early?

T: Session with John.

A: Go well?

T: Still his star pupil.

A: D'aww, that's my boy!

Want to guess who Jackson's taking out tonight?

Hint: Not me.

Another hint: It's Scarlet Duckface Flemming.

T: No second offer for you then, huh?

A: Nope. The dumb bastard.

-

A: I'm taking you out tonight. Suit up and boot up, we're having ourselves some fun for once.

T: Nope. Got plans.

A: Suurrre you do. And I've got a holiday house on Venus! It was an order, not a request. You'll disappear into that bastard computer one day, I swear.

T: Fuck you. Megan's got her dance recital tonight. Both the 'rents are going. Fun family meal after.

A: Oh. Yikes.

Want me to come with?

T: Am I supposed to take that offer seriously with your face like that? No, you're safe, I'm good.

-

A: Ran into Craig today. He actually dragged his eyes away from his reflection in the salon window just to ask after you.

T: And you told him?

A: To go fuck himself, of course.

T: Of course.

-

A: MIKEY ALSTON'S BACK?! Have you seen him yet? What you going to do?

T: Yes, yes and nothing.

A: Nothing? Yeah, right. Totally believe that. This is huge for you, T!

T: It really isn't. And I don't want to talk about it, so hush your face. Now.

-

A: Thinking I might get my lip pierced.

T: Ok. What's your Mum done to piss you off now?

A: Why would you automatically assume she's got anything to do with anything?

T: Oh, right. Cos she's NOT the cause of all your rebellious urges?

A: No. Absolutely not. I resent that you think me so petty!

-

T: Sorry but I'm too tired to follow what you're saying. Something about my mum?

A: Yeah, I saw her yesterday, after she'd visited you. She was really upset. What happened?

T: Shit! Wish she'd just steer clear while I'm in here.

A: Tell me.

TELL ME!

T: She started bawling when she saw my stitches. Then got mad when I blamed it on Mikey. So I sent her out.

A: Are you for real?!

Can't be getting pissy with her for worrying about you, dickface! And blaming Alston for your fall, WTAF?

Seriously, how's that even slightly on him?

I don't understand why you won't just talk to him. Tell him.

T: Cos I don't fucking want to, that's why. I just want him to take the hint and fuck off.

A: You're not –

MY HEAD WHIPS up as a shadow falls across my table. An ominous tension charges the air and my already pounding heart amps up to slam against my ribcage.

Tate stands across the table from me, Adele at his back. Eyes locking mine, his expression alone nigh on annihilates me.

Busted!

My chest feels set to explode.

"Reading anything interesting there, Mikey?" He grits out.

I shouldn't have taken it, I know. It crossed the line. In fact, it was a giant leap way over a pretty damn solid barrier. And now here are the consequences of that move, caught up with me far swifter than expected and intent on my ruin. I'm pathetically unprepared.

Tate's supposed to be in psychology this period. I'd counted on having this fifty-minute slot safely to myself.

Way across the opposite side of the school, I've settled at a study table in the library, one with a clear view of the doors – *just in case.* But my prudent positioning has been for nought, obviously, because I've failed to maintain my caution and he's slipped right on through.

Separating his notebook from the Media textbook I've used to mask it, I close it and slide it across the table toward him. He snatches it up, his grip tight enough to make his knuckles blanch.

He works his jaw, looking set to finish me off with a savage unleashing. But instead, he turns on his heel and storms away from me, out of the library, without another word.

I gape after him, disgusted with myself. Thoroughly.

"Your stupidity knows no bounds, does it?" Adele alerts me to her remaining presence. Jolting, my eyes snap to her. She's looking uncharacteristically flustered, not a hint of smug satisfaction evident on her face. "Up, shit-for-brains, move! Follow him. The two of you are long overdue this hash-out."

I think my body's given up on me.

When it becomes abundantly clear I'm not moving anywhere anytime soon, Adele powers around the table, yanks out my chair and tips me off it.

She continues blasting motivational obscenities and orders at my back as she shadows me out the library doors and along the corridor, herding me toward the Quad.

We find Tate sat atop our usual lunch table, his feet on the bench where I sit. It's raining and everything's wet, his hair's already starting to slick to his head. Headphone's on and the notebook still clutched in one hand, he's leaning forward with his arms crossed over his knees and his eyes trained on the double doors. He gives no reaction when I pass out through them, I get the distinct impression he's been very much expecting me. That makes me nervous.

I leave him plenty chance to speak up first, but he offers nothing, so I start.

"How am I to blame for your fall, Tate? I didn't push you. I wasn't even freaking there! How can you put that on me?" Perhaps I should have eased in with an apology first but screw it.

His gaze flicks from me to Adele, stood just behind me. I'm almost certain he's decided to blank me out, and am about ready to swoop in on him and toss those detestable headphones from his head when he locks his eyes back on mine and clears his throat. "I blame you for triggering the seizure which led to the fall," he says flatly, his lip curling. "And for the further seven I had while in A&E which got me admitted."

My mouth drops open, but I'm given no chance to formulate any kind of response before he continues:

"Ten months I'd gone without a single episode. You show up, crowding me like I'm your fucking life support, and I have eight in one fucking day! Hospitalised and scarred; *you're* the stressor that caused that."

All my words have gone, all sucked away into the dark pit

burgeoning within my chest. He watches me with a painful passivity as I flounder.

"Seizures?" I finally cough up. "Like, epileptic seizures?" What I get from him in reply is a *no-shit-Sherlock* head tilt and nothing more. "How? When? Why...why did you feel you had to keep that from me?"

His gaze is so intensely formidable in its dispassion, I want to hide from it. He doesn't answer me, not so much as a suggestive muscle tick this time.

I throw a glance over my shoulder at Adele to find her mouth moving silently, her fix on Tate so concentrated I can almost believe she possesses a witchy power that's bending him to her will. The instant she notices I've caught her out, her lips press tight.

The pit in my chest volcanoes.

Yes, epilepsy is a crappy hand to be dealt; yes, it permits him some allowance of anger toward the powers that be. But it sure as hell does not prevent him from having friends and a social life. It offers no reason or excuse for his repellent hostility.

"All I've done is try to be your friend, Tate," I blast, whirling back to him, "I just want to understand you. You don't make any sense. I'm sorry I took your notebook, okay? I sincerely am. That was wrong. But, jeezus, what's even the deal with that thing anyway? Every time I've seen you with it, you and Adele have been sat face to face, totally alone, and there wasn't a damned thing I read in there to justify such freaking secrecy. You could have yelled all of that out for the whole world to hear and not a single person would have given a single toss! Note passing should have been left behind in primary school, Tate. It's immature. The pair of you just come off looking goddamned infantile!"

"That's fucking rich, coming from you," he bites back after a torturous moment of cold scrutiny. His tone remains impassive, as do his eyes, but his nostrils are flaring wide and his jaw's set taut. He moves down from the table and closes in on me. "Your head's still stuck in primary school, right, Mikey? Hell-bent on dragging me back there with you."

Every calculated step and cruel word he aims my way beats me down. "I miss what we had, that's all." As quickly as I erupted, I'm spent. "I don't get why we can't still be friends. Why are you so intent on shutting me out?"

He stops just beyond arm's length from me. "Words. So many pointless fucking words. I don't have to. Explain. Myself to you. And I. Clearly. Can't trust you to respect that." He juts his head toward the table where the notebook's been left. I mark the splotches of rain darkening its cover before I fix onto his head-phones, his gaze too hard to hold. "I'm done. Keep clinging to that fucking Pokemon card; you're getting shite all else from me. I'm so done with you, Mikey. Stay the fuck away from..."

"He's deaf!" Adele slices in shrilly over him.

"...me." Tate finishes.

"Deaf?" I echo. Vacantly. The word's meaning is completely lost on me. *Deaf?* It stampedes through my brain, frantic to find its place. Then, *CLICK!* And the whole world slams to a sickening standstill. "You're... you're not deaf."

Tate releases me, locking onto Adele. I can't see what Adele's doing, but his expression turns uglier. His eyes blaze.

It's confirmation enough.

For all I can't fathom it.

"He deserved to know, Tate. You should have told him." Her voice sounds surprisingly calm for someone being rendered to ash.

Never thought I'd see a day in which Adele has my back. I dart a glance behind, dumbfounded, but her attention's tunnelled in on Tate. She's looking far from calm. She's looking closer to terrified than I ever considered her capable of. Lyndsay's tale of a previous confrontation between these two, where Tate threw his fist at a wall, butts itself into the chaos.

"The guy...shit! He decides he's fucking gay and can't keep it to himself – not even for a minute. Goes and announces it to a party-full." He strides on past me to bear down on her and I unwittingly turn, tracking him; my body's working on auto-pilot, my brain buckling under the sudden strain wrought upon it. Adele takes a nervous step back. "Next minute he decides he's in love with me, set to fucking burst with his need to declare it. How long do you think he can hold the lid on this, Adele, eh?"

Now Adele's eyes slide to me, widening in horror with her realisation of the monumental mistake she's made. And our moment crashes to its end.

Eye's drilling in to the side of Tate's head, my vision's blurring. *Has his opinion of me always been that low?* It's a mistake to blink; I'm grateful for the blanketing rain. "So much for your 'I don't care what people say, I'm fine with who I am' bollocks, Tate, huh?" I choke out.

But Adele's cautioning, "Alston," is the only response I get.

Because Tate can't hear. And he's pointedly refusing to look at me.

It's a savage kick. One that's swiftly succeeded by another: *I hate him.*

A terrible reaction. Shameful, even.

Pretty sure I should be channelling my efforts toward processing... working to unjumble the chaos of questions beating against my skull; plying him with reassurances that it makes no difference to me, that I'm here for him still and he can absolutely rely on me to keep his secret.

Can't find any of that in me, though.

Because it wasn't him who let me in; he didn't ever plan to let me in.

Because he doesn't trust me. He's hiding himself away and he doesn't trust me to help cover him.

His betrayal is crushing.

Right now – for that – selfish though it may be – I *hate* him with excruciating clarity.

The desire to hit him blazes; I crave the release of lashing out at him over and over again until he's as destroyed as he's made me feel.

"Alston?"

I wasn't aware I'd started moving until Adele's querying call snaps my attention to it. I don't stop. "I'm *fucking* off."

Tate almost turns, almost flinches, before he once again discounts me.

It's the last time he gets to do that.

"Consider the message received." I shove past Adele, throwing the door wide and passing on through. "The pair of you can stay put in your safe little bunker. Me and the rest of the world will carry on just fine without you."

Neither one of them chases me.

THE BOMBS KEEP RIGHT ON COMING

"*B*unking off class. Tut, tut!" Steph calls, jogging to catch me up as I amble my way along the drive out of school.

"Hey," I greet her, mustering a smile, as she slows to a walk beside me.

I'd been sorely tempted to call an early end to my school day following the confrontation with Tate this morning, escape and put as much distance as I could between us. I didn't though. Because I realised that freeing up time to spend with my thoughts would likely prove dangerously unwise. And so, I went to my classes and I worked hard to keep my mind busy. All except for History. That one I skipped, spending last period in the library, at the same table I'd been caught out at, my watch of the doors keen this time around, making a start on the homework I figured I'd get little chance to work on tonight. It's been a long and mentally-punishing day, and it's not even close to done with me yet.

"So, what's your plans for tonight?" Steph asks, seemingly reading my thoughts. She has her red hair trussed up into pigtails, one side clumsily plaited and the other not.

"Got work."

"Yeah? 'Til when?"

"'Til eight."

"Then?"

I shrug.

"Perfect!" She grins, bumping her shoulder against mine.

Striving to keep the grimace from my face, I curse myself for not having a further excuse on hand. "Why?"

"We've been invited to watch Desperate For Aces rehearse. You'll come, right?"

"Uh..."

"They'll be kicking off at seven, but it's only in the backroom of the Red Bull, right across the street from you, so you could just pop over as soon as you finish, yeah? It'll still be going on."

Assaulting my brain with a blast of live music – *music Tate can't hear* – does actually sound tempting. Drown out the thoughts such as that one from my mind.

"I'm not so sure Lyndsay'll be okay with me being..."

"'Course she will! Yas are all made up now. Hey, Lynds," she throws a call out over her shoulder. "You're good with it, right?"

"What?" Comes the replying call.

"Mikey's coming with us tonight."

"Oh." I turn my head to find Lyndsay idling along several paces behind us. She doesn't look especially enthused by the proposal, but after a small hesitation she lifts her shoulders, flashing a thumbs up and a smile.

"See!" Steph trills, slapping my back.

My gaze slipping beyond Lyndsay, I spot Callum and Alex. And Craig. There's enough of a distance between to suggest Lyndsay's making as deliberate an effort to disassociate herself from them as she is me. Craig looks up from the road, his piercing eyes catching on mine and I'm super abrupt in returning my attention forward.

"So we'll expect you just after eight, okay?" Steph pushes, slowing her step to fall behind me. "I know where to look for you, mind, if you let us down!"

I reach out and catch her arm. "He gonna be there?" I ask, directing her focus with a tilt of my head.

"Who?" She's a little too obvious with her glance back. "Oh, Craig? Nooo, he doesn't really ever hang out with us peasants anymore. Haven't the foggiest why he's shown up today, but he tends to stick to his fancy part of town, kicking it with his older, cooler boy racer buddies in some layby. So..." she grins and winks, "no excuses left, Mikey."

∽

"Did I shout for you out loud?" Sophie turns from the computer screen to ask when my search for my new black work shoes leads me into the sitting room. Her face is scrunched up in complete puzzlement.

"No?" I reply, equally as puzzled.

"Oh." With a shrug, her expression smooths in a blink and she returns her attention to the computer. "Come watch this with me."

A swift glance is enough to tell me it's some annoying kids show. "Nope. I've got work." I scan the floor, "you seen my shoes anywhere?"

She huffs out a precocious sigh of exasperation and, from the speakers, I catch a man's too-chirpy voice enthuse, *"you sign ba-by,"* as she says, "anyone would think you didn't want to learn."

Half-bent to peer under the coffee table, I freeze. *No. Freaking. Way!* "You know, don't you?"

"I know lots of things, Uncle Mikey," Sophie replies, sliding her big brown eyes back to me.

"I mean about Tate."

She stares at me, nonplussed.

"That he's deaf."

"Oooh, kay-kay. Yep, that is one of the things I know. Why?" Her face crumples up again as I straighten and stomp for the door. "Did you not?"

∽

THE BACK ROOM of the Red Bull Inn is cramped and musty. It has its own door in from the street, another door inside which leads through a corridor past the toilets to the bar, and two small, high windows covered in red curtains thick with dust. The 'stage' area takes up half the floor space. When I arrive at quarter past eight, aside from the four band members on the make-shift stage, the room is occupied by only Lyndsay, Steph, Callum and Alex, all seated around one of the six circular tables, in the far back corner. There's two free seats and Steph pats the one beside her, inviting me over with a grin. I settle down, catching the tail-end half hour of Desperate For Aces' rehearsal set.

"They're good, right?" Lyndsay leans around Steph to shout at me as the drums, bass and guitar draw the last song to a close.

The vocalist screams one final "Bury me!" into the microphone before slamming it back into the stand and I cheer along with the others while nodding emphatically. "Really good," I mouth at her. Even I can appreciate how polished and professional their set is. We've basically just been treated to our own private gig here tonight. Bonus: Loud and immersive, the show's achieved exactly what I'd banked on.

My plan's working out pretty well thus far. A hectic second shift at the bistro, where I had little enough chance to breath let alone think, followed by this, my wayward mind has effectively been kept harnessed.

As Derek's bandmates move to settle around a neighbouring table, leaving their instruments on stage, Derek turns up the lights and then heads straight for ours, dropping down on the remaining spare seat next to me.

"Hey gorgeous," he greets Lyndsay, reaching over the table to pinch her cheek, tugging it playfully.

"Get off me, Derek!" She swats at him, her smile flooded with warmth.

Letting go, he pats her cheek twice before leaning back in the chair. "What'd you guys think then? Be honest. But only if it's praise you're offering." He fixes on each face around the table in turn, soaking in the compliments with caricatural gusto. I'm called upon last.

"Enjoyed it, yeah. Brilliant," I offer, tearing my eyes from the winged skull tattooed across his throat and collarbone.

"Derek, Mikey. Mikey, Derek," Steph makes the introductions with unnecessary enthusiasm, gesturing between us and touting the most devious grin I've seen from her yet.

He smiles wide at me, holding out his decoratively inked hand, and I'm seized by the thorny suspicion this whole thing is something of a setup. Lyndsay's face tells me she's arriving at the same conclusion; she does not look best pleased.

With a subtle accusatory death glare fired Steph's way (totally wasted), I take the proffered hand and shake just once before drawing free.

"So, Mikey," he starts, tipping his chair to two legs and folding his arms. Rocking back and forth, his foot taps as though he still hears music. "Your nose. What's the story there? Looks like it must sting a bit."

Callum winces, no doubt reminded of his own bruising, and Alex snorts derisively. Lyndsay pretends not to see the eyebrow waggle Steph sends her, staring off into the middle distance.

"Um, yeah," I keep my explanation succinct, "football."

"Ah." He nods like that's all the information he needs. "Rough." His attention catching on the lanky, long-haired guitarist, who passes by and disappears through the door to the bar, he refocuses on the table at large and I expel a none-too-subtle sigh of relief. He has a tiny tattoo behind his ear too, I notice, a blue and purple fish. "Right, drinks. I'll shout this round. What's the order? Six pints?"

"Hells yeah!" Steph's prompt in answering for all of us, slapping her hand off the table top. "And a Jagerbomb each, pretty please?"

There's motions of agreement from all but Lyndsay and me.

"Nu-uh. No way!" Lyndsay protests before I can.

Derek's gaze returns to me, his brow cocked, and I drop my

head before giving it a slight shake. I was taught a valuable lesson at Steph's party and I fully intend to heed it.

"Oh, fine! A large white wine for m'lady," Steph amends the order. "As well as the Jagerbomb. Obvs."

"I like this one, Lyndsay. Very much," Derek chuckles. I tense, my eyes snapping up, as his arm reaches around the back of my chair. But the move's only to pat Steph's shoulder. "She's an awesome influence on you."

Lyndsay rolls her eyes. "Yeah, sure, whatever."

"I'll just have a coke, please," I speak up as Derek drops the chair to all four legs and slides it out.

"No, he won't," Steph's quick to counter.

Derek winks at Steph and stands, chuckling all the harder.

"Honestly," I call after him as he starts away. "Coke's good enough for me!"

"Coke's not good enough for anyone," he calls back, pulling open the door through to the bar. "Besides, alcohol will help numb the pain."

I'm poised to get up and trail him, requesting a coke from the barman myself if it came to it, until he adds that last bit. I resettle down in my seat. The tenderness on and around my nose is of little concern to me. But some mental soothing, *that* I'm sure as hell all for. One pint, one of these Jagerbomb things, just to take the edge off... in the absence of the head-pounding music, what other options do I have?

"YOU ALRIGHT?" Derek snags my attention with a finger click in front of my face. "You looked about a million miles away then. And I'd hazard a guess it wasn't someplace pleasant."

"Yeah, no," I sigh. "The worst."

No merry buzz for me tonight. A Jagerbomb and three swiftly downed pints later and my edge is sharpened rather than dulled.

Because, clearly, alcohol is evil. Grandad was right to warn me off it.

Just as Lyndsay was right to warn me off Tate. He's not my friend. He's not even an especially decent human being. He's hoodwinked me most my life, but I'm wised up on him now. The Jackass.

"And you've not heard a single word I've said, have you?" I'm broken once more from a trance. Derek looks amused rather than offended, a glint to his affable dark eyes as he runs a hand over his stubbled head.

I grimace, "sorry."

Glancing around the room, I realise I've also been unaware of his bandmates leaving. Their table's empty and their instruments gone, Derek's drum kit packed away and set in the corner. Only our little group remains.

Laughing, he shakes his head and shoves my arm. "You wanting to talk about it?"

"Sorry," I say again, "I absolutely do not."

"Fair enough." He lets it go with a light shrug and I appreciate that greatly. "How about a game of pool then? There's tables upstairs. Closed off now, but Joe'll let us up."

"Sounds good to me," Alex buts in. "Tournament. Me and Steph; Callum and Lynds; and you two." He nods his head from Derek to me. It's about the nearest he's come to acknowledging me since our chat in the library. I continue to blank him.

"Actually, I think I'm best off heading home." I'm all out of distractions here.

"Yeah, I think I'll make a start..."

Lyndsay's cut off as Steph grabs my arm, preventing my rise. "Oh no you don't, Mikey Alston!"

"Steph," Lyndsay admonishes. "Pack in!"

Steph's hold on me tightens. "We have less than an hour left before closing. You may as well stay."

Pinned to the table, I can feel Alex's eyes raking over me and my teeth are set to grinding.

"I'll get you some water, yeah?" Derek offers.

"Someone can get me some water," Callum slurs. Seems that, whatever Callum's reasons for drinking tonight, it's done him just as few favours as it has me. He's slouched back in his chair opposite, glasses halfway down his nose, looking just as miserable as I feel. No one else appears to be paying him any mind.

"No. Thanks, but I'm just gonna...Woah!" In my attempt to wheedle myself free of Steph to stand, I catch my foot on my chair leg and am launched clumsily forward several paces.

Lyndsay hastens to catch me from the front while someone else hooks the back of my shirt.

"You really shouldn't drink," Lyndsay berates me.

"I know," I huff, struggling to get my feet steady beneath me as my face burns.

Steph sniggers unashamedly. "I don't think it's safe for him to walk home alone. Derek?"

"Sure." I hear him respond right behind me. The hand clutching my shirt lets go and a moment later a strong arm wraps around my waist.

Is it possible the guy's in on it with Steph? Does he consider this an actual date? Well, if he does, it sure as all hell must be his worst one ever.

"I'm fine. Completely fine. Just tripped, is all." His arm feels quite pleasantly bracing, and that unnerves me. "I can capably make the walk all by myself."

"Then I'll walk with you just for the much-needed fresh air. Come on. You don't live too far, right?"

Steph shouts out my address at our backs as we make for the exit door: "Just in case he's worse than he looks!"

"You can stop with your stressing, Mikey, I'm not coming onto you," Derek tells me once we're outside the Red Bull Inn. He retracts his arm and puts some distance between us as we start along the street. "Just think it would be good for us to have a chat. Privately, you know?"

I look across at him with some confusion.

"Lyndsay's told me a lot about you."

"Oh?" *Crap on a stick!* I tense up. *Chat?* He's been playing me, the alcohol his calculated attempt to subdue me, and now he's about to beat my brains out for hurting his cousin! That's a cruelly sobering realisation. My eyes begin darting in every direction, searching for a witness or a possible escape route.

Apparently, my reaction is hilarious to him. "She told me you've very recently Come Out. I'm well versed in how tough that can be, that's all. If you're in need of an ear to bend, I've got one."

"So... Steph wasn't trying to set us up?"

"Oh, no, she totally was." He chuckles again. "But you're very clearly pining after someone else and, cute though you are, you're not enough my type for me to go trespassing on another's land." I feel his eyes settle on me. "Also, wouldn't do that to Lyndsay." He doesn't say it as dig, but it buries in deep anyway.

"Huh. Okay." I've no clue what else to say.

When the silence between us tunnels in way beyond awkward, Derek again picks up my slack in filling it, "I didn't go about it quite the dramatic way I've heard you did. I Came Out to my family first. By far the most terrifying thing I've ever done." He pauses as a shudder runs through him. "Worse, even, than my first gig with the guys. And I was sick four times before getting up on stage that night and twice more when I came off.

"I knew my Dad would be alright about it, and he was. I think he already had his suspicions. But my Mum... well, her and Aunt Gina – that's Lyndsay's mum – they weren't as accepting as I'd hoped. Mum's getting better with it. Still looks at me funny, like she's grieving for all the grandbabies she believes I've deprived her of, but we get along almost as we ever did so long as I don't trip up around her and expose the gay. Aunt Gina, though, she likes to pretend I'm dead.

"She has pictures of me up in her house, Lyndsay's told me, only there's none more recent than my year ten school photo."

"Jeezus! That's..." I meet his gaze, my mouth hanging limp as I wrack my brain for a fitting descriptive word.

"Shitty, right?" He lets me off the hook with a knowing smile. I nod and drop my head, watching my feet, as he continues, "for a long while after, I regretted telling them; wished I could take it back. But what kind of life is that? Keeping who I am a secret from those most important to me?"

And with the shake of his head my thoughts plummet straight back to Tate.

That's a concept he's yet to grasp. Cos he's a moron.

Except...

Adele's in on his secret. His family obviously knows. Hell, even Sophie's clued up.

He intended to keep me in the dark. And yet, here I am, continuing not to grasp my blatant unimportance to him.

I'm the bigger moron.

"I feel terrible over how I've treated Lyndsay, you know?" I yank myself back on track. "I honestly didn't mean to..."

"She has a big heart, that girl does. She hurts easy, but she forgives easy too. She won't hold it against you for too long." Derek kicks at a can, sending it skittering along the street. "Have you told your family yet?"

I don't answer straight away. For several beats, I consider not answering at all. It's not something I've really given any thought to until right this moment, when he's asked. Catching up to the can he kicked, I send it on another journey. "My gran's the only person I care enough about to want to tell. But she's not doing so good, so..." I shrug.

"Something serious?"

My brow pinches tight as I force the hateful word out into the crisp night air: "Dementia."

I'm aware of his sympathetic look. I don't acknowledge it, and

I'm glad he doesn't feel the need to accompany it with the typical condolences.

"So little of her there some days. Most days, recently. If I were to tell her and she didn't get it – if I had to keep telling her over and over again only to see the words bounce off, that would…" An arm slams hard across my chest, jarring me back, as a car speeds by us skimming unnervingly close to the foot I have poised out over the curb. "Hurt," I finish lamely, flashing Derek a grateful wincey-smile.

He retracts his arm and we watch three more cars whizz past before we cross the road.

"And if I told her and she did take it in," I continue as I step up onto the pavement, "and she couldn't accept it – couldn't accept *me* – well… that would slaughter me. She's stubborn, there'd be no bringing her round. It's too much to risk; she's all I have." *Grandad would for sure have disowned me.*

"Hmm," is all he says, and then he takes his turn in carrying the silence.

As we turn one corner, cross the street and turn another, I slip into imaginings of sitting David and Mel down for *THE* talk and then, passing by Mrs Branswith's shop, painful musings on how Mum and Dad might have reacted were they still here to care.

Starting along my street, I'm sharp in throwing those unwelcome thoughts right out as Derek finally speaks up again.

"It's a tough call to make, and I don't envy you it. But I think it worth you at least factor in the other possibility: What if you tell your gran and she gets it and she accepts you? There's a chance, right?"

I allow for his words to settle in, but I don't respond.

I don't think he expected me to. "One day, you'll meet someone special. Someone who'll make you feel happier than you believed possible. Who knows, might even be you've found him already – this guy who has your head all screwy – given a good bit of fixing up what's broke. She's special to you too, right? Would you really want to have to hide that happiness from her?"

A snort escapes. "No fix up can be done with him, trust me."

"Ah. That's a shame." His steps have progressively slowed as we've neared the house, his attention trained ahead. Now he juts his chin toward it, slipping me a lopsided smirk. "Cos I'm assuming – though I may be wrong – that's your guy there. And, to me, he most definitely looks to be in a fixing-up kinda mood."

Tate's spotted me before my gaze finds him in the darkness and he's scrambling up from the doorstep to his feet. His expression's unsettling. I could almost believe he's been crying, but Tate doesn't cry. Not ever. He says nothing, just watches my faltering approach.

Derek laughs, the sound startling, and then claps me on the shoulder. "Well, Mikey, suppose this is my cue to leave now. I trust you can make these last twenty or so paces alone?"

"Yeah," I'm only half-aware of myself replying. "Thanks."

"Good meeting you. Come along to our gig on Thursday and I'll shout you a coke."

I attempt a nod, and perhaps I achieve it. He's strode several steps away from me before I recover myself. Ripping my eyes free of Tate, I turn. "Hey Derek? I'm glad we talked. Seriously, thank you."

"Anytime." His grin is broad. "Get my number off Lyndsay. And, hey." He sends his gaze out beyond me, marking Tate – the house – Gran, hidden somewhere just inside. "Best of luck, bud."

30

FIXING UP WHAT'S BROKE

"*W*hat do you want, Tate?" I snap without looking at him, stepping up to the front door.

I'm acutely aware of his move in behind me and when I spare him no further attention he asks, "can I come in? Can we talk?"

My head's screaming 'no, hell no' but my body...well, my body opens the door and motions him right on in.

The house is quiet and dark. I spy a sliver of light under the door of David's office, I'm guessing everyone else is settled down in their beds.

Closing the front door behind me and shucking off my shoes, I say nothing as I pass by Tate and start up the stairs. He says nothing as he follows me.

We've barely made it into my room when, flicking on the light, he grabs my shoulder from behind and whirls me to face him.

He shuts us in with a kick to my door, and then his hand moves from my shoulder to grip the back of my neck while his other hand seizes mine. Before I even have chance to suck in a breath, his lips crash into my lips, his tongue invading my mouth. The excessive pressure is bruising but holy *shit*...

He edges me backwards, toward my bed.

"Tate." I break the contact, pulling my head back. I need air. I need answers. "What...?" My eyes are closed. I snap them open to find him mere millimetres from my face, studying me. A tear – a very real and very obvious tear – rolls unchecked down his cheek. I pull back further, straining against his hold. "What?"

"I'm sorry. I'm so sorry. But I can't lose you, Mikey. I can't. I'm sorry."

It's in defiance of every physical impulse in my body that craves him – fiercely craves him – to force my hand to release his and work up in between us, gripping his wrist and tugging him free of my neck. "You're not...gay? You told me. You said you're not gay?"

Stroking his hands around to bracket my face instead, he shakes his head, "I said I wouldn't fuck my best friend. Shit. Wouldn't fuck things up with my best friend, that's what I meant. But...but forget that. I have fucked up. Please, forget everything I've said to you since you got back." He's breathing heavily. Another tear escapes and I follow its path, fascinated. "And let me try to explain all the shit I haven't... everything I should have said but didn't. Please?"

I stagger two steps back, moving out of his touch. Feeling the bed, solid against my legs, I drop down on to it. I suck in my lips, savouring the taste of him still on them, and succumb to the tidal wave of confusion threatening to crush me. "I don't...I don't understand."

"It's not that I don't trust you," he says, still standing, fixed on me, his arms dropped limp by his sides. "I shouldn't have said that. It was a fucking ass-hat stupid thing to say. But..." His words appear to clog in his throat and I watch his Adam's apple jump as he swallows before continuing, "I push people away, Mikey, it's all I know how to do now. I don't want anyone catching me out. Don't want their pity or their special treatment. And no-one'll guess if they don't care enough to try, right? Was working well for me. Really well. Until you."

"You've pushed me away too. Just like everybody else."

"Yeah," He nods. "I've tried. Fuck me, I've tried."

"Because pity scares you," I surmise, my frown hurting my face.

"You showing up really... *really* fucked me over. I resented the way you looked at me, Mikey; how badly you made me want to go back to who I was, knowing I never could. That me...he's long gone. I'd accepted that. Took just one look from you and, shit, it hurt. Telling you, though... Seeing that look change – seeing you feel sorry for me, consider me *less*..." He closes his eyes as he drags in a steadying breath, reopening them on his exhale, "it's happened. You're doing it now. I can't stand it."

Nope! Not even. It's not possible for anything but utter bewilderment to be showing through in my expression right now. "So you thought it better to make me hate you?" Bowing my head into my hands, I scrub in an effort to clear away all the damning creases from my face. "Adele, though. You let her in. She knows."

His voice cracks, "Mikey, I can't see what you're saying."

My head jolts free of my hands only to discover my vision's become too fuzzy to properly focus on him. What place does pity have when I've barely even begun to unravel the true motivations behind his behaviour? My entire day has been built around keeping those on lockdown. "Why Adele and not me?"

"Wasn't given a choice with Adele." He flexes his jaw and I catch on his hands fisting at his sides. "She was there when it happened, she's been there all the way through."

I wince, and the responding wince from him has me regretting the slip. "How, err, how did it... When?"

"I'll get to that. I'll explain everything, *everything*, I swear," he says. "Just let me..." His pleading eyes bordering on confrontational, he startles me by falling to his knees between my legs, taking both my hands in his. "I was wrong. I can't have you hate me. I probably deserve you to but, fuck, please. Don't."

Staring down at our joined hands, I give all my energy over to ensuring I continue to breath in and out.

"Say something," he begs after a couple of minutes, my stretching silence blasting his attempt at considerate patience. His eyes are on my mouth and he squeezes my hands. "Anything."

"Is it hard?" I manage after a few more beats. "Lip reading?"

His mouth ticks up on one side, his knitted brow smoothing out a fraction, like he's taking my question as a significant first step toward a reprieve. I'm not sure that it is. I'm not sure he's even owed a reprieve; he's reasoned his behaviour to me. How am I supposed to react to this? I just... I need more time. I need more talk. And I need to figure out what the hell else is happening here tonight between us. *Curse my battered brain!*

"I'm getting better at it all the time," he says. "Thanks to John. He's, like, my mentor and then some. He's fucking incredible. But, yeah, it takes a shit-tonne of work. It's not just about the lips either. It's body language, facial expressions... I've got to pick up on all the – the non-verbal clues. Some people are easier to read than others. And the better I know them helps, too. Still, concentrating on any more than one at a time, I struggle."

I nod. "So...you avoid. Use the headphones for cover."

"There's just too much risk. Of making a fool of myself. I don't want people finding me out, treating me like a charity case, but I... I don't want to be looked at as an idiot either. Ignorant loner weirdo," he presses his lips, his brow pinching, "that sits better with me; it's safe. Keeps me in control, you know?"

I'm still nodding, my frown still hurting. "Sign language?"

"Yep." He starts nodding along with me. Letting me go, his hands start to move through the air, touching his face, his body, each other, as he elaborates, "not great. John insists I learn, and Dad makes me use it at home. Adele likes it. She's better than me." Gaze flitting from mine, I get the distinct impression he's uncomfortable with the demonstration, embarrassed even.

He seems skilled enough at it to my untrained eye. Looks impressive. Complicated. *A whole other language he and Adele know, and I don't.* That thought comes with a nasty stab of guilt.

A double thumbs-up is my little-thought-through reaction. He takes it in with a raised brow and I shrug, my hands disappearing between my thighs.

"Who else knows?"

He sucks in his bottom lip, deliberating a moment, his teeth scraping over it on release, and my insides react unreasonably. "Adele's dad knows. It was Mum told him. And Uncle Stevie, though he lives in Bath so...no big deal there. She's told her therapist too. Your, uh – your Sophie." He dips his head, wincing. "Thanks to Meg."

Nudging his foot with mine, I nod to let him know I'm aware of that one.

"Dad had words with her for that. And then she and Sophie swore themselves into a secrecy pact. Think it may have involved pinkies." He manages a strained smile. "Principal Carston – we had to tell him when I decided on returning to school. Mr Garrimay, when I started sixth form. Had to come clean with Mrs Callows after losing my shit in Psych. Cos she was threatening to kick me off the course."

I nod again. Cos, now that he's named them, and now that I know his truth, half a dozen odd incidents and interactions in school come to mind, suddenly making a whole lot more sense.

I give him a minute to add to the list, but he offers none further.

An extremely select few then, all entrusted with his secret on a strict need-to-know basis.

Quite the elite group I've become a part of, thrust into uninvited.

"So," I attempt to clear the lump from my throat, but it doesn't budge. "How?"

Sighing, Tate pushes to his feet and settles on my bed beside me. He nudges my knee with his. It takes a moment to register that he's needing me to angle myself around to him. I'm so totally fumbling this.

"Meningitis," he starts simply – brutally – once I've adjusted my position. "Wasn't caught quick enough."

He's struck me completely off-guard. Again.

"Mum and Dad were away with Megan for the weekend. In the caravan. I thought I'd just come down with a – a bad bug. Or man-flu. Didn't want to worry them." Pressing two fingers to his temple, his mouth twists crookedly down. "But I plummeted fast. Adele found me, I was out cold. Doctors said another hour more, I... I'd have been a goner. They thought I'd be severely brain damaged; told me I should consider myself lucky to have only lost my hearing."

"And the... the epilepsy?" I slice clumsily into his pause.

"You don't need to start exaggerating your mouth movements, Mikey," he chides me gently, and I press my lips tight, flashing a fierce apology with my eyes. "Yeah, the epilepsy was another of its gifts. Four and a half weeks I was in hospital, recovering from the meningitis. Made it out for barely two days before I'm whisked back in, having a – a, uh, *status epilepticus;* one motherfucking almighty seizure that I, again, wasn't expected to... Cos, fuck, I hadn't made Mum and Dad suffer enough already. Stuck in hospital a further three weeks. Lots more tests. Lots more drugs."

His tears have ceased. Gaze unrelentingly intense, he's talking, composed, in a careful tone bare of emotional inflection and it's shredding me.

I remember Laura breaking into pieces at my bedside, after the car crash, clutching my hand and sending out frantic prayers for her unconscious boy to whoever's ears might be listening. I remember Graham losing it with the nursing staff when he was told visitation was over and he'd have to leave for the night, his furious, terrified bellowing causing me to curl up and hide beneath the sheets. My heart's breaking to think of them being put through agony such as that all over again. They nearly lost him, twice more. *I* nearly lost him, and I knew nothing about it; close on 400 miles away, utterly oblivious.

The strain of holding myself together has me trembling. I run my eyes over his face, soaking in his beautiful features, consumed by a scarily excessive appreciation that I can, and I reach to take his hand again.

He smiles at me. I think he means for it to be reassuring – placating. But it feels misplaced, kinda inappropriate, and for perhaps the first time ever, I don't have the automatic inclination to return it. Instead, I draw his hand into my lap and he laces his fingers through mine, his smile fading.

"Laura, your Dad...?" I break off.

Something changes in him. Not so much visibly, but a sudden tension spreads through me from him. "Dad's great, he's been a rock. Much a hardass as ever but he... I need that; he's pulled me through the worst of it. Fought to get me the best help. Fought to make me take it. If not for him, things would be...very different." He bites down on his bottom lip and shrugs.

I wait. But not for long. "Tate?" There's no keeping the quiver from my voice. I don't even put the effort in to try.

His clasp on my hand tightens and then slackens but doesn't withdraw. "Mum... spiralled, blaming herself. Blaming Dad. It got messy." He starts drawing small circles with his thumb over mine. His obvious reluctance to go on has me clenched up taut. "Seeing the changes in me killed her. I could barely communicate... Hadn't only lost my hearing, my brain and mouth forgot how to work together. No one could understand me. I gave up trying. Couldn't skate anymore – balance all shot to shit. Couldn't even fucking walk straight. Migraines. Seizures almost every other day and the medication making me ill. First, she got crazy-obsessed with 'fixing' me. So many doctors and specialists and tests. Found no magical cures, though, and she sank. She was as ready to accept my life was over as I was."

And his blows keep on coming, devastating.

"Then she decided I should be sent to a special school. Insisted I had to give up everything here to start a new life... a life built entirely around my impairment. Dad sided with me, told her no. Said school," he pauses and gives his head a little shake. "He said as long as my school work didn't – didn't suffer, it was my call to make.

"And that was the final straw. Things hadn't been great between them for a while. Ever since Mum put pay to the... New Zealand move really. But there was no working through it for them this time. They were at each other constantly. Mum moved out last year, with Megan. I stayed with Dad. They have their own flat three streets over from us.

"For the best, I think. Me and Dad are muddling our way through things. We're alright. And Mum's actually doing really... really well for herself. Got a job in a bank, worked up to assistant manager. She's getting back on an even keel, and we're slowly fixing things up. But we've..." He trails off as I fight to gasp in a breath. It's only when his fingers wiggle against mine, I register the painful rigidity of my grip. "Oh, Mikey, shit! I'm sorry."

I ease my hold off, one finger at a time, and shake my head. Bringing up my free hand, I scour it over my wet face. My throat's too clogged, and my chest too damaged, for me to quieten my sobs.

His thumb starts up again in its soft stroke of mine. Then I feel the fingers of his other hand settle on the back of my neck, carding through my hair. I stiffen when, laying on gentle pressure, he attempts to manoeuvre my head in to him. I don't know why I do that. Feeling my resistance, he immediately lets up and I sense the cutting sting of rejection I've caused. I lower my own head onto him, pressing my face against his chest. He sighs, his arm tightening around my back as he moves our joined hands into his lap.

"Do you still want me, Mikey?" His whisper tickles my ear.

31

TOASTY

*T*he question buzzes through me, touching every single part of me, filling places I hadn't known were empty. I can't find the words for an answer. But words are pointless anyway, wrapped up in him as I am, my face hidden. A motion is all I need; one simple, well-rehearsed motion. Can't find that either though. Everything feels too *much*.

So completely screwed up, this scene in which I've found myself.

Here's Tate. The one who's almost died. The one left with life-altering damage. The one with the broken family, caught between warring parents. The one who suffers daily, protecting his secrets. He's laid himself bare to me, reopened his wounds and let me probe inside of them.

And yet here I am, the one demanding comfort.

Jeezus! What the hell is freaking wrong with me?

Hurt is etched clear on his face as I extricate myself from him. His eyes flash wide as I tug on his shirt and then push myself up the bed. My nerves climb toward unbearable, placing my head down on my pillow and stretching out, waiting for him to settle beside me.

I know what I'm wanting to do, here. But this all seems so much harder, premeditated.

Locking my eyes on his, I lift my hand from the pillow between our faces and touch a tentative fingertip to his jaw, tracing its curve. His lips creep into a small half-smile. I fix on them, set to thrumming as they kick up further.

Hell yeah, I still want you. I've never wanted anything even near as bad my entire life. My heart flutters in glorious terror.

I thread my fingers through his hair and move in slow, he doesn't back off. My first kiss brushes his lips, featherlight. But that's not enough of an answer for him, he chases me as I draw away. I revel in the pulse-quickening thrill of his mouth, hovering so close to mine, daring me to dismiss my caution. And then I do.

A gratifying moan slips free of him as my second kiss lands without restraint, and a fire ignites beneath my skin. It takes no force to part his lips. Our teeth clash just once before his tongue greets mine and coaxes it into play.

There's a wild urgency to this kiss – our first delved in to with mutual eagerness. My chaotic thoughts dissolving in the heat of it, I surrender every last care. Becoming nothing but *feeling*, primitive and aggressive, I'm fuelled by only the need to be closer to him.

As if of one mind, Tate pushes himself flush against me, his arm a steel band around my back, locking me to him. I tangle my legs with his as my fingers claw into his hair, my hand allowing his head no give for retreat.

My tongue sweeping his, he rocks into me. I feel his arousal. Our heartbeats pound to the same desperate rhythm, and it's like I'm a clock, my time-keeping before this point always off – running slow – and now I'm righted.

But... Sweet. Scorching. Jeezus!

"Getting too close to the edge," I warn him, speaking breathlessly into the kiss.

He disconnects, putting a sliver of space between our faces, and every cell in my body laments my disturbance, screaming for him to close it up again.

We stare at each other in charged silence, a frown creasing his brow. "You okay?" He asks, his voice hoarse and his breath hot on my skin.

Sucking in air so fast that my lungs begin to burn, I manage a whimper. Then I nod vigorously, doubting the likelihood of him reading whimper.

Still, his lips don't return to mine. Instead, he does a thing with his smile that makes my heart spasm before he lowers his mouth to my throat. "Slow this down, perhaps," he murmurs between soft, warm touches along my collarbone.

Biting hard into my swollen lip, I arch my neck to ease his access.

I'M SHAKEN awake from *the* most pleasurable slumber to discover that the gorgeous green eyes from my dream crossed over with me into reality. The pulsing rush of surprise suggests I'd kinda expected him to be gone.

My room's still brightly lit. Outside, dawn's yet to crack the sky. We remain fully clothed on my bed, but we've found our way beneath the duvet.

Tate smiles at me, his head close enough to mine for his cheek to brush the little finger of my hand resting on the pillow between us. No action's required of me in returning the smile, one already stretches my lips.

"Hey," he says.

"Hey." I'm acutely aware of his arm draped over my waist, his hand on the small of my back.

"I don't want to go home."

"Then don't." Feeling bold, I lean in and press my lips to his three firm, teasing times before pulling back.

"Fuck!" He growls, a deep sound that does awesome things to my insides. I feel his fingers claw the duvet at my back. "But I have to. Dad'll go ape-shit if he – if he doesn't see me before school."

I sigh. And then he takes his turn, swooping in on me to steal a kiss. His teeth nip my bottom lip, rocketing a shiver down my spine to the tips of my toes, before he draws away.

His smile widens to a self-satisfied grin. "A few hours, and I'll call for you, okay?"

"Nooo," I whine, and he chuckles.

"Dunno how I'll cope the full school day," I say after a few blissful minutes of zero movement from either of us. "Acting like nothing's going on between us."

His expression shades to a frown. "What?"

At first, I assume he's missed what I said, and I'm about ready to repeat myself, but then he breaks our eye contact. Throwing off the duvet, he pushes up to sit and I catch the muscle jump in his tensed jaw.

Oh.

"Sorry, that was... a dumb thing to say," I start hesitantly, more question than statement, as I scrabble up beside him, "I just thought... see, with you being such a private pers..."

"Most the school already knows you're gay, Mikey. Shit, most the school already thinks something's going on between us." Turning his head around to me, I realise he definitely couldn't have caught any of that stammered drivel he's just interrupted. "Why should we hide it?" His eyes race over me and he looks disconcertingly unsure of himself. I don't like it at all. "You called me on my bullshit, nailed me. I'm not... *so* fucking not okay with so fucking much of who I am. But you, *you*... I don't want us to be another thing I have to – to pretend to the world isn't there. Please? Cos you're the one thing I've got going I'm fucking beyond okay with."

Stunned into a moments stillness, I let his words soak in. Then, compelled by giddy elation, I pounce on him, downing us both to the pillow as my arms encircle his neck in a stranglehold. And, fortunately, that reaction seems to be answer enough for him.

He laughs, his uncertainty dropping away. Angling himself to his side and grabbing my hips, he pulls me in closer. Then he sets me to tingling with a tongue flick and soft nibble to my earlobe. "Not ashamed of being with me?"

I lean my head back just enough so he can see me shake it. In earnest.

For almost ten more perfect minutes, Tate lets me keep him. He teases me with gentle kisses and caresses while we lie wrapped up in each other, not speaking. There's no splinter of a place spared anywhere within, between or around us for our real-world crap; we're on total lockdown. Toasty warm and spectacularly contented, I feel myself start to drift.

Then I'm toppled to the floor with an "oomph", a thud and him half on top of me. He laughs ruthlessly as I flail in the shock.

"Dickhead!" I vent my spurt of indignation with a slap to his arm.

"Just a few short hours, Mikey, I'll be back." The cruel jerk makes little effort to reign in his amusement, clambering free of me.

Once on his feet, he holds out his hand. "Come on, see me out."

When I return to my bed after watching him from the doorstep until gone from view, however, undressed and settled in under the duvet, staring through the darkness at the empty space beside me, my brain wastes no time checking back in. Its several tonnes of baggage chases sleep far, far away from me for the remainder of the night; whole lot of processing to be done.

I've been up, shower-fresh and dressed for the longest two hours of my life when Tate finally comes back for me.

"Not changed your mind, then?" He asks in greeting, with a grin so brilliant it renders me a slosh puddle on the hallway floor.

Stood on the doorstep, tall and lean, his dark hair in shiny-clean disarray, his jeans marked up in black etchings, trainers scuffed and thick coat a faded black, he's regarding me with as much openly affectionate good humour in his eyes as on his mouth, and I swear he hasn't ever looked more goddamn perfect.

The day is icy cold, a layer of glittering frost making the world look deceptively beautiful and the ground dangerous to walk.

Little is said as we dawdle our slow way toward YCS. And I'm absolutely, thoroughly okay with that. Words feel an unmanageable burden – hell, putting one foot in front of the other is proving almost too much – when it's taking such a stupendous whack of my concentration keeping a total freak-out stifled. *A kiss the very moment we turned from view of the house, and now he's clutching my hand so tight.* This shift between us, it's...

Surreal.

Magnificent.

Freaking terrifying!

He's squeezing my fingers alongside flashing me these looks that my brain's translating in his voice, loud and clear, as *'Calm the fuck down, will you, we're good,'* so I'm blatantly not doing too well with holding it in.

The journey takes us twice as long as it usually does, and yet, at the same time, passes far swifter than I'd hoped for it to.

"What a wonderous sight to behold first thing." Adele intrudes on us at the bench outside of the school gates, clapping her gloved hands like a performing seal. The bite of the air has drawn colour to her cheeks and the tip of her nose, and a fraudulent grin contorts her mouth. "So super, duper adorbs!"

Tate doesn't let me unlace my fingers from his. "And it's good to see you, too," he says, smirking up at her.

"Seriously, though, boys. Don't feel like you owe me anything – no thanks, and certainly no apology. Just seeing this beautiful disaster, here, I foolishly helped you into, it's more than enough."

I'm learning fast: I tap my thumb against Tate's, drawing his attention back to me before I speak. "If we ignore her, what are the chances she'll go away?"

Her face takes a foul turn. "My ears work just fine, turd weasel," she fires at me, folding her arms. "And no, not even a slim chance. If this thing, here," a finger peeks out from the crook of her elbow and wags between Tate and me, "is actually happening, you best start playing friendly cos I'm not going anywhere."

Pressing his palm closer to mine, he inclines his head toward her and concedes, "point." And I find myself musing on just how much of her point he could actually have caught. It's too huge of a thing to properly wrap my head around still: What it must be like for him, living his life on constant mute.

I muted the television this morning, tried to follow the newsreader's report using visual cues alone. My head was throbbing within five minutes, and I made out only maybe one word in every ten.

Leaning in and blocking Adele with a hand-shield, I mouth for him alone, "surely it's worth a try, though, right?"

The mare really does have quite the knack for making me feel foolish, and this time it's achieved with the dismissive slide of her eyes and the dance of her hands. Following a keen scan around us, she launches into a complex sequence of sign, her movements fluid and fast. Skilled. I catch none of it, even with her mouth shaping words alongside, and her knowing smirk makes plain this pleases her immensely.

It's a flagrant display of her superior understanding of him; an illustration of the bond that sets them apart.

It has the desired effect.

But Tate doesn't indulge her with a signed response. Instead, brushing his shoulder against mine and rolling his eyes, he translates for me. "She says her tolerance is a fragile thing, and she'd take no less pleasure in your bloodshed, just cos we're together."

"Right. Well..." I let my lip curl to insinuate an appropriately scathing retort to that.

Arching a wry brow, she puts her hands into motion again.

And I am, again, granted Tate's unabridged translation. "It'll be your razor-sharp wit that ends you."

Slitting my eyes as Adele's twisted little mind contemplates a signed insult that he wouldn't be so ready to interpret for me, I swear a promise to myself to get BSL savvy, fast. I'll learn in secret.

Letting Adele fall into a trap of her own making and then burying her in it, that'll be exquisitely satisfying.

"Enough," Tate mildly chides, stilling Adele's eager hands. But then his gaze flicks significantly to me and my mouth clamps shut, comeback trapped inside.

"Pshhht." She scoffs, reluctantly lowering her arms and re-crossing them over her chest. "Moving anytime soon? Bell's about to ring."

Tate and I don't have form room together. After this, I won't see him until second period. I'm not ready for us to part quite yet. A quick glance to him satisfies me neither is he. We both shake our heads.

"You go on in," Tate nods at the gates. "We'll follow after in a bit."

"Already finding you insufferable!" She flips her hands up high, slapping them crisply down on her thighs. "Hope you aren't expecting today to go smoothly, boys." Turning and starting away, she throws back for, what slowly dawns on me, my benefit only: "Really looking forward to hearing just how unsmoothly this all goes at lunchtime."

32

OH, MY HERO! EXCEPT, NOT SO MUCH

'Unsmoothly' is a rather apt description of how the day pans out. A truth that Adele appears to find surprisingly little delight in. Every time our paths have crossed throughout the day – at break, at lunch, in the corridors – she's seemed as disheartened by our reception as I am.

Adamant though I am to follow Tate's lead in blanking out the judge-y looks sent our way, I hit the limit on striking clear the comments accompanying those looks. Try as I might, I can't not hear them. Nor can I let them go. Cos, mostly, they're disparaging of Tate. Brutally so. They wheedle their way deep inside me, curdling my stomach.

Tate wants me the way I want him. He's proud of that. He's embracing that, completely and absolutely. I should be revelling in it. I should be on a high and gloating.

Instead, the opinions of others who mostly don't even matter have me feeling like I ought to be ashamed, like I'm mental for choosing him, like we're doing something *wrong*.

Alex has returned to the stabbing glares and sneers, finding great amusement in the day's upsurge of Tate bashing. And Lyndsay... well, seems this abrupt development in mine and Tate's relationship has her backtracking our road to reconciliation, all the way back to the point of determined non-acknowledgement of me.

Sure, it's not entirely accurate to claim the whole school population has viciously trampled us down. We have garnered some measure of support. Steph, for example, has practically exploded with excitement every single time she's seen us together, cooing proudly, granting herself full credit for the change in our status. And Callum took us in with no more than a blink of his eye, his attitude toward me unchanged and his reception of Tate perhaps warming a cautious fraction. In all honesty, there's perhaps been close to as many comments of encouragement (or the non-reaction of indifference – my personal favourite) as there has those of a negative nature.

But it's disturbing how much heavier the crap stuff weighs.

Several times, I've been caught out with a hurt look trying to pull away from Tate in the face of disapproving attention.

Enough times, apparently, that when we meet up at the school gates following the blessed final bell, he holds back on a move for connection. "It'll get easier, you know?" He says, drawing to a halt in front of me, his hands clenched at his sides and his smile hardly there.

I can't believe he's as ignorant of the things said about him as he makes out. He doesn't hear the words and he chooses not to read them, fair enough, but there's sure as hell no subtlety in their transmission.

I hate it. I hate how thorough he's been in socially destroying himself. And I hate that, this quickly, I'm allowing my elation to be corrupted because of it.

Grabbing his hand and coaxing his fingers loose to wrap around mine, I nod. It's the first time today, I realise, I've initiated the contact and I'm rewarded with an instant disintegration of his rigidity, his smile notching up to obvious. "Sorry," I say, gently tugging him in closer.

My entire body reacts with enthusiasm when he lifts our hands to press a kiss to mine. He passes a slow, questioning gaze over me.

Securing myself to his side, our arms flush, I resolutely don't scan around me as I start us walking.

School's over for the day. Our first step has been taken and, yeah, it was hard but the first always is. I've got time to repair and strengthen my armour for tomorrow, I'll be better prepared and far less easily beaten.

I bump my shoulder against his arm so he turns and looks at me.

His frown breaks smoothly into a crooked grin and the tip of his tongue peeks out, running over his top lip. My breath catches. "We've both had worse days, Mikey," he says when it becomes apparent I have no intention of speaking.

There's nothing I want to say, I simply crave his attention. Because there's something crazy-addictive in the new way he has of looking at me. And because I need the blast of reassurance it's still holding strong.

It is.

Tonight, after my shift at the bistro, Tate's meeting me and we're going to his. Graham'll be at work, not due home until gone midnight, and so we'll have this time for just me and him, alone in his room, with no one to ruin it. And it'll be just as amazing as last night at mine. More so, in fact, because we need waste none of the evening on misunderstandings and difficult talk and tears. My pulse is set to thundering at the sheer thought of...

"OI! LADIES!"

We've made it only around a third of the way along the drive from the gates when the devil decides he's not quite through with us yet, crashing me callously back to earth.

Quite literally.

I'm yanked free of Tate and thrown down on the road with bone-shuddering force.

Gary Tinwell's leering moon-face looms in over me. "Caused a mighty stir in school today, Michaela, flaunting your pervy filth." Grabbing the neck of my coat (and some flesh along with it), he jerks me up toward him before I even get chance to gasp a breath. "What made you think anyone wanted to see that?"

With a sudden, sharp crack, my cheek burns, and my barely-recovered nose is set to throbbing. I taste the metallic tang of blood in my mouth.

It's as I'm attempting a hurried inventory of my mouth with my tongue that I become aware I'm choking. Then I notice Tate's arm around Gary's neck, straining him back. Snapping to my senses, I start scrabbling for freedom, wrestling my hands up from my sides to claw at the beefy ones strangling me with my coat collar.

But Gary releases me of his own accord, rounding on Tate as I crash back to the tarmac. "You've had your free shot at me, psycho! You don't get another one."

"Go!" Tate orders me right before Gary slams him in the chest, sending him stumbling a few steps back.

I feel bile rise up my throat, clogging it, hindering my attempt to get air into my desperate lungs, as I watch with horror from the ground.

"Vile. Fudge. Packer." Gary's on him again before he's recovered himself, launching him clear over the curb into the trunk of a tree.

I force myself into action, hastily and clumsily struggling up.

But before I can manage to get my feet under me, someone else is there, powering into Gary. The first fist, loosed at his head, barely grazes over his jaw as he's jostled by the surprise attack. But the second lands square on target, a jab to the kidney that slams a grunt out of him.

"Fucking scum!" The newcomer snarls in a raspy voice I discover has scratched its own permanent place in my brain.

"Enough, Craig!" Alex then appears out of nowhere, stepping around a stunned Gary to his brother's side. "Leave it! Come on!"

"The fuck, Lawton?" Gary staggers free of Craig, dodging his third blow and knocking into Alex. Alex lurches himself clear.

Quick to recover, Gary widens his stance and rolls his shoulders, knuckles cracking. "You're paying for that."

Sounds around me begin to filter through to my consciousness. Shouts and screams. Pounding feet. Taunts come from Gary's henchmen, Ben and Wayne, who I spot hovering behind Craig, exerting their intimidating presence a nice, safe distance away from the action.

Tate's on his feet, starting toward me, and I resume the effort of picking myself up.

"Your lip's bleeding. Let's go." He darts only one glance toward Gary and our valiant saviour, Craig, immediately attempting to drag me on along the drive.

I resist.

"Think you're such the big man, huh?" Craig's shoving himself into Gary, his face twisted in a way that – in a fair world – should have him looking deranged.

Gary's not budging, and he barks out a laugh. "Look at me, Queer!" A thrust of his belly knocks Craig stumbling back a half-step. "I am the fucking big man."

Alex is getting nowhere in trying to prise the two apart. Amidst the on-lookers, my eyes find Lyndsay, Callum at her back. He's watching her with concern as she watches the ruckus. She looks as dazed as I feel, and I think she may be crying.

Tate lets go of me. "Please, Mikey?"

"Go on, Craig! Pummel the smarmy bellend!" I hear Steph's voice rise easily over the commotion before I see her standing with Ashleigh a few heads to Lyndsay's right, looking poised to pounce into the fray at a moment's notice.

Craig swings his fist again but Gary's ready for it this time. Quick to move, the strike fails to make contact. Securing a vice grip on Craig's throat, his other hand remaining clamped around Craig's forearm, he spits (yes, actually spits in the guy's face). "Careful, now, Lawton. Or I'll be forced to mess up that pretty, pretty face of yours far worse."

"Lay off him!" Alex warns in a tone one disturbing octave closer to a plea. "Craig, mate, this is crazy."

"No." Craig angles his body to land a klutzy elbow thrust to Gary's much-padded gut. "He's been getting away with his narrow-minded bull-shit for way too long."

"You are one stupid bastard," Gary sneers, leaning in close. "We both know what this is really about, right?" Then, his hand moving from throat to jaw, he forces Craig's head to turn as his does and both sets of eyes fix on us. A hefty kick-start to my system, my feet become all too eager to bolt.

Tate's hooked my arm again and is hauling me on before I've even fully turned myself about.

Gary's detestable voice pursues us: "Your boy, there, has himself a new play-thing, so why be his champion now, eh? Look at the pair of them flee, not giving you a second thought. His cock's not yours to suck anymore, dude."

Those words hit me harder than the blow to my jaw.

My step would falter if Tate would let it. His pull is insistent.

"It's true, then? You were with him?"

He doesn't respond. Doesn't glance back at me. Doesn't even ease up his long strides until we reach the end of the drive, burnt-orange and blue school welcome sign beside us. My heart continues sprinting and my breathing's still coming in irregular gulps. But, by this point, my soaring anxiety has crashed through to frustration.

I snatch my arm from his.

He finally stops and turns to me, his gaze zeroing in on my lip, brow pinching tight. "A little further, Mikey, okay? Just around to the church."

"There's something went on between you two," my voice cracks and I swallow, "isn't there?"

His frown deepens. "What?"

"Craig, Tate. You and Craig. Just tell me. Please."

I don't like how his face changes as he shakes his head, an expression betraying a whole host of things I can't even begin to interpret, and it occurs to me in a wretched too-late flash that, of course, he'll be oblivious of Gary's parting taunt. My reaction to it, too. A shaming unease gnaws through my frustration.

But, then... he saw Craig storm to his rescue as well as I did. That act alone was telling enough. So I stand my ground and wait.

He stares at me a moment longer before cutting his gaze away, looking back along the drive. The fight's ended, it would seem, and the loitering spectators are now trickling into view, heading toward us. My heart rate picks up further. I strain my eyes, scanning for a face I recognise, trying to get a read on how it all went down.

"Come on," Tate says, reclaiming my attention but not my hand as he starts away from me. "Church."

My nails gouge into my palms.

He doesn't glance back as he crosses the road, and it's only as he disappears into the alley that I make a start after him.

Settled down on the church's low perimeter wall, he pats the stone beside him. I remain standing.

"Mikey," he huffs out on a sigh, running his eyes over me. "Fuck sake."

Folding my arms over my chest, my tongue slips out to cover the already-caking split in my lip as his gaze comes to rest on it.

Yeah, okay, I'm being deliberately difficult. I'm getting annoyed at myself for it. But not enough so that I'm able to snap free of it.

"I don't know what you want me to tell you here."

He does. I hold my silence.

"Why's it matter?"

"Because," I shrug. "Reasons."

"Reasons?" He echoes. Jaw tightening as I nod, his reluctance is an admission in itself.

"Wasn't even anything serious, okay?" Tate gives in with another heavy sigh, shaking his head and standing. "And no one was ever meant to know. Just two confused kids trying to figure themselves out." His voice is so low, I'm statue-still and barely breathing in my efforts to hear him. Pressing his lips, he swallows and continues on a fraction louder, "we messed around awhile, that's all it was."

I hoped for a denial but hadn't expected one. Not really. And there it is: Thor and Tate, all tongues and hands and thrusts, the image cements itself in the forefront of my mind.

Wrapping my arms tighter around myself, I drop my eyes to his scuffed-up trainers as I feel a disconcerting prickle start up behind them.

"Long done with. Over. History. No more to it, honestly." He steps in to me, his hand lifting and settling on my cheek. "Okay?"

His touch is the gentlest slap back to my senses I've ever been issued. My skin blazes beneath his hand, the heat swiftly spreading over the whole of me, and I melt in it.

I mean, jeezus, what the actual...am I even for freaking real right now?

He's told me only what I've pushed him to. And the inevitable result?

Duh! I absolutely don't feel better for hearing it.

Never to be outdone, my brain is clearly hell-bent on shoving Gary Tinwell down from the Worst Enemy pedestal to reclaim that place as its own. And, damn me to the fiery pit, I'm vigorously and moronically supporting it.

Enough!

I most assuredly will not give voice to its plea for more details. Shutting that right down.

It's my face his hand is pressed against – *mine*; my cheekbone his thumb's caressing.

And, yeah, Tate may well have been rescued from Gary by Craig, but, really, so what? That only came about because he'd first launched himself to mine. *Not without rough consequence either.*

Raising my gaze from his feet, I take my belated turn performing a thorough scan of him. "Are you okay?"

Ain't nothing endearing about a petulant and totally irrational showcasing of insecurity but, when I eventually draw my eyes up to meet his, I find no hint of the exasperated annoyance I feel I probably deserve in them.

Brow quirking up, a grin cracks his grave face and he snorts. His hand snakes around the back of my neck, pulling me in to him. "You can be such hard work sometimes!"

I bury my face into his chest, breathing him in as my arms encircle his waist, and thrill at the reactive kick to his heartbeat. "I know."

33

BETTER BY FAR YOU SHOULD FORGET AND SMILE...

"*Ee*, we got up to such things back then, Ev, didn't we? So fresh-faced and foolish."

I slam to a halt just inside the front door, my half-shirked-off coat dropping the rest of the way to the floor.

I'd know that voice anywhere.

But, oh, my ears must surely be deceiving me.

"And look at this un. Yer dress there, my goodness!"

No way!

I feel my hard-earned good humour of the past half hour start to waver. Today is a day just too damn full of surprises.

"We fell out over that bloody dress." I hear Gran pipe up with a light chuckle, and it rekindles the spark of a smile to my lips; her tone is that of a gran in control.

It's with careful, cautious steps I move toward the kitchen, edging open the door like I've reason to be creeping.

"So pig-headed, ye were."

I peer in. And, whoa, yep. There she is.

Seated beside Gran at the kitchen table, a big cardboard box (*the* box, I notice – the one my help had been shunned in retrieving; the catalyst of Gran's fall) open on it between them, her head's bowed over the mess of papers and pictures spread haphazardly around.

I stare a long moment, rooted, before her blue eyes lift and catch on me. Their corners crinkle as her pink stained lips stretch into a wide smile, and I suspect she's been aware of my presence all along. "What ye hoverin' there for, pet? Come on in and tell me all about yer day at school, eh?"

"Suzy?" I squeak. I clear my throat. "What...?"

"Took your time getting home today," Mel's crisp voice snaps my attention over to the sink. She's turned from it, wiping her hands on a tea towel, to eye me with her typical haughty disdain, poorly disguised by a tight smile. "We expected you in over an hour ago. You need to learn to answer your phone."

Ignoring her, I return my focus to Gran and Suzy, pushing the door wide. Gran pulls out the chair on her free side and pats the seat, grinning at me. I start across the room toward them.

"Oh, now, leave the lad be, Melissa!" Suzy chides in my defence, alleviating all sting from her words with a melodic titter. She winks at me, "what ye been up to then, young un? Mischief with yer new pals? Or you been servin' out a detention for some earlier trouble makin'?"

"No mischief. No detention," I reply succinctly with a dismissive shrug, dropping into the chair on Gran's left.

I've no desire to further explain myself. Time well spent, those few extra precious minutes Tate and I stole alone together at the den. David's call was an unwelcome intrusion, and so I'd turned my phone off.

"That call could have been important, Mikey," Mel persists. She flashes a significant look Gran's way before continuing, "you need to be reachable at all times."

Hitting her intended mark square on, I duck my head in an effort to hide my wince. But, then – who's she trying to kid – as if I'd be spared even a moment's thought should a real emergency occur! Most likely, should I to be told of it at all, it'd be only once all urgency was done with.

"What's all this then?" I ask Gran, motioning at the spread and angling my back to Mel.

"Takin' a bit trip down memory lane," Suzy answers for her. "Ain't we, Ev?"

Mel huffs, tossing the tea towel down on the bench. "Sophie's being a little too quiet, best go check on her," she says with a bright smile I'm not fooled by. "Won't be a mo."

"Here," Gran rifles through the small pile of pictures in front of her and plucks one out. "Take a gander at this un!"

"So what's this about?" I turn on Suzy the minute Mel's swanned from the room. "Why're you here?"

"Michael Spencer Alston!" Gran barks, slapping the photo back down on the table and toppling the stack. "Since when do ye address Suzy in that tone?"

"Sorry. I'm sorry," I relent, forcing a smile for Gran. Her frown dissolves. "Sorry Suzy. Just... it's a surprise, you know? To what do we owe the pleasure?"

Reaching past Gran, Suzy pats my hand. "Mardy little sod that ye are, I know ye've missed me."

Things weren't left on the best of terms between us, and since leaving Newcastle, our communication over the phone has basically been limited to 'I'll just get Gran for you'. But, yeah, I have to concede it's a pretty pointless grudge I'm holding, and I've held it far too long. I have missed her; I needn't deny being happy to see her.

My smile becomes genuine. "Staying long?"

"Well, pet, I..."

"Gracious! Look," Gran interrupts, tugging a rectangular gold frame from the box. "Look at this, Suzy. Thought I'd lost it."

I know what's in the frame even before Gran turns it to show. My heart sinks. It's a cross stitching of Christina Rossetti's poem, 'Remember Me'. Suzy had made it and gifted it to her last year, on the first of Grandad's birthday's after his passing. There's a crack running through the glass, caused during an especially bad melt-down on New Year's Day when she'd thrown it at me, missed, and it hit off the wall; it's following that incident the picture was stored away. I'd hoped to never see it again. I harbour a deep, deep loathing of that poem.

"And you, dear love," Gran continues, transfixed on the care-fully stitched gold lettering as she draws the frame in close. "You readin' it out in church that day, for my Jim, so beautiful. So beautiful."

Beautiful, my reading of it was not. I agreed to do it; thought I could cope; and I tried. But, up front, facing the teary gathering of mourners, seeing Gran falling apart right there in front of me, two lines I stumbled through before I completely lost it.

Gran's blatantly confusing me with David. He'd stepped up and took over while Hannah led me back to my seat beside Gran on the front pew. David gave a perfect delivery, not a crack or quiver to his voice. But, of course, he knew the poem off by heart, word for word, already. He'd read it aloud four and a half years previ-ously, at our parents' funeral. It was one of Mum's favourites.

Keen for a distraction, I lean forward, submerging my face inside the box, and scope out its remaining contents. "Hey, what's this?" I draw back and delve my hands in, retrieving a tattered manila box-folder.

Gran's quick to make a snatch for it, setting aside the gold frame and shaking her head. "Oh no. No, no. That's nout for you to be nosin' into."

Her words come too late. I've already opened the flap and registered its contents.

"I threw these out," I say, flipping through the wad of papers. "How have you got these, Gran? Why'd you keep them?" Letters; cards; photos. From David and Mel, addressed to me. All torn into at least two pieces, they've since been sellotaped back together. "You actually dug these out the bin? Jeezus!"

Gran tuts and makes another swipe for the folder. I whip it away. "Give it here, boy!"

I've spotted a small blue envelope shoved in behind the letters. I pluck it out and open it.

Just a few more old photographs. But these are all of me. And I look so painfully miserable in each and every one. These, I recognise, are the few pictures taken within that first year of me moving to Newcastle. Otherwise known as the year I hated living.

The last four snaps are of my twelfth birthday, an especially dark day. Me, dejectedly opening my impressive stack of presents; me, peeking from my hiding spot behind the patio curtains; me, struggling against Gran's hug; and me, scowling at the Batman cake, candles aflame on top. Taken only moments before I flipped the table over and launched my brand-new Nintendo DS off the wall. That's the day Grandad's tolerance of me broke and our turbulent relationship was secured. I shudder.

A truly uplifting trip down memory lane this isn't turning out to be.

Hastily shoving the photos back in their envelope, and then the envelope into the folder, I fling the folder away from me. "No reason whatsoever for holding on to those. Hardly soul-warming *fucking* keepsakes!" Shame and remorse scorch me the moment the last word has exploded from my mouth.

Suzy's quick to stoke it, raising her voice. "Hey now! Enough!"

My cheeks burn. There is absolutely no call for me to ever snap at Gran like that. No call, ever.

Rescuing the folder and returning it to the box, Gran puckers her lips tight. But before she has chance to respond, and before I can verbalise an apology, the kitchen door opens and Mel reappears through it. David's at her heel.

Taking in my heated expression, he stops just inside the doorway folding his arms, and addresses Suzy, "you've told him then, I take it?"

I can feel the sweep of foreboding take the colour from my

face. "Not again, Suzy!" My head whips around to her. "What is it this time?"

Suzy cautiously side-eyes me and then fixes on David. "No, no. Not yet."

"Ah." He drops his arms to his sides, catching and holding my challenging glare. "Right."

"Tea? Coffee?" Mel asks the room at large, moving toward the kettle.

"Coffee please, baby," David replies, unyielding in our stare off.

"Tea would be lovely, thanks pet," Suzy says, and then: "Maybe the two of ye should go talk in private, David, eh?"

He nods. "Mikey?"

"Suzy?" I entreat her again.

Brow pinched tight, she flicks her hand toward David.

It's a fight against everything in me to not fob him off. Tempting though it is, I know it'll do me no favours. I'll be forced to hear him out at some point, might as well get it over with. *Freaking knew Suzy's visit wasn't string free.*

David walks to his office but I follow only so far as the entrance before demanding, "what?"

With a heavy sigh, he turns, studying me for an uncomfortable moment. Opening his mouth, he doesn't bother cushioning the blow, "Gran's flat has sold."

"WHAT?!" My voice blasts out unnaturally high.

"Taking Suzy back home the weekend after next," he continues on without reaction. "Will be sorting through the remainder of Gran's things and emptying the place. So don't go making any plans, and you'll need to be home sharpish after school that Friday because we want to get away by four at the latest."

"So, wow, again, I get zero say on this?"

"Oh, what a surprise, you're being unreasonable," he retorts with an eye roll. "With the money from the sale, we can arrange Gran a professional carer, and..."

"Unreasonable?" I cut him off, unable to hold onto my last shard of restraint for a millisecond longer. My head's translated the words 'professional carer' to 'care home' and, nope. Just nope. "Have you seen Gran in there?" As if on cue, the warming sound of her laugh reaches our ears. "She's more herself right now, with Suzy, than she has been for even one single other moment since being here. Know why? Cos Suzy is home to her. That flat in Newcastle is *home*. You aren't. This place isn't. Never has been, never will be.

"You can't keep stealing every last bit of her life from her, David! It's not right. Not fair. And like hell are you getting me to help you with it. No!"

I'm breathing hard when I'm finished, and David's just staring at me, eyebrows raised. Screw this, I've wasted enough valuable breath and I'm done with looking at him.

Flipping him off, I turn on my heel. Time I should get ready for work.

"Mikey," his voice trails me up the stairs, tone patronising. "Before you got in, before I got that box down, from the moment Suzy arrived, Gran was flipping out. Shrieking herself hoarse, scratching at her arms and face. She was screaming for you, so I tried calling. Then she attacked Suzy, threatened her with boiling kettle water. When Mel brought Sophie home, though, that's when she calmed down, like a switch flicking to off the minute Sophie appeared.

"This afternoon is by far the worst I've ever seen her. But Suzy's told me she's experienced worse. She told me about…"

I reach my room and promptly slam the door shut on the rest of his drivel. I know exactly what incident Suzy'll have told him about, and I have no desire to suffer his retelling.

My eyes are instinctively drawn to my skates, set neatly side by side under my desk. I've time to spare before I'm due at Citreena's…

Instead, I pull out my phone from my jeans pocket:

Meet me at the den in 15 please?

The reply is almost instant:

Absolutely :)

The lump in my throat swells. Won't he be pleased when I show up an emotional wreck?

I thump my forehead against the door, banging my clenched fists off the frame to either side of it, and suck in several deep calming breaths before I straighten up, throw on my Taz hoody and set off back down the stairs.

34

ELEPHANT SHOE

"Still wanting to move back to Newcastle, huh?"

Tate and I are sat face to face across from each other on the stump's gnarly raised roots. Chewing on my hoody's toggle, I'm running my eyes, slow and deliberate, over the whole of him, committing each and every one of his fine features to mind ready for recall while I work. I've only half an hour before I need to leave, and then we'll be parted for four long, draggy hours.

I watch as his frown deepens. "I asked that out loud, right?"

A smirk kicks up one corner of his lips when I snort out a chuckle despite myself, the toggle falling from my mouth. "Yeah. I mean," I sigh, "no. I mean, yeah you said it out loud, and no," I shrug, finishing lamely with, "I don't know."

"You don't know?"

I almost shrug again, but then, reaching over the space between us, he takes my hand. I'm surrendered his complete and undivided attention, green eyes urging me on, and, jeezus! I *do* know. Of course I do.

"It's just..." I try to sort through the tangled mess of my emotions, enough that I can perhaps explain myself. "I love that flat. Gran loves that flat. Or...*loved.* I miss Suzy and Jean and Hannah. Jody too. But..."

My imminent shift will be only a temporary separation from him, and my chest's already kinda aching. Moving back to Newcastle, putting 400 miles between us again, that's a pain too unbearable to even consider.

Wrapping my free hand over his, I squeeze. He rewards me with a flash of his special, most dazzling smile and my heart skips.

Yeah, there's nowhere in the whole world I want to be but right here, right now. I have him. He's mine. And I don't ever again want to be without him.

His keen gaze holds, waiting for me to continue.

"It's not even really about wanting to move back, it's more that... this, it's so final, you know?" His small nod is all the encouragement it takes to crack me wide open, "I'm angry, Tate. God. Damn, am I angry! Who the hell even is he to do that? Not enough that he plucked us from our home, from our friends, without so much as a by-your-leave. No, he had to throw in this one extra almighty-kick-to-the-balls, really showcase his clout. Gran's been my priority for so long, my world, and I try my damnedest to think of what's best for her, always. But now...hell, that's the worst part, he's got me doubting myself. He's trapped me entirely under his control, taken over everything. And I freaking hate him enough already, I can't hold any more. It's unhealthy, I know it is. I feel like the poison of it..." Running out of steam, I drag in a deep breath before finishing, "I feel like he may actually be killing me."

For the briefest of moments, I float in the solace of all that weight lifted. Registering Tate's strained expression, however, has me sharp plummeting, my gut twisting, and I crash hard. He continues to study me, but he doesn't speak.

Crap! Crap in a wicker basket!

He's right up there as one of my two most favourite people on this entire planet. And he's deaf. And I've just totally spewed ragey word-vomit all over him.

What was I thinking?!

I wasn't.

It's blatant he's tried hard to follow me, but no way could he have caught much of what I said. And if he did — if he managed to even just pick up the gist of my rant, then how selfish must he be thinking me now please? Seriously? He's carrying plenty enough troubles of his own, and here I've gone and unburdened all of mine on him.

Bad enough I did this to him before I knew. Now, it's inexcusable.

I drop my eyes from his, "sorry."

He still doesn't say a word as he abandons my hand and slides himself backwards off the root. My gaze whips back to him. Crossing around to me, he reclaims my hand and tugs.

Welcoming the return of his touch, I obediently clamber up to stand in front of him. His brow remains pinched tight and it's giving away nothing of what I can expect from him here.

"I'm sorry," I say again.

"Sorry for what, Mikey?"

"For being so lousy at this." I flap my free hand between the two of us. My errant glance at his ear does not go unnoticed, he winces and I'm quick to look away. "For being atrociously incapable of..." I stop myself short, realising I'm well on my way to doing it again: Launching off at full speed and losing him. Looking down at our entwined hands, I reluctantly slip free of him. He drops his gaze, tracking my hand into my jeans pocket. I draw out my phone and type: ***For being so pants at giving you the best of me for any more than five minutes at a time. If that.*** His unrelenting watch of me is immensely distracting. ***I just keep right on dishing up those big ol' platefuls of the Hot Mess Mikey Special.***

Passing my phone over, I take up just as close a watch on him, scrutinising his expression as he reads. I blink to his hands as they start moving, fingers typing a reply.

He hands the phone back: ***I'm good for any and all of your***

Specials, dork. I'm 100% in this thing for everything you have to offer.

I'm barely given chance to read it, a timid grin teasing at my lips, before his finger sneaks in under my chin and nudges my head up. A crooked smile softens his frown as he adds, "everything just needs a little bit more time, okay?"

And then he's hugging me. He's wrapping me up in him so tight, I almost believe I can feel all my broken pieces mending back together. My arms snaking and fastening around his waist, I burrow in.

We stay that way, simply holding each other, for a long while – a few minutes, a few lifetimes, I couldn't care to guess – but, still, nowhere near long enough. Pressing a kiss to my forehead, Tate finally releases me and takes a step back.

"You should go," he says, somewhat blind-siding me.

"Err, what?" I check the time on my phone, still clutched in my hand. Not time for me to leave yet; still have fifteen minutes.

"No. To Newcastle. With David."

I narrow my eyes at him. "What?"

"For closure."

My eyes narrow further and I tilt my head. I will him to just shut up now and return to hugging me.

"Or, okay," he smirks as he rolls his eyes. "If not for closure, go for – for the opportunity to catch up with everyone. They'll be missing you too, Mikey. And, fuck, there's no reason for you to cut them out, just because..."

He trails off when my attention's abruptly stolen away from him.

Megan has suddenly appeared in the clearing. Mitted hands clasped in front of her, she picks her careful way out from the tree-line and makes a slow approach toward us, staring. Wrapped up snug against the crisp air, the exposed skin of her face – a thin slice between bobble hat and scarf – rosy, she's kinda resembling a pink marshmallow in sparkly wellie boots.

When Tate turns, following my line of sight, and spots her, she stops mid-step, pouts and stamps her foot down. I get scowled at, and then raspberried. Guess I ruined her sneak-attack.

Grinning wide and chuckling, Tate gestures her closer. "Aha, better luck next time, scamp."

Megan starts forward again, her pace picking up to a skip, and as she rounds the tree stump, he takes another step away from me, drops to a squat and throws out his arms ready for her. She launches herself at him, skinny arms circling his neck, and he straightens, lifting her off her feet and spinning her round. She squeals gleefully. I'm forced into a hasty jump back as her flying legs come a little too close to catching me in the gut. He mouths 'sorry' at me, but he doesn't look it. Behind the kid's back, I flash him the finger.

"So what can we do for you?" He asks, setting her down and remaining on his haunches as she bounces backwards to perch herself on the rim of the stump.

Pulling off her mitts with her teeth, leaving them to dangle from string threaded through her coat sleeves, she brings her hands together in front of her, but then her eyes flick to me and she freezes. She slips Tate a silent question.

He replies to her with his hands, flashing a sheepish smile my way, and her expression immediately brightens. Little though he does, I find it fascinating. I'm astute enough to know I'm the subject, but when I look to him for a translation, another self-conscious smile is all that he offers me.

Megan fires into action now, her signing slower but far more animated than her big brother's, tongue peeking out in evidence of her extreme concentration. Tate appears faintly amused by whatever it is she's saying. He again makes no effort to clue me in. I track her movements keenly, but it's only once she's stopped, cocked her head and then shaken it, mouth screwing up to one side, that I realise she'd been directing at least some of it toward me and I've failed to appropriately respond.

"Oh, err," I smile and nod.

She continues to stare at me.

Tate laughs. "Mikey knows I'm deaf, Meg," he says, flashing me another counterfeit apology with his eyes. "But he doesn't know any sign."

Goddamn... "Yet!"

As if Adele wasn't motivation enough, no way am I okay with being out-smarted by a five-year-old.

There's something a little unsettling in how alike to a young Tate the girl looks when she grins at me as she is now. "Okay," she nods, "good," and then her hands are back on the move. Showing much more consideration than her brother did, she speaks as she signs, "Mummy's here. She sent me to get you."

"Right," he sighs without signing. Straightening up and closing the distance between us, he slips his arm around my waist, setting his hand on my hip. The sweet thrill he sends through me totally makes up for his bit teasing. "Could you... could you go back and, uh, ask her to hang on for ten minutes please, angel?"

Her eyes dart comically between the two of us, studiously deliberating, before she finally gives a decisive nod and clambers up to stand on top of our stump-table. Pouncing off the far side of it, she spins back to us holding up her ten fingers, the impish Tate-grin fixed again on her face as she sing-songs, "elephant shoe!"

"And I love you, too!" Tate calls after her.

Megan cracks up, giggling like a loon as she bounds across the clearing and onto the neglected dirt trail through the trees.

Once she's disappeared, I turn to Tate and leave it to my eyebrow to ask, *'what the hell?'*

"The 'elephant shoe' thing, right? Girl's a mean little trickster. Never fails to amuse her." The fond, big-brotherly smile still curving his lips, he shrugs one shoulder. "'I love you' and 'elephant shoe', they shape the mouth the same way when they're spoken."

"Huh." I try it out – how could I not? – focusing on the movements of my lips for each. *Well, wow, what d'ya know: Totally true.* It gets a second run through, just to be certain. And a third.

"Fuck, Mikey!" Tate smirks. "Don't abuse it. Meg's bad enough, please don't make me regret telling you too."

Mouth halting ajar, a fierce blush floods my face. I bite down hard on my lower lip, berating myself, and then clear my throat. "So what was it she signed?"

"That she found an interesting stone today."

I frown. "And?"

"Then she asked who you are."

"Ah." *Of course. Duh!*

"Yep." He mirrors my nod, his smile stretching and turning ever-so wondrously roguish. Without letting go of me, he angles around to press more of himself against me. "But, anyway, we only have, what? Eight minutes left. Care to remind me where we were?"

"The hug?" I teeter on the brink of begging. No word of a lie, my body's craving him more than oxygen right now. "Let's please go back to the hug?"

"Absolutely," he approves with a grin, tightening his arm around me. "One condition though."

"Yeah?"

"We throw in some lip action too."

"Hell yeah!"

35

LOST AND FOUND

"Come with me," I blurt when a desperate need for oxygen finally forces our mouths to part. "Please?"

I'm done with work and am now at Tate's, in his room, on his bed. Pressed up flush against him, the back of my shirt is rucked up toward my shoulder blades, his hand flat and firm on my exposed skin beneath it. I have the side of his shirt scrunched up in my fist. We're both breathing heavy.

Eyes honed on my lips, his brow pinches in confusion.

"Come with me."

He appears far less, rather than more, enlightened by my second appeal. Something kinda feral enters into his expression as he asks, "'scuse me?"

And, as I reposition my hips in an effort to relieve some of the extreme discomfort going on within my jeans, the penny drops on how my request could be misconstrued, especially in the face of our current situation.

"To Newcastle," I clarify, just a smidgeon mortified. "Will you come with me to Newcastle?"

Tate tilts his head, eyes narrowing, and a lazy grin curves his lips as he makes a prolonged and torturous scan of my face. "Yeah. Okay."

'Yeah'? He said 'yeah'? Really? I hold his eye, questioning. Having filled every free moment at work concocting and rehearsing a persuasive argument, and the past half hour here with him building up the courage to broach it, his easy agreement is proving somewhat hard to digest. I'm at a loss now. "Okay? You'll come to Newcastle?"

He's nodding at me, drawing in closer, his grin turning devilish, and then he's kissing me again, his head angling to deepen it. His fingers skim up my spine, then all the way back down again as he sucks my tongue into his mouth, and – *whoa!* – I discover a whole new glorious galaxy of intoxicating sensation.

Feels like only seconds before we're forced to another halt. This time it has a little less to do with the necessity of an air supply, and much more to do with the sudden blaring chime of my phone. It's the tedious and shrill *'ring-ring'* I've set to represent David. I'm good to ignore it and continue on as we were, but Tate takes that option away, pulling back. Lifting his hand from my vibrating butt cheek, he eyes me inquiringly, and then Mel's words from earlier today whine through my head. I wince apologetically at him and he winks at me.

By the time I've huffed out a curse and adjusted myself to slip a hand into my pocket, the ringing's stopped, but as I slide the phone out, it starts up again.

Tate rolls onto his back and stares up at the ceiling; his intention that of affording me privacy, I assume. While one arm remains caught under me, his other flops onto the pillow above his head. The move rides his shirt up that bit further, exposing the immensely gratifying swell in the crotch of his trousers (*yeah, I did that!*) along with an enticing slip of bare stomach. This area holds my attention hostage as I tap the 'accept call' icon and put the phone to my ear.

"Uh-huh?"

"Where are you?"

I rake my gaze upwards to Tate's face, taking in his still profile. His lips twitch, like he knows I'm poring over him, and he closes his eyes. "Why?"

"You need to get home. Now."

David's tone has my hackles raised, lust-haze instantly cleared from my brain. "Why?"

"Gran's missing."

"WHAT?" I'm bolted upright. "What do you mean 'Gran's missing'?!"

Tate's straight up beside me, eying me with concern. I'm already scanning the floor for my shoes and my hoody.

"Calm down, Mikey," David commands. "She can only have been gone for five or ten minutes, won't have got far. We thought her asleep in her room, but when Suzy's popped in to check..."

"Screw coming back to the house then," I blast over him. "What the hell's the point in that? I'm going out looking for her! That thought not occurred to anyone else yet?"

"Okay, yes, Mel and I are..."

I end the call, hurling myself off the bed. Shoving my phone back into my pocket and yanking my t-shirt straight, I locate my shoes and ram my feet in.

"Mikey?" A hand hooks my elbow as I reach for my hoody.

I rip free of the hold, registering too late whose hand it could only be. I whirl around to Tate. "Gran's gone missing. I'm sorry, I've gotta go."

I'm out the bedroom and pounding the stairs before I'm even sure he's grasped what I said.

Tate joins me at the end of his street. Just about sends me sky-high, planting a heavy hand on my shoulder. I hadn't heard his approach.

"Obviously I'm going to help," he says in response to my wide-eyed look, dropping his hand from my shoulder to my waist. I sag against him. He scans around us. "Where to first?"

"I..." I shake my head feebly and shrug. I've no plan, no clue where to start. It's almost eleven at night, dark and icy cold, and

Gran could be anywhere. Alone. Lost. Scared. *Goddamnit!* My vision goes fuzzy, because that's helpful.

"Head for the high street," Tate takes charge with a decisive nod. His hold on me bracing, he guides me to the road and across.

We take a labyrinthine route toward the town's centre. Tate dons his head-torch to light our way, but we catch no sign of Gran. We tread the high street all the way up one side and back down it the other, closely inspecting every side-street, alley and doorway, but Gran's nowhere to be found there either. David and Mel have had no better luck with their search, and she hasn't returned home – Suzy's promised me I'll be the first person she calls should Gran show; I haven't heard from her.

It's just turned one am. That makes it two hours we've been walking. My stupid work shoes have rubbed blisters into my heels, I'm chilled to the bone, and my eyes are aching with the strain of staying open and vigilant long beyond their duty hours. Worry and fear are all that's keeping me going. And Tate. I'm glad for Tate.

We're at Somerton Primary now, skirting around the back of the school. Through the high fence, in the bright beam cast by the torch, I can see the playing field and can just about make out the playset at its far side.

"Remember that day," Tate suddenly breaks into the night's heavy silence, reigning in my pace yet again with a gentle tug on my hand. It's more his words that have me slowing this time. I turn back to him, stunned, squinting into the light as he continues, "when we found the sports shed unlocked?"

Reminiscing? He's reminiscing? A small smile lifts my lips; this is good. "Yeah, I remember."

"Spent our entire lunchbreak in there, barricading ourselves in, pretending we were the sole survivors of the zombie apocalypse."

"I'd just scored an epic head shot on zombie Gary. We hid in there to escape the vengeance of zombie Ben and zombie Wayne," I follow on, my smile stretching. His does too, his gaze committed to my mouth. "Gary went down hard when that ball hit him. The threat to me was very real."

"Yeah, well." He shrugs one shoulder, squeezing my hand. "Added to the thrill, right? Just the two of us shut up in the dark, plotting for − for lasting our lifetimes alone together in the dangerous new world. Rationing our food supplies. Stockpiling 'weapons'. That lunch hour was pretty fucking brilliant."

"It was," I nod my enthused agreement. It's a good memory, one I'd almost forgotten about. I glide one final scan over the school field before we move on past it, trying to discern the shed's silhouette from the black bulk of the sports hall, and it occurs to me, in a flash of insight, that Tate's deliberately distracting me with this. Clever tactic; worked well for a short while. "Spent way longer than lunch hour in there, though, didn't we?" My attention returns to him as my mind snaps back to Gran. "Missed the bell. Had teachers out searching for us. Came so close to our parents getting a call, and Mrs Jonas was not amused when she saw what we'd done to her tidy shelves."

"I heard the bell. Wasn't ready for our game to end though. Just one of many times I landed you in trouble." His expression's dimmed alongside mine. I frown as he turns to face forward, redirecting the focus of the torchlight away, his grip on me slackening. "I used to love the dark. Because it made me feel like − like anything was possible. Now, though, you know, that's the very same reason I can no longer stand it."

I tense, becoming all-of-a-sudden acutely aware of the pitch blackness surrounding our one beam of light on this eerie stretch of path, and my step falters, pace slowing even further. I catch on the twitch to his jaw muscle, his eyes flicking back to me before he lowers his head.

"Fuck, that was a shitty thing to bring up now. Sorry, I didn't think it through."

Drawing in closer to him, I press a kiss to his shoulder. It's my attempt of expressing wordless thanks for him staying with me tonight. His clasp of my hand re-firming, I think he gets it.

He doesn't speak again as we turn the corner away from the school and cut down a narrow alley that brings us out onto the main road. Not until we've followed along the road some way and the YCS sign glints at the soft fringe of the head torch's range. I'm straining to penetrate the creepy gloom of the school's driveway, debating the worth of crossing to search down it, when Tate jerks me to a stop, pointing ahead. "There."

My head snaps around, following the line of his finger, and it's only his unrelenting hold on my hand that prevents me from charging straight out into the road. And an abruptly realised fear of alarming her that slams my mouth shut on a call-out.

I fix on the bus shelter just beyond YCS's entrance, a street-lamp beside it illuminating the small, hunched figure sat within, and impatiently wait out the passing of one, two, three cars. Tate's hand is lost to me as I make the dash over.

It's not easy to force caution to my approach as I near. Hurts my heart to see she's dressed in her purple dressing gown, tatty slippers on her feet.

"Gran?" I meant to address her softly, had aimed for a soothing tone. Instead, the word erupts from me sharp and shaky. Her gaze startles up as I drop to my knees in front of her and seize her hands from her lap. She feels like ice. "Hey, Gran." My second attempt comes out little better.

There's no hint of recognition in her eyes, wide with fright, as they flit over my face. "Ha' ye found her? She alright?"

36

KEEP RIGHT ON, DOING WHAT
YOU'RE DOING

$\mathcal{I}$t took two hours from finding Gran to get her back to the house. She's now settled in bed, snoring peacefully.

David, Mel and Suzy are sat around the kitchen table, deep in discussion. I can hear their voices but can't distinguish their words. I should be in there with them, weighing in my voice to the decision making. But I'm not up to it just yet. I need a few minutes. Need to collect myself, work through the chaos of my head.

Tate's with me still, sat beside me on the bottom stair, his arm holding me together as I keep steady guard of Gran's bedroom door.

She'd been looking for my mum. Or, more precisely, her daughter of a time before she was anyone's mum. Gran couldn't understand why we were '*needlessly fretting*' ourselves over her, when it was her sweet Elaine who'd been missing all evening; home safe after school, not seen since leaving for work. It dawned that she was confusing my mum with me, but my attempt to explain this had angered her.

That's the point Tate stepped in.

"Evelyn, hi, my name's Tate," he said, moving in to crouch

down beside me; close, but not too close. "I'm a good friend of M..."

"Tate was that?" Gran's attention snapped to him, her brow knitting as she studied him, "Tate...aye, I know that name. Heard all about *you*. Calling yersel' a good friend, are ye? After turnin' yer back on the boy. Hurtin' him. Good friend, pah! Don't bloody think so, lad."

The look of awful understanding in his eyes as he'd glanced across at me, it was torture.

But he stayed, remained calm, persevered.

He was getting somewhere too, talking her down, until David finally pulled the car up alongside. Then accusations of kidnapping flew. Tate got an elbow to the chest, I was kicked in the ankle, and David narrowly avoided a stone pelted at his head.

I feel like I've been put through a mincer today, and tonight has finished me off.

Gran's never gonna get better. I don't know how I'm supposed to deal with that.

Tate's arm tensing around my waist is my first clue I may have voiced that thought aloud. The next comes when querying eyes fix on the side of my face and he asks, "what?"

I turn my head to him, my smile grim, "Gran's getting worse. And I'm useless, there's nothing I can do for her."

His free hand moves up to cradle my jaw. I lean into it and he thumbs a tender stroke across my cheekbone. "You're there for her. You love her. That's all she needs from you, Mikey."

I'm set to shake my head but, dipping in closer, he pins me in place with a cautioning frown. "You can't do more than you already are and, fuck, no one expects you to, okay? Stop punishing yourself for things you have no sway over. Accept the help offered you, you're not in it alone."

Scraping my teeth over my bottom lip, battling its quiver, I jerk a stiff nod. "I'm sorry. Ya know, for what Gran said to you tonight. She doesn't..."

Darting forward, his lips claim mine, effectively trapping the rest of my words in my mouth. His tongue then takes to the task of sweeping them clear away.

Before I recover brain function enough to fully reciprocate, however, the sound of the kitchen door swinging open jars into my consciousness. "Mikey?"

I lurch free of Tate, snatching my hand from his shoulder and swiping it over my mouth. Putting space between us, I become keenly aware of his injured stare. "I..."

"There you boys are." Suzy rounds the bannister. Her eyes dart between us. And even though her smile flickers for only a millisecond, it's enough to give me the distinct impression she has some idea what it is she's just interrupted. *No way she could, though, right?* "I'm about to make some cocoa. Coming in to join us?"

Tate releases his fistful of my hoody, moving his arm from my waist to rest on the stair behind. Now facing Suzy, he side-eyes me anxiously.

"Well?" She prompts.

I swallow. And again; forcing back the queasiness. "Uh, yeah, sure." If she's set on feigning ignorance, then I'm good to go along with that. I catch Tate's eye, "yeah?"

He pushes to his feet. "Actually, I should – sorry Mikey, but I should really get home. Dad's texted me twice already. School tomorrow, you know, so," he shrugs one shoulder and sends a smile Suzy's way.

I stand-up too, green-lighting him with a bizarre salute-type-wave that has me wincing before I'm even through with it. My arm dropping awkwardly to my side, I return full focus to Gran's door.

"Right then, Mikey, pet, I'll leave ye be to see yer friend out." With a pat to my arm, Suzy bustles back toward the kitchen, and I'm certain it's purely my imagination that picks out a weird emphasis on the word *'friend'*.

～

"Jeezus, what?! Lynds, no!"

For the past twenty minutes, Gary, Wayne and Ben have taken it in turns to walk by behind my seat, clouting me across the back of my head each pass. I've pulled off a damn good job of ignoring them thus far, even despite Alex's snorts of amusement. But when Gary sidles up to Lyndsay, following his fourth bonce blow, and offers to buy her a drink, that's well and truly blown. I realise my screw up before the words even finish leaving my mouth.

Gary winks at me, satisfied, as Lyndsay affords me only the merest flicker of reaction and accepts his offer with a tight smile, gesturing to the barely-touched wine glass in front of her, "white, thank you."

"Seriously? *Seriously?*" Callum snaps, bolting up straight in his chair. "Why?!"

I flinch, even though his words – tone as uncharacteristically sharp as his scowl – are aimed solely at Lyndsay.

Meeting his eye, she jerks one shoulder and lifts her glass to her mouth, throwing back half its contents in one go.

It's obvious to me why, and it smarts like a slap to know that she'd undoubtedly have spurned Gary's offer had I only kept my idiot mouth shut.

Alex gets it too. He's doing that thing he does of looking me over like I'm something repulsive he's just stepped in. "Don't worry, Cal," he says, his gaze dissecting me. "She's not dumb enough to drink what he gives her."

"Please don't drink what he gives you," I mutter out the side of my mouth.

At this, Lyndsay drains the remainder of her wine, slamming the empty glass down on the table. Fixing Alex with a defiant, *screw-you* smirk, her gaze skips right on past me as she then turns to Gary and makes shooing motions at him with her hands, "make it a large, would you?"

She's remaining resolutely unthawed toward me; an occasional scathing glance when I dare address her directly, that's the limit of her attention. She has me feeling like my breath should be frosting out, and despite Derek's assurances of eventual forgiveness, I'm beginning to accept I may actually have broken us beyond any kind of repair. My only small solace is that she looks as miserable about it as I feel.

Callum stares at Lyndsay in horrified disbelief as Gary gives my head one final shove before sauntering off – leaving a trail of shoulder barged casualties in his wake – toward the bar.

Sinking down in my chair, I pick my phone up from the table in front of me and wake the screen. It's been at least twenty minutes since I sent Tate the *miss you* text.

Maybe it didn't go through. Maybe I should try again.

I'd invited him along tonight. Well, kinda. I mentioned the Desperate For Aces gig to him in History, and my open invite to it, then left it there between us with my fingers crossed.

Yeah, so I figured a less than slim chance of him latching on to the idea with any level of enthusiasm, but I was hopeful that he'd at least express interest enough for me to work with. Or even put forth an alternative, and more tempting, plan for our evening...

Instead, he'd excused himself with an art assignment he has due in tomorrow and told me to enjoy my night.

I'm doing a truly awful job with that request, has to be said.

Opening my text screen, I tap out *can I come over?* My finger hovers over 'send' for several long breaths, and then I delete it. Setting my phone back down, I instead twist around in my chair to survey the room behind me.

With only around five minutes left until show time, the place is packed to barely a standing space free – seems more rammed, even, than last time. The band's all set up on the stage, and there's a tangible buzz to the air; a buzz that's failing to do any more than tickle the thick blanket of hostility wrapping our small table. Steph's company, as my only vocal supporter, would be much appreciated tonight. She said she'd be here, it's now seeming most unlikely she's gonna show. Grounded again, Alex has speculated.

Adele's out there somewhere, with her group of intimidating friends. I clocked her earlier, when I first arrived. She curled her lip in response to my wave, and that's the full extent of our interactions thus far. Her companions should make her fairly easy to spot, but nope, I see no sign.

"Watch where you're fucking going!" At the boom of his voice, my attention instead snaps and locks on Gary. A pint held high in one beefy hand and wine glass in the other, too soon he's pushing his bullish way back to us.

I scrape my chair back and stand.

"Been apart from your boyfriend for too long, have you?" Alex taunts. "Separation anxiety getting too much to bear?"

Pressing my lips tight against a comeback, I snatch my phone off the table, ramming it into my jeans pocket, and turn my back to him. I'm in need of a blast of fresh air, that's all. I intend to step out for just a few minutes before the gig kicks off. But should my feet take it upon themselves to continue walking once outside... well, I can't say I'll do much to stop them.

The moment I've made it through the press of bodies to see the door, however, I'm reeled to a standstill.

Stood just inside the door, one hand braced against it as if prepared to flee at any least provocation, the other clutching his phone like a lifeline, is Tate.

Even as my gut tweaks at his obvious discomfort, my heart's set to soaring. *Damn, but he's a beautiful sight.* I drink him in, savouring the moment, as he scans the room, oblivious to me.

I jolt forward a step when his head turns my way, and another when his gaze roams on past, missing me. But then the lights are dimming and the room's erupting with cheers.

"Show us the love, guys!" The small frontman with the impressive voice screams into the mic.

I catch Tate lifting his phone and dropping his eyes to it, his thumb put to work on the screen, before those seated around me jump to their feet and he's lost from sight in the uproar.

Lifting to tip-toes, leaning and craning my neck, I manage to just about make out the top of his head. It's on the move, searching again. I hold my breath as I wait for the buzz of a message received against my thigh. Nothing comes through.

As the first notes of the band's first song blasts, I'm jostled every which way by moving bodies. I take out my phone, check it hasn't somehow accidently been set to silent, as I once more start forward, closing the distance between us.

But, just as I stumble-step out into clear view, in the same moment Tate's eyes fix on me, I spot Adele emerging from the crowd off to my right, and her eyes are fixed on him. Grin wide and step bouncy, there's not a flicker of surprise on her face at Tate's unexpected presence.

My eyes drop to the phone swinging in hand by her side, and my heart drops heavily into my toes. *Oh. Right.*

I'm about to allow my ever-ready insecurities to yet again take over brain function when, within the blink of an eye, Tate's body heat warms me, and his arms are circling my waist.

"Missed you too," he mostly breathes into my ear. His lips running a light trail along my jaw, he snuffs out every last millimetre of space between us, and Adele's instantly forgotten.

Too soon, however, my bliss of him is punctured by the pricking awareness of many sets of eyes fixed on us and I remember where we are.

I draw back. He doesn't give me up easily, and that both thrills and shames me all at once. The wounded expression he fails to mask quick enough secures shame the win.

"I wanted to surprise you," he says, recovering himself. Or at least, I think that's what he says: His voice competes poorly against the music.

"Consider me surprised!" I hope that the Cheshire cat split across my face will go some way to alleviate the sting of my move. "What are you doing here?" Yelling to ensure my words carry, I feel my grin twist into something of an embarrassed grimace before I'm through.

The crease of his frown deepens, and I realise, sharply, that it must be as hard – harder, probably – for him to follow the move-ments of my lips in this low light as it is for me to hear him over the band. But then, a sheepish smirk lifts one corner of his lips and he leans in a fraction, directing his shout toward my ear, "I wanted to surprise you, duh! How else could I do that?"

I snort, shoving his shoulder, and his smirk widens. My insides flip-flop giddily. I don't miss the nervous dart of his gaze to the room around us, though; he's so totally not at ease here. *Caught up in a crowd of our peers who blank him at best, watching them all enjoy a live band he can't hear?* 'Course he's not.

"Guess I'm surplus to requirement now then, am I?" Adele brutally intrudes back into my consciousness. She's at Tate's shoulder, waving a hand between our faces.

Tate blinks and turns his head to her, his body remaining in line with mine, and his smile suggests this is, mayhaps, the first he's noticed her hovering presence. "Hey."

She visibly huffs, rolling her eyes.

Tate's wince works as both an apology and a dismissal. She flips him off. And if the pleasure I take from that exchange makes me a bad person, then so be it.

"Whatever." Adele spins on her heel and weaves herself into the crowd.

I watch Tate watch her disappear from view, and then track his gaze on another furtive scan of our surroundings.

Snaking my hand around his, I squeeze, drawing his attention back to me, then nudge my head in the direction of the door, offering him an out.

"No," he mouths, flashing me a quick, tight smile. Jutting his chin toward the stage, he returns my squeeze before letting go and stepping around behind me. Seizing my shoulders, he then forcibly twists me to face Desperate For Aces. "Enjoy your night," his words tickle my ear.

37

BEAST DEFEATED, WE GET OUR HEA NOW, RIGHT?

*W*e've wedged ourselves into a tight nook to the side of the stage. The view's rubbish, and a speaker is blasting a little too close for comfort, but the small measure of privacy the cramped spot grants us...

Tate pressed against the wall, his arms wrapped snugly around me, pinning my back flush to him. Feeling the steady rise and fall of his chest, the rhythmic beat of his heart, the gentle stroke of his thumb across my stomach.

... mmm, yeah, totally works for me.

I barely even notice when Desperate For Aces' set draws to its eventual close, the last guitar note whining from the speaker to its death.

But when Tate's arms release me as the lights lift, and he nudges me up off him, I plummet back to earth like a toppled boulder. Spell broken. The wall of cheering, whistling bodies boxing us in comes into sharp focus and I bolt up straight. A rush of guilt shadows the move.

Giving myself a mental shake, I turn to him.

His smile is everything that's right with the universe. "They're good."

I start to nod. Then frown, because it wasn't a question.

The smile taking on a wry edge, I can virtually feel him tracking my thoughts. "The vibrations," he says, moving his mouth in rousingly close to my ear. "I may not hear the music, but I can feel it. I can see their stage presence, see the crowds' reaction. They're really good."

He draws back, tilting his head, like he's challenging me to dispute his assessment. I stare at him. Taking a moment, I try (and fail) to mentally block off my ears to the room's buoyant atmosphere.

"You amaze me," I blurt.

Now he's frowning. "What?"

I shake my head, face heating.

A quirk to his brow betrays him: He knows exactly what I said, he just wants me to repeat it.

And so I do. Cos it's the truth and I want him to know it. "You're amazing."

Tate laughs – a short, sweet burst of my favourite laugh – and I wish with all my heart I could bottle it. Then, muttering something that I don't catch, he takes my hand and his cheeks take their turn in warming to a soft pink.

"What?"

He doesn't repeat himself.

A sharp shift in his attention has me turning my head toward the stage. My eyes clash with Derek's just as he pounces up to the edge of it beside us.

"Hey, Mikey! Glad you made it." Dropping down to a crouch, his grin bright, Derek slides a pointed glance Tate's way as he smacks a hand down on my shoulder and jostles me. "Catch up in a bit, yeah? Don't go anywhere."

"Um," I start. But he doesn't hang about for me to finish.

"Give me ten minutes to pack up," he says, straightening. A quick nod of his head, first at Tate, then me, and he's moving away.

"Oh. Okay, sure." I call after him.

"So, who's your friend?" Tate asks too soon.

But if Derek heard either of us, he doesn't look back.

"Derek. That's just Derek. He's..." My tracking of his bouncy return trip across the stage is slammed short of him reaching his drum kit.

I catch on Lyndsay. And it's obvious by her locked-in death glare that she's witnessed the exchange. Her eyes narrowing on me, she lifts her wine glass to her lips and tips it sharply. Gary's claimed my chair beside her. He's spotted me too. They're positioned surprisingly closer to us than I thought them to be.

I'm swift in cutting away. "Uh, he's the band's drummer, and Lyndsay's cousin. Seems a good bloke. Gay too." *Whatthehell with that last bit please?!* "We gonna head off now, then?"

A weird and intangible change to the curve of his lips niggles me. "No rush, is there? We can stay for a drink, right?"

Well, now I'm super confused. Thought for sure, with his cover of darkness and noise gone, he'd snatch me up on getting out of this stuffy pub. And anyway... "Alcohol?"

See, I've been doing my reading – on bacterial meningitis and sensorineural hearing loss and epilepsy – a thoroughly head-hurting amount, and one of the many things I've learned from this research is that alcohol and epilepsy medication don't mix all that well together. It's also a trigger for some.

There's a hesitation before he answers me; a miniscule one, but I notice it. "One pint won't do any harm, Mikey, come on." He adds a little chuckle to the end, like that'll help convince me. "Besides, your friend over there," his gaze flicks across the stage, "wants a catch up with you."

"Yeah, but he won't care. I barely even know him," I argue, my gaze slipping back to my former table. "Yours? Mine? The den? Whatever."

"I'll even get them in," Tate deliberately talks right on over me. "Lager? Cider? Or something else?"

I sigh, holding his eye for a long silent moment before I cave. "Fine. Coke. Get me a coke."

That strange look returns to his face as he reaches for my hand, stopping a hairs-breadth short. "A coke?"

I haven't drank anything but water tonight. Deliberately came out carrying no money whatsoever so that, even if tempted to the dark side, I had no way of acting on it. Tate may have more than redeemed himself to me, but alcohol remains my solid foe.

My head gives a firm nod.

Yet, when my mouth opens, what comes out is, "with rum. Rum and coke."

I gasp in my next breath, trying to suck back those words and swallow them. But it's too late, he's read them from my lips and his grin stretches wide and victorious.

Oh, to hell with it! I throw my hands up in easy resignation. *I'm with him. He's here, making an effort, for me.* And if that's not worthy of one celebratory drink, nothing is.

I HAVE my one rum and coke. And then accept another off Derek, because I'm weak-willed. Tate's on his second lager, also thanks to Derek. He's made it very clear he doesn't appreciate my assessing glances, so I'm doing my upmost to reign them in. To be fair, he's giving me no cause to worry; he's trying real hard to relax, to at least look like he's enjoying himself, and I get that I'm not being helpful with that. Still, it's a task I'd find far more difficult if not for the distraction of other happenings – other persons of greater immediate concern.

It's coming up to an hour since the gig ended. The stage has been tidied, and all but Derek of Desperate For Aces have departed. The pub is almost cleared out, only a handful of tables and a couple of barstools still occupied.

Callum's joined us as the pub's emptied. Alex disappeared ages ago. And yet, Lyndsay remains at their centre stage table, enduring the company of Gary, Wayne and Ben.

She's far less tolerant of my watchfulness than Tate is, volleying icy contempt back at me. But there's no let up for her, cos I'm not alone with my misgivings in this instance.

Callum took Lyndsay's wine from her when she snubbed his appeal for moving over to us with him, handing it off to Adele (then seizing it back a moment later to prevent her from throwing it in Gary's *foul toady-face*), and Derek refused to get her anything other than a pint of water on his drinks round.

Fat lot of positive impact any of us have made, though. Already, Gary's replaced her confiscated glass with a fresh one. And Derek's perseverance in trying to coax free the levelheadedness she's intent on drowning appears to be aggravating her almost as much as my attention is.

He's nabbed a chair from a neighbouring table, positioning himself as a shield between his cousin and her nefarious table-companions, his full back presented to Gary. "You've got it rough right now, I get that," My straining ear catches Derek say, "but these guys aren't your friends, girl. They're doing you no good here." Lyndsay's sullenly slouching, arms folded and mouth pouty, and I'm given the distinct impression he may as well be talking at a wall.

I jump as Gary barks out a laugh, slamming his enormous paw down with an audible thud on Derek's shoulder. "Ouch, Dez. Offensive much? Like those fags can watch out for her better than we can – get real!"

Ben and Wayne snigger, and I can sense Derek bristling right along with me. Sitting up straighter, he rolls his shoulders, but he refrains from turning. Lyndsay just reaches for her wine, lips pressing tight.

"I am so through with her!" Callum explodes, snatching me free of Gary's taunting gaze. Perched on the edge of the stage, the heel of his foot slams furiously into its side. "What exactly is she trying to prove? And to who?" He continues fuming to no one in particular, "Tinwell, for shitsake! Of all people – *Tinwell?!*"

Adele huffs, and then snorts. I turn to her, sat across the circular table from me, catching her in a condescending head shake. "The pair of 'em are playing you. How do yas not see that?" She says, arching a dark brow at me. "She's feeding on all this attention. And your reaction's really getting him off. C'mon, get smart."

As though he's heard her, my nerves are again grated by Gary's loud guffaw.

A quick glance back is all it takes to substantiate Adele's theory some: Lyndsay's eyes are stabbing us over Derek's broad shoulder.

Blinking to Callum, I see the same understanding soak into him. He takes off his glasses, rubbing the lenses over his sleeve. "So, ignore them, then? That's what you're saying?"

"Duh!" Adele responds with an eye roll.

"Fine." Returning his glasses to his face, Callum jumps down from the stage and yanks around the free chair next to her. He straddles it, folding his arms over its back and dropping his chin down onto them. "Good. Yeah, leave her to it. Suits me."

"That's the spirit!" Adele ruffles Callum's unkempt hair, "D'aww, puppy dog's learning." He swats her off, blushing fiercely, and she laughs.

Can't say I'm so comfortable with that course of action. I cast another look over, slyly, on the pretence of readjusting in my seat. I mean, what if she's pushed to act out further by the retraction of our concern? *But, then again, perhaps...*

Suddenly registering the chilly absence of Tate's leg against mine under the table, I whip around to him. My eyes slam into his and my breath catches.

Sat to Adele's left, in-between me and her, Tate's studying me in much the same way he disapproved of me doing to him just a small while earlier, only far more intense. He flashes me a smile that doesn't reach his eyes.

Crap! Crap, crapity balls! In my efforts to refrain from badgering him, seems I may have inadvertently given him cause to feel spurned. Again.

I slip my hand from the table top, reaching for his leg underneath. He lets me draw it back to mine, and I give his knee a half-apologetic, half-appreciative squeeze. His expression softens in response and I release my trapped breath.

"You should go talk to her," he suggests, voice loud enough for my ears only. "Or I could try?" A delicious warmth pulses through me.

Stroking my hand from his knee a short-yet-kinda-bold way up his thigh, I side-eye Adele and give my head a swift shake. "Thanks, but, uh..." Gah! These next words ain't gonna come easy. "She might actually be right. Letting Lyndsay work it out of her system on her own – likely the best way."

I know he has good reason for staring at my mouth, but – *oh, sweet jeezus!* – his gaze tingles like a physical caress.

His brow puckers as he considers me, eyes skimming the whole of my face. "It's not your fault, you get that, right?"

I take a hefty gulp of my drink, my throat clenching as I swallow.

My shrug isn't deemed an acceptable response, and he looks ready to say more. I don't give him the chance. Swooping in on him, a soft brush of my lips seals his.

His leg jars against my hand, a soft *'Gnnyr'* escaping him.

The wide-eyed bewilderment I'm greeted with on drawing back has my heart rate spiking. I grin, goofily.

"Wow," he starts, "that – that was..."

I strike again. Pressing a little harder this time, lingering a little longer.

And again. He hums gratifyingly against my lips. His hand covers mine on his leg and our fingers lace.

And again...

"You filthy fuckers!"

Gary's voice thunders venom through my veins.

Tate must feel me tense – my mouth stilling; my fingers clamping to stab nails into his thigh – but I don't let him break away.

Screw it, screw everything. This is my moment to step up, to act for me and me alone. And I'm goddamned taking it.

Winding my free hand around his neck, I secure him to me. I tease his lips with my tongue. He willingly lets me in and I deepen our kiss, giving him exactly what he deserves of me.

It's exhilarating. I feel powerful!

A chair screeches over the floor. "Knock it the fuck out before I knock you the fuck out!"

Closer, another chair squeals. "Just try it, Tinwell!" Adele blasts, "I'd love to crush any chance of you reproducing."

"Shut up, you miserable bitch. As if you could."

"I feel sick," I barely hear Lyndsay announce above the sounds of more chairs on the move. One topples to the floor with a crash.

Violently swatting back my flight instinct, I wrench my own chair in closer to Tate's, my hand venturing that bit further up his thigh, up to about where I know he has Deadpool's mask drawn on his jeans. I focus on his accelerated heartbeat, perfectly in synch with my own.

"Uh, guys," Callum pipes up, his voice shaky. "Maybe you should..."

"Stop!"

Tate yanks himself free, gasping in a lung's fill of air as his leg lurches away from me.

"Stop," Adele repeats, and my eyes fly open to find her hand gripping Tate's shoulder. His head twisted around to her, his profile displays a wild, disorientated confusion. Letting him go now she has his attention, she flaps her hand out at the room around us, "this is about to get real messy."

"What...?" Tate glances at me, frowning, before he turns to take in her meaning. My gaze follows.

"Hey, no, please, don't stop on our account," Derek calls out, catching my eye. There's a strain to the grin that accompanies his words, but then, it's clear he is exerting a great deal of energy into holding Gary in place. Squared up, he has one hand pressed firmly to Gary's chest, blocking the beast from an attack on us he looks all too eager for. His chair is on its side next to him. "Congrats on working it out," he adds with a wink. "The two of you look great together."

Gary shoves his bulk into Derek, sneering. "Get your faggot-loving hands off me!"

"Yeah, cos it's contagious," Derek retaliates with a sneer of his own, pushing back on him and catching up a fistful of his shirt. "And I truly am a massive faggot-lover. Especially when one has their mouth wrapped around my dick."

"Shit, Mikey." The flat tone in which Tate utters my name pulls me back to him.

Adele has her hand on his arm, running her eyes over him. "Okay?" She mouths.

He nods. But his face contradicts him.

He looks kinda sick; peaky. And... *Angry? Scared?*

I used to have a far easier time reading him. He's learned to hide so much.

Leaning in, I press my lips firmly to his shoulder. *So tense.* It's a notable age before he reciprocates, his kiss to my forehead feather-light.

I straighten. "We could..."

"Oi, oi! None of that!" My peripheral snags on the barman's hasty step out from behind the bar at the same moment the distinct sounds of a scuffle hit me.

With Derek's wrist in a vice-grip, Gary's bearing in on him. "If only you'd had the sense to get out of my face," he taunts, his other hand raised in a fist.

"Drama," Tate breathes out on a sigh. And then, louder: "It shouldn't be this fucking hard!"

He won't look at me now. I catch Adele's eye and our perplexed expressions are a match.

"I've already given out one black eye to a queer this week, but I'm real okay with giv...*GYNNAaah!*"

I miss how it happens. But somehow, suddenly, Derek's behind Gary, and Gary's arm is being savagely twisted up around his back.

Someone at my table gasps. Perhaps me.

"Pervert," Wayne spits, surging to his feet. He does no more than stand there and posture, though, when Ben fails to act on his signal. Ben's gaping, apparently dumbfounded by the power switch.

Lyndsay... uh, Lyndsay appears to have gone. *Where? When?*

The barman hovers at the edge of the bar, ready to intervene should it be necessary. "Chill time, yeah?"

"Sit. Down." Derek growls close to an ear as he presses in, wrenching the arm up further. I can't help my lips kicking up in satisfaction as Gary's bent almost double, twitching like a shored fish. *About time he met his match.* "Now."

Finally, knees buckling, he staggers back under Derek's coercive guidance to drop down into the chair behind him.

Looking every bit as smug as he should, Derek releases Gary's arm and then gives his cheek three sharp slaps while crooning, "Good. Little. Homophobe."

No sooner has he taken a step away, however, the beast rises back to his feet.

"Any more trouble and you're out!"

"Relax." Gary flashes the barman a wide and far-from-reassuring grin, circling his wrist through the air and flexing his shoulders. "I'm so done with this shit. Going for a smoke."

Crossing the pub for the doors, his swagger is as cocky as it ever is – like he hasn't just taken a major beating to his pride – and that unnerves me.

38

TRIGGER WARNING

"You!" The grin Derek sends my way kick-starts a nervous fluttering in my gut. A justifiable reaction, it turns out. "You just create chaos wherever you go, eh?" He chuckles. Pulling out a chair at the table beside ours, he copies Callum in straddling it so he's facing us. His finger then waggles between me and Tate, "nice bit of PDA there, though, boys. Awesome."

My face heats. "Uh, thanks?"

He shoves my shoulder.

Tate's eyes are grazing over Derek's colourfully inked sleeve, all the way up, pausing to inspect the skull at his collar before skipping to his amused face.

"Looks of an angel, your boyfriend has," Derek continues to poke fun, speaking to Tate. Even as I will him to stop and turn his focus elsewhere, his use of '*boyfriend*', said for the first time in a none derisive way, has my heart thrumming. "Most deceiving. Those big browns of his hide a devilish spirit."

Tate's hesitation before he flashes a small, lopsided smile, however, makes fast work of dulling that. I study him as he shifts in his seat and takes a drink, his face upholding the half-smile while Derek's playful teasing runs on. I take in the slight furrow to his brow, and the tightness of his grip on his glass. He darts me a glance when Derek says my name, and – *Oh.* It finally clicks: *Derek's talking fast. He's not following.* That ends the thrum completely.

I slip my hand into the narrow gap between his chairback and him, flattening it on the small of his back. He leans into it and his smile ticks up, just a little.

"I jest, obviously," Derek says, giving my shoulder another shove. "But, hey, bet he does keep life interesting, eh, Mac?"

"Tate," My correction slips out automatically. I wince when Derek inclines his head in apologetic acknowledgement. But, see, no one ever called him Mac before I left. Mac's the name of a stranger; a hostile stranger, mocked and ignored. And that name needs snuffing out, not spreading. *Damnit, Lyndsay!*

Thinking of whom...

"Interesting?" Adele snorts, replying in Tate's stead (because of course she figured him out before me). "Okay. Sure."

I narrow my eyes at her.

"'Scuse me." Moving free of my hand, Tate pushes his chair out from the table to stand. I track him up, questioning, and then make a move to stand, too. He puts his hand on my arm, halting me. "We're not girls, Mikey. I don't need a bathroom buddy."

Derek's set off laughing again. Adele joins him.

"Lyndsay left already?" The question bouncing on the tip of my tongue is stolen and voiced by Callum. I blink away from my watch of Tate's journey toward the toilets, returning attention to the table. "I didn't see her go."

Shaking his head in reply, Derek points his finger after Tate. "Actually, damn, I should have asked your boy to check on her." He scrunches up his nose and bites into his bottom lip, turning to the only girl at the table. "She's taking her sweet time. Would you mind?"

Adele heaves out a sigh, like she's been mightily put-upon.

"She'll be puking." Callum finishes off his Budweiser, slamming the empty bottle down on the table. "And fingers crossed she manages to purge all the stupid from her system."

So much for being through with her, eh?

"Yup," Derek nods his agreement, instantly sobering. "I've never, ever considered slapping the girl, until tonight. He's a nasty piece of work, that one."

With a heavy sigh, Callum then pushes to his feet and moves to collect his jacket from the corner of the stage. "You don't know the half of it."

"Where you going?" Adele asks, watching him zip up.

"Home." He leaves the 'Duh!' hanging in the air unsaid but does roll his eyes as he shoves his hands in his pockets. Moves himself up in my estimations, right there. He nods his farewell to each of us in turn, "catch yas in school tomorrow. And great gig once again, Derek."

"Aim to please. Thanks for coming."

As he skirts by our table, Adele springs up.

"Just checking she's not dead, yeah?" She asks Derek. "Cos I'm totally not okay with holding her hair out her face and stroking her back."

Derek studies her a moment, entertained, his brows high. "Let me know she's still breathing and conscious, that's all I ask."

"Right you are," she salutes. Then, falling in beside Callum, she says, "you've been friend-zoned for way too long to ever get out of it, surely you get that, right?"

Callum's retort sounds more like a legitimate apology, "I'm sorry, I don't recall asking for your opinion."

"Hey, no need to be sorry. You absolutely never did. But you're getting it anyway, you lucky thing," Adele's badgering continues as they weave together around the empty tables. "Gotta quit being her doormat, Cal. It's making you miserable. And to the rest of us, you come off as pathetic."

One hand reaching out for the door, he pauses and turns to her. "You're one helluva bitch," he says, grabbing and yanking the handle. I catch myself nodding. Derek snickers.

"Why, thank you!" A smirk stretches her mouth as he whirls his back to her and steps outside. She calls after him, "I do try."

The door has barely closed behind Callum, however, Adele only two strides further forward, when an ear-splitting scream has us all on the ceiling.

Across the far side of the pub, the door through to the toilets swings wide, crashing off the wall behind it. Gary hurtles out.

"Lyndsay?!" Derek bolts into action first. "If you've fucking hurt her, Tinwell... Shit! Lyndsay?"

Then Adele.

I'm half a beat behind.

"Gaz?" Wayne shouts. He and Ben hastily stand, chairs skidding back. "Oi!"

Gary doesn't react, not a flicker for any of us. There's something disturbingly vacant about his face. One hand cradling his other against his chest, his eyes lock in on the exit and he charges for it.

His move from the doorway reveals Lyndsay behind. She's supporting herself on the corridor wall, her chest heaving as she staggers forward. "He tried... I couldn't..." She gasps. "OhGodoh-GodohGod."

With a bestial growl, Derek makes a sharp change of course, vaulting over a table to intercept Gary. "I will fucking end you!"

"Mikey." Steadying herself in the doorframe, Lyndsay finally gets a fix on me as I swerve around the table Derek's just cleared. I take in the tears streaking her cheeks. And then the blood staining the sleeve of her powder-blue shirt as she gestures frantically into the corridor at her back. "Help, Mikey...Please. It's Mac."

"Tate?" My chest begins ticking fast toward explosion. "Tate!"

Every damn chair impedes my terror-driven dash. Blocking. Bruising. Tripping. Doesn't help that the ground won't stay firm beneath my feet.

Adele reaches Lyndsay first. "Breathe. Let me past." *How can she be so freaking calm?!*

My leg sends another chair toppling. I'm a lot further than half a beat behind now.

"Mac tried to help," Lyndsay gushes, working hard to make herself coherent. "But – it all happened so fast – he got slammed off the wall, then he – something's very wrong with him – and Tinwell wouldn't..."

"MOVE!" Adele orders, dropping every last shred of patience. Grabbing her shoulders, she shoves Lyndsay from the doorway and storms past.

I see Derek lunge as Gary veers last minute to avoid his attack.

I hear him call out to the barman, "Joe! Get him out of here! Tweedledum and Tweedledee over there, too. The three of them, they're now barred, right?"

And then I'm pitching into the corridor behind her.

"Tinwell blocked me in the toilets. Said it was time I repaid him. For – for all the drinks he'd got me," Lyndsay picks up her garbled explanation at my back, her every breath pulled up in a sob. "I tried to get past him. He grabbed me. Dragged me back, and I hurt my arm – it was the lock, I think. I don't know. Then Mac's suddenly there. What might've happened if – oh God!"

My gaze barely touches on a hunkered Adele before dropping to the figure at her feet, prone across the doorway to the 'Ladies'.

"Oh God, Mikey, what's wrong with him? I told him to get help. To just get help. I didn't..."

I stop listening to her.

"Stay back!" Adele warns as I launch myself for Tate. "Just give him space. He's going to be alright."

He sure as hell ain't looking like he'll be alright.

Unconscious. Body jerking. Skin ashen. Breathing laboured.

It's terrifying.

Nothing about this scene is alright. And Adele's face is doing nothing to reassure me.

What if it's another status-elep-whatever? He's been out too long already. And Tinwell slammed him into the wall, that's what Lyndsay said, she said he was slammed against the wall. He could have hit his head – off the wall; off the floor. It's been a lifetime since her scream. Is anyone timing this? My mind's whirling. *How come Saunders gets to be beside him, but I can't?*

"Shit, whoa!" Derek startles me, grabbing me from behind, holding me up before I can drop to my knees at Tate's side. "Epileptic?" He asks softly into my ear.

I don't know if I nod or not. But I'm mighty aware of the painful sound lacerating my throat as he hauls me back against him.

"This is my fault. This is all my fault," Lyndsay whimpers, "I'm sorry, Mac. Mikey, I'm so sorry. He only tried to help."

"ALSTON! WEBB!" Adele's dark eyes pierce me, and then Lyndsay. "Couple of minutes – tops – and he'll be out of it, okay? Get a grip!"

"Just let me go," I plead.

Derek doesn't let me go.

"Take it easy, Mikey. There's nothing you can do right now, just let him be," he attempts to soothe, securing his thick arms around my waist. "Lyndsay, angel, hush. Take a breath."

Neither of us take the advice. Until, at the count of 32, the spasms wracking Tate's body stop. He groans and his eyes flutter.

Wordlessly, Adele arranges herself cross-legged on the floor and eases Tate's head into her lap. His breathing's steadied, and, already, colour's returning to his face.

"Ah, see," I hear the smile in Derek's voice. "He's back."

Lyndsay's babbling ceases with one last sob.

Relief torpedoes me into hysterics.

"DRINK," Derek orders, nudging my rum and coke toward me. "Now."

We've returned to the table; a forlorn trio. Derek's sat across from me in Adele's former chair. Beside him, in Callum's, is Lyndsay. 'Last orders' has been called, and aside from Barman Joe, we're the only ones left in the place.

"Go home, Mikey," Tate'd said. But they won't let me. They're worried home wouldn't be the place I'd go. And they'd be right. So, they're keeping me here, minding me. I suspect I'll be here 'til we're kicked out, and then Derek will insist on escorting me home.

Lyndsay's recounted the whole awful string of events leading up to Tate's seizure. Several times. Until Derek felt enough reassured that Gary was interrupted before anything happened that could only be avenged with murder, and Lyndsay fully absorbed just how close to a bullet she'd put herself tonight. He's successfully calmed her down now. She's sipping her water, sobering up, and acting almost herself again.

But not me. Nope. I'm not even close. Any second now, I could explode into a million jagged shards.

Derek's not giving up, though. "My music teacher in college, Teddy, he was very open about his epilepsy – would talk about it with anyone who'd listen. Still, the first time he had a seizure in class – scary as shit. Most the class panicked, much like you did, me included. It's okay. Understandable."

I pick up my glass, roll it between my fingers for a moment, then put it back down and shove it away.

"He told us," Derek continues, "when he comes to, he always feels disorientated and drained, needs to take a bit quiet time to regroup himself. Tate's likely the same, right?"

I remain unresponsive to him. My gaze holds firm on the door; on the point I last had eyes on Tate as he let Adele lead him out and away from me. My hand's splayed on the seat of his empty chair, pretending his body's heat still warms it

"Just talk to us, Mikey," Lyndsay implores as Derek sighs. "You'll feel better for it, honestly."

Rubbish.

I don't trust myself to speak. One word is all it could take to detonate me.

Because, yeah, Tate was confused and, yeah, he did say he

needed sleep; I knew to expect all that. But he was also angry. At me. And it was, without doubt, anger that moved him to leave me behind, not a wish for alone time.

I'm even angrier at myself.

See, I thought I'd prepared myself; I've worked so hard to be ready.

Tonight was my big test, and I failed. Freaking out was the worst possible reaction I could have had. I let him down, and now he thinks I'm not up to dealing with it, not strong enough to be there for him. I saw it in his face, the guardedness returned to his eyes. Heard it in his voice when he told me to *'please, just back off'* and give him *'some fucking space'*. Felt it in his shirking of my touch.

I've sent him three texts. Derek snatched my phone from me when I attempted to make it four. He promised he'd let me know if I got a reply. I'm still waiting.

"You blame me, don't you?" Lyndsay breaks into the settled silence. "And that's okay, I deserve it."

My eyes almost shift to her. Almost.

"Lyndsay," Derek gently cautions, "stop it."

"No. I do. I totally deserve the silent treatment, too. Payback, right? I've been such a bitch. And I don't even know what I was thinking tonight, messing with Tinwell. Stupid! I hate that I got Mac in..."

"*Tate.*" The muttered chide escapes through my clenched teeth, cutting her off. It's a slip I regret.

For several long breaths, she holds quiet, and I can feel her expectancy like a weight on my shoulders.

"Seriously, stop," Derek urges. My peripheral catches the movement of his hand reaching for hers. "Mikey, please, can you just tell her this isn't necessary?"

But I don't have that for her. I really don't dare give anything.

I press my lips. Swallow. Focus on my breathing.

"You have every right to be mad at me, I know. But, Mikey, I can't stand it!" She eventually picks up again, her voice wobbly. "I miss you, and I'm so, so sorry. I just want us to be good again. What will it take?"

I sense her headshake, "I've messed up. *I'm* messed up. And you're with Mac now, and" – *tick, tick, tick* – "okay; that's okay. But... does it have to mean you can't still be there for me? I was hurt, too. And scared. Mac's not..."

Tick.

"DAMNIT!" I finally blow. "You know what, Lynds? Fine. Here you have it, okay? Yes, I do blame you." I turn from the door now, focusing the impact of my blast. It feels good. Her stunned, pained expression has zero effect on me. "*Tate* went for a piss and got caught up in your screw up. He got slammed off a wall and trig-gered into a seizure all because you've been so hell-*fucking*-bent on punishing me. *Tate* by far came out the worst from this! And, yeah, he may not have swooped in with any grand heroics, smiting down the villain. He may be still as much the scorned outcast he ever was. Fine. But he did save you. And, for that, you owe him far more than a feeble pity-hurrah." I see her nostrils flaring. "He can't stand anyone's pity."

"Pity-hurrah? I don't pity him!" She launches into her rebuttal before my mouth's even shut. "I'm sorry he got hurt, sure. And the epilepsy thing, that's rough. But there is absolutely nothing feeble about my gratitude for him stepping in tonight!"

I lift one cynical brow and she pinches in both of hers.

"He's got you believing he's some poor, bullied victim, right?" She snorts. "You've been had. Trust me. Mac turned on us. Not the other way around. He shut himself off and made quite sure we all kept our distance."

Following a pause I only scowl through, she goes on, "I don't like him, okay, I admit it. I have many reasons, but mostly... I can see he's bad for you."

"No. He's not."

"Yes." She tries to convince me with her stare. "He is. Honestly, I wasn't wanting to get into this with you tonight – not after all that's went down, but I'm worried about where your head's at. He treated you like crap, just like the rest of us. Worse, even. Yet, still, you chose him. And now he's changing you, Mikey, we've all noticed. You're letting him cut you off. You're becoming just as isolated as he is."

I'm shaking my head in furious objection. "I came tonight, didn't I?"

"Right. And then he showed up."

My gaze flicks to Derek. His eyebrows are rising up his forehead as he studies us. It's like he's hearing out each side before he chooses which one wins his support.

"Because he's trying..."

"Oh, please!" She scoffs. "Open your eyes! Mac came to check up on you. Demonstrate his claim on you. Show us all you're never off his leash. That kiss, it wasn't subtle, was it?"

It also wasn't his doing, I choke back. Her words (the extreme wrongness of them) are stabbing into me like knives. I should have held my silence.

"Wow, yeah, you're super grateful!" I spit out in a vicious whisper.

"I am."

"Not the greatest timing for this, little cuz.," Derek mutters, giving her hand a squeeze. Her flushed wince feels like one mini, flickering victory.

And then he turns, joining the attack: "Look, I'm not going to pretend like I know your boy – and I'm absolutely not about to judge him on what I've heard from Lyndsay. Not taking anything away from what he did for her tonight, either. This is purely an observation, for whatever its worth, okay?" He does at least look immensely regretful for what he's about to wound me with. I slump in my seat; worn down. "He's a tough fella to engage in conversation. And I didn't see him making much effort with anyone besides you and Missy Sharp-Tongue. I mean, maybe he's just shy, or perhaps..."

"Tate's deaf." A quiet voice hits me like a freight train.

What?! Bolting to my feet, I fire up to refute it, argue. Two pairs of stunned, wide eyes on me, however, douse the hot words from my throat; extinguish every single word I've ever known.

"Uh, what?" Lyndsay's voice whips a gash through the dense air.

Derek's mouth is frozen in a half-grin, half-grimace; not quite sure what to do.

My head floods with the memory of Tate's reaction to Adele when she spilled his secret to me. *'How long do you think he can hold the lid on this, Adele, eh?'* His words strangle my heart.

I latch on to that half-grin like a lifeline. Force out a chuckle.

It works against me.

"Mikey...?" Derek softly prods, his face now all puzzled solemnity.

It takes very little more than that and I crack; give up everything.

Tate's gonna hate me.

39

BEWARE THE WOLVES AND THE BEARS

"*W*hatcha doing?"

With one skate on and my left foot poised to slide into the other, the soft sing-songy voice at my back has me toppling to the floor. I curse. Wince. Then I whisper-curse.

"Going somewhere?" Turning my head, I find Sophie, dressed in a unicorn onesie, rocking on the balls of her feet and hugging a pink giraffe. "Can I come?"

I groan. *Busted.* "None of your business. Yes. And nope."

She purses her lips, giving me an indignant once-over. Then, her cocoa eyes take on a challenging glint. "Guess I'll have to just tell daddy on you then."

"Guess you will," I bat back.

Disappointment dulls her face. "Fine."

"Fine." Shifting my position on the floor, I get my second skate on and start fastening.

"Good."

"Good."

Sophie hovers a moment, watching me through slits, and then starts stepping backwards toward the living room.

"Hang on a minute," a thought sparks belatedly, stilling my

busy hands. I angle back around to her, my own eyes narrowing, "what are *you* doing?"

Stopped in her tracks, her mouth forms a tight, little 'O'. The glance she throws over her shoulder at the slightly ajar living room door is shifty as all hell.

"Ah," I smirk. "Guess I have something to tell your daddy too, then, huh?"

"Umm..." She gives her head a frantic shake, her eyes bugging, "No. I don't think so."

I tilt my head, pretending to consider. "Or, instead," pushing myself back up to my feet, I turn fully to her and cross my arms, "perhaps neither of us have anything to tell your daddy?"

"Oh." She hums, her eyeballs sweeping from side-to-side before her shake switches to a nod. "Kay. Yep." The extreme crookedness of her second glance back has me almost intrigued. A grin spreads wide across her crafty little face, "I like how you think, Uncle Mikey."

As she spins on her heel and disappears back into the living room, I'm thinking I should perhaps be more concerned. But I have far bigger things on my mind.

Moving around to the front door, I gently open it, step out, and ease it closed behind me. The slap of the crisp air makes me shiver, but at least the night is clear and dry. I glance up at the blanket of stars and heave a sigh.

It's 1.23am. Sophie's up to something incredibly suspicious in the living room. And I'm on my way to Tate's house.

I have no clue exactly what I'll do when I get there. Don't plan on ringing his bell, that's for sure. He'll almost definitely not still be awake. But I just couldn't stay in bed – or even in that suffocating house – any longer.

I've a letter in my pocket. A full confession of my betrayal tonight. I guess...I'll post it through his letterbox and hope that Graham doesn't get to it before he does (but, hey, it's illegal to open mail addressed to someone else, right?), then... then I'll head back and hope for some small amount of shut-eye. I just need the weight of it off me, that's all. Whatever happens after, well... I won't give him up easy.

I slip a hand into my pocket, checking for the umpteenth time, my fingers stroking over the seal of the envelope and, then, the indent of his name penned deep across the front.

A letter is the smart way to tell him, I'm still working on convincing myself. Considerate. Not cowardly. It has nothing to do with the fear of watching the change in the way he looks at me as I try to explain myself to his face. He'll have a far easier time understanding the whole of the situation from my letter than he would from having to follow the bumbling, stuttered words tripping over themselves out my mouth. Plus, this way, the warning will be there, waiting on the doormat for him, the moment he wakes up; giving him the most possible time to absorb and prepare himself.

I'm about halfway to his house when I feel my phone, tucked in behind the letter, vibrate against the back of my fingers.

My heart beats free of my chest.

Hooking a lamppost, I skid myself around it to a sharp stop and yank the phone from my pocket.

I've texted Tate a further four times since Derek returned it to me on my doorstep. Received not a single reply. Until now.

If you're still awake, I need to see you. We need to talk.

'We need to talk'?

I stare at my phone screen, reading that last part of his message over and over again, the rest of his words fuzzing out in the face of them. A sickness wells up from the pit of my stomach.

Nope. Not ready for this. Can't do it. Can't face him. Can't take it.

I've let go of the lamppost and spun to head the way I've just come when my phone dances again in my hand.

And it's like he knows I'm still up, and he knows, yet again, exactly what's going on in my head right now.

I'm so sorry. Den? Please?

Not exactly reassuring.

Okay. I take a deep, fortifying breath.

Already on my way. Be there in 5.

~

AT THE DEN, Tate's made a fire and put up a tent. Unexpected enough that I almost face planted the ground when it came into view.

I've now joined him on the blanket he's spread out across the front of the tent, seating myself to face him. A bright lamp's illuminating us on one side, while the tame fire crackles merrily on our other and the stars glint above. It's cosy perfection; heartening. My spirit's lifted considerably. "Hey."

"So, here's the thing," Tate leads in with, cautiously, as I take to the task of removing my skates, "please don't panic."

I stiffen, panic instantly blazing. I let my guard down way too soon, obviously. Something dark twists my insides.

His cheek ticks, an almost smile that I almost miss. Then, flicking a glance to the shadowy trees surrounding us, a soft chuckle escapes him. "I've set no perimeter traps. We're wide open – completely vulnerable to bear and wolf attack."

A snort's surprised out of me, a bucket's worth of tension launched out with it. I glare at him, tugging off my second skate and tossing the pair over beside the lamp, but I can't keep it up. A grin teases. "Dick!"

"But, honestly, I believe our chances of being mauled tonight are fairly slim, okay?" He kicks up the sleeping bag he has opened-out over his legs, inviting me under. I give his socked foot a sharp tap as I eagerly take him up on the offer, skooching forward and stretching my legs out by his. He grins, "if we are, I'll be the distraction. Give you time to run. Promise."

I wrap the warm cover tight around my lower half and roll my eyes at him. "Totally holding you to that."

"I insist on it. But, hey, at least my tent's not yellow. Not like the sun this time, right?"

"You're freaking hilarious."

"True."

Studying me as I study him, he seems to be in no hurry to say anything more.

I'm really not keen either.

But there's things need saying. And, so, I suck in a deep breath and start in on them. "I'm sorry, Tate. For tonight. I..."

He's shaking his head at me. "No."

"I shouldn't..."

"No," he says again, sterner, his face sharp becoming deathly serious. "Don't."

I swallow past the rapidly formed knot in my throat.

Then his hand's wrapping over mine on my lap. "You've nothing to be sorry for."

I allow for a brief moment of duping myself that, yeah, we don't need to talk about it. We could absolutely just stay here like this, together, his hand on mine, and not give voice to a single one of the hard words crowding in to divide us.

But I can't hold it.

There's an odd sort of off-ness to Tate, despite his bit joke and soothing touch; something to his vibe that seems to be adding an extra chill to the already bitter night air that neither the fire nor our sleeping bag can alleviate. And then there's the guilt spilled to paper hidden in my pocket, getting heavier and heavier with each passing minute.

"Please, just let me..."

"Seriously, shut up!" His interruption cracks out as an edged command this time. I blanch. "You should be fucking pissed at me, not apologising."

I stare, mouth gaping, not understanding. But the way he said it has my blood whooshing loudly in my ears and the knot expanding in my throat. "What? For what?"

"I lashed out at you."

"I lost my head."

"You were scared for me."

"I knew what to expect, Tate," I snap, a sudden anger flaring. My reaction was not okay, and we both know it. He can't be letting me off so easy, like it didn't ever bruise him. He surely wouldn't be if he'd only give me chance to confess what came after. "I should have held it together better!"

"I was angry with myself," he says with a laden sigh, his fingers curling around underneath mine and clasping, "not you."

His admittance is bewildering. I recover swiftly. Bend my knee until it brushes his. "Well. That's stupid."

His lips crook, but not in a way that lightens his face. "I just couldn't handle it: Seeing you like that, and knowing it was my fault."

"Stupid," I repeat, frowning. "It's not like you did it on purpose. You could hardly have prevented it."

"Exactly."

"Exactly what?"

Tate sighs again, glances away at the fire, closes his eyes for a slow count of three, and returns to me. "I tried so hard tonight. Just wanted one night to be... to prove to you I'm not..." He teeters off with a soft groan. His hand slips from mine, and from the cover, taking with it all my hopes that, actually, we'll be okay. He scrubs over his face. Carding his fingers through his hair, he starts over, "I'm broken, Mikey. And as much as I don't want to be – as much as I *try* not to be, I can't change it. That's all tonight fucking proved. Just a couple of hours acting normal, and I couldn't even pull that off. Then I behaved like a massive jerk – again. Made it all a shit-tonne worse."

I'm holding my breath, I realise. My chest burns. I feel like I'm hanging over a precipice. And then:

"I told them."

He stares at me, and I watch a subtle range of emotions flit across his face until he settles on confusion.

I feel about ready to puke my own heart out. "Lyndsay. Derek. I told them everything."

His gaze intense, he waits on me continuing. But I've got nothing. The rest of my words are jammed, clogging my throat.

My letter.

Leaning to one side, I delve a hand into my jacket pocket. My fingers hesitate, reluctant, before they pinch the slim envelope and snatch it out. I thrust it at him, "I'm sorry."

Tate stills in a way that makes my whole body tremble. His eyes jump from the letter to me and back again. He opens his mouth.

"Take it," I scrape out, shutting him off. "Read it. Please."

Mouth closing, he nods once, the motion so slight it almost doesn't count.

I kinda want to watch every nuance of his reaction as he reads my confession, but not anywhere near as much as I really, *really* don't. So, I turn away as he plucks the envelope from me, fastening my gaze on the little campfire.

But the flickering flames rile me rather than soothe – their bright, spirited dance wholly unaffected by the rip and rustle of the letter being freed.

The air around us gets thick and ugly.

It's an excruciatingly long while (far longer than one read through should take) before he offers up any reaction.

"Well. Shit."

I brace myself, turning back to him, as he finally lifts his head to face me. I see no horror in his expression, though. No sign of rage or revulsion simmering, either. I've no clue what to make of him, nor how's best to proceed. "Yeah."

"Your handwriting's as bad as it ever was."

What?! "What?" I frown at him, cos I need him to be straight with me here and we both know his curse had nothing to do with my penmanship. *Unless...* "You couldn't read it?" *Oh, sweet jeezus, please say you could read it!*

"It's okay, Mikey," Tate says, but the slant of his mouth tells me otherwise.

"No. It's not."

"You needed to talk. I fucked you up tonight, left you in a state." Dropping a glance to my scrawled admission, he tries nodding to convince me. "It's good that they were there for you."

"But they know now."

"They do."

"And there's no taking it back."

He hikes a shoulder. "Got a time machine handy?"

"I'm such an almighty screw-up. You were right, I can't keep a secret to save my life."

"Yep. I totally called that."

"Stop it, Tate!" I bark, getting annoyed. "Stop pretending like this is no big deal to you."

Pressing his lips, there's a stiff pause before he responds. "You've told me, here," he jiggles my letter, "they've promised to keep it to themselves, right?"

"Yeah. But..."

"And like you said, there's no taking it back now, is there? It's done."

"I'm so sorry," I deflate, "so very, extremely sorry."

What happens next, happens incredibly fast. I have only the briefest moment to register Tate's exasperated growl before he's throwing off the sleeping bag and launching himself across the space between us. Knocking me flat on my back, his weight pins me to the ground.

"We're taking a break from talking now," he says, his words a warm breeze over my lips, "okay?"

Dizzying arousal sweeps through me.

40

THERE WAS ONCE AN ODD-BALL CALLED TATE...

"Your're still chewing on it, aren't you?" Tate shifts, and I can feel his gaze fixing on the side of my face.

"No?" I venture the answer I know he wants. And then, realising that, in lying on my back, staring up at the clear sky, he probably won't have caught it, I turn my head and smile for him like I'm honestly not beating myself up inside.

Rolled over to his side and propped up on his elbow, he's giving me an assessing onceover, and his expression is unconvinced.

Our break from talking has been delicious. A most vibrantly absorbing time-out. But now the necessity for air and restraint has forced space between us, and my brain is refusing to stay shut down. Pretty certain, though, I'm not alone here in waging an inner battle against returning chaos: Tate's become just as fidgety and restless as I am.

Guess the lead's mine to take.

"No more apologies," I first aim to reassure him some more. Then, "I'm just...curious..."

But at the same time, Tate says, "I've been out here all night, thinking."

"What?" Follows from us both a beat apart.

I work up another smile for him.

Again, he doesn't smile back.

His eyes narrow a fraction, brow pinching. Then he shakes his head. "Me first?"

"What?" I think I repeat, but my mouth is suddenly desert-dry and there's every possibility the word withered on my tongue. Moving myself around to mirror him, I take a moment re-tucking the sleeping bag in around me, and another finding an unlumpy area of ground for my elbow. I nod.

He chews on his bottom lip, deliberating, and my stomach flutters. I welcome his hand on my hip, fiercely distracting though it is. His eyes continue to roam over my face, and his follow up is long enough coming I begin to lose focus on what I'm waiting on from him. I snap to when his grip on me tightens, fingers digging into the flesh of my hip, and my chest constricts.

There's something big brewing here, I can feel it. His mood's taken a sharp and disturbing turn, it has me all kinds of twisted up.

I tap his arm – a gentle prompt.

Then I get impatient. "Just tell me."

"Mikey..."

"Please."

Jerking up to sit, he swerves around to frown down at me. Opens his mouth. Closes it. Swallows. Turns toward the campfire. Then, setting his jaw, he shoves the sleeping bag off his legs and gets to his feet. "I don't even know where to fucking start!"

I push myself up. "Tate?"

But he's no longer looking at me. He disappears around the side of the tent. Mystified, my heart rises from my chest into my throat where it catches, swells and chokes me. Fairly sure I don't breathe until he returns into view.

He steps out from the tent with an armload of firewood clutched to his chest and his tatty backpack dangling by one strap from his elbow. He still doesn't look at me.

Crossing to the little fire, he sets down the bundle of branches, drops his backpack, and lowers himself beside them, staring into the flames.

I watch him feed the wood to the fire, one stick at a time. He's at it a long while, and it's blazing and sparking with a worrying ferocity by the time he deems himself done. The smoke and ash escaping from it is making my chest tight. *Definitely just the smoke and ash.* Moving his bag onto his lap and sliding open the zip, it's only then that he turns my way.

"I'm no good at this talking shit," he says, his hand rummaging. "I'm sorry."

"No apologies," I rasp out, "remember?" But if he's at all aware I spoke, he shows no sign.

He's drawn out a notebook and pen, and with the backpack flattened out as a makeshift lap-tray, his attention's shifted to the open page.

Putting pen to paper, he starts to write.

There's only a few small steps between us, but he feels miles away. And though I don't time him, I'd swear several lifetimes pass us by as he frantically scribbles. His words seem to be flowing without pause, like an unfiltered stream of consciousness.

Finally, he closes the notebook over the pen, shoves his bag to the ground, lifts his head, and clambers to his feet.

I track his approach, trepidation jittering through my body.

"If you're about to break up with me, I don't accept," I warn him, my voice disgustingly shaky, as he retakes his place beside me on the blanket. He crosses his legs and I pull the sleeping bag up further around my torso – protection.

His expression is anything but reassuring as he holds the notebook out to me.

I glance down at it but make no move to take it from him. "Derek and Lyndsay, right? That's what this is really about?"

He shakes his head, but what he says is, "well, sort of. A bit. But not in the way you're thinking." The notebook's thrust toward me twice more. "Your turn to read now. Please."

Despite his insistence, he doesn't eagerly relinquish it. He then moves the lamp in closer for me.

Opening the red cover to the pen page-marker, I'm assaulted by two full pages of his handwriting, sloppy and cramped and disorganised. It takes a great deal of mental preparation before I can make my eyes focus on the first line. They're instantly set to stinging.

'It keeps me up at night, thinking of you hurting and alone out here. You must have left thinking I didn't care. That kills me.

'I cared. So much. More than I could handle.

'After all we'd been through, all you'd lost, I just wanted to cling to you and never let go. But I couldn't stand seeing the pain you were in, knowing there was nothing I could do to fix it. No fucking Pokemon card was special enough to bring your smile back this time. And the goodbye between us, it felt fucking toxic.'

I bite down hard on my bottom lip.

'I begged Mum to take you in, you know? She offered, too. But your grandad didn't think it would be in your best interest to stay around here.'

No – did not know this. I whip my head up to him, gaping. Guarded eyes lock on mine and he gently nods, as if he knows exactly which point I'm at (probably, he does. He's teased me often enough about how my lips move as I read), then he drops his head.

'I felt powerless and I gave in to it.

'I'm well aware of how fucking pathetic that sounds, believe me. Selfish and weak. But there's the truth of it. You only ever really needed me to be here for you and I let you down because I wasn't strong enough. And I won't ever forgive myself for that.'

I glance up at him again. His head's still bowed. I nudge his arm three times before he looks at me.

I can't tell him that it's okay, and that he didn't crush me. Because it's not, and he did. There's no pretending like that night doesn't cause a debilitating ache in my chest whenever it's recalled. Instead, I say, "we're here now. Together."

He nods as he casts a fleeting scan around us. But, returning to me, he says, "too little, too late."

"Better late than never," I counter. "We were just kids. Tragic, messed-up kids."

"Always so fucking quick to excuse me, Mikey."

"It's done," I toss his own words from earlier back at him. "Only this, here, and onwards really matters, right?"

Dropping his head back and closing his eyes, he huffs out a laugh, a bitter exhalation of sound. "Well played."

I remain fixed on him for a few breaths longer, but he holds firm on the blanket of stars spread above.

'Then you were gone. And nothing was the same without you. I wasn't the same without you. My best friend – my only friend. More. You were my everything, and I'd let you go thinking you meant nothing to me. No more hiding from my feelings after that. They fucking tortured me. Ate me from the inside out.'

My stomach flip-flops even as I give that paragraph two – three – four read-throughs, unsure of exactly how much meaning he intended for me to take from it. His clenched jaw enlightens me none.

*'The worst part? I could have contacted you at any time, tried to explain, but I didn't. Convinced myself that you were better off letting me go along with the rest of this shitty place. Honestly, though, it was more because I didn't dare risk you saying that you **had** let me go and were doing better without me.'*

I take a break, digging the heels of my hands into my burning eye sockets.

"Got bad enough," Tate startles me, "that when Dad got that job offer, he told me it was either we take the do-over across the far side of the world, or he kicks me out." He's side-eying me warily. "I mean, I guess I knew he didn't mean it, but he made the threat sound real enough. It was the wakeup call I needed."

"I don't understand what you're getting at with this, Tate."

"Keep going."

'I'd only just made the start on sorting myself out when the illness struck, finished me off. Left me the empty shell you came back to. And you expected for us to simply pick up right where we left off. The six years apart

had ruined me, but you'd pulled through them unscarred. Hardly changed at all.'

"I've changed," I mutter.

"No," Tate catches me out again, "not in any of the ways that matter."

I snort.

'I couldn't give you who you wanted. I'd only drag you down. You truly were better off without me. That's what I told myself – how I justified shutting you out. But you wouldn't let up. Stubborn as ever. Now we're here, an 'us', and I can't even begin to wrap my head around how that happened. I've done nothing to deserve all the chances you've given me. Nothing. And I think, possibly, I ambushed you into this that night I turned up on your doorstep, wrecked. I gave you no space to think through what you'd be taking on with me. You've barely even started to figure out who you are. And this whole relationship thing, I'm feeling mighty unprepared for it. Fucking clueless.'

The hurt caused by his words is beginning to agitate the hell outta me.

There was nothing even remotely *clueless* about any of his moves on me just a short while earlier...

...I'd argue Craig *prepared* him pretty damn well.

A sweep of nausea joins the mix.

But, no. Hell no. I stomp the breaks on that line of thinking.

'Being with you tonight, at the gig, it was tough. Already, I'm failing you, exactly as I feared I would. I can see you shutting your friends out, Mikey, and it's not right. Lyndsay's been good to you, far better than I've been, and now you're not talking. Because of me. Then, there's Gary. I'm making everything so fucking difficult for you.'

Glowering down at the page, I'm shaking my head.

'What happened – how I behaved after and the way I left you, I feel like the biggest piece of shit. Worse because you're hoarding all the blame. I can't even promise you that'll be the last time. I hate not being able to rely on myself! Then you hand me that letter.'

Knew it! Here we go...

'And you were so fucking afraid of how I'd react. Do you even realise

how messed up that is??? You shouldn't feel that way. Not ever! But, again, that's all on me. You have plenty enough with your gran to deal with, and I've asked for too much from you.'

I dart him a glance but he's apparently too fascinated by his jiggling right foot.

'All I keep thinking about is how much more you deserve. Someone you can relax with, who'll take some of your strain rather than add to it. Someone to look out for you. Like Derek did tonight.'

Wait. What?

"Derek?!" I blast him, tossing the notebook down beside me. I've had quite enough of this. "Tell me I did not just read what I think I did!"

He doesn't respond cos his foot continues to have him mesmerised.

I kick out at him, catching him on the heel, and repeat myself when his head snaps up.

His brows draw down to darken his face. Yup, I've finally caught him off guard. He acknowledges the discarded notebook with a sigh. "You've not finished it, have you?"

"Gonna need more explanation here," I steam on over him. "You think I should be with Derek?"

"Fuck!" He winces. "No, that's not it at all. Derek's just... just an example."

"But we're a mistake, right? A guaranteed train wreck? You're fit only for the scrap heap, and I'm still way too much the immature, naïve kid to handle you?"

He heaves out another almighty sigh, flicking a nudging glance down at his letter.

I ignore it. Continuing to stare at him because, hell, he's gotta give me more than that.

After a long moment of silent study, he leans in pulse-quickeningly close. But the move's only to snatch up the notebook. Smoothing out the page, he scans over it and mutters, "my writing's almost as fucking illegible as yours." His twitchy little smirk kinda makes me wanna hit him. Then, dropping back, he clears his throat and, in a voice too flat for comfort, says, "I'm not going to look at you as I read this out, so there's no point you talking."

He starts, "*This is me, opening up and letting you in.*"

Then he stops. Rolling the notebook into a tube, he lifts it, drawing it back past his shoulder, and sends it flying toward the fire. "Fuck it."

The notebook narrowly escapes its doom, landing a little short and too far right. My peripheral catches its good fortune as I remain locked expectantly on Tate.

His gaze barely brushes mine, one side of his bottom lip pulled in between his teeth, before he lies himself down on the blanket and stretches his arm across the space between us.

"Come here," he urges. The tremor to his voice flips my pulse to racing again. "Please."

I do.

Laying my head on his shoulder, I nestle into his chest. He pulls the sleeping bag over us and snakes his arm around me, wrapping me tighter in to him. Bypassing conscious consent, his breathing and his heartbeat begin to allay my nerves. I flatten a hand over his stomach and he presses a kiss to my forehead.

"Try this a different way," he murmurs into my hair. His free hand moves over mine, weighing my palm into the ridges of his abdomen. "Okay?"

I incline my head, tucking it in under his chin.

"Naive and immature? Yeah," he startles me from my count at eight heartbeats. His arm around me tenses as the words hum softly through his throat. "A little bit. Overly sensitive, completely neurotic, and awkward as all hell sometimes too."

"Hey!" I jerk, creating a wedge of space between us, and he takes in my baffled face with a cautious smirk.

"You're also smart, and you're funny." His lips kick up further. "You have the brightest, most genuine smile. And fascinating eyes, so dark and deep I feel like – like I could lose myself in them. You hide nothing. Even when you try, your face gives you away. So openly expressive, I love that." My heart catches the exact same moment his voice does.

Love.

The simple word fills his brief hesitation, and I become acutely self-conscious of my flushed cheeks.

"You're my happy place, Mikey," he continues after a steadying breath. "You've always been my happy place."

A delicious heat floods my entire body. "And you're mine."

He halts my eager move in toward him with a minute shake of his head. "Loyal to a fault. You've never turned your back. Not once." The affectionate curve to his mouth slips and my brow pinches. "Against all good sense. Forgiven me far too easy for far too much. And now this? I just... I can't make sense of how... It's more than I dared hope for. But I'm worried − fucking terrified − that this might be the absolute worst I've ever done to you. A push too far." He leaves no pause for my objection. "I've held so much back from you, and it's all stacked up against us. I can feel it ready to crush me at any minute. I can see myself destroying this − destroying you."

I don't let his headshake hold me off this time. Closing the distance between us, my mouth takes his without finesse, without restraint, without a single further thought.

He resists me at first, pulling back to groan my name against my lips.

"I chased you, remember?" I whisper back on his. He won't know what I said. But that doesn't matter. I thwart his attempt to sever our contact. "I'm not letting you go."

His surrender comes the instant my tongue strokes his. Then, in the next instant, the play of power switches.

There's an edge of desperation to his kiss; a search for reassurance. His need for that from me is my own reassurance, and I give myself over to him, forcefully shutting off my brain.

Pushing me into the ground, he moans as our bodies meet. He rocks into me and the motion awakens an excitement I have zero control over. I feel his heart beating as rapidly as my own. He's all strong arms and sure hands, decisive lips and deft tongue.

When he breaks away, my head's swimming.

He's breathing hard, his parted lips swollen. Dipping his head, he licks a stripe along my collar bone before leaning a little away and raking his gaze over me, one questioning brow arched.

Mighty aware of his fingers tracing the skin along the waistband of my jeans, I'm just barely able to nod my consent.

Tate doesn't break eye contact as he undoes my button and fly, then his.

My heart swells, crushing my lungs, as his hand returns to me, sliding under my jacket and shirt to stroke up my chest. He moves in, and I feel his teeth nip the soft skin of my earlobe. His hand trails slowly back down my torso and I shudder.

When he follows the line of hair leading from my belly button into the band of my boxers, however, my hand snaps to his wrist, locking around it. The play of his fingers over my eager tip stills abruptly and he jerks back.

I'm as alarmed by my reaction as he is.

I want this. I want this so freaking bad.

I can barely withstand his careful assessment of my face.

He knows what he's doing. He's done this before. Perhaps many times.

The exact moment he deciphers my expression is made obvious by his sharp intake of air, and I suddenly lose the ability to draw in any air at all.

I release my hold on him and he's quick to pull away. Clambering up to his knees, he reaches over me and, as I watch him unzip the tent's entrance flaps, my attempts at breathing cease altogether. Until, that is, he turns back to me, grins wide, and grabs hold of the sleeping bag.

"Come on," he says, "it's been a heavy night. Let's get some sleep."

Oxygen rushes my tight lungs as I follow him inside.

Snug. There's an airbed filling the small space. I wait at the foot as Tate crawls over it, switches on a lamp hanging from the dome's centre point, and settles on the left – always his chosen side. He spreads out the sleeping bag and motions me in beside him.

"I'm in no rush." He turns to face me as I lie next to him. His arm slips comfortingly around my waist. "This'll go at your pace. Okay?"

My boxers remain exposed, I remain rock hard inside them, and I'm thoroughly despising my brain right now.

I swallow hard against the tangled lump in my throat. Then: "Please don't ever again tell me what I should and shouldn't do; what I need and what I don't. I have enough people doing that. We're gonna work out, Tate. It's the only thing in my life I have absolute faith in."

He frowns, his expression too complex to read. I figure he missed most of what I said, but then he tips his head in closer, sliding his hand free from under it to cover my racing heart. "Your turn. What are you curious about?"

"What?"

"Earlier. You said there was something that had you curious."

Ah. Right. I remember. *Your tale of self-discovery.* I shake my head. *No longer in a fit state to pursue that line of enquiry.* "Doesn't matter."

His gaze probes my face for a minute or two. And then he bursts into verse:

"There was once an odd-ball called Tate,

who was mad at his very best mate.

Cos his mate kissed girls,

let them play with his curls,

and forgot to come out for a skate."

"What the...?" I snigger. In a bewildered and unglued kinda way. I can't help it. That was bizarre. "Sweet Jeezus! What the hell, Tate?"

"I wrote that after I'd caught you kissing Bridget behind the slide," he goes on, dropping his gaze. His lips kick up on one side in a way that instantly sobers me. "When you'd gone off with her to play on her trampoline. Instead of coming back to mine. Not shitting you, I was furious."

"Bridget? Bridget Morris?"

"Yeah."

"We were, what? Ten?" I nod, rooting out the dusty memory. "You... you stopped talking to me."

"Because kissing girls just – I don't know. I mean, it's not a thing I'd really ever thought too much about. But then, suddenly, you're kissing Bridget... and you're choosing her over me... and I'm left feeling like there must be something wrong with me."

"The next day, her friends made fun of her and she told me she hated me," I wince. "That was the day Gary ripped up my Gyarados card." A grin softly ghosts. "And you gave me your Lucario."

"Yeah. A particularly shitty day for you, that one." His fingers slip under the bottom of my coat to massage the small of my back while his eyes seem to be fighting to stay open, skating over the lines of my face. "You weren't smiling, and I missed it. Felt fucking empty without it. That card brought it back. So bright. And I guess," he hesitates, fixing on my mouth, "I guess that *that* was the first moment of realisation – of a sort, anyway."

I stare at him, stunned.

"Too much?"

I open my mouth, but only manage to shape, "no."

Whatever it is my face is doing appears to convince him well enough. Yawning, he finally lets his eyes drift closed. "Always been you."

41

THE WALL

I stayed awake a long while, simply watching him.

The moment he pulled me closer in his sleep, entwined his legs with mine and puffed out a contented sigh: That made life complete.

What felt like mere moments after I'd allowed my own eyes to drift shut, I was awoken by the touch of warm lips on my throat.

Voice hoarse, Tate told me he needed to get home before his dad woke up.

We emerged from the tent to a frigid world not yet lightened by dawn. The fire had burnt out and the lamp on the blanket was dimmed close to death.

He offered to walk me home. My sleep-fogged head screamed *YES!* but my mouth said "no." Instead, I walked with him the short way through the trees to his back-garden gate, and then we parted ways with a tame press of lips.

I managed to catch another hour of sleep in bed before my alarm gave me a far less pleasant wake-up call.

I'm now in second period Study, sat alone.

Tate didn't call for me this morning, and he's not in school. I've texted him but he's yet to reply. And Adele blanked me when I called out to her as she headed into her form room first thing.

My brain's already drawn the conclusion that, perhaps, we're not as 'sorted' as I thought us to be. I keep fixating on that moment I slammed the brakes on his move for more, and on our unsatisfying goodbye kiss at his gate.

If I wasn't so scared of discovering myself right, I'd be ditching school to hunt him down.

There's plenty of gossip buzzing around the classrooms and through the corridors today, and my one source of relief is that, for once, Tate and I aren't the focus of it. Gary's another extremely conspicuous absentee today, and Steph is out for his blood. I've noticed Ben and Wayne actively dodging her.

Derek accompanied Lyndsay in this morning, they had a long meeting with Principal Carston. Our mild-mannered Head looked thoroughly agitated when he escorted Derek out afterwards. Then Lyndsay spent the entirety of first period in the small Student Counselling office with Miss Desdree. I saw her disappearing into the girls' loos just before the second bell sounded, her eyes looked puffy and red. Need to find her as soon as this class is over; we need to talk.

I've been staring at this same page of fraction problems for over half an hour, my pencil's marked no more than a single dot on the paper. I'm done with even trying to concentrate. Instead, I'm listening in to the conversation between the three girls at the table behind me and slying regular glances down at my silenced phone.

Alice Brent is telling her friends that she'd overheard Principal Carston talking with Mr Garrimay. Apparently, Gary's blown all his chances, he's getting thrown out of YCS. I'm hoping with everything crossed that she's overheard right.

IT'S lunchtime before I hear back from Tate. His text simply reads:

I'll see you after school :)

The smiley face definitely curbs my anxiety some.

"Aww, that's loverboy then, is it?" Steph coos beside me, bumping her shoulder off mine. We're ambling our way toward the lunch hall. "Look at you all goofy-faced! And you've gone bright red now. That's adorable."

"Shut up," I mutter, tucking my phone away in my trouser pocket.

Hooking my elbow as we turn a corner, she laughs.

Then, with a jarring abruptness, she stops. "No. Way. You have got to be kidding me!"

We're passing by the windows looking out onto the quad. I follow her gaze out over it, and my pulse automatically thrums with anticipation of finding Tate there. But, of course, he's not.

Our usual table isn't empty though. I see Adele. And Callum, sat in my space beside her. And they're the cause of Steph's sudden distraction.

They are an unexpected pairing. I'm pretty sure they've not shared more than a word between them until last night. Both have their backs to us, so little can be made of their interaction but the space separating the two is slim.

"What's Cal thinking of?" Steph's pulled us up to the window and she's glaring. I frown at her, not at all grasping what exactly her issue is. "Her? Really?"

Ah.

"Good for them." Lyndsay's voice at my shoulder scares the living bejeezus outta me.

I'm slow in turning to her. I haven't seen her since she slipped into the toilets, and I don't know what reception I should be preparing for from her.

My lips twitch into a nervous smile. "Hey."

"Hey, Mikey." She smiles back. An audible sigh of relief streams from my mouth as she moves to my free side and I feel her fingers gently brush over my arm. "You okay?"

"What you asking if he's okay for?" Steph cuts over me before I even get a word out. "And you can't seriously be okay with *that*," she goes on, flapping her hand toward the glass, "I'm not buying it."

I snap my mouth shut, my gaze darting from one girl to the other.

Lyndsay looks genuinely baffled. "Why wouldn't I be?"

"After what happened last night? The minute you actually need him to be there for you, and he suddenly develops a wandering eye. Come on, girl, so not on."

"I don't need him. I'm okay. Good, actually. Tinwell's totally screwed himself, and we'll all soon be rid of him. Besides, Callum's just talking to her. For all we know, he's helping her with homework."

Steph snorts.

"Me and him weren't ever going to be a thing, Steph."

"Fine." Rolling her eyes, Steph drops my elbow and starts walking. "Keep living in denial, little dove. Come along, I'm starving!"

One step forward and I'm pulled up short by Lyndsay grabbing hold of my sleeve. "You can trust me. Your secret's safe."

The fierce rush of gratitude her soft reassurance incites knocks me dumb. I almost hug her.

But she doesn't hang about. Releasing my shirt, she hurries on past me after Steph, calling back: "Last one there gets the broken chair!"

I ACKNOWLEDGE a distinct pang of disappointment when I come out of school and Tate's not waiting for me. It's the first I realise that I'd even been expecting him.

The afternoon has dragged, History class feeling like the longest fifty minutes of my life, and I can't stand the thought of yet more waiting.

I walk home with Lyndsay and Steph. And Alex, a step behind. I'm acutely aware of his eyes branding my back, it has me tense.

Lyndsay doesn't say much as we walk side by side. She hasn't said much all day. And nothing more whatsoever on the events of last night or what I revealed about Tate. Despite her claims to the contrary, it's obvious she's still shaken up. But she's trying with me; brushing off my verbal blow-out on her, she seems keen to work on re-establishing our friendship. This extra chance she's giving me, her understanding and her promise, it's not something I'm taking for granted.

Steph's more than up for filling the silence. Her dialogue requires no contribution from others, and she appears entirely unconcerned by our inattentiveness.

When we reach the end of the long driveway, we find Derek waiting.

"What are you doing here?" Lyndsay snaps as he joins us. But she doesn't mask herself quick enough and I can tell she's pleased to see him.

He catches her out on that, too. Grinning, he throws his arm around her shoulders and squeezes her in to him. "Did he show up?"

"Nope," Alex answers him as Lyndsay half-heartedly tries to squirm herself free. His gaze roams around us as a bodyguard's would. "No sign."

Scrunching up her face, Lyndsay sends her cousin clear warning to drop the subject.

Derek dips his head at Alex before dragging and pinning an enthusiastic Steph in to his other side. When his gaze lands on me, I duck.

He may be Lyndsay's cousin and, seemingly, a decent guy, but I don't know him anywhere near well enough for him to have so much on me. It strikes me now how unsettling that is.

It's not until we've passed the park, once Steph and Alex have veered away from us toward the View, that Derek turns to me again.

"I'm taking Lyndsay for a coffee. Fancy coming?"

"Oh." My eyes flick to Lyndsay and she shrugs. "Thanks. But I... I already have plans."

"With Tate, I'm guessing? You boys solid again, then?"

"Yeah." *He ended his text with a smiley face.* "I think."

He nods, and I can feel my face colour under his friendly concern. "Well, another time then, yeah? And, hey, don't forget, if you need to talk, anytime, you have my number." Then, flashing a smile, he starts leading Lyndsay away.

"Thanks," I call after them, meaning it. "Enjoy your weekend."

"See you Monday, Mikey," Lyndsay volleys back.

I'm feeling pretty good by the time I reach the house. I've decided I'm gonna slip in to check on Gran and then I'm heading straight back out for Tate's. Everything seems to be working out in my favour for once, but until I get firm assurance from him that we are, in fact, absolutely solid again, I'll not be able to fully relax.

"Mikey? That you?" Gran's voice belts out from the kitchen the moment I shut the door behind me. A moment later, she's bustling into the hall. "Jesus wept, boy! Where on earth ha' ye been?"

Dropping my bag to the floor, I take in her flustered glower and my heart sinks like a brick. "School, Gran. I've been at school."

"Ye can haddaway tellin' me fibs!" She snaps, throwing her hands up. "Ye've a friend here for a playdate. All bloody day he's been waitin' on ye."

"What?"

"Gran?" I hear David. "Come on, your egg's getting cold."

Her eyes narrow on me in a way I've learnt to fear. "Four cupsa tea Suzy's fetched him. What're ye playin' at, eh?" She moves closer. "Ye canna go about makin' plans wi' folk and then disappearin' on em!"

"Tate?" My voice comes out too high. "Is he still here?" I ask, taking a careful step toward the stairs. Then another.

"Tha's not how I raised ye," Gran's scolding chases me. "I'll be havin' a proper word wi' ye later, mind. Best have a bloody good apology ready!"

There's no talking to her when she's like this. She'll just wind herself up angrier and angrier if I were to try. Then things would get thrown, and it'd end with one of us in tears. Or both.

I bump into Suzy at the top of the stairs. She has an empty mug in her hand and she uses it to gesture toward my closed bedroom door. Her face tells me that Gran's been at her most challenging for a while. I hesitate. With an understanding pat to my shoulder, she squeezes past me. "Go on. Ye'll sharp be smiling, pet."

~

"Nowhere near finished." Tate says, his eyes fixed on the side of my face, making my skin tingle. I don't need to turn to know my reaction has him grinning smugly.

I can't stop looking at it. So much detail and colour. Every time I scan across, I'm discovering something new. It's magnificent.

"Was a touch cocky to think I'd be done in a day," he adds. "Not disappointed, are you? That it's completely different to what was here before?"

"Disappointed?" It's a wrench to turn myself away from the stunning art adorning my wall, but for all he may have said that with the lightness of a joke, something in his voice has me thinking he's genuinely unsure. For a moment, I do no more than absorb the delicious heat of his gaze. Then I'm crashing into him, driving him back towards my bed.

Our fall onto my mattress is clumsy and a little painful. But, as I adjust to straddle him, pressing him down under me, and seize his lips with mine, I don't think my immense appreciation could possibly be made any more non-verbally clear. He groans into my mouth, and I become keenly aware of his erection nudging against mine.

I'm forced to ease up off him, just a bit. Our positioning is far from comfortable.

"Thank fuck!" He murmurs with a chuckle once he's managed

to catch a breath. Grabbing my hips, he gracelessly rolls us over, so that we're lying side-by-side, eye-to-eye. "I've been stressing over that design for days."

I track his hand's move down into his trousers, watch him readjust himself, and my gaze lingers a little too long to appear unaffected by the action. When I drag my eyes back up, it's gratifying to find he's as flushed as I know I am, his pupils blown.

I swallow. "So, that's why you stayed off today? To surprise me with this?"

"Partly," he shrugs a shoulder, sucking in his reddened bottom lip. Then he jets out a breath. "But, no, not really. Dad caught me sneaking in this morning. And when I told him about last night, he went ballistic. Made me stay home. Sent me back to bed. Lack of sleep, stress, charged emotions – all big triggers, you see. So, yeah, I slept through most the morning. Then, when dad went to work, I saw the opportunity and I took it. Been here since about eleven. Suzy's taken very good care of me."

I force my thoughts away from Gran's attack when I came in, and Suzy's weary expression as she passed me by in my escape. Not ready to bring myself down, not yet.

Darting forward, I credit him another kiss. Swift but significant.

Then, I'm skipping back through what he's said.

"You... you told your dad?"

His smile tweaks into something almost coy and his brow pinches. "I did."

"Just about your seizure or...?"

He slowly shakes his head. "Everything. I tell my dad everything, Mikey."

"Oh." Stricken, I become incapable of anything more than staring at him.

I suppose I should be feeling fortunate that I'm still breathing. Though, chances are, I won't be for much longer.

Tate's now apparently decided this is amusing. "He's not out to kill you. Promise."

But he hates me, I blink.

"Dad only wants for me to be happy," he says, moving his hand from my hip to trail up my spine. It's wonderfully distracting. "And he knows you make me happy."

I'm working my mouth for quite some time before I manage to rasp out, "Laura?"

My heart starts pumping way too fast when he nods. "Remember when Meg interrupted us at the den? She was very quick to tell that I wasn't there alone."

Jeezus! "But... Meg doesn't know who I am."

"Fuck, Mikey, Mum knows I'd not be there with anyone else." He leans in, luring me closer. "Besides, her description was unmistakeable: Blond and goofy looking."

My hand smacks off his chest.

His laughter finally escapes him. "Mum adores you. Always has." He dips his head to recapture my straying gaze. "And she's been pestering for a catch up, driving me mad over it ever since she heard you were back. So... Guess now's actually a pretty good time to ask you about that."

"Ask?" The blood is whooshing in my ears way too loud for me to think clearly. "Ask what?"

42

NO POINT CRYING OVER SPILT ORANGE JUICE

'*Think I've figured out what I'm getting for Megan and Laura.*' I write on a clean page of my English notebook. '*Just something small each, before you start rolling your eyes. But you have to help me out with your dad. Please, I beg you. A few suggestions to work with, that's all I'm asking.*'

Ripping out the sheet then folding it in half, I nudge Tate's shoulder until he turns and then pass it to him.

He frowns at me, questioningly, before straightening to face front again. I study the back of his head as he drops his gaze to read my note.

Principal Carston's called a full-school assembly, taking us all out of fourth period early. My class was one of the last to arrive at the auditorium, Mr Bell having fought against the disruption to his maths lesson, and I found Tate already seated in the third row, hemmed in on both sides by year eights and nines. While my year twelve classmates headed straight for the back, joining the rest of sixth form, I nabbed myself a spare chair two over from his on the row behind.

It all kicked off this morning.

Tate was summoned to the office midway through Study, asked to give his account of what occurred at the Desperate For Aces gig. He hadn't returned by the end of the period, and so I hovered around reception, waiting on him.

That's when I saw Gary arrive, escorted into school by his grim-faced parents. And he looked downtrodden enough that I almost – *almost* felt a little sorry for him... until he nailed me with a pitbull sneer.

Moments later, Tate emerged, and Gary was whip-sharp in redirecting his malice to the floor. I half expected to be called in for my statement too. But, no, we were promptly shooed on our way.

Mr Tinwell apparently didn't take well to the news of Gary's dismissal from sixth form. Word is, the police were called in and he had to be forcibly removed from the grounds.

The auditorium was abuzz with excited murmurs when Mr Bell led our class in, and my nerves were set to jittering. But as Principal Carston took to the stage and launched into an anti-bullying lecture, drumming in the school's zero-tolerance policy, complete with PowerPoint presentation, the mood of the assembly has quickly dimmed to bored chatter. Carston's now preaching on the dangers and severe consequences attached to underage drinking. No names or specific incidences have been directly addressed. Quite the anti-climax for most, but I'm relieved.

I lean forward in my chair as Tate pulls his pen from behind his ear and starts scribbling me a reply. I'm forced to stretch when he bends his arm up over his shoulder to pass the paper back, darting me a sidelong glance and a smile.

'If you're so absolutely determined, gift Megan a little something as a 'well done' after her recital. No one else needs anything, I've told you already. We're just going for a pub meal. And I want you there to make the evening more bearable for me as much as anything else. Stop stressing.'

Not helpful. I huff out a frustrated sigh as I put my pen to the paper once again:

*'Stressing is what I do best, you know this. I'm not just your best friend anymore, Tate. I'm your **boyfriend**. And that's a big deal. Thursday feels like I'm about to meet your family for the very first time. I need to win your dad over. You need to help me. Please?'*

The bell sounds, marking the start of lunch, just as he takes the note back from me. All around, pupils begin gathering their stuff and readying themselves to leave even though our Principal's spiel continues.

I stay seated, awaiting a useful response.

I don't get one: *'You bring out my good side. That's enough.'*

"Your every action has a consequence. Think on that." Principal Carston bellows into the microphone, wrapping up over the swelling noise of inattentiveness. "Now, enjoy your lunch, everyone. You're excused."

The pigtailed redhead to my left is stood glaring at me, waiting to get out. Muttering a few obscenities under my breath, I crumple the note up in my fist, snatch up my bag, and stand.

Tate's rumbling chuckle halts my shuffle along the row. "Coffee. Dad likes good coffee," he concedes with a shake of his head. I narrow my eyes at him, unconvinced by the suggestion, but his raised brow cautions me not to quibble. "The beans. Not the instant shit. And the stronger, the better."

Right. Good. Workable, perhaps.

We meet in the aisle and I take his offered hand, letting him guide me into the exiting traffic. I regain his attention once we make it outside. "You coming over mine again tonight?"

We've – *he's* – worked hard on my wall all weekend. To my eyes, it's completed to absolute perfection. But he's insistent there's more to be done. I can't get enough of watching him work, so I give him no argument. He's also spent some time over the past two days teaching me the basics of sign. Although reluctant to at first, once he discovered my efforts to be hilarious, his enthusiasm sharp climbed. He's welcome to laugh at me all he wants, I've decided; I really like that I have that effect on him.

"Sorry," he winces. "I'm game testing tonight."

"Ah." My disgruntled pout makes a return. I drop my head to hide it.

His yank on my hand comes without warning and I pitch into him. Someone passing by gasps as I yelp. Then, using his body, he backs me up into an alcove. "But, hey, I have the house all to myself 'til ten."

"Sooo..." I drag in an unsteady breath, cursing my instinctive sweep around us. "I can come watch?"

"Can you promise not to distract me?"

"No."

A smile curves his mouth, promising wonderful acts of misbehaviour. "Any time after five."

GRAN'S HAD an exceptional couple of days, lucid and chirpy.

On Tuesday, the sun shone, and Suzy took her out. They walked through the park, feeding the ducks and enjoying ice cream, rounding the day off with a cream tea sat outside the riverside café. Gran was eager to tell me all about it right from the moment I arrived in from school. We talked for hours and she made us both beans on toast for tea.

Yesterday, I came downstairs following a shower to find Tate'd come over early. He was sat with Gran at the kitchen table, and I stood quietly in the doorway for a long while, savouring the scene. Gran was regaling him with the tale of the time Grandad Jim asked for my help building a wardrobe and, not five minutes in, I'd broken his foot with the hammer. Wasn't funny to any of us at the time, that. Still isn't to me (Grandad was convinced I'd done it deliberately). But seeing Gran and Tate laughing over it made me smile. When I did finally interrupt the pair, Gran had nothing but good things to say about my '*handsome friend*'.

I haven't been able to enjoy this precious time with *my* Gran as much as I realise I should, however. Because ever present and nagging is the knowledge that her upswing can't last. She's not better; won't ever get better. And any given moment could be the one in which she slips back down.

It's today that dreaded moment comes. Thursday. *Freaking Thursday!* The day my nerves have more than enough reasons to be fraught as it is.

I'm up in my room, just finished packing for the Newcastle trip tomorrow and about to make a start on getting ready for my big '*re*-meet the family' date, when Gran's scream shatters the peace.

"GERROFF! I SAID NO. YE CANNA MAKE ME, WOMAN!"

"Stop that, Evelyn!" I hear Suzy say, her voice raised and razor sharp, as I pound down the stairs. "Come on now, yer going to hurt yersel'!"

"YE THINK ME DAFT, IS THAT IT?" Gran continues to shout, and I can tell she's worked herself to tears. "I'M NOT DAFT! I SEE WHAT YER BLOODY DOIN'!"

I burst into the sitting room just as something smashes off the wall close enough to the right side of my head that I career left to dodge, smacking my elbow off the bookcase.

"Oh, dear love, thank goodness!" Gran launches herself across the room and seizes my arm before I've even had chance to get my feet back under me. She stabs a vicious finger at Suzy. "She wants me dead! I heard 'er plottin'. She's try'na poison me, Mikey."

Yep. She's slipped, and she's fallen hard.

Suzy's clutching on to the back of the sofa, staring wide-eyed at the shattered glass strewn across a soaked patch of carpet beside me.

"Suzy? What's going on?" It's so hard to hold an even tone. Gran's clawing hold on my bicep is painful and she has me pinned up hard against the bookcase. "Where's David and Mel?"

I watch her mouth open and close several times before she recovers her voice. "I... I sent them out for family time. I'm sorry, pet. I'm so sorry. They've took the bairn out to the pictures."

"LIES!" Gran screeches over her. I recoil, swerving my ear away from her. "Ye canna believe a word she says! She's a liar! She's wicked!"

"Shh, Gran," I attempt to soothe, my eyes sending her a desperate plea, "it's okay. I'm here now, and nothing's gonna happen. I won't let anything happen."

"I'm sorry," Suzy repeats, her bottom lip trembling. If not for the sofa propping her, I doubt she'd still be standing. "Ev's been doin' so well. And all today, all she's gone on about is spendin' the night relaxin' with her shows. And I thought, wey, I'm off home the morrow. May as well give them a night out afore I'm gone. Ye know?"

I don't react fast enough as Gran releases my arm and bolts forward. "YE WILLNA FOOL HIM!"

Suzy doesn't budge. Whether standing her ground or petrified to the spot, I'm not sure.

I manage to snag Gran's shoulder just before she makes it out of reach. Wrapping my arm around her waist, I haul her back. She crumples into me, sobs wracking her frail body, and I tighten my hold on her.

"Go, Suzy," I say, my voice thick as my own tears break free. "I think you best leave us."

She starts to shake her head, but the objection's weak. I jut my head towards the door and she obeys.

"Only orange juice. Freshly squeezed orange juice," she says, edging past us and waving her hand toward the messy breakage. "Was always her favourite. This'll need cleanin' up."

I'd reach out to her if my arms weren't all that's holding Gran up. "It can wait. I'll sort it." I raise a cautioning brow as she looks set to protest. "I've got this."

Feels like all my strength follows Suzy out. The moment the door clicks shut behind her, my legs threaten to buckle. I manage to manoeuvre Gran around to the sofa and we collapse down together onto it. She curls into me.

I FELL ASLEEP.

Heart jackhammering in my chest, I take the stairs two at a time. My phone's in my room. I need to text Tate, explain.

Goddamnit! Gran and I fell asleep on the sofa. Sophie woke us, barging into the sitting room, singing, when the three of them returned from the cinema. Mel took over with Gran, leading her off to bed. The broken glass and spillage had disappeared – Suzy, I assume. Wish she'd woken us. I'm now beyond late for dinner. Likely missed it altogether. *Crap, crap, CRAP!*

Barrelling into my room, I trip over my suitcase as I dive for my phone on the desk. My knee smacks off the bed frame and I flop forward onto the mattress with a howl of pain.

Hurts. Like a. *Bitch*!

Really do not have the freaking time for this!

When I finally retrieve my phone, I find nine unread messages and three missed video calls.

*17:36: **You on your way yet? Need to leave in about 20mins x***

*17:44: **Oi! Where you at? X***

*17:45: **You know you're meant to come here first, right? :/ X***

*17:59: **Can't wait on you any longer, sorry. Meet us at the hall? Show starts at 6.30. I'll hang back for you in the lobby x***

*18:11: **You missed a video call from Tate.***

*18:14: **You missed a video call from Tate.***

*18:28: **I'm going in now. We're sat halfway along third row. Text me when you get here x***

*19:02: **Worried now :/ What's going on? X***

*19:35: **Ok, heading to the Ship. Hopefully see you there.***

*19:53: **You missed a video call from Tate.***

*19.55: **Nice. Real nice. Half expected you'd fucking bottle it, but thought you'd at least let me know.***

*20:10: **This isn't like you. Everything ok? Your gran? Hoping you're just grounded or some shit. And you've lost/broke your phone. I'm coming over.***

He's on his way over. Good. That's good.

But...the time is now 20:40... He should be here already...

Shoving my phone into my jeans pocket, I change my t-shirt, throw on a hoody, jam my feet into my skates and snatch up the bag of McAllister pressies from the floor. Then, taking a pitstop in the bathroom to splash my face with water and to blast some deodorant, I'm out the house into the wind and rain.

HOLD THE SUGAR-COATING

*R*eadjusting my grip on my skates, I shiver in my damp clothes, glancing around the quiet inn. The atmosphere tonight is far removed from what I've experienced here on gig nights. Aside from the two of us, there's only seven other people in. "Thanks for meeting me."

"No problem." Derek hands me a pint glass and gestures with his own toward a door I haven't noticed before, set in an alcove between the bar and the stage. "Come on."

Dropping my eyes to my socked feet, I follow him across the sticky carpet through it and up a long flight of bare-wood stairs. *Should have worn shoes.*

At the top, he reveals a key in his clenched fist and opens a second door with it, leading me into a long room furnished with little more than two shabby pool tables. "So, stab in the dark here," he says as he flicks on the lights, "you're finding this relationship shit tough? You and Tate hit on another obstacle, huh?"

Thrown by his no-nonsense approach, my head's nodding before my brain okays it to. I slam the breaks. "That's not what I want to talk about."

"No?" He turns to me, cocking his head, his gaze curious. "Then, please, enlighten me."

This was a mistake. I drop my skates down beside the door and sweep my gaze over the dingy room. It feels so wrong to be up here, so totally alone with him. *I shouldn't be here.*

But after what I've just witnessed – after what's just happened, I couldn't face returning to the house. I needed someone to talk to. And, well, Derek did offer. What it is I want to talk about, though, I actually have no idea.

Some preamble would have been appreciated.

"Do you have a boyfriend?" I finally query as my eyes continue to wander.

"I do not."

"But you've had a boyfriend before, right?"

"Nope. Not really."

My glass lifted, I jerk it to a halt just before it reaches my lips, eyes narrowing in on him dubiously.

"Just coke," Derek assures me, missing my point. He smirks at me as I nod and take a sip. And then, with a shrug of apparent unconcern, he adds, "I'm what many would consider a 'slut'."

I sputter, struggling to swallow.

"Careful there," he chuckles, giving my back a spine-jarring slap before striding away, circling the nearest table. "I haven't found my someone special yet." Stopping at the far end, he puts his drink of *just coke?* down on the table's edge, beside the corner pocket, then bends and retrieves the triangle from a slot underneath. "But I'm thoroughly enjoying the search."

"Oh." I move to the large sash window, place my coke down on the peeling off-white sill, and lean back against the wall beside it. "Okay."

Folding my arms across my chest, I watch him as he collects and drops the balls into the triangle. And when I say watch, I mean appraise.

His colourful ink's hard to ignore, drawing the eye over some mighty impressive muscle definition; charming cheek-dimples accentuate his playful grin and spirited eyes. Drummer in a band with an intriguing 'bad boy, good heart' vibe about him, comfortable in his own skin... *Yeah,* I'm sure Derek has very little trouble finding willing bodies to warm his bed.

He lifts his gaze, catching me out, as he rolls the balls into position on the table and removes their plastic coop. "Look, Mikey, you want to do something other than talk, you need only say. I'll take you back to mine right now."

Whoa. My eyes flash wide. *What?!* I blink away to the window, gawking blindly out onto the well-lit street below.

"Genuine offer," Derek continues. "I'd look after you well and teach you plenty. Distract you for a while."

I slowly slide my eyes back to him and regret the decision, instantly baking inside my skin.

He waits for me to respond, his fix on me unsettling. I open my mouth, but no words come out. And that appears to be the reaction he expected.

His face relaxes into a broad grin. "Then, I'd send you away with the black ink of guilt blotting your soul, and so would end our budding friendship." He collects two pool cues from the wall rack beside the table and tosses one to me. "You can break."

Still several bewildered steps behind him, I fumble the catch and the stick clatters gracelessly to the floor.

"We would also, most certainly, crush Lyndsay. Daresay, she'd cut us both out. Your boyfriend, too, I imagine."

I snatch up the cue and stalk up to the table, glaring across it at him. "What. The. Hell?"

"You're a real mess, tonight."

"Am not!" I lie as I slam the cue point hard into the felt instead of the waiting white. "That one doesn't count."

"You know your elbow's bleeding through your sleeve?"

"Yes."

"And your jeans are filthy. You're also limping a bit."

"Yes."

"So, if we're not going to screw," he winks, "think you could just cut the shit and tell me what you called me here to?"

I focus way harder than necessary on lining up my second shot. Manage to hit the white this time, aggressively, and it scatters the balls every which way. But none find a pocket.

"Orrr you could assault this innocent, old guy." He goads, patting the table while giving his head a sorry shake as the balls batter themselves off the cushions and each other.

"Tate was with his ex, tonight," I bite, stomping the cue butt against the grubby floorboards. "In his car. And they almost ran me over."

"Wow. Yikes." Sucking in a sharp breath through his teeth, his face turns very solemn, very fast. He scrubs a hand over his shaven scalp while his other wafts over me, "so, that's how...?"

I shake my head. No, that earth-shattering blow caused only internal damage. All my physical is the result of the epic tumble I took on my way here; my first skating blunder in a good long time.

"Right. Well, then. Fancy running me through it from the start?"

With a heavy sigh, I cave.

We play as I talk. Lashing out at the balls proves most therapeutic, even if I do keep losing – badly. I begin my tragic tale with Gran's meltdown, and he listens without comment or question.

Up until I reach the point in the story where, two streets away from Tate's, a black car almost stole me away to the afterlife:

"Take a breath, Mikey," he says. "You've stopped making sense."

I heed his advice, but it doesn't especially help. My head's throbbing with the terrifying chaos of screeching brakes and blaring horn, savage headlights blinding me.

Derek prompts me on, "but you weren't hit?"

"Do I look dead to you?" I snap, a touch unfairly, as I strike the blue striped ball (not even mine) clear off the table.

"A little bit," he teases in a weak attempt to lift my mood. "Someone really needs to teach you some road safety, kid."

Taking another undue – but uncontested – turn, I leave him to go retrieve the fleeing ball. "Made it to the curb. Car stopped a short way past me." And it's just after this point I kinda wished I had been obliterated. Like my bag of stupid gifts, accidently sacrificed to the road in my panic. *Damnit!* "Craig got out the driver side, hurled abuse at me. He was fuming and I was shaking. I tried to apologise. But then... Tate."

"Right." Again with the sorry headshake. "So, what did he say?"

"Nothing."

"Nothing?"

"Couldn't stay there, could I?" I sag. "Not when he's stood there with Craig, glaring at me like I'm a *fucking* nuisance. Obvious what was going on!"

For a moment, Derek studies me silently. Then, bending, he takes his shot. Two balls go down. "The car wasn't parked up and rocking with steamy windows, Mikey." He lines up his next pot. "You see Tate's head bobbing at Craig's crotch?"

My grip on the cue stick tightens.

"Craig zipping up his fly when he got out the car?"

I'm sick a little bit in my mouth. "Shut up!" As if my mind's not fractured enough as it is.

"No?" With another of his balls disappearing from the table, he flashes me an insensitive smirk. I snatch up the chalk. "Then I don't follow. What was so obviously going on?"

"Tate's mad at me. Craig's god-like. They were together," I spell it out for him. "Rekindling."

He guffaws. "Holy shit! I'm so glad I didn't take you home."

Ouch!

Chalking my cue tip secures my full, undivided attention.

"Give me your phone."

I ignore him.

"Let me see it a sec." His hand reaches out over the pool table, fingers snapping. "C'mon."

In my mind, I'm stotting the chalk block off his head.

"Hand it over."

"No!" I blast, putting down the blue cube and backing away

from the table as he starts around it toward me. "You're not getting hold of my phone again, Derek."

Stopping in the space I've just vacated, Derek snags up the chalk as if that was his sole objective all along. "You know, I'm really happy with how the band's going right now," he then randomly boasts. "We're tight, and all the hard work we've put in finally looks to be paying off."

"Okay." My backside bumps the windowsill and I perch down on it. "What?"

I don't even register his spring-loaded move, but I'm suddenly pinned against the glass and his nimble fingers are lifting my phone from my jeans pocket.

"Hey!"

The thieving prick's speedy in putting the full length of the room between us. "Oh good. No passcode. That makes things easy. Aaand you've got five new messages."

Lurching to my feet, I give chase. "What you doing?"

He doesn't let me get close, skipping clear of my every advance. "Stick with me here, Mikey. I'm about to get real deep."

"Quit being a jackass!"

"Hasn't always been so great. We've had our fair share of fall outs, took some knocks."

"Phone, Derek," I growl over him. "Now."

"Shane once punched me in the face, knocked a tooth out. One dumb misunderstanding too many that got out of hand. Could have so easily marked the end of us, right there. I could have walked away, cut the ties, joined a new band. But, no." His eyes finally lift from the screen, thumb shifting to its edge, but he continues to dodge me. "Cos, you see, I've made a commitment to the Aces; bound my future to them. And I know that, no matter how rough it can get sometimes, what we're building together is worth fighting for."

"Yeah, okay, I get what you're saying."

"Do you?"

"But it's hardly the same."

"Is it not?" My phone buzzes in his hand. He glances down at it and his grin splits wide. "You don't consider your boy worth fighting for, is that it?"

"No. I mean, yes. I mean...*Fuck!*"

"You've a real knack for taking something complicated enough already and ramping it up, don't you?" Giving up his cat and mouse play, he presses my phone into my palm and then pats my cheek twice. "Come on, drink up while I clear the table. Our session is over. He's expecting you."

44

SLEDGEHAMMERED

"*O*h, thank goodness, Mikey!" Laura swings the front door open on me before I've even dropped my finger from the bell, and she has me locked in an embrace by her second word.

Heartening signs that she, at least, isn't foaming mad at me for this evening's ruined plans.

"Hey, Laura," I wheeze into her hair, my nose tickled by the fine fly-away strays of her bun.

"In you come then." She doesn't let me go until she's steered me inside. The warmth of the hall is glorious. "You're drenched through."

In my attempt to shut out the sodden night behind me, I trip over the doormat. But as I catch myself on the wall, my eyes catch on the floaty emerald scarf draped loosely around her neck and I'm immediately thrown to staggering again.

Feeling one hand on my elbow, helping me steady, I watch her other lift to finger the bright strip of fabric trailing her cream sweater. "It's beautiful. Very thoughtful, thank you."

"How...?" I break off as I lift my gaze to meet hers. My mind switches track in a heartbeat. "Is Tate... Everything okay?"

"Oh, yes. Yes, everything's fine." Darting a telling glance up the stairs, she works harder on her smile, but it still fails to quite touch her eyes. "So I keep being told." At the soft titter she tacks on, a shiver runs down my spine and I hunch into my damp hoody in a futile effort to combat it.

"He's...?"

"You've got ten minutes, boy," Graham's booming voice then amplifies my bone-deep chill. He appears in the kitchen doorway at the end of the narrow hall. "It's late."

Megan squeezes around in front of him, yawning wide. Still dressed up in her pastel pink ballet attire, a small bear's head peeping out of her cropped cardigan, she fastens her sleepy eyes on me and lifts her hands.

My stomach flutters. I'm being tested on my promise, her challenging little smirk tells me. It's dismal how little I'm able to decipher, slow as she signs. But, as she pats the teddy's head and then spells out B-E-T-S-Y, I take a stab at signing back *'you're welcome'*. My efforts score a beaming grin.

Graham's quirking eyebrow is the ultimate pass, though; I think it's possibly the biggest gesture of approval he's ever awarded me. I experience a fleeting warm fuzziness before his all too familiar glower returns and he grumbles, "sloppy."

With a squeeze to my elbow, Laura mercifully breaks me from his stare-down. There's no fondness in the look she's sending her *ex*-husband, and it has my insides tying themselves up all the tighter. The house feels revived, just by having her in it, but she's in black stilettos, not her fluffy slippers, and she somehow no longer looks at home here. "Go on up, sweetheart," she urges me, "he'll be glad to see you."

Not so sure about that.

"The bedroom door stays open." I'm warned in a tone only a fool with a death wish would dare dismiss as I bend to tug off my skates.

It's on jelly legs I climb the stairs, actively avoiding any further eye contact with Graham. I hear the two of them squabbling in hushed tones at my back, and despite not making out a word of it, their every hostile murmur scores like a fresh wound. How often had I wished, as a kid, that my parents were more like Tate's? Sought refuge here when the angry words were flying like bullets at home? *More restraint should be shown in front of Megan!*

I've reached the top step when Graham's voice lifts, booming. "For petesake, woman. Fine." Then, raising it another few notches, he calls up after me, "thanks for the coffee."

"No problem," I squeak. And instantly squirm in the discomfort of my lameness.

Tate doesn't look away from his trio of computer screens when I let myself into his room. I know he knows I'm here, though – he'll have been alerted by, first, the flashing green LED on his desk when I buzzed at the front door, and then the blue when I pressed the button outside his bedroom before entering. No clue what game it is he's playing, but it isn't one he seems to be especially engaged in.

"I rescued your presents," he says in lieu of a greeting. "All unharmed, amazingly." His tone's flat. Not encouraging.

"Yeah, I gathered," I reply pointlessly to the back of his head as I remain hovering and fidgety just inside the open doorway.

"Well, all except for the funsize Mars bars. Mine, I assume? Their fate was unfortunate."

I'm halfway across his floor and preparing myself for hijacking his lap when he finally swivels his chair around to face me. I stop mid-step. "Tate, about tonight. I get that you're mad I missed..."

"Dad dropped me off at yours after the meal," he shuts me down, shaking his head. "I spoke to Suzy. You were sleeping, she said, and she wasn't keen to disturb you."

"Oh." *Goddamnit! She should absolutely have disturbed me.*

"I was told about what happened – with your gran," he continues. Sympathetic understanding softens his voice a fraction, but it does little to soothe the tension from my shoulders. My mouth screws to one side and I nod. "I'm not mad that you missed it."

"But you are mad?"

If I'd somehow managed to miss all the clues in his reception, body language, voice and face, his next words would have sledge-hammered me:

"I'm not coming to Newcastle tomorrow."

As it is, I still find myself woefully underprepared for the savagery of his blow.

"What?" My eyes zip to the floorspace beneath his desk, where a fat blue duffel bag has been stashed, packed-up ready, for almost a week; it's still there. "Don't say that. Yes, you are."

He raps his knuckles off his knee, one – two – three times, and then sighs. "Suzy's not even aware you've invited me, Mikey. David neither, right?"

"So."

"So? So, what, I'm supposed to just show up tomorrow with my bag? The unwelcome tag along. You seriously thought that would be okay?"

Restarting my feet, I perch myself on the foot of his bed and Tate rotates his chair, bringing his leg within inches of mine. "Suzy's not gonna mind. And I really don't give a toss how David takes it. I want you with me. If he has a problem, then that's tough."

"Un-fucking-believable," he mutters. "Using me to get at your brother." Head dipping, his fingertips rub circles over his temples. "You were about to drag me into the crossfire, and you couldn't give a shit."

I lean forward and reach a hand toward his chess-piece adorned thigh, but a curling of his lip warns me off. "That's not how it is."

"Really? Then how is it?"

"You wanted me with you tonight to act as a buffer between your parents. It's the same thing."

Barking out a hollow laugh, he catches up a fistful of hair and tugs. "For starters, both my parents knew you were coming. And secondly, they are also fully aware of our relationship status."

I gnaw aggressively at the inside of my cheek as he holds me in a bruising stare. With a stiff shrug, I fold, "I'll clear it for you, okay? Tonight."

But that's not enough for him. "This thing with David, it's toxic. You need this weekend. You need to at least try to work shit out with him."

"Please, Tate. We've made plans already. I'll ring the prick right now."

He's unswayed, his mind set, "I'd only restrict you anyway. I'm not coming, Mikey."

"This is such bull!" I snap. Launching to my feet, I put distance between us. "It's Craig, ain't it? Bet you're cursing me for catching you out."

Eyes widening like I've slapped him, he shakes his head. "Really hoping you did not just say what I think you did."

The blast of regret for my accusation is instant, but I make no attempt to take it back. Instead, I fold my arms across my chest and push on: "What were you doing with him?"

"Craig caught me on my way home from yours. He offered me a lift, to save me from the rain. That's it. He's nothing to do with anything."

"And?" I spur him on. He sure as hell wasn't taken straight home, or he'd have been back way before I set out hunting him.

"You actually believe something happened, don't you?" His eyes interrogate my face for any least hint of denial. "I regretted getting in the car the instant I shut the fucking door. Knew it was a mistake."

The corrosive seed of insecurity is just too goddamn deeply imbedded in my gut. "Would you even have told me? If I hadn't seen?" I feel it sprout in his hesitation to answer. "Well?"

"He just wanted to talk," he reluctantly surrenders, side-stepping my question. "Apologise, I guess." And then he flares. "He held me hostage in the car, okay? Wouldn't let me out or take me anywhere until he'd fully fucking unburdened himself. I've no clue what he hoped to get out of it, but he sharp dropped his bullshit when I fucking seizured on him again. And then, for the grand shitfest finale, bam! There you are, gunning for a mow down. So close! Vanishing in the next blink."

"He...You..." My words jam, clogging my throat.

Apology.

Seizure.

Again.

"...What?"

His frown crumples into a grimace as I drop back down on the mattress.

I wait for him to elaborate; long for him to just reach out and touch me. But, mouth flatlining and body held rigid, he does neither.

"Tell me."

"He wasn't ever anything more than a dim blip of light in a long stretch of dark," he barely whispers. "No threat to you."

"Tell. Me."

The silence becomes thick as tar. I watch him grind his teeth for a long while until:

"Craig's only ever cared about Craig. That's a truth I realised too late."

All the hairs along my arms leap to attention.

Flexing his jaw, he continues. "He turned on me when Gary outed us. Told me I was a mistake. Said I disgusted him. Made me feel dirty. Worthless. But even then, I didn't see it."

There's no disguising the injured look that passes over my face, giving me away, but he's reinforced his guard and it's holding strong.

"I was struck down sick right as all that shit was still very fresh. Wasn't until I got back to school – after – that my eyes were forced wide-open to him. My reappearance stirred up the old gossip-pot, and he wasted no time laying into me for it. Had zero lip-reading skills then, but he made himself clear enough. Blamed me for fucking him over. For ditching him to take all the flack. He wasn't interested in where I'd been. Or what'd happened to me. Wouldn't hear me when I tried to tell him. Just got angrier and angrier, all up in my face. I snapped, then; decked him. That's the last of my time I spared for him, and a week later, he... he'd switched YCS for college."

"So, suddenly – out of the blue – tonight, he's overcome with regret?" I steal uneasily into his next pause as his eyes stray from mine, ranging over my face. "Why now?"

He hushes me with a twitch of his jaw and a slow shake of his head. "The day this happened," he says, leaning a little to one side and inching up his t-shirt, just enough to flash a peek of the nasty gash scoring his torso, "Craig... he saw it. He's the one who took me to the hospital. And he stayed with me until my dad got there."

My heart stutters painfully to a stop and plummets to my feet.

"I was a fucking mess. Because of you; because of how effort-lessly you... you wrenched-up everything I'd worked so hard, for so long, to fucking bury. Because of the savage end to my seizure-free stretch. He witnessed two more on the short drive to A and E, and a fourth right outside the doors. I made a bad call – letting him stay... letting him in. But in that rock bottom moment, Craig was the only one there with me. And he was being great. I slipped, remembering him as the first boy who'd liked me the same way I'd liked him; how he – in the beginning – had made me feel alright with who I am." He drags in a breath through his nose and barks out a jarring laugh on his exhale. "Slammed to my senses sharp enough when... when at the end of it, he ranked my damage – the wreck of my head – beneath the fucking blight of our incurable gayness. As self-absorbed and deeply closeted as he ever was. And when Dad showed up, he scarpered – seriously, Dad worships you in comparison. But, since then, he's been, uh...unshakeable."

I dig my knuckles into my thighs, my nails gouging my palms. Clearing my throat, I finally dislodge my voice. It scrapes out, rough and raw. "So. Not only is Craig in on your secret, he's also very much *not* 'history'. And you deliberately didn't tell me."

"Cos I knew how you'd react. And there's really nothing to it worth you stressing over."

"Okay for you to take issue with me keeping David in the dark, but I'm being unreasonable, is that it?"

Bolting to my feet, I dodge his reaching hand. Too late for that now. I'm done. And I desperately need to get myself out of this intolerable pit tonight's thrown us into. "Enjoy your weekend."

"Mikey, don't." He's up and on my heel, failing another clumsy attempt for contact. "I'm trying... Fuck Craig! I only got in the bastard car to shut him down – put an end to it."

I slam his door on him and hurl myself down the stairs.

45

AIN'T NO PLACE LIKE HOME

"*H*ey, Miktard," Jody drops heavily onto the dilapidated sofa beside me and prods at my shoulder through the hole of my Wile E. Coyote tee. "Why so glum, chum?"

I swat her hand away before I look up from my phone. We've been here, in Leeson's squalid flat, for less than an hour, and already her pupils are so dilated, I can make out only a slim band of blue around them. "I'm not glum."

"Yeah? Fancy telling your face that, then?" She laughs as she lets her head thud against my arm. My nostrils are irritated by the sickly-sweet smoky scent she's wafting up them with her every move. "Smile, man. You're the guest of honour here tonight!"

Hardly, I roll my eyes.

I persuaded David to set off early this morning, rather than hold off until after school. Surprisingly, he took very little convincing. Suzy needed slightly more. But by eight am we were on our way. Though tedious and strained, the long journey was hiccup-free, and we arrived in Newcastle just after three. I spared only the time it took to drop my bag in my old room – bare and depressing – before I legged it the hell out for Jody's.

I had it all worked out in my head, how I was gonna come out to her; played through the whole spectrum of ways I thought she might possibly react.

But my big news didn't make the impact I'd anticipated. Cracking up, she congratulated me for finally catching on. And when told about Tate, her only query was whether I bottomed or topped. Then she forced me into tagging along to this dive. I've been granted little more than a handful of minutes with her since we arrived.

"Thinking of maybe having a mosey out to town in a bit," Flynn announces as he saunters over to join us, perching down next to Jody, on the sofa's broken arm. "Yeah?"

"Perhaps," I reply, with a non-committal shrug, before realising his invite hadn't been directed at me.

Jabbing my ribs with a sharp elbow while sluggishly angling around, Jody frowns up at him, "Why would we go out?"

"For some fresh air, babe." He leans in close, his hand trailing up her inner thigh, and I'm quick to look away. "Some good, clean, sobering fresh air. You need it." I then hear a slap, to which he reacts with an amused, "OW, woman!"

Chip-shop Paul is no longer Jody's other half, I've discovered this evening. That honourable position now belongs to his former best mate. There'd been quite the messy fallout, apparently, though Jody had got a blatant kick out of the two blokes fighting over her.

And another, far more alarming discovery I've made tonight: I always felt uncomfortable around Flynn because I totally had a thing for him. Glaringly obvious, now I understand myself.

Although it's not a flame that still burns, this unlocked awareness of it has, infuriatingly, hiked up the discomfort I feel around him rather than expelled it. Being the third wheel between him and Jody – my first – isn't helping, not when I'm feeling pathetic and lonely and wretched enough as it is. But then, also... his dark hair, his lanky frame, his easy grin... *damn!*

My phone vibrates in my hand and my gaze whips down to the screen. Message nineteen of the day. Mostly unread, and none replied to. Neither Tate, nor David this time, though. It's Lyndsay. I open it.

Missed you today. I know you're away in Geordieland, but if you get a chance can you give me a call please? X

Jody startles upright as I spring to my feet and tug my jacket free from behind her. "Tit!" She berates me. "No rush. We ain't going anywhere right this minute."

"Just gotta make a quick call," I say as I pick my careful way across the cluttered and littered room to the door. A glance behind me finds Flynn commandeering my seat. He wastes no time in bodily pinning Jody to the sofa, devouring her face. I hurry out the stifling flat into dank and forbidding fog. The drastic change in temperature immediately has my teeth chattering.

"Thought you'd be far too busy with your old friends to call me tonight." Lyndsay picks up on the second ring. Her sweet voice magics a comforting trickle of warmth through me. "Everything okay?"

With only the narrowest of footpaths separating Leeson's flat from the busy road, and a fast-moving trail of headlights all that's visible passing by on it, my back presses flush against the rough wall of the run-down three storey. I hug my free arm around my chest as I fib, "yeah, all is well."

"Much changed up there in your absence?"

"Nah. Not really." Sucking in a lungful of dense air, I huff out a cloud. "What about down your end?"

Her tinkling laugh fills my ear. "Oh, you know. Gone less than a day, and the town's slammed into shutdown without you, Mikey."

"Ha. I'd expect nothing less." _This is good._

"I've had quite the eventful day, actually, though."

_Uh-oh._ "Yeah?"

"Umhmm," she hums. "Craig showed up outside school this afternoon."

Heart stuttering, my words trip over themselves. "For what? Tate? Why?"

"No." I can hear the frown in her voice. "Me. I assumed he was there for Alex, cos he's done that plenty before. But he seemed keen no one else saw him. And he said some really weird stuff."

"Like... what?"

"Well. Like how he wished that I was what he wanted, and how great we could be together if he wasn't so wrong in the head. He blasted me with this crazy, tortured outpour, then. Just. Hugged me, said 'don't know what you both see in him', and walked off."

"Huh," is all I've got as my fingertips gouge my ribs.

"Told Derek about it, and he suggested I should speak to you. So, uh, here I am."

A strained moment's silence settles over the line.

Then, "I... Honestly, Lynds, I've not the foggiest what's going on with Craig. All as I know about it is..." Breaking off, I bite down hard on my lip.

This isn't something I can talk through with her, I've learnt that lesson. She's specifically asked me to keep her well free of mine and Tate's relationship business.

"Okay, look," she says, realising I don't intend to finish, "I get that it's to do with Mac." No attempt is made to correct her slip this time. "Seriously, what's *not* to do with him these days? But. Craig, he...it was messed up. And disturbing. So, as much as I already regret asking, will you clue me in please?"

I need no further prompting. Taking another deep breath, I fill her in on the events of last night.

Wrapping up my tale at the here and now, lost in the fog on an unfavourable street, I wait out her prolonged and mute digestion of it.

I've over-splurged, the unsettling hush makes plain, and she's likely considering me a worthy rival for Craig in the 'disturbed' stakes. At no point had she asked to hear about Gran and David-the-dick, nor how miserably ill-fitting I now find my once-comfortable life here to be.

Just as I'm about to apologise, Lyndsay finally breaks the seal with a sighed, "oh, Mikey."

"I don't know what to say," she continues after a further

weighty pause. "I knew you were having a tough time. But, wow, that's too much. Way too much."

"You only wanted an explanation for Craig. I'm sorry."

"Pfft! Stuff Craig. He dropped me without a second thought. Besides, there's nothing anyone can do for him until he's ready to do something for himself." An acute vibe of wariness travels the vast distance between us before she goes on: "You're not especially helping yourself either, though. I mean, I get how you feel about Mac and everything..." Again, my jaw tensing, I give her a pass. "Please don't take this the wrong way. But... neither of you are in a good place right now. And, maybe, you should be thinking about..."

"Still with this? Seriously?" I explode over her, stricken. "Tate's not a sacrifice I'm willing to make!"

"No, that's not what I'm saying!" Her attempt to placate is lightening-fast. "You can't think me *that* cold, surely? Just that... well, it's crazy to think you can carry his weight on top of everything else going on, Mikey. You can't support him anymore than he can, you. If you don't give yourselves some space to breathe – to live a little outside of each other – you've got to see the risk it all falling apart, right?"

My spine's rigid against the wall. I've already endured much the same crap she's spouting from Tate, that night by the fire at the den. *Breathing space*, that's what he suggested for this weekend when he ditched me on it last night. Smarts just as bad coming from her as it did him. A furious shake casts the words from my head and I imagine them dissipating in the fog. "Was he in school today? Did you see him?"

"Skulking around like a vengeful spirit, yeah."

Dropping my head back on the coarse brick, I squeeze my eyes shut. We fall into another lull. I'm about ready to call it, say good-bye, when Lyndsay pipes back up.

"You can at least stop giving Craig a place between you. Cos he's not any kind of threat." Glad she can't see my sceptical lip curl. "And all that other stuff – with your gran and your brother... you know, even if all the good I can serve is to lend a listening ear, you can count on me, okay? But, honestly, if you and Mac hope to really make a go of it together, I think your biggest hurdle is his whopping great secret. To stand any chance, he needs to give it up."

"That's not for anyone but him to..." I'm interrupted by the snick and creak of the flat's front door opening. Leeson tumbles through it first, hacking his lungs up. His zombie-esque friend slouches out on his heels. "Hang on a mo, Lynds."

I catch Jody's arm as she and Flynn bring up the rear. "Hey, think I'm gonna head home now."

"What? No!" She flaps a hand at Flynn, instructing him to close the door. He obeys. "The night is young, Miktard, and we're going for kebab. Come on!"

I shrug, "Just not feeling it."

"You are the *least* fun."

"That I am."

"We'll catch you again before you go, though, right?" Flynn says, delivering an unnecessarily hearty fist to my bicep before pulling his pouting girlfriend in close and steering her around. "You've been missed, man."

"Sure." My reply hits his back as he guides Jody along the street without a second glance after Leeson and the undead. Within a few steps, the night's ghostly veil has swallowed them. "If you fancy a skate tomorrow, Jody, give me a bell."

"Will do, rabbit stew!" Her disembodied voice calls out as I return the phone to my ear. "Laters loser!"

"That was Jody then, huh?"

"Yup. And her new slave." *My old crush...*Man, it feels like a whole other life. Straightening up off the wall, I start walking. "I can't make Tate tell. It's not my place to."

"I know. I know it's his decision to make. And I won't leak a word of it, I swear. Keeping a secret like that, though, it's so not smart. He's stunting himself. You and your relationship right alongside. Surely you see that?"

"Pushing him on it would do more harm than good."

"He was okay about me and Derek, right?"

"Cos I had your promise it'd go no further."

"Hey! He's got to be due more credit than that. I'm worried about you. And the hard truth is, if he truly cares about you as much as he should, he has to be prepared to start taking down all those walls he hides behind."

'You were so fucking afraid of how I'd react.' My mind snags again on that letter he penned me. *'Do you even realise how messed up that is??? You shouldn't feel that way. Not ever!'*

A fine drizzle starts, and I huddle deeper into my jacket, tugging up the hood. "And just when did you become so wise?"

"Meh, it comes and goes."

"You're a damn good friend, Lynds."

"I am," she agrees, the trace of a smile in her voice. "And hopefully someday I'll find someone who can see me as more."

Lyndsay stays with me, a welcome companion on my treacherous journey through the shrouded streets, saying goodnight only once I'm safely delivered to my front door, fumbling the key into the lock.

Takes some major steeling to step inside my sad, empty shell of a home. More still to carry myself along the hall to the kitchen, where I'm yet again met by the unsightly scene of my brother sat with Suzy at the table. I don't quite make it through the doorway.

"Thought you had a hotel room?"

David rakes a disparaging eye over me before he shakes his head. "There's a lot to be done this weekend. You were brought along to help."

I bristle but hold my tongue.

"Where on earth have ye been all night, pet?" Suzy chimes up. "Flyin' out like a bat from hell a minute after ye've stepped in."

With a glance from one to the other, I pry up a sullen shoulder and turn my back, "I'm exhausted. I'm going to bed."

"He can't keep this up forever," David's voice trails after me, "can he?"

~

SOUL DESTROYING WORK, this: Sorting through Gran's stuff and packing it away in boxes. All that remains here are the things deemed not worth bringing with us in the move, pieces there's simply no room for in Yoverton, so most of it is marked for a trip to the charity shops. I've put aside a few items; bits Gran may have forgotten about but possibly would want kept. Now, though, I'm trying not to look too closely or think too hard.

The sitting room and my room have been done. Currently, I'm sat on Gran's bedroom floor, going through the drawers of her dressing table.

It's proving remarkably easy to keep my mind distracted. Cos since 7pm yesterday, I've heard nothing from Tate. I finally caved last night, in bed, and read through all his texts. Leading in with remorse and concern, they got progressively less tolerant in tone the longer I'd blanked him. His final one simply said: *See you when you get back.* I tried video calling him, but he didn't pick up. So, then I messaged, *I've been a gigantic asshat. Unusual for me, right? Missing you like crazy and will speak to you tomorrow. Goodnight x*

Called him twice today, but seems he's now fixed on doling me out some payback. At least, I hope that's all it is.

Just as I'm about to drop a Roses tin full of buttons into the half-filled box beside me, Hannah's hand shoots out to snatch it from me.

"Where in hell is your head at, boy?" She scolds when my eyes bolt up to her. "Chuck this in there like you were about to, and you'll smash the mirror to bits. Seven years bad luck that'd curse you with. Christ almighty!"

"Pining after your special gentleman friend, eh?"

I whirl around on Jean. "What?!" My voice shrills out, a painful surprise even to my own ears.

Remaining busy at the wardrobe behind me, Jean chortles. "Suzy's told us all about it."

All the colour drains from my face, collecting and transforming into bile at the back of my throat. "What?" I repeat, barely a whisper this time.

"Oh, you daft sod, relax!" She finally extracts herself to peek around the door at me. "We may be old biddies, but we ain't old fashioned. This Tate of yours, he's a lovely fella, by all we've heard. Good looking, and well-mannered to boot."

Gaping at her, I open my mouth but nothing comes out. I snap it shut, cough, and try again. "You're okay with it? Me being... gay?"

Hannah starts braying like a donkey and slaps my leg. "Listen to him, Jean. Sounds like he's admitting to being a hunted criminal!"

"Admirable that you're learning sign language for him." Jean's given me far too little time to recover before dealing me this second blow, and all remaining wind is slammed from my lungs. "You should let me introduce you to Roger. He's been deaf more'n fifty year."

Need... need... *a drink?* Yes. Desperately. Not the bottle of water next to me. Something unwise and potent to dull the edges, loosen the knots. *Because that's always worked out well for me.*

And then the door opens and Suzy bustles into the room. "What's happenin' in here, then?" One look at me seems to be answer enough for her. "Ah. Right."

"How? How did you find out?" I rasp, eyeballing her.

"If that was yer best attempt at subtlety, pet," she replies, her expression turning defensive, "it were bloody awful."

Head dropping, my hands whip up to conceal the total collapse of my face.

"All as any of us want," I hear Jean above me, her voice now solemn, "is for you to find your place in this world. If this lad of yours is helping with that, then we're glad of him."

Words fail me, but Suzy's quick to pick up my slack. "Smitten, the pair of 'em. That wall the boy did for him, made even my toughened old heart turn gooey."

I feel exposed. Like they've peeled away my clothes, rendering me stark naked, vulnerable and defenceless.

The prickle behind my eyes is levelling up to a white-hot burn.

"Oh, hey now, come on, kid." An arm wraps around my shoulders and then I'm being drawn into Hannah's side. She squeezes me, her soft body jiggling with poorly repressed laughter. "Ain't no need for this."

She's right. I realise this. These three women, friends – *family*, they're not attacking me. I'm not ashamed of who I am, not anymore – nor what Tate is to me. And their awareness of Tate's secret is nothing I need fear (even if they didn't live across the far side of the country from him and all who'd care). It's just that...

Screw the drink!

Giving my face a vigorous scrub, I twist myself free and clamber to my feet. "I... I, um..." I'm incapable of meeting their expectant gazes.

I need an immediate escape from this roasting room.

Jody hasn't been in touch, but she's about to have me knocking anyway.

I need to skate.

"Go on, pet," Suzy urges me, nudging her head from me to the door. "I'll take over here."

I hesitate for barely a heartbeat.

As we pass by each other, she hooks my elbow and leans in close. "Yer gran'd be chuffed for ye too, ye know?"

46

COS MAKING UP IS HARD TO DO

*S*lamming my bedroom door, I sag back against it and close my eyes. The ninja-assault of conflicting emotions has me reeling, and it's a good, long while before I feel up to... well, anything.

When I do finally reopen my eyes, and fix them on my skates, sat lonely on the floor space my desk used to fill, I can muster no drive to cross the floor and collect them. My energy's sapped.

Relief is what I should be feeling at their ready acceptance of me, and 'thank you' is what I should have said. Except, they hit me unawares with it. And with such force. It's just...too great a thing to wrap my head around; a stupefying mind-fuck.

If Gran was here, where she belongs, her keen mind and rightful throne within the coven restored, and her reaction was a match for Suzy's claim... *Crap!* The thought, alone, makes my chest squeeze all the tighter, but I'd give anything to have her banging my door down right now, demanding we have a heart-to-heart.

Suzy's word is likely the closest I'll ever get to Gran's blessing, though. Because Gran's been stripped back, just like my room, and there's no recovering what's gone.

Maybe I should call her. Just to check in, hear her voice. This is the first in a long, long time I've gone more than a day without her.

Maybe I should try Tate...

The rhythmic '*rap-rap-rappity-rap*' at my back has me springing free of the door, an almighty kickstart to my system.

It's not Gran. Obviously.

Whirling around to see the handle depress and the door crack open, I'm well aware of who it is on the other side. "Don't," I find my voice. "Just needing five minutes to myself, okay? Get lost."

But, like the dick that he is, David invites himself in regardless. "Give me a freaking break!"

"Thought you might like to see this," he says, closing the door behind him and holding something out to me.

I determinedly don't look. "You thought wrong. Sod off."

Lifting his offering higher, he continues over me, "I found it at the bottom of a shoebox. Buried underneath a load of thimbles."

There's no ignoring the damn thing now, held right in my line of vision.

It's a crimson leather-bound folder, long and narrow. A photo album, I'd guess. I don't recall ever seeing it before. And, oh, how I'm now cursing him for piquing my curiosity. "What's in it?"

"Photos."

"Duh."

"Of Mum, as a kid." His lips twitch into a sardonic smirk as he skirts around me and makes himself comfortable on the edge of my bed. "And a few of her as a teen."

Resting the album across his legs, David opens it. I catch a teasing peek of a petite, feral-haired blonde before I prise my eyes up to glare at him, barricading off the impulse to lunge and snatch it from his hands. "Right. Well, leave it there. I'll look at it later." *The very minute you've skedaddled outta my space.*

He starts flicking through the image-filled sleeves, stopping on one toward the end. "She's about your age here, look. Seventeen and heavily pregnant with me. Think that might be Dad's hand on her belly."

"What exactly is it you're trying to do here, David?"

"Not a brilliant photo. So much for the pregnancy glow; she looks miserable."

"Seriously?"

"Mum and Dad were never ones for taking pictures," he steams ahead, unfazed. "Doubt there's enough of me growing up to fill even half of this book. Far less again of you."

I gape at him, incredulous. The arrogant tosser's delusional if he thinks he can draw me into this conversation. Nope. Definitely not now. But, also, not ever. "Leave."

"We weren't ever much a happy family, do you remember?"

"Sweet jeezus!" My desire for escape reignites. "Fine." Fuelled by spite and defiance, I blast across the room to my skates. "If you won't go, then I will."

This secures his attention. "Mikey. Please." Snapping the album shut, he abandons it on the bed, then stands and takes two steps. Toward me, though, not the door. "It wasn't my intention to eavesdrop on you, honestly, but I heard what was said next door, there."

Fire turning to ice in a heartbeat, I freeze. I'm crouched down, one foot raised and ready to slide into my boot. A far from comfortable position to find myself stuck in.

"Some I already knew. Some I…"

"'scuse me?"

"Sophie." He shrugs and flashes me another of his infuriating smirks before elaborating, "when I collared her about the overnight glitter explosion in the sitting room last week, little rascal thought nothing of dragging you under the bus with her. It was a card for you she'd been making, by the way. She plans on giving you it when you're nicer. One with a rainbow on the front. Cos Megan told her a rainbow is much better than a heart for showing she loves you."

The floor claims me, and I land hard. "Megan?" *Of course.*

"Those girls do like to gossip." His soft chuckle grates. "And now I finally understand her obsession with sign language. Was starting to drive me batty, that puzzle. He wasn't always deaf, though, right?"

"Wow, *fuck!*" Broken free of my stupor, I ram my foot into the skate and yank hard on the fastenings. "You *accidently* listened in to the entire conversation, huh? Well, that's just great. Awesome!"

"Look, I didn't plan on saying anything. Your business is none of mine, you've been very clear. And, believe it or not, I'm trying really hard to respect that."

I snort, cos that's hilarious.

"But enough is enough, Michael," he yet again slights me. "We can't go on like this. You have to at least hear me out."

"I don't have to do any such thing," I retort, snatching up my second skate.

"Just ten minutes of your time, can you give me just ten minutes? Please?"

I fumble, the heavy boot almost slipping from my fingers. David hasn't ever before requested something of me without command in his tone.

"I'm not asking for your forgiveness. Don't expect it. I've made too many mistakes, and done too little to fix them, I get that."

Whoa! That admission takes me several breaths to process.

"I'll give you five," I bite out after setting my skate aside, crossing my legs and swivelling around to face him. "But it's for Tate, not you. Cos in return, you're gonna keep to yourself what you've no right knowing about him, okay? He's not ready to be outed on that yet."

He's frowning, but nods along with me, "fair enough."

"And your time starts now. Tick tock." Feels a whole lot like I've taken control as I watch him chew over his starting point. Seems he wasn't prepared for me to give him the floor. Not gonna lie, it's kinda satisfying.

Heaving out a sigh, he takes another step closer and then lowers himself down to the worn carpet in front of me. His long legs stretch out and he leans back on his arms. "My decision to send you away, it's not one I regret. I still believe it was the right thing to do; you needed the fresh start – the clean slate, and I wasn't in any position to..."

"I've heard this speech before, David," I slice through him. "Many times. Use these minutes wisely, eh? Tell me something I don't already know."

Pressing his lips, he wastes a long, precious moment considering me before changing tack to something equally as redundant. "It bothers me, the way you are with Sophie. She's done nothing to deserve your attitude. But, also..."

"Really? Wow, noted."

"*But, also,* I'm sorely aware that I was always a lot the same with you."

"Yep."

"*Because*... I got little enough attention from Mum and Dad as it was, and I resented having to share that."

"There's a point here somewhere, I assume. And you're going to reach it soon?"

"If you let me just speak, yes," he says with another sigh.

Our eyes locked, dark on dark, I tilt my head, urging him on. *This wants to be good.*

Deliberation loses him another moment. Then: "When Mel told me we were going to have a baby, I was terrified. We hadn't been together long enough to take on parenthood. I couldn't be a dad. Never wanted to be one."

My lip curls, unimpressed, but I bite my tongue.

"The kid was a mistake, just as I was. And they'd grow up feeling that every day, like I did. It would be my undoing and, in all honesty, running was all I could think about."

"Arsewipe!" I slip.

With a flex of his jaw the only sign he's heard me, he stays on track. "The day I heard that precious, fluttering heartbeat, though, and saw Mel's beaming grin, everything changed. My entire outlook on life brightened. Still, I felt like running, but not away from Mel and our baby anymore. *With* them. I wanted to cut all ties, escape the labels I'd grown up bearing, and start over fresh with my own family, free."

"Then our parents went and died. Left you with only me to ditch. Score." The jerk's making it too damn hard for me to keep my trap shut.

"The accident happened just six days later. But, no," he gives his head a weary shake, straightening and drawing his legs in. "Contrary to your belief, Mikey, I'm not heartless. They were my mum and dad, I loved them. In no way was that crash taken as any kind of a blessing. I grieved them, and I hurt for you. It crushed me, seeing you so broken."

"Too crushed to bear for any longer than a couple of weeks, huh?"

"I wasn't your best option." The subtle tremor to his voice stalls my next retort. "Besides, Grandad would've never let you stay with me, even if I'd fought for it. I was the ruin of his daughter. I'd caused the ruin of Mel, too, so he said. Over his dead body would I get to influence your path."

And, so, here we are...

If not for David, Mum wouldn't have thrown away her dreams; if not for David, she wouldn't have followed Dad across the country, breaking Gran's heart. Grandad Jim hadn't ever made a secret of that deep-rooted grudge. My brother hadn't ever – before now – seemed to care, parrying every barb doled out with a whip-sharp one of his own. "He's who you figured my better option?"

"No, not him. Gran."

I flinch, teeth nipping my tongue.

"She adored you. And Grandad adored her. He may have been a cranky, mean bastard, but he swore to see you right. For her sake, if nothing else. I was giving you the new beginning I'd hoped for myself, that's how I saw it." He lifts his hand from his knee and I'm quick to reposition myself clear of his reach. "You're in a much better place because of Gran than I could have ever gotten you to. Can't tell me you're not glad of those years you got to build that bond with her, little brother. The relationship you two have is special. Enviable. It's a relationship I've wished many times I'd given Sophie the chance of forming before..."

"Enough." My gaze swoops to his bouncing foot. "Time's up." It's not. I'm shutting him down early. This is no longer satisfying. The cracks of vulnerability in David's cool façade are just too obscenely alien for my eyes and ears to withstand.

His foot stops. "Must everything always be a fight between us? It's not like I came in here expecting a few words would solve all our issues or anything, Mikey, I accept I've created too big of a divide for that, but this really can't continue as it is. No one knows Gran the way you do, and I need you to... I need for you to let me help. If you can manage nothing else, we'd be stronger support for her if we were at least working on the same side."

His closing statement is met with silence. I feel him watching me as I snatch up my skate and resume fitting it on.

"Gran's gonna need to be in a nursing home," I eventually give in, remaining attentive to my fingers' battle with the laces, "I realise that. But not yet, okay?"

"Not yet," David agrees with a jarring tenderness. "And when the time comes, that's not a decision I would ever make without you. I promise."

MY SKATE with Jody hits the spot dead on. And I'm reminded of our friendship's pivotal value. Sometimes you just don't want to talk about anything significant. Sometimes you need an escape into frivolity. It's good to take a break from expectation and responsibility every once in a while. She gives me that.

"YOU LEFT WITHOUT EVEN SAYING BYE."

"I was still pretty mad at you."

"You ignored all my texts."

"I'm stubborn. You know this."

With a twitch of his jaw, Tate pushes up off the tree stump and takes a few steps toward me, but not enough to bring him within reach. He hooks his thumbs into his jeans pockets, and my nerve endings are set to tingling by his scrolling gaze, head to toes and back again.

Heavy rain saw David and me out of Newcastle this morning, the rising sun dim behind a bank of grey, weather as dismal as my mood. We arrived back in Yoverton mid-afternoon, welcomed by a flawless cobalt sky. After dropping off my stuff and checking in on a napping Gran, the den was my first port of call. Tate was already here, waiting, just as I hoped he'd be. The tent's up again, like this was a pre-arranged rendezvous, even though we've had zero contact since I stormed out on him Thursday evening. I'd not fully grasped just how worried I've been about us until the sight of him relieved me of it. And, *damn*, only now am I appreciating the day's glorious transformation.

Mirroring his deliberate scrutiny, my stomach twists in longing. I can feel the distance between us with my whole body, six endless steps across the grassy clearing. "You didn't reply when I messaged you back."

"Couldn't."

"Why?"

"My phone broke."

"What? How?"

"Threw it at the wall."

My eyebrows shoot up to my hairline and he bops one shoulder, looking mildly abashed. "Tried Skyping you."

"Dad took the power lead from my computer."

I open my mouth but only blink at him.

"To punish me. Cos, apparently, fucking my phone up wasn't – that wasn't punishment enough."

"Oh."

Picking up his approach, an apostrophe appears at one corner of his lips. "Said he refused to watch me winding myself up stupid all weekend. Over you." He stops in front of me, almost toe to toe. "But, of course, I had no way to tell you that's what was going on. And nothing to distract me. So... winding myself up stupid all weekend is all I've fucking done."

A dizzying thrill sweeps through me at the soft press of his lips on mine. It's a tease more than a kiss. Too soon, he pulls back.

He takes my hands, eyes heating a trail over my face, the wry turn of his mouth inquisitive.

Although inwardly groaning, I concede a nod. "David knows. About us. We talked."

"And?"

"And..." *He knows about you, too. Everything. They all do. Except Gran.* I shrug. *None of it happened on my terms.* "You were right. I guess I feel better for it."

A flicker of uncertainty follows my admission.

I will tell him the whole of it. But the drama and discord of my weekend is so entirely not where I want my headspace right now. Time aplenty for all that later. After an altogether different kind of 'catching up' has been thoroughly addressed...

Taking the last small step that separates us, I lean in. He takes no convincing, bending to meet me halfway. I let his mouth brush mine, featherlight and for only a moment; my turn to tease. A gratifying hum escapes him as I withdraw, and his grin cracks wide. My body reacts.

Fuck, I've missed him!

Heart pumping faster and faster, I tug on his hands and lead him over to the tent.

47

ASSIMILATE: TO ABSORB MENTALLY;
TO BECOME ADJUSTED.

*W*hen I'm summoned to a family dinner on my return from the den, it doesn't entirely take me unawares.

See, talk happened between David and me during the cross-country drive today. More than we've ever attempted before, *and* we both made it back in one piece. Okay, sure, it wasn't the kind of talk that brotherly bonds are formed with, but he heard me out on how I needed to be more involved with Gran, to be included in all decisions concerning her, and he seemed to take it on board. In return, I accepted that things really couldn't continue as they were, fuelled by resentment, and agreed to work toward an adjustment in attitude.

What does come as something of a surprise to me, however, is that the meal isn't actually feeling much like a chore.

I've laughed out loud at Mel's spray tan tale of horror. Not ironically; not mockingly. But a proper, genuine guffaw born of genuine amusement. And hard though it is to admit, I kinda liked earning one of her real smiles for it.

The food is David's handiwork: A Sunday beef roast with all the trimmings. Boxing day at Suzy's was the last time I sat down to anything even near as impressive. I draw the line at verbalising a compliment for him, but I'm making no attempt to stop Gran's busy feeding.

In between slapping my elbows off the table and reminding me of my manners, she's piling up my plate as steadily as I'm shovelling it.

May just be the soaring high spirits of my afternoon spent with Tate at play, but I'm feeling decidedly okay about... *this*.

Sophie plops back down in her seat across from me. Uncharacteristic enough to be of note, she's been quiet this evening, her mind seeming faraway. And now, from somewhere along her toilet excursion, she's acquired a writing pad and pencil.

"No, Sophie." David leans across me to shake his head at her. "No doodling at the table. Put that away."

Shoving her gravy-flooded plate to one side, the kid proceeds to set the pad down in the cleared space and flick it open. "I'm not doodling. I'm authoring," she challenges, curling herself over the page, "and I really gotsta write down this thought in my head afore it gets away."

I snort when David throws Mel a plea for help, but it's Sophie who glares at me for it.

Mel explains, "it's her home-learning. She has a story to write."

"A superhero story," Sophie elaborates, putting pencil to paper. "At night, I become Indigo Sparkles."

Another snort threatens. I choke it back. "Wow. Well, that's..."

"My mask and cape are indigo, cos that's my new favouritist colour. And I woopah the baddies with my star-whip."

"...*Inspired*."

"Sounds wonderful, little pup," Gran chimes in, and then pats my knee, like she's totally on to me. "You used to love writing stories, do ye remember, dear love? Ye were so good at it."

I turn and flash her an indulgent smile. She starts to hum as she moves a Yorkshire pudding from her plate to mine.

In truth, I've only ever wrote one story – with any real enthusiasm, anyway. Also set as a homework assignment, way back in year eight, I'd gotten a smidge carried away. I went beyond the wordcount by 13,000, beyond the deadline by eight days. My teacher refused to mark it. I can't recall all that much about it. Some sort of mystery, about a boy whose best friend goes missing. Turned out, the boy's friend hadn't been kidnapped at all. He'd just decided to become a pirate. Was utter tripe, I'm sure. Gran swore blind to anyone who'd listen, though, that it was the most amazing tale she'd ever read.

I wonder if a copy still exists somewhere, perhaps stored safe away in the cardboard treasure box of old photographs and melancholy cross-stitches and letters addressed to me.

"You're in my story, Uncle Mikey," Sophie snaps me back to her. "You're called Boy Whiz-Whoosh."

"Boy...'scuse me, what?"

"Whiz-Whoosh," she nods, barely looking up. "You have jet-powered skates and a gigantic laser-sword."

"O. Kay." I do laugh now. I can't help it. Cos even as the kid's cutting me down with insult, she tries to please me. "I'll bite. Robin to your Batman, huh?"

"Huh?"

"Never mind."

But, then, her next words have my good humour taking a rapid nosedive.

"You're my evil nemesis."

Going back a week – hell, even just a few days, that statement would have had me all the more amused. But now...

"You keep trying to disappear me, but it won't work. Cos the bad guy never wins."

I don't need to look to know David caught the exact moment his comment yesterday, voiced hundreds of miles away, finally struck its mark. I'm feeling his eyes boring into the side of my head, and I can picture the shaming crook to his mouth.

"Mummy, how do you spell Twonklet? And, also, what does it mean?"

"You can spell it N-O, sweetheart," Mel frowns, gliding her

own significant look my way, "meaning you'll be in big trouble if you use that word ever again."

And, *curse it all* – being cast as her villain just as David is mine – I am ashamed.

I contemplate the Yorkshire pud and two roasties that remain of my dinner, then push the plate away. It clinks against Sophie's.

The worth of her glittery rainbow picture no longer seems all that negligible...

~

"HEY! HEY, WAIT UP!"

Steph's shrill call yanks me to a halt. Tate takes another few steps before he, too, stops and turns. A slight frown creases his brow as Derek lopes over the road toward us with a giddy Steph attached to his back, her arms in a death-grip around his neck, her legs bracketing his hips. I suspect they've just left the Red Bull, so there's a substantial possibility they're sozzled.

"Where's Lynds?" I ask, scoping them dubiously, when Steph reins Derek in beside us and slides herself down off him.

"Nice to see you too," Steph rolls her eyes.

Derek rolls his shoulders and then his head. "Don't know for sure," he starts his answer on a sigh. "But I suspect her plans to meet me were discovered and my dear aunt waylaid her."

"Oh," is all I can think to say, wincing. I feel bad for him, and for Lyndsay, especially as my all-around messy and unintentional *outing* is panning out so comparably smooth.

"Yeah, '*Oh*'. Her mum is the. Worst!"

"Lucky for me, Steph was here to save my night."

She beams. "True story!"

They are, perhaps, a little merry, I decide, but not drunk.

"No word of a lie!" Playfully shoving her, Derek repositions them both more fully inside the streetlight's glow and flashes Tate a grin. The intent behind his manoeuvre doesn't escape me, and I greatly appreciate the subtlety of it; inconsequential to the one person of this party not in the know. "What you two up to, anyway? Mighty dangerous, walking the streets after dark."

I give Tate the chance to include himself in the conversation, but a glance across at him finds his lips thinned and his furrow very much still in place. He's skirting an uneasy fingertip over the orange headphones encircling his neck.

"Work. I've just finished work."

"Ah. Citreena's, right?" Derek turns back to me.

"Yep."

Tate ate alone at the bistro tonight, waiting for me to get off. I think he got a real kick out of me serving him, and he left a lousy tip, but he did keep slying me bites of his banoffee waffle each time I passed. Now, we're headed to his to make the most of a couple hours alone time while Graham's out working. Every second of this time is precious, and it occurs to me in a flash of insight, we're wasting it here.

I sidle up close to Tate and guide his hand down from his throat, sliding my fingers through his. He gives a gentle squeeze, which I read to mean, *'yes, do it'*. So, I do. "It's true enough, though, this night does feel alarmingly perilous. We should probably..."

"Absolutely," Steph blindsides me, pouncing and hooking herself to my free side, "Lets walk!"

"Uh..."

She lurches me forward. "We'll talk as we go."

"Nah, leave 'em be, girl," Derek swoops to my aid, taking up the hint Steph (deliberately?) missed. He nods toward our joined hands, "tell them tomorrow."

Then, of course, I go and shoot myself in the foot: "Tell us what?" *Sweet. Freaking. Jeezus. WHY?!*

"Aha!" Steph croons, gleeful. "See, they want to know." Forcing another step from me, she seizes Derek's arm and I lose my hold on Tate. "Onwards, my queers, and I'll reveal all."

Derek flashes me a pitying *I-did-try* kinda look, moving beside her on his own steam and tugging on her wonky pigtail. "Everything Lyndsay's told me about you is entirely true."

Grinning like he's just paid her the best compliment, she kicks straight in. "So, Mum thinks that by leaving it til the last minute to tell me she'll be away for the weekend, I won't have enough time to plan fun. I mean, it's like she doesn't even know me! I'm owed a birthday party, right?"

I reach out behind me for Tate. He leaves me hanging.

Angling around to discover him unmoved, now several paces away, I'm hit with a peculiar look that throws me off kilter. Lifting my outstretched hand, I wiggle my fingers, beckoning.

"Can't," he mouths and drops his gaze, being illogical, difficult, frustrating.

And I feel the night's promise tarnishing with every extra step I take from him.

"Like I'm gonna let this chance go untaken, pah!" Steph continues, barely taking a breath. "Two days is plenty time for me to pull together something epic, with help from my amazingly awesome friends... What the...?" She doesn't make it easy for me to wheedle my arm free of hers. I back up and swerve. "Mikey?"

"Sorry."

"Rude!"

"They have other plans for their evening, Steph." I hear Derek mutter. "Don't even pretend you didn't clock that."

My gut tells me those plans have now changed, though I've no clue exactly why or how.

"Yeah, well." Voice switching from grumble back to shout in a single breath, she rattles my spine: "Wimp out on me Friday and there'll be hell to pay! That goes for the both of you!"

"I JUST DON'T GET it, Tate."

We walked to Tate's in silence, his gaze remaining stubbornly fixed on his feet. Now we're in his room, the house deadly quiet around us, and between us there's a gaping absence of heated touches and kisses and closeness. I'm hacked off.

The desk chair squeaks as he sinks down onto it. "It's dark. She was walking and talking. And all I could fucking see was the backs of your heads."

"That's not what I mean!" I shut the bedroom door with a little more force than intended and then do away with the space dividing us. "You're gay, right?" His brows dip, head cocking slightly, as he watches me perch down on the end of his bed. I wait for him to reposition the chair and I trap his leg in-between mine. This is volatile ground I'm about to lead him onto. "You're perfectly happy for everyone to know that. Couldn't care less if people take issue with it."

"Bigots can go fuck themselves."

"Exactly," I nod, holding his eye. My finger nervously traces over the Queen, Bishop and Pawn doodled on the thigh of his faded jeans. "Anyone unwilling to accept you for who you are – and for what you can't change – can just do one."

It takes only six beats worth of probing study for Tate to catch up with me. Yanking off his headphones and tossing them onto the desk, he huffs out a flat laugh, shaking his head.

"Tate..." My hand claps down on his knee as I sense the threat of him bolting, feeling tension in his muscles and warm skin through the wide rip in the denim under my palm. I edge forward. "You're not about to stop being deaf any sooner than you are being gay. Why...?"

"Don't."

"All this effort you put into hiding it – everything you're giving up..."

"Don't," he warns again, sharper. His jaw tics and his eyes implore.

But, *Goddamnit*, "I can't stand watching you shut out the world, Tate. Especially when it doesn't have to be that way. Derek tried to include you tonight, did you even notice? Hell, Steph did too, in her own way – it's not her fault she doesn't know. And Lyndsay thinks that..."

"Enough!" Jerking upright, he slams his chair back against the desk, his knee escaping my hold, and this risky venture takes the turn I've been dreading. "Fuck, make up your mind. The opinions of others: Either they matter or they don't, which is it?"

"... What? No. Just. Things'd be easier if..."

"Ah. Right. The 'special snowflake' treatment, that'd be better for me?"

"You can't tar everyone with the same brush. Not..."

"I totally called this. Remember?" He stands and turns away. "You rushed in with no idea just how much you were taking on with me." Stalking to the door, shoulders squaring as his eyes return to mine, he opens it. "Well, the out's still here if you want it, Mikey."

I stare at him. He stares back, a challenge. And, okay, now I'm furious. "You're not hearing me!"

"Because I fucking can't, can I? That's the whole bastard issue."

"That is so not the issue."

"Bullshit it's..."

I'm across the room and slapping a hand over his mouth before he can finish. This is not gonna go the same way our last 'conversation' in this room did. Heated words sear my throat, and I take a slow breath in through my nose before I let them spill. "You've faced off with Death. And won. More than once. You've put yourself back together. Adjusted. Learned how to talk with your hands and listen with your eyes – to read people beyond the words they speak. You're by far the most determined and resilient person I've ever met.

"The issue isn't that you're *damaged beyond repair*, Tate. It's that the damage has become all you see." Fingers curling around my wrist, his head twists. I firm my grip on his jaw and move into him, determined. "And, yeah, you can fault me on how much stock I put in others. But don't even *dare* try to tell me your opinion of yourself shouldn't matter, cos..." Another, deep, fortifying breath. "Cos I love you. And nothing else matters to me more."

I feel the moment he takes the hit, his entire body locking up against mine. Then, my breath catching and my heart panicking, I take my hand back from him.

He opens his mouth, but I'm not done yet.

Because they're the truest three words I've ever spoken – because I refuse to chance misunderstanding or dismissal – because he needs to accept them, even if he takes nothing else from this, I point at myself, press both hands over my chest then jab him hard with an index finger as I elaborate, "I'm in love with every single creative, thoughtful, *fucking* brilliant, perfect and imperfect part of you. I'm with you completely. With the whole of my heart. Only," I press my eyes closed, "that's never gonna be enough if you can't stop hating on yourself."

A bruising crush of my lips on his ends my declaration. Then I leave. And I take the control out with me.

PUSSYFOOTING

*T*here's an elephant on my wall.

An unobtrusive little fella at first glance, stood just above my power socket, to the right of the door. But I've been staring at him for what feels like hours now, and the artful intricacies of his design have become all I can see.

The infinity symbol replaces nostrils at the end of his long, grey trunk; his ears are outlined with a complicated Celtic knot design; and on his chest is a smudge of red – two overlapping thumb prints shaping a heart. Most cleverly of all, where body joins legs, fore and hind, the crease lines of his skin suggest two faces in profile, looking at each other. And, on one hind foot, he wears a clumpy green boot, laces untied.

Elephant shoe...

...I love you.

Except, Tate didn't look at all as happy as a guy in love whose boyfriend loves him back should, today.

He was kinda distant, quiet. And he seemed keen to pretend our talk last night never happened.

I let him. Now, moping alone in my room, phone silent on the bed beside me, I'm wishing that I hadn't.

~

"W ANT to know what I've been thinking?"

"Um..." I side-eye Steph as she settles herself against the shed wall beside me. Gaze sweeping over the activity of her garden, she's wearing the grin I've learnt to be wary of. "Not sure that I do, actually."

An elbow to my ribs punctuates her chortle. "Smart arse!"

By far a tamer affair than the last party she hosted, Steph's birthday celebration still consists of an unwise volume of teens and alcohol (an opinion I'm keeping to myself, along with my decision to remain sober). But at least I recognise a majority of the faces here this time, and have a few more names I can attach to them. The fairy lights are twinkling prettily again, it's a clear night, and almost everyone has congregated in merry little knots across the lawn. The music pounding through the house is almost endurable out here.

"I'm thinking you really didn't give him enough of a chance," she informs me anyway, leaning in close as if sharing a secret, the fur of her coat's hood tickling my ear, "and what a terrible shame that is. He'd be *sooo* good for you."

"Who?" I ask, even as my eyes dart across to Derek. Just a few feet away, he's huddled under a blanket beside Lyndsay on the wooden swing seat, invested in an animated chat with her about... squirrels, I think. But, of course, he picks this moment to glance up and catch me out. His grin barely registers before I look away. "And why on earth would you be thinking that?"

"Cos you're allowed to have fun, Mikey, you know? You're allowed to *be* fun. Derek can totally make that happen."

Her amplification of his name zaps like a taser. "Tate makes that happen." I glare at her when she snorts. "He does."

"The guy too busy being ignorant and angry to even show his face here tonight? Yeah, okay then."

My voice is a tight, warning hiss, "Steph, encouraging me to cheat on my boyfriend just because he hasn't come to your party, it's a little harsh, don't you think?"

"The cat's away, why shouldn't the mouse play?"

"I am so not..."

"Whisper, whisper, whisper!" Lyndsay startles me upright, guilty-looking as a kid caught plundering the cookie jar. "Leave him be, Steph, would you?"

I feel myself flushing scarlet while, with another flash of her wicked grin, Steph bops one shoulder and straightens up from the shed. "Simply reminding him of his options."

Oh, what a shamelessly fickle beast she is.

It's not until I realise she's crossing for the walled flower bed where Alex and Craig are once again perched that I desist in lasering the back of her head. I'm determined not to draw unnecessary attention to myself tonight and blanking out their existence strikes me as a wise move toward achieving that. It's going well thus far – they seem equally as disinclined to acknowledge me.

Derek laughs. "Relax, Mikey. You'll cause yourself an aneurism if you're not careful."

I deflect my scowl down to the grass at my feet rather than target him with it. "Goddamnher!"

"Honestly, just ignore her." There's sounds of movement and then Lyndsay's beside me, hooking her arm through mine. I feel her shivering. Lovely as she looks in her soft blue dress, the silky shawl she's wearing over it can't be affording much protection against the air's chill. "Steph may be my best friend, but even I know she's awful."

Truth is, though, it's not so much Steph that's bothering me. She's hit a nerve, sure. But it's one that's already been worked tender these past two days. Just... More fool me, I suppose, for trusting in my heartfelt proclamation to accomplish anything. Something other than the return of a bruising sense of imbalance.

I'm fairly certain I can feel the scrutinizing rake of Adele's eyes on me, from where she stands with Callum between a monstrous stone gargoyle and the barbeque, but I don't turn to check. Apparently, Tate's spoken more to her about our talk than he has me. I'm not sure of how much, but within five minutes of me arriving here, she had me cornered:

"Be careful. You push him too hard and you risk causing damage instead of repair."

I'd bristled. "So, what? I'm just supposed to pussyfoot around him? Stand by and stay quiet as he buries himself behind his stupid walls?"

"You're not the only one worried about him, Alston."

A part of me kinda wants to slam Lyndsay with an '*I told you so*' – after all, it was her advice that had emboldened my tongue. Except... what glory is there to be taken from that? Instead, I let her turn me toward the house and press herself in closer to my side.

"I need another drink," she says in answer to an unasked question, angling her face up to see mine. "Come with?"

Considering she already has us on the move across the garden, there seems little point in voicing a reply.

"I'll have another Magners!" Derek calls after us. "Actually, bring me two. And a slice of pizza if there's any left. Thanks, Cuz, you're a diamond."

This is the closest her and I have been since the last time we were here together, and I'm acutely aware of feeling kinda weird about it. But then...

"So, hey," Lyndsay murmurs low, darting a glance and an obliging salute back at Derek. "Just to make sure we understand each other here, though, Mikey: Something happens between you and my cousin, that might just be too much for us to bounce back from, yeah?"

"What? Yeah. Jeezus, no, nothing will. Promise. I mean, Derek's great and all, but..."

"Good." Her hand joins mine in my jacket pocket. "That's all I needed to hear. Thanks."

I flash her a smile and get a grin back.

...to have this from her despite the happenings of and after that night, I'm also feeling pretty damn blessed.

Reaching the house, the bass booming from the stereo inside thrums a vicious assault on my whole body. And when Lyndsay opens the back door, the blast of sound that hits us has my teeth vibrating.

Screw it all! What can I change by stressing? I'm at a party and I'm in great company; I owe myself a break for the night.

"Fancy taking over the music and maybe having a dance?" I lean down to shout into her ear.

"Oh boy, do I!" She laughs, nodding, and yanks me inside.

THE SCISSOR SISTERS are halfway through *Gay Bar* when I drag Lyndsay from the centre of our makeshift dance floor toward the front door. We're both sweaty and giddy, and I'm in desperate need of fresh, cool air.

We've been throwing out moves to a playlist of all the cheesy party greats for well over an hour, the front room steadily filling around us, and my body is now threatening collapse.

Weaving through bodies and around furniture, Steph catches my arm in a vice grip as I try to steer us unseen around Alex. She gives an insistent tug and I shake my head, but in liberating myself from her clutches I crash, staggering, into a solid someone bouncing too close behind. Alex's guffaw breaks over the music.

A colourful arm drapes over my shoulder, another snaking around Lyndsay's, then Derek's head appears between us. "Sneaking off, are we?"

"Taking a breather," Lyndsay shouts back at him, shimmying lithely free of his hold, dodging the magenta whip of Ashleigh's hair, and taking the lead. "We'll be back!"

"Promise?"

"Do I ever lie?"

He laughs and releases me.

Another handful of steps, skirting the overturned coffee table, and Adele's next to obstruct our progress, her questionable dance moves landing an elbow into my ribs. "Ooof."

"Watch where you're going, Turd-features!" She spins around to snarl. Seeing it's me she's wounded, one satisfied brow arches and her eyes flick to Lyndsay. "Switching sides again tonight, huh, Alston?"

Callum flashes us an apologetic smile, inclining his head, before he takes her hands and guides her a safe distance away.

I see him lean in, saying something close to her ear, and then she's snatching a hand free of his hold to slap his chest, looking affronted.

Those two, together, make no sense whatsoever. Not to me, nor to anyone else. They've rarely been seen apart this past week, but all they ever seem to do is bicker and name call and wind each other up. Much as I can figure it, Adele's getting her kicks from torturing the poor bloke, and Callum's a sucker for punishment.

Gay Bar is fading out by the time we make it to the door, sagging against it, gasping and giggly.

As *Time of My Life* croons in, Lyndsay groans and drops her head back. "But I love this one!"

"We'll still be able to hear it outside," I say, nudging her up and seizing the door handle. "Not so sure I can pull off that lift, mind."

"Not so sure I trust you enough to try."

Despite my overexerted and cramping chest, I laugh.

But as the door swings wide and we step out into the chill night, that laugh withers in my throat.

The sight of my boyfriend out in the road is not one I was prepared for. That he's pressed up against the side of a familiar black car by the unreasonably perfect body of its owner, his ex-boyfriend, is a sucker punch to the gut.

Lyndsay grips a firm fistful of my jacket sleeve. But I'm immobile anyway.

"He's nothing. We both know it. Nothing but your rebound and my wake-up call," Craig's fierce rasp carries across the quiet street, and the noise of the party at my back seems to fall away. "You win, okay? I'm jealous. That what you want to hear?"

Tate's not fighting him. "This isn't a fucking game."

"No? Then, what is it we're doing here, T?"

I force myself to take them in, and my heart freefalls wildly on the observation of Tate's hand delved deep inside Craig's jacket pocket, Craig's hand clamped around his wrist.

"Good question," I finally find my voice. It quivers, but like hell am I fleeing without answers this time. No matter how sick I feel.

Craig whips around, startled.

Tate echoes the move. His wide eyes lock on mine. He holds himself as still as I've been rendered. "Mikey."

"Tate?"

I jumped to conclusions last time. Surely, I'm doing the same thing now. *Or perhaps I'd been right all along...*

"Hello again, choir boy. Such perfect timing."

My nails dig into my palms, a grounding pain.

Their bodies flush, it must be the vibration of Craig's voice that snaps Tate aware of his position because only now does his attention leave me. He jerks, trying to shove Craig back, trying to wrench his pocketed hand free.

The sneering change to Craig's face is as glorious as it is hateful. I watch, horrified, as he bears in closer. "We've got heat, T. I know you feel it. I know you. All of you. Can't tell me *he*..."

"Alex! Wait!" Lyndsay's warning comes just a beat before I get roughly shoulder barged off balance. Alex storms down the driveway, his posture menacing. And it's the fear of his intention that jump starts me moving. My jacket gets left behind in Lyndsay's hand. "No, Mikey," she groans.

Tate hasn't wasted the moment of distraction. A slam to the chest has sent Craig sprawling. The bottle Craig's had propped on his car roof falls and smashes on the road at Tate's feet, speckling beer dregs over his jeans. He doesn't seem to notice.

Expression morphing into one of blazing fury, it's the first I've seen on Craig with no appeal. "I've gone through fucking hell because of you!" He clambers back to his feet looking unhinged and dangerous. "What more do you want from me?"

"Nothing." Tate curls his lip and raises his arm. Fist opening, he jangles the set of keys hanging from his index finger. "Nothing but these." His voice is as unsteady as his legs as he scrambles up from the car, but he doesn't cower. "I'm done with your shit, Craig. But I won't let you kill yourself. And I won't keep on taking the blame. You need to get help."

"Bastard!"

My stride hitches and then hastens as Alex catches his brother mid-lunge, restraining him. I see Craig struggle, spewing obscenities, his face twisted and his muscles as taut as a strung bow. Alex secures his arm-pinning clamp, wrenching him back a half-step. "You're drunk," he growls.

"Not drunk enough."

"Too drunk to drive. Fuck, bro, you promised! Knew I shouldn't have brought you here tonight."

Craig's sneer returns, and he snorts. "*I* brought *you*. Bro." For a split second, it looks like he's about to slam his head back into Alex's face. Instead, he futilely jerks a shoulder, straining forward. "*I* did *you* the favour. Piss off back to your bitch and mind your fucking own!"

Tension's radiating from Tate, but the instant I cautiously step within his reach, he grabs me and pulls me in to him. Arms twining my waist, his head tilts to rest his cheek against my temple, and – that simply – for the spell of a single heartbeat, I lose grip on my every least care.

"I'm sorry," he whispers softly into my hair.

Then, Lyndsay's holding my jacket out toward me, her brow pinched with concern; Alex is snatching the keys from Tate, gritting out a "thanks" through his teeth as he wrangles a foul-mouthed Craig around to the passenger seat; the music swells from the house as the front door swings wide, and I'm swiftly reawakened to everything that's wrong with this situation.

49

FOR WHAT IT'S WORTH

"*A*s I live and breathe, it's T-Mac. The great Tatey Macster. Tacmoody Mactoody. Here. At my party. Oh, lordy-lord, I'm honoured!"

The shrill call has jolted my head up from Tate's chest, and I feel his frown on me, bewildered for a moment, before he, too, turns his attention to the house. Steph's bounding down the driveway toward us.

Lyndsay groans. "I swear that girl's fitted with a drama-radar."

She's on us before I can even think of escape, dancing around us like a crazed lion eyeing up its easy prey. "So, what've I missed, peeps?"

"Nothing," I shrug to a reception of shrewd scepticism as Tate shuffles his feet, tightening his hold on me, and Lyndsay pastes on a smile. "Nothing exciting."

Steph's grin turns pouty, and I steel myself for something wildly inappropriate to be released from her mouth. But just as she drags in a predatory breath, Craig's car starts up, revving loudly, and her attention is abruptly whipped away. "Where's Craig going? Is that *Alex* behind the wheel? Aw, hell no!" Launching herself at the driver's door, she yanks on the handle and slams her fist against the window. "Open up, Alex. Open up and get out!"

Lyndsay shoves me from my bemused stupor. "Don't just stand there, dope." Making shooing motions with her hands, she hurries to Steph's side. "Escape."

I don't need telling twice.

As Steph screams, "YOU'RE SUPPOSED TO BE STAYING THE NIGHT!" and Alex blasts the horn over her, I lead Tate away, around the side of the house, to the back garden.

We pass by four blokes who look too old to be here, sat in a circle on the lawn and blatantly passing around a joint, and I spy a couple, wrapped up in each other, half hidden in the tight space between fence and shed, but otherwise, the pretty, fairy-lit garden's now empty. Aerosmith can be heard keeping the party going inside.

The swing seat rocks as I drop down on to it. Curling one leg up so I'm angled sideways, I wait for Tate to settle across from me and then I clear my throat. "Why...? What?"

He doesn't answer immediately. Looking a little uncertain and a whole lot uncomfortable, he first pulls a blanket out from behind him (the thick fleecy one Derek and Lyndsay had huddled under earlier) and shakes it out over us, taking his time to tuck it in around himself. "What Craig said... I don't know how much you heard, but...you know you're not my rebound, right?"

My mouth dries. That is so not how I expected him to start. I try for a nod, only my shoulder bobs more than my head manages to.

His eyes probe me, unsatisfied, but I've nothing else for him. Huffing out a curse, he doesn't push it. "I saw you dancing. Through the bay window." One corner of his mouth kicks up as I stiffen, my fidgeting fingers curling into the blanket. "You were really going for it, enjoying yourself. I watched for ages, like a fucking creeper. Until Craig caught me out. That scene you walked into, Mikey... he was drunk and angry, and making threats to..." a wince; a head shake; he covers my hand in both of his. "I couldn't let him get in the car. That's all it was. Bastard was talking all this shit, and I couldn't trust that he was bluffing."

Takes me a little while to collect myself. "Why didn't you come in? Or at least let me know you were here? I'd've..."

"You'd've left with me."

My nod comes easier this time, but it lands worse.

There's no levity to the bark that escapes him. "I came tonight with the plan to make a grand announcement."

"What?"

"Put everything out there, all in one shot. A spectacular confession, much like yours, and fuck tomorrow."

I'm horrified. "No."

"Lost my nerve, though. Minute I got here. Kept thinking about that gig. And you – you just seemed so happy. Didn't want to ruin it. To let you down again."

"Tate, no. No, you haven't let me down." I lean in to him. "If this is because of the other night – jeezus, that's totally not what I meant for you to take from it. I love..."

"Yeah. No, I know," he cuts me short, dropping his eyes. My heart twists. "I got what you said, and I've thought of little else since. I just...I wanted to make things right again between us. Couldn't think of any other way."

I've got one. I bite down on my lip and allow him his sweep of the garden.

Two girls have just emerged from the back door, dancing and giggling. A smouldering butt and a distinctive tang to the air is all that remains of the four stoners. The loved-up pair can't be seen from here, but I can hear them in our silence.

Cupping my free hand over Tate's cheek, my thumb nudges his chin until his eyes return to me. "I don't need you to do anything like that. Please stop thinking those thoughts." I stroke my pinky over the silky soft hair around his ear while the pinky of my trapped hand caresses his palm. "All I'm asking is that you stop shutting out the world. And you start to recognise your worth. Just...accept that people deserve the chance to know you."

He says nothing in response to that. For a long while, he simply looks at me, his green gaze penetrating, expression indecipherable, and then, "it's late." The soft kiss he presses on my mouth is warm and lingering and delicious. I breathe him in, close the distance between us, and my body reacts. But just as my eager tongue slips past his lips, he pulls back, releasing my hand. A weird noise wrenches free of my throat. "I have a worse fate than turning into a pumpkin if Dad gets home at midnight and I'm not there."

The seat's set to swinging as he moves to stand. And again, as I sink back into it, deflated and hurting.

"Hey, Mikey?"

My eyes snap open, but I don't trust myself to speak and I don't lift my head. What even is this talk? *Proof of the damage I've caused us by pushing too hard, that's what this is.* When will I freaking learn?!

"I – I have the house to myself tomorrow. From three. Would you...? Can you come over?"

I inhale deeply and exhale slowly. "I've promised to teach Soph how to skate."

"Yeah?" A half-smile brightens his face, like a peek of the sun through a break in the clouds. "Lucky Soph."

"Yeah."

Could be exactly as it seems: He's glad I'm giving time up for my niece. But there's no quieting the whispers taunting that it's a relief to him I'm not free.

He nods, sobering, and turns away. "Okay. Well. Maybe afterwards. If you want."

SOPHIE'S top half careens ahead of her bottom. Catching herself on the fence before she faceplants, her legs are then pitched into a wild dance out from under her; Hello Kitty skates gone rogue. "Woah, hey, no, stop!"

I dart to her aid, offering my hand, but what I get for the effort is: "I got this!" So, stifling my amusement, I leave her to flaunt that self-reliance and topple to the ground. Her glittery pink helmet thuds off the fence panel as the paving slabs greet her knees. "Ouch!"

"Yep. You totally had that."

She doesn't cry. Jutting out a defiant jaw, she clambers gracelessly back to her feet. "Stupid." The insult could have been meant for her skates, or herself, but I get the distinct impression it was aimed at me.

"This is supposed to be fun, remember?"

"I *AM* having fun!"

Chuckling just a little, I retreat a few steps to the bench. Gran pats my leg as I settle down next to her, but her gaze remains locked on the baby apple tree across the far side of the spacious garden. *Grandad Jim's tree.* Don't think I'll ever get used to the weird ache of missing her when she's like this: here, and yet not. Still, there's a contentedness to her, an ease to her silence, and after the ups and downs of my past week, I'm feeling some comfort in that today.

"Try and try again, kid, come on. Quitting's for the weak."

Following a grumbled, "I'll show you," Sophie resumes her trundle along the path to a chant of, "push, push, gliiide."

"That's the spirit!" *Wilful brat.* She's doing pretty good, though; coming at this with far more mettle than I did, that's for sure.

I wrap my hand over Gran's and lean back, my eyes closing against the washed-out sky. The green freshness of Spring scents the air.

My first time out on skates, I'd felt jittery as all hell. I was seven, the day was wet, and Tate was scary expectant. It took me under a minute to fall, and as my butt hit the pavement, I decided I hated it.

Decided I couldn't do it.

Decided I was best friends with a lunatic.

Decided I'd quit.

I came so close to condemning myself a lost cause. If not for Tate...

"Don't you dare give up on me yet, Mikey," he'd laughed, dragging me back up to my feet. "Here, keep hold of my hand, okay?"

Every time I put my skates on, Tate's there; the two are so intrinsically woven together in my mind, it's impossible for me to not think about him.

I really wish, though, that I could stop imagining him sat alone at his desk right now, in his empty house... while I'm teaching – *encouraging? – aggravating?* – my niece, just as he had me... staring at his three damn computer screens.

Gran shuffles, pressing her weight down on my leg, and I jolt alert. She's levering herself up from the bench. "Gran?"

"What?"

"Where you going?"

She mutters under her breath, fires me a stern look, and then starts away toward the house. My frown follows her to the back door before I turn to acknowledge Sophie's shout.

"Look at me now, Boy Whiz-Whoosh! Push. Push. Gliiide. Just try and catch me, I dare you!"

"That's it, sweetheart!" Mel's swift to praise, emerging from the greenhouse and clapping the mud from her gloved hands. "Excellent!"

"Yeah." The kid's now beaming in delight, moving at snail's pace along the path past me, arms pumping at her sides. "Excellent. I'm totally excellent."

Rising from the bench, I nod my encouragement and give her the thumbs up as I manoeuvre myself in close beside her, then clip my gait to keep us level. "Steady," I instruct in my impressively authoritative teacher-voice, "and there we go."

My hand reaches to take her elbow, but she jerks away from me and sends herself to teetering again, face twisting in panic.

"'Sake, Uncle Mikey!" I'm berated in the aloofest tone she can muster with body wobbling and skinny limbs flailing out wide. The stink eye she darts has me rolling back a step. "Couldn't you see I didn't need you?"

I flash her my palms in a show of contrition, "sorry." But sucking in my cheeks fools her none.

"No, you're not."

"No. I'm not," I concede, releasing my amusement with a snort as she admirably regains her balance and pouts. "Your face though!"

"Yeah. Well. What about your dopey-looking face?" Is her masterful retort.

And it's quite pathetic how close to the bone it cuts. "Harsh."

Tilting her head, she takes diligent measure of me. Then, switching the side of her tilt, she adds, "It's like it just doesn't know what to do. Silly mouth...droopy eyes. Are you happy, or are you sad?"

"I'm just dandy, thank you very much."

"Dandy?" She scrunches her nose.

"Yep," I nod. Then, I cross my eyes, stretch my grin wide, and poke out my tongue. "See? Dandy."

Erupting into a wild fit of giggles that have me grinning for real, she manages to upset her balance again. "Oof." She snatches up a fistful of my hoody, instantly sobering, and pulls herself upright. "You absolutely gots to stop dis-acting me now!"

And then she squeals. Because I've ducked in behind her, bent, and seized her around the middle. "Sorry, Indigo Sparkles, but no can do." My fingers tickle and she squirms giddily against me, her hands in a vice grip on my wrists, as I start skating backwards, hauling her along for the ride. "For this is all a part of my evil masterplan, you see? Your hero days are over, prepare to meet your doom. Mwaha..."

"Tryna do me business and the're knock, knock, knockin'!" Gran's loud return to the garden stops me short. "Canna get a bloody moment's peace!"

"Oh dear." I hear Mel as she hurries from the greenhouse toward her, tugging off her gloves as she goes.

I'm careful to steady Sophie, giving her a moment's breather, before letting her go and straightening. "You okay, Gran?"

Stupid question. It's like someone's flicked a switch on her.

"Heaven forbid any bugger else'd get it," her rant continues, undisturbed. "And who was it? Trouble, that's who. Didna fool me wi' that charmin' smile. I see what he's hidin'!" She's all askew, with her tights halfway down her legs and her skirt caught up in them, looking equal parts befuddled and furious. And... she has a bottle of Lucozade Sport in her hand. *David's Lucozade Sport.*

I groan. Pretty sure that's his last one she's taken from the fridge. "You'll be straight in his bad books with that, Gran!"

"Yep," Sophie chimes in her agreement beside me. "Nobody touches daddy's running juice."

"Evelyn..."

"Electrolytes!" Gran hollers over the top of Mel. "For the boy." She jiggles the bottle around in front of her. "He's got demons need riddin'!"

I stare at her, feeling as adrift as she looks. "Who?"

It's not Gran I get the answer from.

"Hey," Tate's voice yanks like a lead.

He steps out the back door, Megan trotting dutifully at his heel, and I'm already halfway across the lawn.

Stopping at the edge of the grass, a few paces from him, I open my mouth, close it, and then I state the obvious: "You're here."

The beguiling crook to his grin has the butterflies in my stomach rioting. "I am."

I will never ever become immune to the effect his look alone has on me.

He takes a step closer. "Is that okay?"

I nod.

And my hands itch to take hold of his. There's not a single other thing I can think to do with them.

Are we okay?

"Canna look after me own bit self now, is that it?" Gran intrudes on the moment, a brutal jolt from the spell. My spine's

414

snapped rigid as I turn to find her irritably swiping her skirt free of Mel's fussing hands and quickstepping toward us, jabbing the Lucozade out at Tate. "Here, lad. Take it."

I'm acutely aware of the fierce blush scorching my face as I respond to Tate's confused frown with a headshake.

"Ye can pack in wi' that look!" Gran scolds me, stopping at my side. She thrusts the bottle into Tate's hand and his frown drops down to it. "Like I'm one card short of a deck. Fixin' him's as much for your sake as his!"

Her words prick delicately at something inside me, but before I can investigate it further, Sophie clumps awkwardly through us, narrowly missing my toes. "Megan, hey! Are you here to skate?" Then, she erupts, "WHAT?!"

"Gracious!" Gran's hand flies to her chest.

And I use the distraction to snag the Lucozade back from Tate's limp grasp.

"But it's so much fun!"

Megan shrugs, shying away from my niece's bristling indignation. "I just don't want to."

"You're such a baby sometimes."

"Am not."

"Are to."

Mel's up off the bench and at Gran's side. "Behave, child."

Flapping a dismissive hand at us, Sophie's chin punches out again. "Well, I don't want to do anything else 'cept skating today, so, probably, you shouldn't have come."

I've watched the pucker to Tate's brow deepen as he's followed the exchange, and his little sister's looking dangerously close to tears as he squats down level with her. There's only the barest sheepish flicker my way before he lifts his hands and starts signing.

Gran mumbles something indecipherable into my ear and, with a nip to my hand, reclaims the bottle.

I barely even flinch. The siblings' brief and silent interaction has me transfixed, trying to memorise every movement, shape, and sequence. The scowl vanishes from Sophie's face. I assume David must have caught Mel up on his weekend discovery (despite his promise not to), because she, too, watches without comment. I'm grateful to her for that.

Megan looks notably happier when Tate straightens up and gives her a gentle nudge. He remains fixed on her as she steps forward.

"I could learn you how to dance," she says, timidly, "real ballerina dancing?"

Mel's quick to pipe up as Sophie gives the suggestion careful, slinty-eyed consideration. "That sounds like a brilliant idea, angel. What do you think, Evelyn?"

"What?" Gran snaps. "Dancin'?" And then her whole face brightens in a blink. "Oh, yes. My Jim would always tell me I moved like a sprite."

"Uncle Mikey?"

I grin at Mel and she winks at me as Gran surrenders the sports drink to her without a further thought. "You'd make an amazing sprite, Soph."

That approval is all it takes for Sophie to give the nod. "And after, Megan, can you learn me more hand-talking?"

"Yep," Megan eagerly agrees. "I know lots more now."

"Help me get these off then."

Gran's humming and swaying as she follows the two nattering girls to the bench. Turning back to Tate, I find him most pleasantly entertained, too.

"Guess I should take my skates off as well. You gonna help?"

"Why?"

A darting glance marks Mel walking away from us. ("Would you like to stay for tea, Megan? I'll ring your mummy.")

"Obviously, I don't need your help. I was being cute."

"You're absurdly cute," Tate smirks. "But that's not what I mean. Why do you need to take them off?"

"Cos..." I'm lost, and my frown tells him so.

At no point have I thought to pay attention to his backpack until he now shrugs it off his shoulder. He may as well be pulling out a dragon's egg for the level of awe I'm struck with as he exposes a pair of brand-spanking-new blades. "I'm feeling brave. Pupil turned teacher – you up for it?"

Screw restraint! I hurl myself at him, arms locking him against me. The world narrows to the warm gust of his startled laugh against my lips.

50

THAT'S ALL FOLKS!

"*F*uck, Mikey. That was terrifying!"

I shake my head, grinning like a certifiable crazy person. "You said 'amazing' wrong."

Tate's demons are far too deeply rooted to be exorcised by the electrolytes of a Lucozade Sport (though I have to give it to Gran, she'd certainly been on to something there). It should have occurred to me way before now that, of course, his remedy is the same as mine. Okay, so, our afternoon skate may not have 'rid' him of them, but it sure as hell seems to have at least shaken the corrosive blighters loose.

He was a little rusty, sure; more cautious than he used to be, and his performance caused him some frustration. But once his nerves had settled enough for his passion to reignite, it was like I witnessed him transform from grainy black and white to full HD colour. And it. Was. Glorious!

After three and a half hours, I've finally convinced him we need a break. We're outside his house.

He's flushed, breathing heavy, his body practically sparking with energy, and I have him pinned to his front door, my arms bracketing his head.

"You know, I saved up for months to get these blades," he murmurs, so close. "Christmas money, birthday, chores. Besides my computer, they're the most expensive thing I own. Got them just two days before I...before I got sick. Wore them once. And after, when I got out of hospital, I was so determined that me being... I just couldn't let the Meningitis take anything else away from me... but, shit, I could barely stand in them, never mind skate. Then, strike two. Landed myself straight back in hospital with the mother of all seizures. Only kept them, really, as a reminder of why I gave up all I did. Never, ever thought I'd find the courage to put the fuckers back on." His words are so sad, but he looks so happy. "Amazing is definitely another word for it."

Leaning in, covering his mouth with mine, emotion swells my heart so that it feels too big for my chest. I can feel the grin still cracking his face, the adrenaline pulsing through him. He's given me far more than I think he realises today, with this. For all that I am possibly his sole motivation for putting on the skates, it's the impact that act has made on him that means the most.

I tilt my head, deepening the kiss, and he hums into my mouth as our tongues meet. His arms wrap around me, hands fisting my hoody at the small of my back.

He's made things right between us in a way his plan of throwing himself to the wolves at Steph's party never would've. In a way that's given us both something we're better for having.

I lift a hand from the door and card my fingers through his wind-ruffled hair, pressing in flush against him. The graze of his teeth over my bottom lip incites a hiss. Arousal powering my body, I rock into him, and hiss again as he thrusts to greet me. Hard and panting and eager for...

But, no! I stop, sudden realisation jolting me back. My fingers curl into Tate's thick hair, preventing his chase, and I gulp in air. Because this, it isn't enough. What I'm feeling – what I need for him to understand – is a whole world beyond the limits of this kiss on his front step. "Inside?"

Kiss-bitten and heavy-lidded, he stares hungrily at my mouth, nodding. His hand moves from my spine to his pocket, delving in for the key. Then...

...Then the front door swings open on us, Tate falls backwards, crashing on his hallway floor with an *ooof,* and I'm pulled down on top of him.

Several envelops flutter to the floor around us. "Oh my!"

Wheezing, my head whips around, gaze zipping from shiny black heels, grey trousers, white blouse and emerald scarf, up to Laura's startled frown. My face instantly flames.

"Mum!" Tate snaps. He nudges my chest, but no way am I moving yet. Can't. It's obvious enough what we've been up to without showcasing evidence.

There's a strained and awful eternity of stunned gawping, none of us sure how to react or proceed. But, then, Laura's travelling eye catches on the tangle of our skates protruding outside, and what begins on her face as an anxious pucker sharp gives way to a wide grin.

She laughs. "Well, this is...unexpected."

My heart flutters in wild panic as I take her offered hand and finally scramble up off Tate. And once I'm on my feet, she doesn't immediately let me go.

Instead, she draws me into a hug, bringing her mouth close to my ear, and murmurs, "knew you could bring him back. Just... look after him, please, Mikey."

I nearly tumble again when she steps back. Bending to retrieve the dropped mail, she leaves me to help Tate up.

"Mum? What are you doing here?" His hand's crushing mine.

"Oh, don't mind me, boys," she says, straightening. "I just called in for the post before I go collect Megan." No hint of her frown remains as she pecks Tate on the cheek and pats my chest before stepping past us out the front door. "Enjoy the rest of your afternoon. But your dad'll be in at midnight, Tate, remember."

Tate and I stand and stare at each other in mortified silence for a long while after the door slams shut behind her. Then Tate busts out laughing.

And in the next minute, I'm laughing right along with him. "So. That was awkward."

"Ya think?"

"For a moment, there, when your mum noticed the skates, I honestly thought she was about to do her nut."

"You've nothing whatsoever to fear from my mum, Mikey."

"Your dad, on the other hand..."

He snorts, finally releasing my hand, and I flex the life back into my poor, mangled fingers as he turns to flick the latch on the door, locking us in. "We have until midnight."

I've never removed my skates quite so fast before. By the time Tate stands after taking off his own, he finds me halfway up his stairs.

"Keen?"

In place of a reply, I flash him a grin and take the remaining stairs two at a time.

~

"OKAY. ENOUGH. STOP," Tate pants, trying – and failing – to unhitch himself from me. His shuffle across the bed does nothing but trap him against the wall. "Please."

"No," I murmur, my friction-tender lips moving obstinately over his jaw, "not yet."

"Fuck, Mikey!" A fistful of my hair restrains me and then he flops onto his back with a groan. "You're killing me here. Just. A minute. I just need a minute."

It's not a request, and there's no point me answering anyway; not only has he turned his head away from me, but he's closed his eyes. Instead, I nuzzle in tighter against him and press soft kisses to his neck.

His chest vibrates with a soft chuckle. "Help me out here, please. I'm trying really hard not to push you too far."

He's just being stubbornly obtuse now. For the ten minutes or ten years that we've been here, in his room, I've given him zero cause to believe I'm opposed to being pushed. But, *damnit,* that unwitting reminder of my inferior experience needles a hole straight through my lust haze, a dispiriting puncture.

"Thank you," he breathes when I grudgingly detach myself from him. Dilated pupils anchoring on me, a delicious grin relieves my sting. "You've no idea how fucking close you came to trashing my good intentions."

My move to immediately erase the fresh sliver of space between us is halted by the firm press of his hand to my chest.

"Need longer than that."

"Sweet. Jeezus!" I relent, kicking out at the rumpled duvet by our feet. "*Fuck!*"

Takes several moments of deep breathing, savouring the taste of him on my lips, and a herculean force of will to get me moving up off the bed.

As I pull off my hoody and chuck it over the desk chair, Tate returns to his side, propping himself up on one elbow and splaying his hand across the warm space I've just vacated. "What're you...?"

He trails off, his eyes flashing wide, dark brows disappearing into the messy hair falling over his forehead, as my T-shirt follows my hoody and I unzip my fly. And when I kick off my jeans and socks, he bolts upright.

I hesitate, my jaw clenched so hard my teeth feel at risk of shattering, giving him the chance to raise objection. Silence reigns.

Then, I lose my boxers and straighten.

Little Mikey does me proud even as my confidence slips.

Never have I ever been more acutely aware of the scrawniness of my body: the pale, rangy plane of my torso; the sharp jut of my hip bones. And as I watch his dazed eyes start to roam, feel the heat of his gaze licking over the whole of me, it takes every ounce of my self-control to remain still and exposed. But there can be no misunderstanding here.

For Tate more than anyone, action wields greater power than words. He's demonstrated that with my bedroom wall, with the camp set up at our den, and then again today, giving me an afternoon close to perfect. And so what if he's not quite yet in the same place of unquestionable certainty with us as I am, it changes nothing. He owns me; I'm his, utterly and completely, and I'm ready to show him that.

"Fuck, Mikey," he breathes.

Nerves raging and legs unsteady, I return to the bed. He drops back onto his pillow as I settle myself in the still-warm space beside him, and the intensity of his stare locks me in. I see him swallow, his Adam's apple jumping, before he lifts a hand from his hip and tentatively lays it on mine. The skin-on-skin contact scorches a trail straight to my core.

My body could not be any less subtle in telling him what I want, so I stay quiet and focus on continuing to breathe as he becomes a little bolder with his touch. The tingles are almost unbearable.

He doesn't stop me this time when I move in and kiss him. Nor does he stop me when I rid him of his top. And once I've success-fully fumbled his jeans undone, he takes no persuading in working them down his legs and kicking them off.

I'm fascinated by the way his wiry muscles flex with each and every move he makes, and his reaction to my riveted study is empowering. I circle a fingertip around his nipple and he shudders, burying his face into my neck.

But as I make a move on the thin cotton tent of his boxers, his hand slams down on mine, trapping my palm against his lean abdomen.

"Fuck, Mikey," he says again, only this time it sounds more like a pained groan. "No."

My heart trips over itself, like I've missed a step going down-stairs. I bite down hard on my bottom lip.

Shaking his head, he rushes on as I try to wrench myself free from him. "Don't. Please. Just..." He secures my hand more firmly to his body and glides it up over his torso. His chest is rising and falling like a storm-touched sea, and then, in its depths, I feel the pounding beat of his heart, its rhythm as zealous as my own. "I want to. Fuck, do I want to!"

"But...?" Is all I manage to rasp.

"But..." He leans in close again, his breath scalding hot on my jaw, "not yet." I feel a light nip on my earlobe and then, in one fluid movement that slams the air from my lungs, he's pinned me hard to the mattress, bare skin to bare skin. "Not while you're doubting me."

I'm barely able to draw a breath, never mind adjust to this sharp turnabout; all my senses invaded and fully intoxicated by him – by his weight, his heat, and the hard-earned tangy musk of his sweat – by his erection insisting itself on mine, only a thin stretch of fabric between.

What. In the name of the demon king. Is he freaking doing to me here?!

"You have no idea how infuriating it was for me, Mikey," he goes on before I have chance to de-stupefy myself. Arms propped either side of my head, he's staring down at me, "the other night. When you caught me off guard. Stole my thunder."

I open my mouth. A weird noise escapes.

"I've waited so long...tested the words out on my tongue so many times... And then, what? I'm suddenly left with just tacking 'too' on the end? Fuck that shit! Might just as well say 'ditto'." Bending at the elbows until his forehead's brushing mine, he gently bucks his hips and his eyes drill into me. I only barely hold myself together. "I imagined and I planned and I held off, waiting. Cos I wanted you in my arms, much like this. Even better, in my bed. Only for you to... you took my moment and – I'm sorry, but – you fucking ruined it."

The force of an impetuous and wholly ridiculous grin threatens to split my face in two, and my heart starts doing crazy, beautiful things inside my chest. Wrestling my arms free from between us and throwing them around him, I may – *unintentionally* – claw across his shoulder blades. But his whole-body shudder is insanely satisfying.

"The night of the gig-to-be-forgotten, I came so close. But..."

"Just spit it out, already!" I snap, cutting him off with an impatient flick to the cup of his ear.

He smirks, a wickedly intimate smirk, and pauses. Then, "I fucking love you, Mikey Alston. Have done since before I could even understand my feelings for what they were. And I thank fate – and your brother – every fucking day for bringing you back to me."

In the next moment, I've rolled him off me, clumsily relieved him of his undergarment, and slotted our bodies tight together.

My hands get brave and my mouth gets smart.

"Ditto," I murmur against his lips before I suck his tongue, hard, through the welcoming gap between mine.

The air around us grows combustible.

ABOUT THE AUTHOR

J.S. Edge remains adamant that when she was a kid she could fly.
Pfft to the nay-sayers.

Born and raised in the North-East of England, J.S. Edge graduated
from Northumbria University with a BA(hons) degree in Media
Production, a script writing major. She and her husband now live
in the beautiful South-West, sharing their Devonshire home with
four 'spirited' children and a menagerie of furry friends. J.S. Edge is
a terrible cook but an exceptional dreamer, and Elephant Shoe is
her debut novel.

Twitter: @JS_Edge
Instagram: @edge_joanne
Tumblr: @jedge9-blog

WANT TO READ SOMETHING COMPLETELY DIFFERENT?

BLOOD MOON RISING BY SILVERFOOT

After a horrendous and brutal attack, star student and good girl Dia awakens in a grave to find herself changed, her sheltered and safe life gone forever. She's gained surprising new powers, astonishing strength and speed, but she has new vulnerabilities and new enemies.

As she learns to navigate her changed world, she must exercise caution. Vampire life is not what she envisioned and comes with a unique moral code limiting how she can use her newfound abilities. The consequences of failure are catastrophic.

It is 1961, and the country has a charismatic new president, the civil rights movement is gathering strength, beatniks are becoming hippies, communal living and free love are making noise. Sex and drugs and rock'n'roll, baby!

Against this backdrop, she and her creator hunt her killers so she can find justice. Along the way, she finds new friends and allies and awakens to the social issues of the day, struggling with them right along with the rest of society.

On top of this, she must resolve her personal issues about what she has become and how it has affected her moral code. Is she a monster or not? What can she say—it's complicated!

34235657R00256

Printed in Poland
by Amazon Fulfillment
Poland Sp. z o.o., Wrocław